The Knights Dawning

The First Book in the Crusades Series

James Batchelor

ADVANCE UNCORRECTED
READER'S PROOF
FROM PENDANT BOOKS

Pendant Publishing

Salt Lake City

The Knights Dawning
A Pendant Book.

First Pendant Publishing Edition, November 2011

All rights reserved.
Copyright © 2009 by James Batchelor

Library of Congress Control Number: 2011916213

No part of this book may be reproduced, scanned, or distributed in any printed or electronic form without written permission. Please do not participate in the piracy of copyrighted materials in violation of the author's rights. Please purchase only authorized editions.

ISBN 978-0-9840044-0-9

This is a work of fiction. Names, characters, places, and incidents either are the product of the author's imagination or are used fictitiously, and any resemblance to actual persons, living or dead, events, or locales is entirely coincidental.

Printed in the United States of America

ACKNOWLEDGMENTS

This book would not have been possible without the effort and support of a great many people, but the following should be mentioned specifically:

My wife, Elizabeth, for her support and for never letting me give up.

Denise Mason, for her editing skills that she so willing donated though it took time away from her own family.

Dan Cutler, who's patience in tirelessly hashing and rehashing these subjects borders on the miraculous.

And finally to the individuals in the reading groups, most of whom I do not know, for being willing to read new material and not being afraid to give their honest feedback; and especially those who were willing to endure multiple versions of the same work that they did not even like the first time through.

To all these people, I say thank you.

For Jared:

For everything he wanted to be,
For everything he could have been,
And for everything he was not.

AUTHOR'S NOTE

A word regarding the history and the language used in this book:

Though I had always enjoyed reading it, I had never particularly wanted to write fiction (at least not in my adult life; as a child, I thought that was all I would write). So when the idea for *The Knights Dawning* came to me, the way I salved my conscience over writing a fiction novel is that I was writing historical fiction. Well, very early on in the project, it became clear that either the history or the story was going to have to give. While most of the major battles referred to by name as well as the historical figures such as Prince John and those surrounding him are all real, the history was not lining up. I found it would be necessary to sacrifice the story or bend the dates and experiences to fit the story I wanted to tell.

Nevertheless, I refused to abandon the historical aspects altogether because I feel the story is lent a certain validity by having it occur against the backdrop of a very tumultuous time that actually occurred in our history. Even so, given the many liberties I ended up taking, I thought I should mention some important details. Everything referenced in the story: Damietta, The Magna Carta, King Richard, the Norman conquest of England, King John and his feud with Pope Innocent III, etc. are all true historical events that occurred during this period. Where the liberties were taken is in the details. The dates of Richard's death and the battle of Damietta, for example, do not exactly line up with the time I needed them to occur in order to make for a smooth-flowing story. They were a few years off, so I ignored that fact.

VIII The Knights Dawning

The armor presented another challenge. The full suits of plate armor as we typically imagine knights wearing did not exist in that form until sometime later than this story takes place. But I wanted traditional knights for my story, so the armor obligingly jumped back in time to accommodate me. The size of the horses is also a matter of some dispute. It appears that destriers were not the massive draft-type horses I have depicted herein, but there was just something about a knight charging into battle on a Shetland pony that was distinctly underwhelming, so that fact, too, changed.

Dawning Castle is another particular worth mentioning. When I planned this story out, I thought I would find a specific Norman castle in England that I liked and base Dawning Castle's design and location around that. But I could not find any that suited me, so I created one from whole cloth.

Most of these items are probably not a concern to the recreational reader, but the history buff may get hung up on these details. In the end I could not really call this historical fiction, but I still value the historical aspects of the story, so it was important to me to preserve them.

The Language:

While writing this work, I was confronted with some difficulty regarding the language the characters should use. My problem is that to preserve the feeling of the period as well as the beauty of the language, I felt the need to incorporate the use of the first person, informal form of the language (i.e., "thees" and "thous"); however, I believe to the modern reader this language lends a certain level of inaccessibility and keeps the characters at a distance. It was essential to the story that the readers feel an understanding of the characters involved as this is a very character-driven story; so I was struggling with a mode of preserving both of these elements.

While grappling with this difficulty through multiple rewrites, I hit upon the idea of using formal speech as the Japanese do. The Japanese use their "Teinei," or formal speech, in different levels according to whom they are addressing. They use formal speech with bosses, strangers, or figures of respect, and very informal or "plain form" (so designated as it is bereft of all the additional honorifics that make polite speech polite) with close friends and family members.

While the Japanese language has many levels of politeness, English traditionally only had two (with one form falling out of use some five hundred years ago). As a compromise, I chose, eventually, to use the first person informal language where the situations would call for formality or excessive politeness, thereby trying to preserve the sense of this period in history and some of the beauty that once lent itself to this mode of speech. While the characters are speaking to each other, they use more colloquial-sounding language to help bring the story home to the reader.

Unfortunately, much of the reading group found the transition between the two forms of speech jarring and said it tended to remove them from the story. The version you now have in your hands has had all the first person informal language stripped from it.

With that, please enjoy *The Knights Dawning*.

X The Knights Dawning

PROLOGUE

Mount Alamut

It was midnight when they removed the blindfold from Amir's eyes. He was in a dark cave lit only by a few torches lining the stone walls. A brazier glowing red from the coals within stood before Amir. In the coals sat an iron pot filled with a liquid bubbling in a rapid boil and emitting an acrid odor. Twelve men stood with their backs to the cave walls, facing in toward Amir. They were largely obscured by the deep shadows in the cave, and all Amir could make out was their silhouettes. Amid the exhaustion, hunger, and intense thirst Amir was experiencing from the grueling series of initiation rites he had been subjected to, he felt something else now that he was not accustomed to feeling: fear. He began to fear what might lie ahead. An unusually large man, Amir was not wont to feel such emotions at the hands of other men, but he knew well the penalty for failing his initiation.

One masked man in a long hooded robe stepped forward into the light of the brazier. He handed Amir a book that the huge man knew well. "Throw this to the ground," he said. Amir hesitated for only a moment to perpetrate this action that would be viewed as a stoning offense to most of his friends and family. He himself had never particularly subscribed to these traditions, but it was these very traditions and rituals that surrounded and infused the education of his younger years. These actions contradicted everything he had been taught. The heavy book hit the ground, sending a puff of dirt up into the smoky cave. "Spit on it!" the robed man ordered. Amir

XII The Knights Dawning

hesitated a moment longer before following this order. Was it possible that this was part of the test of the initiation and by obeying he was failing? "This book is a dead law." The robed man was pointing a bony finger at the book in the dirt. "The only law is the word of Imam Hassan Ibn Sabbah. If you have not accepted that then you do not belong among us."

Amir did as he was instructed and spit on the book with the little spittle he could muster from his parched mouth. "Grind it beneath your heel!" The masked man ordered. Amir placed one massive boot on the cover and twisted his heel, breaking the spine and spilling the pages out on the dirt. "Who is the law?"

"Imam Hassan Ibn Sabbah," Amir said.

"Who is the law?"

"Imam Hassan Ibn Sabbah," Amir said louder.

"Who is the law?"

"Imam Hassan Ibn Sabbah," Amir yelled with all the strength he could rally.

"Who do you obey?"

"Imam Hassan Ibn Sabbah," Amir shouted again.

"How will you find your way back to paradise?"

"Through the word of Imam Hassan Ibn Sabbah!"

The robed man produced an old wooden cup from within his robe and filled it from the bubbling liquid in the pot. He dropped a handful of dark powder into it that sent an abundance of steam hissing from the cup. He then extended the dark brew to Amir. "Now you will experience the pleasure of paradise through the word of Imam Hassan Ibn Sabbah. Drink!"

Amir looked at the cup skeptically. What did this man mean by 'the pleasure of paradise'? Did that mean he had been found unworthy? Was this how they dispatched candidates that failed the initiation?

"Drink!" the robed man ordered, obviously becoming impatient with Amir's hesitance. Amir accepted the cup in acknowledgment of the fact that his life was in the hands of these mysterious men regardless of whether he drank this offering or not. He poured the burning liquid into his mouth. It had a bitter, acrid taste. He fought back his gag reflex and after several attempts swallowed it all down.

It took only a few moments for Amir to identify the effects of the drink. He became light headed and euphoric. The cave swirled around him and he fell back on the cool dirt. He did not know what was happening to him, but it suddenly did not matter any longer. He was happy. The cares that brought him to seek out the Nizari, the worries over his raped country and the European devils who seemed to come in an endless torrent were of no concern now.

He was vaguely aware of the men from beyond the torchlight closing in and lifting his limp frame from the ground. He felt the cool night air replace the stuffy air of the cave as he floated up to a softer, gentler place. Amir seemed to slip in and out of dream. He vaguely remembered being carried up the steep mountain trail that led to the fortress of Alamut. Then he was in paradise. He lay in a lush garden surrounded by beautiful women. Some of them were playing soft music while others tended to him. The foreign devils would be dealt with in time, but for now, Amir was nestled in Allah's bosom.

XIV The Knights Dawning

CHAPTER ONE

Iberian Peninsula

Richard unconsciously gripped the shaft of his lance tighter as he watched the Moors crest the hill beyond the valley. They were swarming like so many insects. And like so many insects, they would be ground under his heel. One more conquest, one more victory; an infestation that had gotten out of hand, quelled. Richard and his army had cut deep into the Iberian Peninsula marching under the banner of the Pope, though the Pope had not sanctioned this particular crusade. They were reclaiming the Iberian Peninsula from these filthy invaders, and he had driven them from village to village, town to town until he had pushed them against the Mediterranean Sea. Those remaining had combined their forces to make one last stand.

    His men stirred. Richard looked over the line of hired mercenaries surrounding his huge black warhorse. He hated these dirty, thieving, backstabbing whores almost as much as he hated the Moors, but they were a necessary evil to achieve his aims. The mercenaries were essential to achieving victory—to achieving glory—but they were also greedy, vicious, and treacherous, and they were all very overdue for payment. The booty Richard had counted on collecting during these raids had barely covered the expenses of feeding and maintaining the army. He had neglected to mention while enlisting their services that he did not have the money on hand to pay them. Should they discover his treachery... Mutiny was always an option for men of their ilk.

But all that would soon be over. He would shortly eradicate the Moor scourge from this part of the country and the spoils available to his men would more than make up for what he owed them. They could have it all. It was not wealth that motivated Richard. He wanted the glory, the fame, and the power. This would prove once and for all to his family that he was indeed imbued with undeniable greatness. He would show them that he was worthy of all the respect his toadying lackeys gave him— a respect he was denied from his family. This would truly seal his reputation as the greatest warrior in the world, if not in history.

He broke from his musings and turned his gaze back to the opposite hill and the business at hand, and his heart skipped. The entire hill was alive with bodies, and they were still streaming in from the far side of the hill top. He looked over his force scarcely a thousand strong. They were battled-hardened veterans, but they were also fatigued from this five year campaign.

The enemy hill had to have at least five thousand men. He had not anticipated that so many Moors yet remained. But it wasn't just Moors, he reminded himself. In the five centuries since the Moor conquest of the Iberian Peninsula, many of the unfaithful had interbred with their heathen conquerors and were now fighting for them as part of their families; they were therefore worthy of the same fate. Nevertheless, Richard was not oblivious to the strength of such numbers. The Moors must have received reinforcements. Richard's scouts had reported nowhere near these numbers even in their latest report. Five to one, how could he triumph with such odds? Yet this battle was the culmination of six years of preparation and five years of nonstop fighting. If he turned back now it was all for naught. He could not pay his men; he would have no glory; he would be disgraced. Victory was the only option.

He glanced back down at his men who were looking at him uncertainly. What did it matter if he lost most of them? It was their privilege to die in this great struggle. None of them really believed in the Christian cause that they were fighting for anyway. Richard was no different, but he believed in himself and he would make a stand here.

He wheeled his horse and spurred it into a gallop across the front line of his men. "This is it, men!" He shouted, standing high in the stirrups. His blood red armor glowed in the pre-dawn light. His massive frame that stood almost seven feet emerged larger than life over the lines. "This is all of the enemy that remains! They are scared and weak. Most of them are just boys that can hardly hold a weapon. You are battled hardened veterans. You are strong! They are weak! We will finish it here and return in glory to our homes where we will be greeted as the heroes that ran this vermin from our lands and took back what was rightfully ours. We will do what no one else could do in five hundred years! You have never failed and you will not fail when it matters the most.

Richard held his lance aloft, the church's banner fluttering from the end of it just below his own crest. The men followed suit and raised their weapons aloft. "We will stand strong this one last time for everything we have fought for and for everything we believe in."

A great shout of support rose from his army. Richard donned his wicked looking helmet. The iron outer shell of his helmet was dyed red to match his armor, but the mask was devised to look like a face comprised mostly of bone. It was fearful to behold and gave this intimidating figure a fearsome presence indeed. This helmet added to the impression that he was something otherworldly, a demon sent from hell to collect souls.

Movement on the opposite peak had slowed till hardly a stir rippled through them. They were watching the crusaders, and the crusaders were watching them. An electricity hung in the air. The first rays of the morning sun touched down on the field of battle and the excitement, anxiety, and anticipation were impossible to contain any longer. As it always did for Richard, the electricity welled up in him from his chest until it escaped his mouth in a great war cry. "For glory!" He roared and spurred his horse down the hill.

The Moors on the opposite peak responded in kind and with a terrible racket came rushing down the opposite hill like a great avalanche of people. Still shrouded in the shadow of early dawn's timidity, the entire hillside seemed to be alive, undulating and rolling toward Richard and his small army.

Richard and the front line of cavalry raced out ahead of the infantry. At this moment in the battle, as he always was, Richard was possessed of a strange sensation as if he were floating outside his body, merely a spectator to the ensuing events. The noise of his men and the approaching army seemed to fall way. He no longer heard the horse's ironclad hooves on the ground or his armor clinking in the saddle, but rather he felt his horse's muscles rippling beneath him. He felt the cool morning air rushing through the seams in his heavy armor. He felt the weight of his weapons pulling on him. With no thought and almost in a daze he performed the motions he had done thousands of times before. He raised his lance from where it was resting in his stirrup and dropped the point of it, hooking the handle on the crook of his right arm. The line of cavalry followed suit in one well-rehearsed motion, all the attached flags of the individual banners dropping in a smooth line.

The advanced cavalry reached the enemy line well ahead of the infantry. There was a great rush around him, and Richard's inexplicably serene moment exploded into chaos, abruptly pulling him back into his body and into the fray. Richard dropped the point of his lance and took the first enemy in the chest. His lance snapped off in the chest as his unfortunate victim was torn to shreds.

Richard was dismayed that it had broken so quickly. But he raised the remaining five foot stub and brought it down in a massive blow atop the head of the next enemy within reach. Meanwhile his mighty stallion rode over two more hapless peasants who had the misfortune of being placed in the front lines to precede the more experienced warriors; survival here had nothing to do with strength or skill; it was plain and simple luck. The sword of Damocles hung over all in the front line with one inevitable conclusion.

Richard discarded the last bit of wood and ripped his massive sword from its sheath, kicking another assailant square in the face with his ironclad boot as he did so. He glanced over the line to see how the others were fairing and was startled by the number of empty saddles. Just then his foot soldiers arrived and with a mighty clash charged into the melee, cutting down everything before them.

The Moors began to fall back before the mercenaries like the ocean tide receding from the beach. Richard continued to cut and slash violently toward anyone that came within range. One mighty blow smashed the inferior weapon of one man, tearing the flesh of the body that it failed to protect. Another blow cleaved the helmet of an unsuspecting Moor that had dropped his guard after dispatching a mercenary. Richard's uncommonly large destrier, which stood head and shoulders above most of the Moors, reared up and brought his hooves down on the shield of a Moor soldier standing before them. The overwhelming concussion shattered the Moor's arm and elicited screams of pain that were silenced by the same hooves trampling over the suffering Moor.

Richard dealt death at every blow, his terrible presence inspiring awful terror in all who ventured to withstand him. His prowess as a warrior alone is what kept his underpaid, overworked men in check. Fear of his wrath and a desire to be part of a legacy that this man was surely destined for were all that kept them going in the face of overwhelming odds such as this.

Richard continued to cut deep into the enemy ranks. Tirelessly he decimated everything in his path until he was swinging at retreating backs as a void opened up around him. All saw that it was certain death to face this demon warrior whose blood red armor now ran thick with the lifeblood of all that came near him. His massive black destrier barded in plates dyed to match the plate of its rider seemed to have leapt from the very pits of hell itself.

20   The Knights Dawning

The battle wore on. The sun was high in the sky when Richard drew his mount up to take a breath and survey the battle field. He first noticed that he no longer saw any other mounted riders. He quickly scanned the situation, seeing only dark faces surrounding him. Fifty yards behind him he saw the battered remnants of his line being pushed back. He was deep behind the enemy lines alone, and his men were about to retreat. He cursed himself for not being more aware of the battle at large. He was the General after all. It was his responsibility to see to the direction of his men. But he had become so accustomed to always being victorious, to always routing the enemy, that he had neglected to properly lead his men. He had fallen into the habit of merely being a gallant banner for the men to follow, and he only concentrated on eliminating the enemy. His cavalry was gone, and the remnants of his foot soldiers were desperately fighting to escape, not to win.

If his men fled, he would be left alone in a sea of enemy faces. Mighty warrior though he may be, Richard did not like those odds. He had to act quickly. Wheeling his mount, he began to charge back toward his own line. But as he did so, his line of crusaders began to crumble as the surviving mercenaries fled. The Moors pursued them and continued what had ceased to be a battle and was now a slaughter. All at once the crowd surrounding Richard's warhorse became aware of just how outnumbered he was. Those that had been giving him a wide berth before took heart and turned on him. The Moors knew well who he was. They knew it was he that had led this campaign, butchered their people, destroyed their towns, and kept them living in fear for all these years. They knew that it was he who led the relentless onslaught, and they knew that they now had him trapped. They would exact a terrible justice on him.

Time seemed to stand still as each of the players realized their separate positions. Nobody moved for a long instant, as if time had fallen behind the moment. Then with jarring suddenness it jumped ahead as Richard let out a mighty battle cry and cleaved into the army, determined to cut his way out.

The Moors rushed him, encouraged by their vast numbers. Richard cut and hacked furiously in every direction, his nearly four foot blade cutting the soldiers before him like wheat. But they continued to press in upon him from every direction. They stabbed at his horse, his arms, his legs—any exposed bit they could find. Richard's giant blade became a hindrance as there were too many bodies to cut through all of them. Then with a terrible neighing whinny, his mount's hind legs were hamstrung and gave out. The massive destrier's back legs buckled, dumping Richard off of its back. Richard stumbled backward out of his saddle but managed to retain his footing.

Though this was the perfect opportunity to finish him off, the individual soldiers were still instinctively afraid of this massive, inhuman figure that somehow seemed all the more intimidating toe to toe. At this range , it was impossible to overlook exactly how much bigger he was than the average size frames of the Moor soldiers. Even as he stumbled to regain himself, this monster was unfathomable. The bone face of his helmet that was caked in the blood of their comrades showed no pain, no fear, no fatigue, only unyielding cruelty. And the blade, the mighty blade he wielded, was massive enough to require two hands to heft for most men. He was a monster, and now this monster was angry.

One soldier took courage and charged towards Richard's right rear flank, spear extended, determined to find a chink in the wicked armor. Richard regained his balance just in time and swung his sword down to deflect the spear, but the momentum of the soldier's charge propelled him straight into Richard's chest. The Moor was too close to effectively cut him down, so Richard did the next best thing: he slid his sword arm under the soldier's arm, pivoted around and hurled the soldier into the sea of befuddled Moors, landing him across three of them. They collapsed in a painful tangle. Richard then spun and continued his grim death march toward freedom. With no hint of fear, he tore into anything that came within range of his bloody sword point.

Twenty yards, thirty yards, he left a trail of dead and dying. It began to look as though he was going to make it to freedom. The Moor army redoubled its efforts. The crowd pressing in on the circle of hesitating soldiers surrounding Richard actually became an impediment to their own men. Those closest to him were shoved forward, throwing them off balance and depriving them of the opportunity to time their attacks. The Moors were terrified of this creature that they were sure had risen straight from hell as a scourge to their people. Nevertheless, the army as a whole possessed a will that superseded that of the individual.

***

Naim had been a farmer only a year before. He knew nothing about soldiering before Richard's army had arrived one fateful night in his village. They had plundered, pillaged and burned everything. His wife, his children were all dead or missing, and Naim no longer had a reason to live outside of standing against the crusaders. That was his sole purpose for being now, and he had fought in virtually every battle waged against Richard's army since that time. Now here he was at long last, with Richard trapped before him. Naim was on the inner circle facing Richard. The crowd behind him undulated as an unstoppable force threw him forward in front of Richard. Though Naim had faced Richard's army many times, he had never been near him in the battlefield. Naim's eyes widened as he saw the slaughter of the others taking place a few scant feet away. He was suddenly acutely aware that his small stocky frame, insufficiently protected as it was by a mismatched helmet and breastplate, was nothing compared to the goliath before him. He desperately pushed back into the crowd as the path of destruction turned his way but was violently shoved forward once again.

Reluctantly he braced himself to face this foe. His arm felt very weak as he raised his sword, hoping against hope that this ever-spinning, pivoting demon would not turn on him. But Richard did turn on him, and for just a moment Naim looked into those black eye sockets and that evil bone face that was drenched in the blood of his friends and family. His hand went limp. His sword dropped to the ground.

Richard, however, did not hesitate. Naim's terror produced not a moment of hesitation or pity in this ruthless warrior. His sword came down with a great overhand swing and cleaved through Naim's clavicle. The force of the swing may have cleaved the whole top section of his body off had it not been for Naim's rusty breastplate. Richard's sword cut deep into the breast plate and lodged there. He attempted to slide it out, but it was wedged in the now twisted steel and bone of his victim. Furiously he jerked his weapon back and the stuck body of the soldier was whipped around like a rag doll.

***

The solid end of a heavy cudgel came down on the back of Richard's sword wrist, breaking his grip from his weapon, the steel of his gauntlet being all that saved his hand from breaking.

Another soldier raised his sword overhead in both hands to finish this dreaded knight once and for all. At the last minute Richard lunged toward the swordsman, knocking him over and rendering his blow ineffective as the two were entangled on the ground.

Others quickly stepped up to dispatch him but could not safely distinguish Richard from their fellow soldier in the fray. Dropping his weapon, another man leapt in to assist his comrade in subduing this massive beast. He threw his whole body onto Richard's, wrapping himself around Richard's huge right arm as Richard rolled on top of the smaller Moor. Richard hurled the Moor attaching himself to his arm back into the crowd and brought his fist down hard on the exposed face of the soldier underneath him, smashing his nose and breaking teeth under his gauntlet in a bloody mess.

Now many others were on top of Richard, hitting, kicking, and wrestling him onto his back, where his heavy plate armor put him at a serious disadvantage. At last they had him pinned down with two men holding each arm and two more on each leg.

With some effort, Richard's bone helmet was yanked violently from his head, revealing long black curls and sweat pouring down his face, dripping from his square jaw. His deep brown eyes were set in an indignant glare at the heavyset, bearded man who stood over him with rage-filled eyes. The man did not speak, but his lips quivered with an exultant excitement; Richard was completely at his mercy. After a moment he merely spat on Richard and raised the point of his blade, determined to drive it into the face of the hated knight.

"Stop!" Another man in a full suit of armor with long stringy black hair stepped up. He was a giant among the Moors, even taller than Richard himself, though not as massively built. He was clearly a person of consequence as they all parted to let him through. "An honorable soldier's death is far too good for this animal."

Richard sneered at the giant. "I know you, don't I?"

The Giant looked down at him coldly. "Hello Richard," he said and then barked orders to bind the prisoner.

The soldiers hastened to obey, keeping him well in check at every moment. Many men stood over him with weapons poised. The slightest bit of resistance earned him a sharp strike to his now exposed head.

When his bonds were secure, they picked up the mighty knight and dragged him to a captured horse. As they threw him over the back of the horse on his stomach, the last vision he had was of the Moors stabbing his suffering steed.

CHAPTER TWO

Egypt: Damietta

"William, good," Gorm said, looking up from where his squire was helping him gird his suit of armor around his increasingly rotund figure. William stood by the entrance of the tent flap as if ready to flee at any moment. Gorm sucked in his paunch to allow his sword belt to be fitted around his waist by his squire. "William, time is short, so I shall be brief. I want you mounted and riding with the chivalry tonight when we ride against Damietta," he said to the young man.

"Begging your pardon, sir, but I am not a knight," William said simply.

Gorm's curly beard that hung to his chest in a coarse tuft began to twitch as it was wont to do when he was agitated. "Why do you insist on remaining in the infantry?" Gorm demanded, flabbergasted by William's repeated rebuffs. "The infantry's fate is not of their own making. You know better than anyone that an errant arrow, a well-placed enemy lance, or overwhelming odds, spells the end for an unlucky infantryman. It is merely a game of chance in the front lines that inevitably ends the same way for all who remain there long enough. If I did not know better, I may take it into my head that you wished to perish in battle."

William shrugged calmly. "What could be nobler than to perish in a righteous crusade serving the Holy Pope himself?" Gorm was never quite certain whether or not William was being sarcastic or genuine, and said nothing. William, taking the hint, continued, "I'm afraid I have never taken to the noble equestrian activities. The last time I charged on horseback, I ended up meeting the enemy with the wrong end of the horse before me. Neither rider nor animal was satisfied with that, I can assure you."

Gorm paused to survey the young man standing before him. His skin was smooth but darkened from the long days in the sun in this part of the world while his ordinarily dark brown hair was a fairer brown now, the sun having worked the opposite effect on its pigment. He stood some five feet eight inches, but he was powerfully built across the chest and shoulders. His chin was square and his face much too handsome for this life. The years as a knight only brought scars and disfigurement to the lucky ones and death to the rest. He was outfitted differently than Gorm had ever beheld in his many decades of campaigning. His long shirt that hung down to mid-thigh was composed of many small overlapping plates that were designed to afford maximum mobility without sacrificing much protection. His legs were protected by mail leggings with heavier greaves on his shins for extra protection. He was typically bare-headed in battle, a point that Gorm did not agree with but could not argue about given his fierce prowess on the field. He had a sword on his back, which rarely came out in battle, and a dagger in the small of his back with still another tightly affixed to his left thigh. He sighed. "Who are you, William?"

William grinned. "I am William of York, sir."

"You still refuse to reveal more than that, eh?" Gorm asked, being further irked by not only having his generous ovations rebuffed but also by the young man's repeated refusal to confide in Gorm despite his best efforts to take him under his wing and mentor him.

"I have told you all that I remember, I'm afraid," William sighed. "My father was a tanner, and my mother a fishmonger. We were poor, and when they died they made me swear that I would serve God nobly and honorably." He looked so affected by the recollection of this emotional moment, one could have believed it had happened only yesterday; but Gorm was not impressed.

"Last time, your mother was a tanner and your father a fishmonger, and only he was deceased. Your mother was waiting anxiously in prayerful supplication for your return."

"Oh?" William looked surprised. "Well, that's what I meant, of course," he said quickly. Then reassuming his former air of mourning he said, "They so shared in each other's burdens that one was inseparable from the other."

"They even shared the burden of dying?"

"Sir, do not the scriptures say that a man and woman must cleave to each other, becoming one flesh? My parents had obeyed this so thoroughly that when my mother died, isn't it only fitting that I may say 'they' died?"

"Father died," Gorm reminded him.

"Right!"

"Very well, keep your secrets if you will, but that does not change the fact that I expect my lieutenant to be mounted beside me when we ride on Damietta at first light."

"Your Lordship does me too much honor, but I fear the infantry would be lost without me, and at this most critical of battles, we cannot risk such confusion. Your Lordship has no need for me to remind him that this battle more than most will rely on each army doing their part."

"Are you refusing a direct order?" Gorm demanded angrily, turning his large frame directly to the young man.

"I'm afraid I must risk a lashing at my master's hands according to the laws of chivalry, by which I am not bound, not being a knight," he responded in an easy manner, seemingly not the least bit concerned by Gorm's formidable anger, "lest I incur the responsibility for the failure of tomorrow's initiative by not speaking my mind now."

"Confound you, boy!" Gorm roared, pounding a meaty fist on the table in front of him. "Why do you refuse the honors I would shower down upon your head? We would not even be at Damietta's gates if not for you. The Church has sought Damietta for a hundred years. Why will you not allow me the pleasure of championing a brilliant young man and a ferocious warrior, as is befitting?"

"Oh, I fear you ascribe to me much that is not deserved. In battle I mostly find it convenient to hide behind others until the battle is finished. I believe my noble lord's mount has been my shield on more than one occasion." Gorm reddened even more and pounded the table again. "Sir, I but fear that the simple heart of a peasant as beats in my breast would swell with such honors, and like fateful Icarus, I would fly too close to the sun of chivalry, only to have my dreams dashed on the rocks of reality for my vainglorious aspirations." Gorm grinned despite himself.

"I know you are having sport of me, William. I should lash you for that alone."

"My back is ever ready for your noble whip, Sir Knight." he said, and began fiddling with the ties of his armor as if he would remove it for his lashing. "But I fear the weather has made this armor unmanageable, and I cannot remove it."

"Confound you, William," he said, laughing aloud. "Well then, what would you have me do for you?"

William did not speak for a long moment, then said simply, "When the day is won tomorrow, I must beg leave of you."

Gorm stared at him to determine if he were sincere. "You will leave us?"

"I believe my work here is complete."

Gorm looked sadly at the table before him. "How long has it been now? Four years? I cannot conceive of going to battle without you after all that time. I never thought I would be saying that when that brash young man came riding up to join the crusade all those years ago." He smiled self-deprecatingly. "But I suppose I managed without you for fifty years before we met, and I can continue when you have departed. Very well, if that is what you wish, then it shall be as you say." He smiled. "I still remember when you joined our band. I was not sure what you were. Come to think of it, I guess I still am not sure what you are, but I know you are a Heaven-sent scourge to the Moors."

"Scourge to the Moors, perhaps," William allowed. "But I'm afraid you do err greatly in your assumption that I am your good angel. Not I, Sir Knight. Does not the Lord use the wicked to punish the wicked?"

Gorm did not respond. William nodded, satisfied that he had been understood, and turned to leave. "William, stay a moment," Gorm said quickly, aware that William was retiring without being formally dismissed. He had always afforded this boy far too much license, but it seemed impossible to discipline William as he might other soldiers. William turned back to him expectantly.

"Though you insist on playing the buffoon," Gorm said, "I see that your intellect is keen and your skills are unparalleled. There is much good you could do from a seat of power. Stay with me and let me put you at the head of my armies," Gorm blurted suddenly. "Train my men, lead them onward to glorious victory over the Saracens!" He said the last with great passion, envisioning his men standing over the Holy Land in flames with his banner raised above all others.

William did not respond, and Gorm realized himself in time to observe William's heaving chest as he tried to stifle his laughter. Gorm's eyes flashed dangerously. "Forgive my impertinence, milord, but can you imagine me at the head of armies? I am as unfit to command as your daughter," he said, grinning broadly.

"I do not have a daughter," Gorm growled.

"Exactly," he said, still grinning. "You have earned the love and respect of all who serve you through a generation of gallant service and brutal combat. I cannot claim any such accolades of my own and therefore neither command nor deserve the respect afforded you."

"Your men worship you," Gorm objected.

"My men follow me because they are mostly untrained soldiers. I wear a pretty suit of armor and they therefore assume that I am someone worth following. You are a leader; I am merely a novelty. I need not explain the difference to you."

Gorm dropped his eyes, disappointed that he had been unable to entice his young ward to remain with him.

William crossed the tent and placed a hand warmly on Gorm's shoulder. "You do me much honor. I will never forget your kind hand and understanding heart. I hope that I may be guided by your example all the days of my life."

"I will feel your loss mightily, William," Gorm said, tears springing into his eyes.

"That is only because you have a mighty heart. Spare me not a moment's thought," William entreated him and squeezed his shoulder warmly. "William," Gorm called as he departed to prepare for the battle to come. "If you ever need anything, remember that I am here."

CHAPTER THREE

Persia

"**H**enry, over here, over here!" Henry heard the voice through the clash of the battle. He searched desperately to see who it was that was calling for him but could not locate the sound amidst the din. Slashing his wicked-looking scimitar through the man in front of him, he raced toward the source of the sound.

Ramming through a press of men, he arrived to see his young lieutenant, having lost his weapon, leap at a Moor opponent. Surprised by the act, the Moor did not respond in time, and they grappled briefly until the Moor threw him off, landing his light frame in the dirt. Henry charged at the Moor. The Moor raised his sword high.

"NO!" Henry shouted instinctively, hoping to draw the Moors attention, but the Moor did not look up as he performed his dark deed. Patrick, his lieutenant, curled up on the ground and shielding himself as best he could, did not see the blade that entered his back and pierced his heart. Henry reached them in a few more steps and swung his scimitar so hard the Moor's head was removed from his shoulders before he even had a chance to pull the sword from Patrick's body.

Henry dropped to his knees beside his lieutenant, yanked the weapon free that had stolen his young life, and angrily hurled it clear. He slowly rolled Patrick over, afraid of what he would see. The young lieutenant had a surprised look on his face. His eyes were lifeless and blood was trickling from his nose and mouth. Tears came into Henry's eyes, and he beat his fist on the ground. The battle raged all around him as his men were being driven back. The spot he currently knelt on had been the front line but was quickly becoming enemy-held territory. He hugged the boy's body to his chest, briefly wondering how he was going to explain this to Patrick's family. Though only a few years older than Patrick, Henry had felt responsible for him since he had joined them en route to Persia. He had met the boy's aging mother, who had demanded an oath from Henry that he would protect her last remaining son.

Henry was a battled-hardened veteran at that point and never doubted his ability to command when his own commanding officer had fallen during their previous battle only two weeks before. When Henry took over, he had taken the boy under his wing, giving him a post of lieutenant to keep him where he could watch him... for all the good it did him.

An enemy soldier noticed Henry kneeling over the body of his friend and aimed to take advantage of it. He charged at him. Though preoccupied, Henry was very aware of the battle raging all around him. As the Moor swung his mace in what he expected to be an easy kill, Henry's scimitar parried his blow with so much force the soldier could scarcely retain his grip on his weapon.

Henry rose, the fury showing plainly on his long face. The Moor soldier suddenly regretted his decision. Though lean, Henry stood a head taller than the average Moor and was clearly possessed. Henry drew his sword back for a brutal swing. He made no effort to conceal the blow from his opponent. The terrified Moor raised his mace to block it but was again shocked by the ferocity with which it was delivered. Henry was not engaging in battle with this soldier, we was swinging to finish it. The Moor's wrist gave way under the blow and the edge of the scimitar cut deep into his throat.

Through the tears that were welling in his eyes, Henry could see that his men were falling back quickly. Henry cut down the next two enemies who stepped too close to him and began a measured retreat with his men.

The Moors took heart to see the crusaders retreating and redoubled their efforts. Before he knew it, Henry was losing control of the situation. The Moors were pressing on them hard, and his men were about to break.

"Stand strong, men, remember what you are fighting for!" He yelled even as he himself had to retreat a few steps before the onslaught. "This is for God and the Holy Land!"

Whether Henry's men did not hear his words or were simply unable to respond, he did not know. But as if by some unspoken mutual consent, his men gave up, and the measured retreat turned into a full scale routing. Crusaders on all sides turned and ran from the Moor army. Henry held the line as long as he could, trying to assess the situation. He dispatched another two Moors and tried to call his men back, but they did not hear him. In their haste to retreat, they left themselves open to their enemies and were being cut down in droves.

"You fools, turn and defend yourselves!" Henry cursed them, but no one was listening. He fell back several yards before the onslaught, turned to try to fend off his attackers, and then fell back again. All was chaos now. Those who tried to stand and fight stood alone and were overwhelmed. Those who fled were easy targets. Henry tried to find an equilibrium between the two in order to execute a measured, controlled withdrawal. He had to stay near his disintegrating line or he, too, would be overwhelmed, but he watched as his men were cut to pieces right before his eyes, and he felt powerless to stop it.

It frustrated him that his men were doing it to themselves. If they would only act as a united front, they could have executed a retreat without it turning into a slaughter. He had tried to drill that discipline into them, but he saw now that men would behave ultimately as they were at their core. Not for the first time, he wished for a solid corps of knights rather than the militia and semi-skilled soldiers that comprised most of the ranks. "Lord, let them see what they are doing. Please protect them and the cause we are fighting for," he silently prayed in desperation.

He ran back again and again turned to face the advancing enemy. His frustration was quickly growing into desperation as he fenced with two more pursuers. After a few minutes he was unable to get the advantage and retreated another ten yards. He could not afford to get involved in a long battle and lose his line all together.

To his left he saw Charles, one of his officers, also attempting to fight. Charles was literally overrun as if by a pack of dogs. There were just too many of them, and they swarmed over him. "Charles!" He screamed helplessly. He tried to cross the short distance to help him but his way was barred and he knew it was already too late.

To his right, Alston, one of his sergeants, was only just holding off the Moors. If only he could get to him, they would both have a better chance. He started to push in that direction. "Alston, to me! To me!" he shouted, but Alston, who was completely occupied with survival, gave no indication that he heard Henry. Henry fell back a few steps. He was determined to get to him before it was too late. He redoubled his efforts, slashing and cutting and stabbing. He drove the Moors back before him, but they were pressing hard against him now, and he was still behind Alston. Someone screamed from his left. Another of his men went down in a spray of blood. He had to get to Alston. Another groan and another man lost; they were falling all around him. But Alston was a seasoned veteran. He was strong, and the men respected him. Maybe between the two of them, they could rally the men and survive this slaughter. Another man fell.

Two Moors appeared directly in front of Henry. He sidestepped a swing and cut the left one down. The other stabbed at Henry's belly but jumped back, stumbling to stay clear of Henry's rapid riposte. He tripped and landed in the dirt behind Alston, who was still furiously engaged in a struggle for his life. The way was clear now and Henry lunged forward, but he did not get two steps before his way was again barred by two new challengers bent on dispatching an English knight. The first Moor that had tripped and fallen jumped up from the ground at Alston's back. Henry saw what was coming.

"Alston, behind you, behind you!" he shrieked desperately. But whether Alston heard him and was simply unable to respond in the face of multiple opponents or had not heard him at all was impossible to tell. In desperation Henry plowed into the two men standing between him and Alston's would-be assassin. He knocked them off balance and dodged their clumsy blows to pass by them only to see the back of the assassin disappearing into the ranks of his comrades. Alston had already dropped to his knees with a nasty wound in his back. He was finished.

"No!" Henry could not believe any of this was happening and on his first battle when he was fully and completely in charge. It was like some horrific dream from which he could not awaken. He scanned the area desperately for some stronghold of his men that were still fighting, some haven to which he could flee in the chaos of this vicious sea. Nothing. He could not see any of his men anywhere. His tears of grief and anger had turned to tears of frustration at his impotence. Impulse turned him and sent him into a full sprint now. There were just too many Moors, and he was a dead man if he did not escape.

Henry heard them pursuing him and knew he did not have much time. If he kept running they would catch him and kill him. But if he turned to face them, they would overwhelm him. He was not strong enough to take on multiple opponents for very long.

"Father, please... Rescue us from this. Spare your servants that they might live to fight another day. Rescue me."

Just then he caught site of a small band of his soldiers that had formed a small line. They were being driven back but were still fighting. He made a break for them, his entourage of enemy soldiers pursuing vigorously.

He cut down two Moors from behind to gain access to the group. "Take heart, men, we may yet prevail!" He shouted as he turned and joined their lines. Surely, this was an answer to his prayers. Then the group of Moors Henry had brought with him were upon them. The line that had been barely able to hold before folded under the stress of the additional enemies.

"So glad to see you, Captain, a voice muttered through teeth clenched in exertion." Henry did not see who had said it, but it did not matter because they were fleeing again. Eight of them turned as one and ran. Another small group of crusaders that were attempting to regroup raced over to reinforce the seven that were with Henry. Only four of the eight survived until the reinforcements made it to them. They turned and fought again, twenty strong now.

Henry fought beside his men. His energy was flagging, and he could see the exhaustion in the faces of his men also. Victory was energizing, but losing had the opposite effect. It was demoralizing and had a way of making a soldier feel inferior and weak against his enemies. He forced himself to surge. He fought hard and stepped out just in front of his men so it would appear as if he were actually pushing the enemy back.

His men seemed to take heart and struggled to push up to where he was standing. Then they pushed past him and Henry dispatched the enemy soldier he was fencing with and found himself behind his own men. He looked back and saw three groups of men milling about as if unsure of where to go or what to do. If he could just gather them to him, they might have enough of a force to survive the day.

He broke into a run toward them, "To me, men! To me!" They did not seem to notice him. "Men!" he shouted, but still no response. Henry glanced back at the line he had left. Seeing their leader running from the line, the group had become muddled and confused and broke down. They were cut off from each other and were being slaughtered.

Henry ran a few steps back toward them to assist them but realized that by himself he was going to be powerless to help and he, too, would be killed. He needed to gather his men. He turned back and continued toward the other group of milling soldiers, shouting to them. But his shouting had roused the attention of the Moors and they were a step ahead. They swarmed into this new group of men and destroyed them before they had a chance to organize.

Henry cursed loudly. He felt an uncontrollable rage seize him and he felt his legs of their own accord charge toward the nearest group of enemies. "This is over," he heard a voice say, and came to a halt. He glanced around, but there was no one in the immediate vicinity. Yet all at once he knew the voice was correct. There was nothing more to be done here. The day was lost, his forces were crushed, and nothing he could do would change that grim fact. He hesitated for just a moment longer before changing his course. Instead of charging into the line of Moors, he veered off and retreated to find any of his men that had survived. As he ran by a group in the midst of a losing skirmish, he heard, "Captain! Captain!" He looked over and saw one of his soldiers on the verge of being overwhelmed shouting for his help.

He stopped in place, unsure of what to do. The group was done for. If he jumped in now he might be able to stave off their deaths for a few moments but then all of them would surely die. On the other hand, could he leave a brother in need? He took a step toward them and stopped. This was suicide.

"Capt—" the shrill cry was cut off sharply as the soldier was cut down.

Henry cursed in frustration and continued to run from the field. The day was lost. "Why have you forsaken your soldiers on your errand?" he demanded of God through the tears of anger and guilt that were blurring his vision. From the hilltop surrounding the battlefield, he cursed Persia and the Moors. Finding no one waiting for him with which to rebuild a force, Henry cursed himself for being alive and fled in shameful defeat from the field of battle.

CHAPTER FOUR

England: Dawning Court

"You feeble-minded child!" John spat at Lindsay. Her angry words had given way to tears now, but this only enraged John further. "I cannot believe that I was so foolish as to marry an idiot peasant. I must have completely taken leave of my senses altogether!"

Lindsay was the daughter of a villein, a partially free peasant, from the outskirts of Dawning Court. As a peasant from a family that lived off the land, she was a poor match for any nobleman; but for the eldest son of a baron and the heir of Dawning Court, it was an unthinkable one. If it had been a younger son, the family might have looked the other way, but for the eldest son with the keys to the family fortune and the weight of the family reputation on his shoulders, this was absolutely unacceptable. The eldest son was expected not only to marry appropriate to his station, but to accept a match that would increase the family fortune, not diminish it.

Nevertheless, John had never been entirely comfortable with the scheming females at court. He instead had fallen in love with a guileless, simple peasant and married her the previous year, and in consequence was subject to the family's wrath. His mother was furious. She was looking to John to replenish the near empty coffers of Dawning Court, but instead he had acted purely on impulse. They had fought, and she threatened to cut him off if he did not comply with her wishes. In anger he took his bride away from Dawning Court. His family had made no official attempt to contact him, and he had been living in poverty on a tiny patch of land tenanted by Lindsay's father ever since. John had tried to farm but did not have enough land or knowledge to be successful at it. He was a knight from a warrior family within a warrior class, and that was all he knew how to be.

Now the crops had failed and Lindsay was angry with him that with all his education and breeding he could not even manage the simple act of bringing in a crop to feed the two of them. "Even the lowliest serf could manage that," she had said in anger, and John had exploded. They were not happy and argued frequently. "You behave as if you are so high and mighty, but what do you have to show for your life? You're not even as good as the lowliest serf," Lindsay repeated the dig. She was no match for John intellectually and was pleased that remarks in this vein had gotten a rise from him in the past, so she tried it again. And again it had the intended effect. John took a long step toward her and brought his hand up to strike her.

Lindsay cowered and John stayed his hand. Seeing her shrinking in the corner, he was suddenly cognizant of a terrible reality that he could not accept. This could not be his life. He was miserable, he had made her miserable, and whose fault was it? Whose fault could it be?

John turned and stormed from the dilapidated old cottage, up the rut-filled road and into the town square to the tavern. These days his time was divided between home and the tavern, with the lion's share spent at the tavern indulging his endless thirst, as was attested to by his ever growing belly. John was larger than most men and very strong, but as he tried to live the life of a farmer, he had neglected his training and turned soft.

Murray was using his dingy grey apron to clean the cups when John walked into the tavern. Murray looked up expectantly as the door opened, and his shoulders slumped in disappointment when he recognized John. John never had any money, but the bartender knew well who he was and knew that he did not want to risk making an enemy of a man that may one day return to prominence and take his place as the baron of Dawning Court. In an effort to secure his own future, Murray allowed John to drink for free. John's insatiable thirst, however, consumed the tiny profit Murray's pub turned. Murray shook his head at the irony that by trying to avoid being closed down by a vengeful baron at some possible future date, he may be sacrificing his livelihood then and there. Nevertheless, he wordlessly slid a cup of cheap wine toward John. John took it and dropped heavily on a stool.

"Why do you wear such a troubled countenance?" a hard alto voice said from behind John.

John looked up in surprise. He had not noticed the solitary figure sitting at a table upon his entrance. "Is it that obvious?" John chuckled humorlessly, trying to see around the drawn hood that obscured her face.

"What could make such a mighty warrior with so many conquests under his belt and a barony at his feet so troubled?"

"A mighty warrior?" He asked casually, turning in his stool to face her and leaning back against the bar.

"I know you, John. There is no sense pretending that you are other than you are. Even in these humble surroundings, your greatness cannot be hooded."

John was unsure how to respond. Something told him to be wary, but the wine and his depression both agreed that this was the first good thing he had heard in a long time, and he wasn't willing to turn his back on it just yet.

"What weighs you down?" She pressed.

"My current situation defies description," he said dismissively and took another pull from the cup.

"Perhaps articulating on your troubles would be a salve to your heart. And it certainly would sound better over a drink," she said, gesturing toward her empty cup suggestively.

"Yes, well, I don't think—" She pushed back her hood and John's heart leapt into his throat, choking off his words midsentence. The refusal he had been working on never emerged. Her dark hair was pulled back from her black almond eyes, and her high cheekbones were covered in the perfectly smooth olive skin of a beautiful Saracen woman. "Murray, two more of these!" John ordered.

Wordlessly Murray set another cup beside John's and filled them both. He looked meaningfully at John, but John did not notice his gaze. His attention was rapt on the portrait of beauty before him. She was still looking straight ahead as if she did not notice she was being gawked at.

"What may I call you?" John tried to sound casual as he set the drinks on the table and sat in the chair opposite her. His heart was still beating very fast and he felt flustered, like a schoolboy trying to strike up a conversation with the object of his affection.

She took a sip of the cheap wine, ignoring his question. "Now tell me, what has brought John Dawning, the mightiest of all the Dawning men, to this?" She gestured slightly to indicate the dank tavern.

"Your knowledge of my situation does seem to be beyond that of a casual observer," John observed rather than answer her question.

"Everyone knows of you. Everything your family does is significant as the local economy rises or falls on when the Dawnings empty their bowels."

John's eyebrows raised slightly at the crass expression. "Look, I never asked for that!" John insisted defensively.

"Why does that matter? None of us asked for the lives we were born to, but that does not absolve you of the responsibilities that come with it."

"I don't have to take this. I came in here to get drunk and thought some company might be nice. Seems I was mistaken about the second, but I can still have the first." He started to rise.

She leaned across the table and placed a soft, slender hand over his large, calloused one. "It is not too late for you. Your life may yet still have meaning. You may use that power that was so unwillingly inherited for something great!"

John hesitated for a moment. "Ah, no. But I thank you," he said, pulling his hand free and picking up his drink as he stood fully erect. "I thank you for providing the perfect end to a perfect day."

"You were not meant to be a farmer," she said urgently to his retreating back. "You were meant for greatness. Will you content yourself to live in the shadow of your younger brothers when it is you who should be the head of the family?" There was a note of desperation in her voice.

John stopped in his tracks. She had struck a nerve. He turned back to her slowly. "What do you know of these things?"

She stood and moved closer to John. She was taller than most women, and stood to his chin. "I know there is more in store for you than you have ever imagined if you will let me but prove it to you." She looked intently into his eyes.

John considered her words. She definitely had her own motives, but was he in any danger? Probably not. What good would killing the disgraced son of a nobleman do? Especially when there were many more sons to take his place. She was so beautiful, what harm could there be in listening to her?

"Perhaps we can go somewhere we can... talk," she suggested seductively.

"I cannot be seen to escort you anywhere until I have learned your name," John said lightly.

"Anisa," she said simply and turned and walked toward the exit.

John stood rooted in place, admiring her form as she glided to the door. He suddenly realized she was getting away and set his drink down quickly in order to follow.

"Uh, sir," the tavern keeper called as he was exiting on her heels. Anisa and John both stopped and looked back.

"Uh, Sir John, there is the small matter of the bill, if you would be so kind." John was annoyed; of all the times to bring this up. Murray had never called in his tab before. Why now?

John looked down at Anisa, who looked impatient. "Pardon me a moment," he smiled at her.

John walked slowly back to the bar. He knew he did not have any money or any way of getting money. He was going to look ridiculous in front of the woman who thought he was rich and powerful. He reached the bar across from Murray, unsure of what to say. He opened his mouth to speak, hoping something intelligent would come out, but the tavern keeper cut him off. "I am sorry but I thought you should be aware: that woman has been coming in here every night for days and has never spoken to anyone until tonight," he said quietly.

John glanced over at her and saw her standing, watching impatiently. "And?"

"She is a Moorish woman. She may have designs on your noble person. I would advise caution."

John looked again at the tall, slender form in the doorway. She was so beautiful that he found himself angry at the tavern keeper's insinuation. "Have you ever been over there? Have you ever fought the Moor— Saracens, or lived among them?" he demanded.

"No, Sir John." Murray looked down at the cup he was absently wiping dirt on with his filthy apron.

"And yet you do arrogate the right to advise me? What license have you to hold a prejudice against a people you do not know?" John continued angrily. "I have been over there! I have talked with them and fought with them. I have had friends struck down by them. If I can overlook that prejudice, then what excuse can you make for yourself?" John pushed himself back from the bar.

"Yes, Sir John. I am sorry," Murray apologized quickly, not looking up from the cup he was wiping. "I only wanted to make you aware."

John was still angry but realized the tavern keeper meant no harm. "I am sorry," he said more softly. "I know you were only conducting yourself as a loyal subject, and I thank you for it."

"Yes," the tavern keeper said, somewhat relieved.

"Put it on my tab," John said casually but loudly enough that Anisa would hear as he walked back to join her at the door, and they departed into the evening together.

Anisa immediately struck out of the square and down a lonely road in the diminishing light without speaking. Finally John broke the silence. "I am as yet unenlightened as to how you are going to restore me to my former glory."

"I never said I would restore you to your former glory," Anisa said simply.

"Ah," John said, expecting their conversation to ultimately come to this, just not quite so quickly.

"I will help you achieve far greater glory than you have ever dreamed."

"Ah..." was all John could manage.

"Did you have dreams as a child, John?"

"Dreams?" he asked. "You mean like nightmares?"

"I mean daydreams of glory and power, and what you wanted from your life."

John shrugged. "I concede that I did."

"And in those dreams," Anisa asked– casting her arm over the dirty town square behind them and the serf huts littering the countryside before them, interspersed among fields in various stages of crop growth–"did you ever imagine that your purview would be limited to a simple field in the lands of another man... or woman?" John knew what she meant, of course. He was now nothing but a villein to his mother, who was holding the seat of Baron in the absence of a worthy male heir to take his father's place.

John shrugged again. "Not likely, since I always knew I would be Baron, assuming Richard didn't find some way of doing me in first."

"So how did you end up here? How did it come to this?" Anisa pressed. John only answered with another mute shrug.

"You could have stood up to Martha Dawning and demanded your birthright. Yet you did nothing. Why was that?"

"My mother has not had an easy life, and it did not seem right to deprive her of all that is left to her of her husband and her legacy," John said uneasily. Anisa rounded on him, her dark eyes boring into his soft brown eyes until he dropped his gaze.

"Left to her?" She asked, her voice a mix of confusion and consternation. "Left to *her*? John, Dawning Court belongs to you. Have you not accepted that?" John felt like a child under the scrutiny of this foreign beauty. His embarrassment made him want to lash out at her, but perhaps it was time he started to ask himself these questions.

He shrugged again, still unable to meet her gaze. "I am not going to kill my own mother over a position I am uncertain I could fill adequately." Anisa stepped forward and shook his arm to get him to meet her gaze.

"Of course, why would you desire to upset the woman who has contrived literally from day one to make you nothing—less than nothing?" She demanded sarcastically.

"Contrived?" John said, stepping around her to continue walking and take her focus off of him. "What nonsense is this?"

"Nonsense?" she said, catching up to him. "Is it nonsense, then? Ask yourself, who has kept you from your inheritance?" She did not wait for a reply. "Who brought you up to be a great warrior and then stripped you of the right to do that?" John could not help seeing the sense in what she was saying. He was a warrior from a long line of warriors, and it was all he knew how to be. By disavowing him, he was no longer a knight of Dawning Court and could no longer march with their army or receive rewards as such. "What other skills are you equipped with?" she pressed. "Are you a farmer, or a thatcher, or a tailor?" She let that sink in before again stepping in front of him in the road, drawing tantalizingly close to him. "Martha Dawning did not simply deny you your rightful inheritance; she took every opportunity away from you of living a productive, useful life. She robbed you of every opportunity of a warrior's glory, of a warrior's noble death. Instead you will simply rot away out here until you are dumped in a pauper's grave after being crushed by a plow horse or expiring from consumption."

John stared at Anisa for a long moment, turning her words over in his head. "What are you proposing?" he asked cautiously.

She smiled at him, and John felt his whole soul excited by it. She stepped so close that John trembled to feel her against him and his nostrils were filled with the scent of her perfumed hair. But she did not touch him. "Think about what I have said. Think very carefully. What is your own life worth to you? If you do decide you are worth something after all, then meet me back here tomorrow night." She went up on her toes until her lips brushed his ear when she spoke. "I know you are great. I just need you to realize it."

With that she turned off the road and disappeared into the darkness. John watched her go, her scent still in his nostrils, and the feeling of her lips still warming his ear. He snapped out of his meditative contemplation of her beauty when she had disappeared entirely. "Wait a minute!" he called. "Meet you where? Here?" He looked around at the empty road. They had passed the last of the serfs' cottages and were now on an empty stretch of road that led to Baron Braddock's lands in the neighboring barony. "Why here?" he called but got no answer. "And when tomorrow night?.. If I choose to return," he suddenly added, afraid he was sounding too interested.

It was not lost on John that there were still many unanswered questions, but he could not seem to focus on those at the moment. All he could think about was the contrast between the beginning of his day and now. In the last two hours he had not only met the most beautiful woman he had ever seen but also found that she was very interested in him. And now, because of her, he was beginning to see the beginning of a possible escape from this dismal life he had carved for himself— or rather, this dismal life he had been thrust into.

CHAPTER FIVE

Egypt: Damietta

Tahir stood with his men amassed by the gate. He tried once again to keep them silent, but with so many men assembled, even the smallest sounds each individual might make were multiplied upon each other and seemed a great racket: A chink of armor here, a cough there, the hard tang of metal bumping metal. All these sounds played particular havoc with Tahir's tensed nerves as he waited behind the gates of Damietta. He listened for any indication of how his men fared outside the walls. Were the crusaders being driven back into the sea, or were his men being crushed? Of course he did not really expect that his men were prevailing as it was only half his force outside the walls. The real power was behind him, waiting for just the right moment to strike. Yet he prayed for their success.

The hair of Tahir's head was grey with age, but his arm was still as strong any of his men, and he had been protecting his city from the endless sea of crusaders for as long as he could remember. He wondered vaguely where they all came from and if they would ever exhaust themselves on the rock of his arm. Though one looked much like another, he had observed that they had gotten smarter over the years. Each new army was more clever than the one before. Tahir feared for how much longer he could keep his people safe. He feared for the day when he would not be able to outthink the enemy, but that day would not be today.

Many of the town elders had insisted they remain inside and wait out the crusaders by a lengthy siege, but Tahir had convinced them his plan was better. The city was not prepared for a long drawn-out siege. They had not expected an attack this late in the year, and if they allowed a siege to begin, the crusaders would simply be able to starve them out. But the crusaders would never expect an ambush upon their ambush.

Today he had the upper hand. While half his army was out meeting the first wave, he was lying in wait to cut the second wave in half. His informants had revealed that the crusaders were planning a two-pronged attack: one by sea, and a second by land. But because of this advance information, the advantage was now his. There was nothing left to do but wait until he heard the signal from the lookouts that the cavalry of the land forces had attacked. Then the gates to the city would be flung open for the briefest of moments while his men flooded out and then quickly re-secured. His contingent and those already defending against the attack from the sea constituted all the fighting men in the city other than a skeleton crew to maintain the defenses.

***

William of York leaned on his spear as he watched the sleeping city of Damietta. He wondered idly as he had so many times before if this was the end. The Angel of Death was circling the field now as he certainly must be, but was it looking for him? Was he already dead, as he knew so many of his men were? He could read similar thoughts on each of their faces. William repeated the inner monologue he had asked before a hundred other battles just like this one. Would he know if he were about to die when the time came? Would there be a warning in the air? Would he feel a sense of foreboding, or would death strike at him the way William had lived his life, rashly and unaware? He entered each battle expecting God's judgment would be passed on him for his many crimes, and yet from each battle he was delivered with rarely more than a scratch. He was ready to die. He deserved to die for all he had done. Surely he could not continue to live, and yet here he was after all these years, still standing, stronger than ever, while all around him better men than he were struck down.

Damietta was a dark mass against the grey dawn. He wondered if those who had first settled this area for its choice location at the foot of the Nile River, where it met the Mediterranean Sea, realized what a target they were destined to become. Damietta was the key to this part of the world. He who controlled Damietta controlled the Nile, and he who controlled the Nile controlled Egypt. He had been working for this opportunity for a year now, and he was not going to let it slip. The city was surrounded by Christian soldiers. William's detachment was part of the second wave of assaults. The first were men landing from the Nile itself. As soon as they were engaged, they would charge the adjacent side of the city from the initial assault. It was calculated to break the back of the resistance once and for all. It should work, provided the surprise of the attack was preserved and had not leaked to the enemy. But they had taken the utmost care to protect this, with only the generals of each army knowing what was planned and misinformation deliberately being leaked to the men to throw any would-be spies off the trail.

William was largely responsible for this plan and loved it for its simplicity. An army was a massive beast that was infinitely dumber than the lowest rodent, infinitely slower than the slowest insect, and yet more powerful than a wildfire; and it needed to be manipulated accordingly. Overly elaborate plans rarely worked in the mishegoss of battle. But small subtleties often went a long way against an opposing army.

Just before the sun crested the hills, the roar of the assault from the Mediterranean side washed over William and his men. He looked to Gorm, who now sat at the head of a host of mounted knights. They were a majestic sight with their silver armor glittering in the early morning light and their pennants fluttering in the cool air. Gorm raised his sword high in the air. "For God and country!" he called and spurred his destrier down the hill toward the city.

The cavalry rushed toward the battle in the first rays of dawn, when it was only just possible to distinguish friend from foe, with William's infantry close on their heels. The soldiers from the city were well engaged on the Mediterranean side, and the cavalry led by Gorm cut a swath of destruction from their unprotected flank. Everything was going exactly as planned. William's infantry were charging down the hill, a large gap having opened between his men on foot and the much faster cavalry, when the early dawn light was almost completely obscured by an immense dark cloud that arose suddenly. William almost missed it in the low light, expecting no opposition other than the forces that were before them. It was almost too late when he roared over the din of the field, "Cover!" Not a moment was lost, not a man hesitated before throwing his shield overhead and crouching down as the hail of arrows from the city wall clattered around them. They plinked off shields and armor, they embedded themselves in the ground like stalks of wheat, and for those who were not careful enough or well protected enough, they cut into unprotected flesh.

William was surprised they would have left so many archers on the walls when their army was making its last stand. It was also strange that the darkened city still seemed to sleep while its army fought for survival. He would expect it to be alive with activity. Nevertheless, when the hailstorm stopped, he shouted the command to resume, and they charged ahead until the sky was once again darkened with the massive volley of arrows and the infantry was once again forced to take cover. When they arose this time, however, the gates of the city were open and a sea of soldiers was streaming out upon them.

"Ambush!" he roared. It was a trap and they had fallen right into it. William cursed himself for his oversight but hunkered down again as the archers protected the approach of Damietta's men with yet another volley. Once they were engaged, it was difficult for the archers to shoot effectively, but they could keep an advancing army off balance enough that the defenders could gain the initial advantage.

The moment the last arrow had dropped, William roused his men and charged into the sea of newcomers. Like two mighty waves colliding, William's company crashed into the Moors that were still pouring from the gates of Damietta. William charged into the army, hurling his shield at the unprotected head of a nearby Damiettan. A whirling disk of death, it slammed into the side of his head, and William impaled his first hapless victim on the end of his spear. He felt the familiar rush of the battle, and strength surged through him. On an impulse, he raised the dying man up on his spear and shouted, "Death to the Moors that have corrupted our lands and perverted our religion!" He flung the body off into another approaching Moor. The enemy soldier stumbled in an effort to avoid the grotesque projectile. William spun his spear in his grip and drove it deep into the Moor chest as he tried to avoid the body.

Whirling, William stabbed at a soldier's exposed face. The unusually long reach of the spear often took the average sword-wielding soldier by surprise. However, this Moor instinctively jerked back, only receiving a deep gash on his cheek rather than the promised fatal wound. William instantly closed the distance. Stepping forward, he swung his spear in a wide arc around his head, catching the same man in the side of the head with the heavy oak shaft. He crumpled instantly to the ground.

Then, as it always did, the way opened before him and he had to take it. William charged deep into the enemy line. It was the challenge he had issued so many times before—a challenge to death himself. He pushed far into the opposing lines until he was surrounded by enemies on every side, completely cut off from help. He was throwing the gauntlet down before the Heavens, challenging them not to kill him. He had to know if the Angel of Death could not be enticed to take his soul as it should have so long ago. He wanted Death to take him now, while he was prepared, rather than at some future time when he least expected or desired it. He charged into a thick of soldiers.

It was him and only him against the enemy. He had to know if God was fighting for him or against him. William ran the point of his weapon through the ribs of a Moor who had made the fatal mistake of failing to notice an enemy so far behind his own lines.

When William had first joined Gorm in his crusade as scarcely more than a boy, he had ideals about noble combat and glorious battle; he truly believed there was honor in war and the rules of chivalry would be abided. His eyes were quickly opened, however, to the ugly truth that in a battle it was kill or be killed. One did not let a soldier retrieve his weapon only to be stabbed in the back by that same blade. When an enemy stumbled or dropped his weapon, he had lost. There was no such thing as a fair fight. In fact, William did everything in his power to ensure that battles were not fair. Keeping the odds overwhelmingly in his favor ensured that he would lose fewer men, which meant more victories.

Now William tended to see the enemies as a thick forest that needed to be removed. His movements became almost mechanical, as that of a lumberjack who had felled so many trees he did not see the individual tree anymore but only the large brown mass that remained to be cut before the day was done.

Jerking the end of his weapon free from the body of his latest victim, William closed the distance on another enemy, caught his sword slash on the side of his spear, and spinning, pinned the man's sword arm between his own arm and body. With his free hand, William swung the back end of the spear under the Moor's feet and swept them from underneath him. The Moor hit the ground hard, and William finished him with a quick thrust of his weapon.

Still another Moor was standing over one of William's own soldiers whom had tripped. His man was helpless. William could not cover the twenty feet in time to rescue him. On impulse, he hurled his spear at the Moor. Hit! The end sunk into his kidney, and he dropped his weapon and arched back in agony. The prostrate soldier was immediately on his feet and back in the fight.

The enemy saw William unarmed and quickly advanced on him. William locked eyes with the advancing peasant made soldier overnight. He drew his katana from its sheath slowly and deliberately, letting the slightly curved blade sing as it left the sheath. He let the finely crafted weapon catch the light and highlight the waves that ran in close lines down it from the hundreds or even thousands of times the metal was folded by the swordsmith. He let all this work its effect on this boy that was younger than even William himself. The Moor boy stopped short. What had only a moment ago seemed an easy kill now looked menacing indeed. They were only a moment thus locked on each other's faces when William knocked the blade of another soldier aside and whirled. Dropping low, he sliced a deep cut in the side of the Moor's thigh. The now helpless Moor dropped, and William leapt over him to the boy.

The boy's weapon was raised high, ready for William. William feigned a stab at his face. The Moor's downward defensive swing dropped too fast to control. It missed William, who had stepped just out of range, and the blade dug itself slightly into the ground. William slammed his boot down on the middle of the blade, wrenching it from the Moor's hand. The boy was defenseless now. There is no such thing as a fair fight.

William stepped over the boy's body in an effort to reach his spear, still embedded in the body of the fallen enemy. Besides being his preferred weapon, it was extremely valuable, and if it were picked up by someone else on this immense field, he may never find it again.

***

Tahir rushed out the gates ahead of his men. They were aiming to separate the second wave of infantry from their cavalry, which was already entangled in battle with what they presumed to be the entirety of the Moor army. Typical Christian arrogance to assume Muslims lacked any cunning or forethought, like simple animals that were fit for nothing but extermination. It was all too common for the Christians to disdain his people and assume they were weak and stupid. This was a prejudice that served Tahir very well.

Tahir's men crashed into the infantry of the crusaders, determined to cut their way through them before the Christian cavalry could return to reinforce them. The enemy realized what was happening too late for any but a thin line of foot soldiers to turn and meet Tahir's men head on. Tahir himself was in the section of his line that hit the back of the Christian infantry, which was largely unprepared for the strike on their flanks. He cut into the enemy with relish. He had dispatched three enemy soldiers before he realized part of his own line to his left had collapsed and there were crusaders streaming behind his line. He rushed over to provide support but stopped short. His heart froze for the briefest of moments as he beheld an angel sent from Allah himself, and he was fighting for the crusaders.

There, some fifty paces to his left, deep behind his own line, was a figure that glowed in white and gold armor in the early morning light. Tahir was mesmerized as he watched this being that seemed to have materialized behind his line. He wielded death with his spear like nothing Tahir had ever seen. He watched the spear whirl seemingly of its own volition and the figure leap and spin and jump as a dancer in some elaborate performance.

An angel? That was ridiculous. Tahir forced himself to snap out of his trance. This was nothing but a European devil that was cutting through his soldiers like blades of grass. He was greatly concerned by this, not only because of the men they were losing but also because the crusaders seemed to be heartened by this dramatic display. This white man seemed to know in advance what each of Tahir's men would do. He had to be stopped, and it seemed that his spear was where his real advantage lay. Tahir watched as the white knight hurled it and killed a man not far from Tahir himself and immediately began fighting his way toward it. Tahir knew he had to get there first.

With a dramatic thrust of his mace, he doubled the closest Crusader over, then crashed the mace into the back of the Christian helmet. The sizable dent convinced him his job was done as the Christian collapsed. He took a few rapid steps towards the enemy spear. Several of his men intervened to keep the possessed knight from reaching his favorite weapon. Tahir breathed a sigh of relief. He was almost there. An ironclad knight suddenly stood before him in full armor. Tahir cursed at him. "Get out of my way!" He ordered in Arabic. But of course the European did not obey. The Europeans never took the time to learn anything about the people they were trying to destroy. Even so, he now had a problem. European knights were encased in iron, and dispatching them could be a long and frustrating ordeal. It could take even the most skilled warrior some amount of time to find a weak spot and exploit it. Tahir was not afraid, but he was vexed at this delay. "Move aside!" he ordered again.

The knight raised his sword. Tahir roared angrily, smashing the knight's blade aside and going on the offensive. These knights were the reason Tahir had taken to using a mace against the crusaders rather than his preferred blade. Often the blades were ineffective against someone completely clad in iron. But the maces were a different story. He swung again and again, furiously driving the knight back. Tahir could see his men continuing to drop before the white knight not far away. He knew he and the Christian were both racing for the same objective. He had to get there first!

Tahir's opponent tried desperately to defend against this crazed Moor, but the end came when his heel caught on the body of a fallen man and he tumbled backward. Tahir was instantly on him, smashing his visor repeatedly with heavy blows until the knight stopped moving.

Tahir looked up, panting, from where he stood over his victim as the white knight was just dispatching the last man in his way. Tahir was triumphant. He had beaten the white knight to his weapon. The very body that had tripped up his opponent had been that Moor with the spear stuck into him. Gleefully Tahir jerked the weapon from the corpse and turned on the white knight. He was looking at this knight as if he were the heart of this evil scourge that lusted after Tahir's city.

Tahir had only used a spear a handful of times. He felt it was a clumsy weapon given to the unskilled, expendable foot soldiers. But then he had never seen anyone use it the way this man had. It was a refined instrument of death in this knight's hands. Watching him, the advantages of it were obvious. Holding the weapon in both hands, Tahir leveled it at the white knight's chest, halting the knight's charge at once. Tahir stepped forward and swung the weapon in a wide arc at the knight's midsection, trying to duplicate a move he had just seen him perform moments before. But the awkwardness of the weapon carried it well past his intended target and left Tahir's flank open; The white knight took advantage of this and flicked a quick blow at Tahir's side with his long, curved sword blade, cutting a jagged gash in Tahir's flesh.

Tahir looked down at the wound in surprise and confusion. Rethinking his strategy, Tahir made a savage but clumsy thrust toward the knight's chest, but the knight was expecting it. He parried the blow to his left with the sword, stepped in close and seized the shaft of the spear with his free hand while he put his right foot on the Moor chest and shoved him violently backward, landing him in the dirt. Before the Moor had a chance to collect himself, the knight was above him with his foot on Tahir's chest, the spear point held at his throat, and his sword poised over his head, ready to strike the Moor. It was the end. Tahir looked up at his executioner and all at once realization dawned. This was no angel of death but a mere man. What's more, it was not just any man. "I know you," Tahir spat. "Have you come here to finish the murdering and pillaging that your villainous father began so long ago?"

The white knight's eyebrows lifted in surprise. "You knew my father?" he asked.

"He himself tried to take my city on several occasions and failed. Just as you will fail."

The knight only grinned at him with no trace of humor. "When you get to Hell, give Braden my regards!" Tahir made as if to reply and instead kicked hard at the young knight, lifting him off the ground and sending him stumbling backward. Tahir snatched a weapon dropped onto the earth and was again back in the fight. He now knew something about this knight, and this was a fight he was determined not to lose.

***

In the heat of battle, it was always difficult to tell exactly which side was prevailing. For William, the strength and morale of his men was gauged more by feeling than anything else. He trusted to a sense garnered from the men around him and how hard he himself was fighting. The Moors had surprised the Pope's forces and successfully divided them. They were using that to their full advantage. Each force of the Pope's was smaller than the Moor army they were engaging, and as a result they were being pushed back by the greater numbers of Moors.

The crusaders were fighting for a noble cause, but the Moors were fighting for their homes and families, which was the strongest cause of all. Whenever possible, William would keep his campaigns from reaching this point. As long as their homes and families were not at stake, the soldiers always fought as if they had something to lose–tentatively, and not overly committed. But when their backs were up against their own front doors, they fought like lions, as they did this day. It looked as though the day would go to the Moors again. That the people of Damietta would repel another invasion as they had for so many centuries. But the crusaders had one more trick to play.

William was sparring with a particularly able Moor. William's pride had forced him to respond glibly to his opponent's comments about his father, but suddenly he found himself very curious to know if this Moor had actually known his father. Braden died when William was very young, and William had very few actual memories of him.

William blocked a stroke on the shaft of his spear and returned a strike at his opponent's head; the Moor ducked. Continuing the momentum, William spun around and swung another blow at the Moor's legs, who jumped just in time. The Moor then jabbed a quick thrust at William's chest. William was forced to lurch back to avoid the blow.

In the short pause this created, William had to decide. With sudden clarity he realized how distracted he was with this opponent and how precarious the situation of his men actually was. His decision was made. William shouted to his lieutenant, "Sound the signal! Sound the signal!" His opponent advanced on him with malice in his eyes. William's lieutenant dispatched another enemy and fumbled with the horn tied over his shoulder. Putting it to his lips he blew a great long note. Then, after a short pause, he blew another. It was answered by a distant note from a similar horn.

Most of the men were far too involved in the battle to pay any heed to the horns, but William's opponent heard it. The intensity in his eyes drained away and was rapidly replaced by fear. He realized what was happening and turned toward his own line of men. "Retreat!" He shouted. "It's a trap, retreat!"

Fearing he would alert the Moors to the imminent third strike that was about to take them by surprise, William lunged at him. The Moor's attention was no longer on William but on sounding the alarm for his people. He drew breath for another call and William's spear sunk deep into his lung. He gurgled something unintelligible and dropped. None of the men of Damietta had heard his warning call, and they were not prepared for the new force that fell on them.

The new wave of crusaders swept down onto the field, and the tide turned quickly against the defenders. As the last of the men were being routed, William paused amid the chaos. He looked for the Angel of Death, but he was not interested in William on this night. Perhaps now, through all these years of service, William had atoned for his wrongs. Perhaps he had been forgiven after all, and there was mercy and peace while still in the flesh.

CHAPTER SIX

"*M*ilady, I thank you for seeing me unannounced." Leah glided into the room followed by her handmaid, Edith.

"Of course, Henry. What is it?" she asked, noting with some concern his paler than usual complexion and agitated manner.

"It is an exceedingly personal matter, milady, and I would beg leave to speak with you alone," he said, looking between Leah and Edith. His request was quite unorthodox and not the sort of request a respectable lady would frequently grant if she intended to remain respectable. Nevertheless, Leah turned without hesitation to address herself to Edith.

"Edith, my dear, would you be good enough to leave us for a short while?" she asked in an apologetic tone. Edith looked as though she would protest but only flicked a dark glance at Henry and withdrew.

"Please sit down," he said to Leah as soon as the door had closed, leaving them alone. She did as she was bid while Henry continued to pace in a feverish manner.

"Henry, please, sit a moment and rest, for you are discomfiting me with your manor." He sat down rigidly on the extreme edge of the sofa.

"Henry, what is it that has you so upset; are you unwell?"

"No. Or rather, I am most unwell, milady," he said, grasping at this to try to articulate his thoughts.

"I must call someone to tend to you at once." Leah started to rise.

"No, please," Henry said, quickly extending a trembling hand to her shoulder to urge her to reclaim her seat. But he did not dare allow himself to touch her, and withdrew his hand. "What I mean to say is that I am most unwell, but there is no medical man whose arts could have any power over my ailment. My sickness is of a very different kind. Please," he interrupted her protest. "Please do not deign to speak until I have said what I came to say, for if I do not express what I have purposed to express here and now, I may never find the will to do so." Leah remained quiet with a solemn expression of concern furrowing her smooth brow.

"As you may be aware, I will be departing for Persia on the morrow to combat the Moor scourge on that quarter..." Henry was once again pacing, pulling on his fingers anxiously. "I am giving myself over, as it were, to the whims of fate and do not know but that I shall be overcome and struck down by the blade."

Leah put her hand to her mouth in a gasp of shock. "Do not say such things, Henry."

"Please," he said. "Leah, you are of too wise a temperament and pragmatic a disposition to dispute such a point. And I only state the former as a motivation for appearing before you now in such a barbarous fashion, not as any call for remonstrance." He sighed and sat again but was just as quickly on his feet a moment later.

"Leah," Henry's voice was trembling. "In this last year since William left—" He hesitated, cursing himself for the slip of the tongue as he always made an active effort to avoid mention of that name to her. "In this last year, I have come to value your friendship very highly. I regard a word from you more highly than anyone else, I dare say." He laughed nervously at this admission.

"Oh Henry, I too am grateful we have had the opportunity to become friends. It would have been my misfortune if I had never come to know you better." She smiled warmly at him.

Henry was encouraged by this. "You are like none other I have ever met. In the all too few moments I have had the *pleasure of your company, I have never heard you utter a single ill word against anyone. Your fair countenance is rendered moreso by your delightful disposition."* Leah blushed and dropped her eyes at this.

"I am afraid you do me too much credit," she returned. *"I am afflicted by a great many flaws that you are too good to mention."*

"Never!" Henry almost yelled. *"I could never hear a word uttered against you, not even from your lips. You are too good and too wonderful. I cannot and will not brook such villainous lies."*

Her fine eyebrows perked up a bit. *"Surely you would not deny me the privilege to acknowledge my own faults."*

"No, milady. I cannot hear such things. If fault there be with you, you must keep it to yourself, for it is not for mortals as myself to cast aspersions at the gods."

"Henry, what is it that has worked you into such a state?" She laughed lightly at his behavior but at once quelled her mirth, sensing the impropriety of it.

"Please, Leah," he said with a pained expression. *"Please do not laugh at me now. While your laughter is musical and delightful, at this moment it cuts me to the very core."* He rushed on before she could reply. *"I have thus to say as my heart compels me. But I fear at once that my lips would take it back before it is uttered."*

"I have found the mind to typically be the better judge in such moments than the heart," Leah interjected, but he did not listen.

"I leave tomorrow and may never return. I must confess what is in my heart." A tear of emotion stood in his eye as his voice quaked and trembled. He dropped onto one knee before her and took her left hand in both of his. Leah unconsciously recoiled slightly at the action, but did not dare interrupt him in such a passion. *"I have said I am unwell, Leah, but it is because my heart is no longer my own. It has been wrenched from my breast as surely as any enemy may have done. I have endeavored to ignore the emptiness the absence has left. I have*

thought to control the emotion by force of will. But Leah, on this, the eve of my departure into the wastelands of the Saracens, I tell you that I could die a happy and contented man if I but knew my heart was held by one in whose esteem I was held equally high." Leah was not aware of the expression of horror that involuntarily crossed her face. Henry noted it and hesitated, but plunged on despite his crumbling resolve. *"Leah, I know you are an honorable and true maiden above all others, and you would never pledge yourself falsely, believing you might one day turn back to another. I am down on my knee before you, lady, to pledge my undying love and devotion to you. Will you accept this gift? Humble though it be, a deeper, more heartfelt gift I never could offer to anyone."* Henry bowed his head before her as if awaiting his sentence.

Leah took a few moments to recover herself, and when she spoke, she did so very carefully. *"Henry, you have done me too much honor to offer such a gift as your devotion. Such an offer of a nobleman, a scholar, and a knight would be the pride of any woman in England to accept. And while you have my deepest admiration both as a man and as my friend, you do not have my heart."* Henry's head sank even lower, but he did not speak as the emotions overwhelmed him. He feared lest speech would betray the wound he had just received. *"Trouble yourself not, Sir Knight, over one such as myself. I pray you not to give this one moment's reflection upon your departure."* She gently raised his chin to gaze into his tear-filled eyes. *"You are too good and too noble. I am not worthy of you."*

Henry quickly stood and wiped his eyes. *"You say any maiden would be honored by an offer of such a pledge and that you are not worthy."* His voice had a harsh edge to it now. *"And yet you have rejected me."*

Leah sat back in surprise at his words. *"I assure you, good sir, that I spoke sincerely,"* she said, her voice echoing the same surprise that showed on her face.

"Why do you rebuff me? Is it for William?" he demanded angrily. *"He is dishonored and disgraced. If he is not already dead, he can never return here. He will never be anything but a*

cravenly dog. Would you give your heart at the expense of your name and the honor of your own family?" Leah put her hand to her bosom in shock at this abrupt change in manners. *"Would you sacrifice everything on the vain hope of a memory of a departed child?"* She crimsoned at this in anger and only bit her tongue and bowed her head humbly.

"Foolish woman," Henry said, his shame making him angrier still. *"When I walk out that door, my offer is withdrawn forever. I suggest you consider this carefully."*

Leah slowly turned her beautiful hazel eyes up to Henry's fuming countenance, her silence saying more than words could have. Henry turned and stormed out of the room angry, humiliated, and soul sick, feeling that perhaps Persia was not far enough for him now.

CHAPTER SEVEN

Annie stared up at Thomas, her mouth hanging slightly open, her dull eyes revealing nothing. Thomas returned her stare levelly. He was unsure if she had understood him or even heard him at all. "Do you understand?" he said, enunciating each word as if she were hard of hearing. "The children are playing in the wallow again. You must keep them out of there or they will get sick."

Annie's expression clouded over. "You don't think I'm a good mother?"

Thomas rolled his eyes. "We are not discussing your abilities as a mother," his voice rose slightly, but he forced himself to contain his anger. "I am trying to keep my children safe." Annie turned away and did not respond. She was pouting. Thomas bit back a sharp comment. "Will you please fetch them?"

"Why don't you?" Annie responded in a sulky voice, hiding her round face behind her unkempt black hair.

"Because I need to call on my mother."

"Of course. You walk out on your family at every excuse," Annie said, still facing the wall.

"What are you saying? My mother is my family, too. I swear, Annie, sometimes I feel like I have three children. Just take care of Hannah and Harry and stop whining!" His irritation was clearly showing through now. He took a deep breath to collect himself. "Look, I will get them out of the mud and send them inside on my way out. Will you please see that they are bathed?"

Annie did not respond. Thomas took that to be as close to consent as he was likely to get when she was in this mood. He turned and walked out the large front door of his small estate house and around the side of the stone building to where a few animals were kept in pens. "Hannah, Harry, get out of there!" he said to his three-year-old daughter and his son that was almost two. His voice was louder and angrier than he intended even in his own ears. It occurred to Thomas that he sounded that way a lot lately.

Hannah looked up in shock as if she had just been apprehended selling state secrets. Her bright red hair was completely covered in mud. Chubby little Harry grinned at him from where he was sitting naked in the mud. "You will get sick if you keep playing in there! Now go inside. Mother is going to give you a bath."

"No!" Hannah screamed defiantly and threw the mud in her hand at him.

"Get inside now, or I will beat your bottom!" Thomas did not bother to try to control his anger at her reaction. Harry grinned and smeared mud all over his bare belly.

Hannah ran for the house, letting out a blood curdling wail. "Moooother! Father yelled at me!"

Thomas went to the fence and attempted to pick Harry up, but he was just out of reach. Cursing to himself, he took a step into the ankle-deep mud, leaned over, and snatched his filthy son from the mire. Extending his son out in front of himself at arm's length, he carried him back inside. At times like this, Thomas frequently pondered on the irony of a great warrior doing such menial and silly tasks. This was beneath him, but he knew if he did not do it, no one would. He really needed to employ servants like his mother did at Dawning Court, but other than the cook and the maid, his mother would not fund anymore. She always claimed she could not afford loan requests from Thomas, which they both knew he would never pay back, but then she lived in the lap of luxury with ten times the number of servants in her house as occupants. Nevertheless, because of her unwillingness to give up any of her own personal luxuries, Thomas was forced to live on a small estate on the outskirts of Dawning Court with only two servants, one of which he had to pay himself. It angered Thomas that he had to pay his own way simply because he was not the first son. Of course, John had not fared too well either, marrying that peasant girl as he did. But that made it all the more detestable that his mother was withholding support from Thomas even after denying John the inheritance that was rightfully his.

Thomas scowled at his muddy boots as he rode toward Dawning Castle. His boots were expensive, and he did not know if they would come clean. Some spectacle of a nobleman he must be, knee deep in the mire. That did not fit his image of what nobility was all about, but then he was not so sure *he* fit the image of what nobility was all about. He often wondered if it had not been some accident at birth that landed him in nobility. While he felt entitled to a life of privilege by his right of birth, he did not feel he shared the attributes of his brothers that gave them distinction over the common man. John and Richard were brave warriors that nature had imbued since birth with great size and strength. Thomas was the only brother who was overweight and who had always been so. Henry and Edward had sharp intellects, and William had fine aristocratic features to which the girls had always been partial. One female in particular showed a keen interest in the fortunes of Thomas' youngest sibling. Thomas, it was said, was the funny one. Though he had served honorably in a crusade of his own, he had returned without distinction. He had been knighted for his efforts, but he felt in his heart that he was not as good as his warrior brothers. Though he was no coward, he had always preferred to avoid battles rather than charge into them as his brothers seemed to. He had served the minimum time required by honor and returned and married quickly.

His brothers still in the field, however, had all far exceeded their requisite time, and new stories of their heroics poured in each day. As their reputation grew, Thomas's diminished in his own eyes, not only because of their exploits but because he no longer wielded a lance. He stayed at home with his family, tended his estate, and petered into oblivion. His own exploits, few though they may have been, were noble and had been trying for him, but who remembered that when Richard was taking on armies of Saracens with only a handful of men like some biblical prophet, and William was being dubbed the Saracen Scourge? They were unstoppable forces. That is what noblemen were supposed to be, but Thomas had never felt that he fit into that mold. He privately wondered if it was to be taken as a sign that he felt more at home in a tavern with the commoners than with his own kind.

Thomas rode up to Dawning Castle on the pretext of acquiring news regarding his family. But he was actually escaping the frustration he was feeling for his life. Ordinarily he sought out John's company when these moods beset him. John was of similar sentiment to his own and could commiserate, but invariably they just ended up drunk. Thomas was yet grappling with his problems and was not yet prepared to surrender to vice. Later, perhaps, but not now.

Thomas found his mother in her customary spot in the library at her writing table, clothed in her gray dress with her widow's cap in its usual place atop her graying head. It had been so long since he had seen her in anything other than drab colors, he began to wonder if she owned anything colorful any longer. "So what's the news?" He asked without preamble upon entering and dropped heavily down onto the leather sofa. He was currently the only Dawning boy that routinely saw his mother, and much of the formality was gone, which was fine with him as he stretched out over the length of the sofa, putting his muddy boots up over the arm.

Martha Dawning looked up from what she was doing. "Hello, Thomas. William of York was a holy shadow on the battlefield at Damietta and single-handedly routed the entire town's foot soldiers." Martha repeated the news as it was relayed to her, but was unable to keep the irony out of her voice. They both knew the stories, as they filtered over the hundreds of leagues between them and the Crusades, were distorted, but there was real information to be gleaned from them. One could learn from this tale that William, if this was their William as his description had led them to believe, was alive. The Christians had won the day, and he had, at least to some degree, distinguished himself on the battlefield.

"Great," Thomas grunted, feeling even worse about himself. "Anything else?"

"Richard's band of mercenaries came up against a frightful horde of Saracens and were defeated."

"Is that so?" Thomas lifted his head, suddenly interested. "And Richard?"

Martha shrugged, trying to look disinterested, but was unable to hide her apprehension for her son's well-being. "No word, as yet, on his fate." She changed the subject. "Please don't get mud on the furniture, dear."

"That is not mud, it is the battle scars of parenthood, thank you very much."

"And how did these particular scars come to be marring my furniture?" Martha Dawning asked, with no particular interest.

"Rescuing my children out of the mire," Thomas explained.

"Again?" Martha was still looking over the sheaves of paper before her. "Perhaps you should just relocate the nursery to the wallow and be done with it."

"I'm glad you think it's funny," Thomas said, annoyed. "My wife seems unable or unwilling to keep them from playing in there."

"You chose her for your wife," Martha said absently.

"I am aware of that, Mother, but who else would have had me?"

She looked up at Thomas, who immediately realized he had revealed far more than he intended, blushed furiously, and looked away.

"Why would you say such a thing?" she asked simply.

"Oh, Mother," Thomas began with emotion that he had not realized was so close to the surface. "I hate my life. I never intended it to become a long series of tradeoffs between monotony and misery. I blame my wife and station and house, but mostly I just wish I were doing something to improve it, something to increase my standing."

"And why would you say such a thing?" Martha asked him again. "You have served your God and your country. Your obligation is finished. You married and settled down. What is so dishonorable in that that requires increasing your standing?"

"I am miserable. Surely I must do something to affect a change in that condition."

"And increasing your wealth is the answer to your misery, is it?"

"Are you suggesting it is not?"

Martha shrugged. "I have seen many things in this world, but I am not sure I have ever seen anyone find lasting happiness in wealth."

"Well, perhaps my mind is so occupied with that which I do not have that I am unable to focus on those things that truly need addressing in my life," Thomas suggested only half-ironically. Martha stared at him expectantly. "You know I wouldn't be covered in mud if you would do your job as a parent." He meant this last statement to be light but it came out as accusing.

She sat back in her chair. "I fail to see how the mud on your clothes is any reflection on me as a parent, other than the fact that I obviously failed to instill proper manners in you—bringing your muddy clothes into my library."

"There is no one to keep them out of the mud—the children, I mean—so I have to chase them all over." Thomas ignored her comment.

"No one? What about their mother?"

"Do you listen to anything I say? She does not do it. She allows the kids to run free. Her time is consumed by sleeping or socializing," Thomas said in an elevated tone that was very nearly a yell.

"I am still failing to see how this is my fault," his mother said calmly. She was very used to Thomas's manipulations by now and did not get worked up over them very easily.

"If you would house us in the style befitting the sons of the most powerful baron in England then this would not be a problem."

"House you? I see. So your lamentations over you station in life were not born out of a desire to improve your situation but to have your situation improved for you? So far as I am aware, you are not exactly starving."

Thomas crimsoned, taking this as a reference to his rotund figure. "I am an heir of Dawning Court, and I should think you would be interested in my presentation around the area, particularly given how few heirs remain in good standing. One lousy house servant is all I have. One! While you sit here in this house that is practically empty save the butlers and cooks and stable boys and ladies in waiting. I have my wife and children to think of ; you have only yourself."

"So tell me again why it is that you think you are owed something. You have life better than most people in the world." Martha's disgust was plain, and her anger was causing her not to guard her words as she ordinarily would have done. "And how do you want me to pay for it? Dawning Court is nearly broke. Many hard years of rebellions, crop failures, and let us not forget Edward's ill-judged 'holiday' have left us with very little in reserve."

"The measure of my status is not relative to every peasant and serf that eeks out his existence from the land but measured among my own kind. And against such, I may as well be counted among the serfs, for that is how I would be perceived." He was on his feet now in his passion. "I am entitled to better!" he shouted and slammed a meaty fist on a nearby table for effect.

"Why are you entitled? The younger sons of noblemen always have to make their way in the world."

"Perhaps, but I am a full knight. I could go anywhere and receive lands and wealth for my pledge of service, yet I am rejected by my own, who leave me floundering in indigence."

"Pledges of fealty? You are a Dawning!," Martha exclaimed in exasperation.

"Furthermore, I am not just the younger son of a baron any longer. I am the heir to the birthright." His passion gave voice to that which he had hitherto been afraid to say.

"Oh?" Martha asked, mildly amused. "And your brothers?"

"You have taken care of that for me, Mother," Thomas sneered unabashedly, gaining confidence as he spoke. "You arrogantly presumed to judge John and cut him off because he married Lindsay." Thomas held up his fingers, ticking them off as he listed each brother. "Richard has run off to strange lands, he is either dead or living a new life with the money that he absconded with, and will not return. Edward," he dropped a third finger, "has disgraced the family and run off to live in the fleshpots of the mainland somewhere. That only leaves me. I have been true. I have married well. I have served the Church honorably. I am the rightful and remaining heir to the Dawning fortune and the vacant seat of the Barony."

"Thomas, you must believe me when I tell you there is no fortune!" Martha insisted, trying to make Thomas see the facts. "It is gone, all gone." Her amusement had darkened into anger at Thomas' insinuation that she was responsible for her children's misdeeds. "But whether or not you accept that, the one thing you have overlooked in your impertinence is that none of your elder brothers are deceased. Therefore, their claims to the Dawning birthright cannot be discounted. You are correct, I do not know where Edward is and I sincerely hope the rumors about him are not true. But even if they are, Richard could return at any time and make a claim to the seat and, of course, anyone currently occupying the seat would be an impediment to such a claim. Is that a fight you want?" she asked, looking Thomas squarely in the eye. She knew she was challenging his pride, but she also knew that Thomas had always silently admired and feared Richard.

Thomas glared at her for a moment and dropped his eyes so as not to inadvertently reveal anything that he did not think his mother already knew. "And as far as John is concerned, do not speak of things you know nothing about! John made his decision and chose to shirk his responsibilities."

"Why? Because he married a Saxon?" Thomas challenged, echoing the words that John himself had said a thousand times. "You are a Saxon, Mother! I cannot conceive of a greater hypocrite than you."

"You insolent fool!" she hissed at him. "Do you think I am so petty as to concern myself about the Norman-Saxon prejudices when all that my husband left for the support of my family is about to collapse into dust? That foolishness is for vain youth and old men trying to cling to antiquated traditions." She was saying more than she intended, but in her wrath she was slow to restrain herself. "If I cherished such prejudices, would I have married Braden Dawning, the epitome of proud Norman nobility? Yet his children are doing no justice to his legacy. His children are not nursing their aging mother, in fact. Each in his turn is a burden on me. John, Richard, Edward, all continue to disappoint me, and now you show up demanding concessions you think you are entitled to. Why do you think anybody owes you anything?"

Thomas could not meet her gaze. "You cannot lay all that at my feet!" His tone was one of shame mixed with anger. "You mean the way you laid it at mine only moments ago?" she demanded hotly.

"It is not my fault," he objected weakly.

"No, your brothers' actions are not your fault, but your own actions are certainly your responsibility." Feeling that he was suitably humbled, his mother changed tones to one of reassurance. "You are building a good life for yourself; do not get discouraged now. Keep it up and you will come to the end of your life happy and fulfilled by all the good you have accomplished."

Thomas stood in silence, looking at the floor. At last he decided to try a different tack. "Mother, aren't you the undisputed Baroness of Dawning Court? Can't you do as you please?" has asked seriously.

Martha looked at him, not comprehending his meaning. "Why not distribute the land now, so it is not an issue later?"

She snorted a mirthless laugh. "Because it would be an issue later. Primogeniture," she said simply.

"I do not understand."

"The Law of Primogeniture says that a father's wealth in its entirety will pass to the firstborn son upon his death. Therefore, even if I were to divide the land among you, John could claim the divisions were illegal and make a claim on any land I may give you. I cannot be responsible for the civil war that would inevitably ensue."

"John would not do that," Thomas protested.

"Thomas, you must understand that I have control of Dawning Court because my sons have not yet contested it. But at any time, John or Richard could rise up and make a claim on the seat, and I would have a fight on my hands. Do you think either of them would be disposed to allow you to keep a present of land that would have gone to them?"

"No, I suppose not." Thomas dropped his eyes to the floor in disappointment.

"I will make sure you get something," she assured him. "If it's in my power," she added, "you will get something."

Thomas said nothing but did not leave.

Martha sighed, feeling guilty for having reacted to her son's childishness with anger. "Tell you what, return home and I will have one of the kitchen staff report to your house going forward to help with some of your wife's domestic duties."

Thomas smiled up at her, his darker emotions instantly replaced by excitement. "Thank you, Mother," he said, taking her by the shoulders and kissing her cheek.

"Yes, yes," she said dismissively, "I spoil you too much, and it will be your downfall."

"I have no problem with that," Thomas replied, grinning over his shoulder as he exited the library.

Martha watched him go and knew that all that she had said was lost on him. He had gotten some of what he wanted and would forget all that led up to it. She wondered from where he had inherited his sense of entitlement. Several of her sons felt the world owed them something. She wondered where that came from. Perhaps it was from never really having had to work for anything. All of them knew how to work hard, but they had never had to work such that their livelihood depended on it. That was a regret that this life of privilege had brought her. She could not impart the wisdom that growing up as the daughter of a humble woodsman had brought her. Her sons did not know what it was like to go without, to not have enough to eat. They always knew they would be provided for, no matter what. She idly wondered if Thomas would come to terms with that sense of entitlement before it led to his undoing.

CHAPTER EIGHT

"Henry, help me," Leah screamed at him through the clash of metal and the screams of men. How had she gotten here? He knocked down his opponent and raced toward her, but another enemy appeared in front and brought him up short. This enemy he knew very well.

"Patrick," Henry demanded. "What are you doing? Move aside!" But Patrick only stood there, his sword held at the ready, his lifeless eyes showing no emotion. Leah screamed again and Henry disarmed his young lieutenant and attempted to push past him. But Patrick wrapped his arms around Henry and clung to him. Henry was shocked by the weight of this lithe young man. He could not seem to move at all. He tried to disentangle himself from him, but they only became more tied up as he struggled. Leah screamed again, and Henry watched as a man in white picked her up and spirited her into the crowds of dying men. Henry screamed in frustration but could not get past his lieutenant to reach her. He could not find her or see how to get to her; he was held in place. He looked down at his burden and was staring directly into Patrick's dead eyes. Patrick stared silently back at him and he did not utter a word or make a sound.

Henry sat bolt upright in bed. He rushed to the window for reassurance that what he knew to be a dream was just that, a dream. He had dosed off on his bed while awaiting the start of the feast being held in his honor, and the dreams had returned here, too. He had not been able to stop these terrible dreams since that fateful battle, and he awoke each morning feeling more exhausted than when he had retired. The dreams he was used to, but Leah was a new addition. Returning home was stirring up many old emotions in him he had thought gone forever.

He draped his tunic over his bare shoulders, sat on the bed, and braced his hands on his knees. The last thing in the world he felt up to was entertaining. He had as little inclination to socialize as anything he could think of, but he knew it was expected. His mother was not doing this to inconvenience him; she was doing it to honor him, and he was obligated to play the gracious recipient.

But how could he go into a room full of people celebrating his return home when all those that rode with him, that depended on him, were left in the earth of a distant land? How could he look into the eyes of his family? How could he look into the eyes of his friends, into Leah's eyes, and not see the reflection of his own guilt? Surely, they must all think him a coward that had only been cautious enough to ensure that he escaped with his own skin intact. Was that what they would see? Was that what he was?

His head was in his hands now when a knock came at the door. "Sir Henry?" It was Sebastian, the head servant's voice. "The guests are all assembled. Have you made yourself ready?"

Henry suddenly realized that he was only half dressed. "I—uhh—I will be ready momentarily, Sebastian."

"Very good, Sir Henry."

Henry quickly laced up his silk tunic and pulled on the soft boots. He had his sword half-way buckled on when he remembered himself. The finery of court felt strange after three years of armor, but not half so strange as not having a weapon on him. That just seemed foolhardy. "I am never going to get used to this," he said to himself. Another knock on the door roused him, and he followed the silver-haired Sebastian to the main dining hall that was set in formal regalia for this occasion. The hall was full, and everyone stopped and turned when he was announced. A thunderous applause went up from those assembled upon his entrance, and Henry crimsoned. All his life he had been imagining this moment, his triumphal return after his glorious crusade. Yet it all seemed hollow to him now. It was as if everyone was merely pretending he was a hero for his benefit.

Martha Dawning met him at the door wearing a slightly more formal gown than she customarily wore but still of black. Her widow's cap still had a place on her head, only now it was set atop her hair that was pulled up in a tight knot. She seemed older than Henry remembered. She hunched slightly as if the weight on her shoulders was physically felt and had stooped her. The lines in her face had deepened and the skin seemed to hang more loosely from her aging face than he remembered. For the first time, Henry found himself wondering if she had been beautiful as a younger woman. She had always just been his mother and she was what she was. She put her arm through his. "Smile, dear," she muttered through lips that did not move. "You look like you are attending a funeral."

Henry forced a smile onto his face. The assembled guests started to come forward to greet him. "I'm very proud of you," his mother said quietly to him before they were surrounded and Henry pulled from her in a sea of well-wishers.

Roland was the first welcome face that Henry picked out among the many assembled. "Roland!" Henry called, and Roland came forward. "How are you, Henry?" he grinned somewhat foolishly. He was very skinny and tall and usually seemed awkward in his own skin. Henry embraced him, which was uncomfortable for both of them as neither cared for public displays of affection.

Thomas was the next significant face to appear in the crowd. "Welcome home, little brother," Thomas said with a massive bear hug that squeezed the breath from his much thinner younger brother. All the bones in his back cracked in succession under the powerful grip. "There," Thomas said, grinning, as he set him down. "I just put ya right."

"I think that was the sound of my ribs cracking," Henry said with forced good humor.

"It might have been." Thomas laid a meaty hand on Henry's arm. "You didn't fatten up a bit over there."

"I had one or two other items to occupy my time," Henry told him.

"More important than food?" Thomas said in his customary loud voice. He was in entertainer mode in a room full of people, so he was always careful that everyone could hear what he had to say. He slapped his belly. "There is always time for food!" he laughed loudly at himself, and Henry could not help laughing at him also. His irreverent attitude was infectious.

Then she was there, breaking through the crowd. Henry could not keep from gawking. He remembered Leah being attractive, but if she was beautiful before, she was stunning now. Time had only served to turn the features of a pretty young girl into those of a beautiful woman. She wore a pink dress that had a series of ties running from the waist to just beneath her perfectly formed chest. Her brown hair was pulled back on the sides, cascading down past her shoulders with a strand of hair hanging carelessly in her hazel eyes as it always seemed to. Henry drank in her beauty, his resolutions of the last three years concerning Leah temporarily forgotten. All her features, even the ever so faint spray of freckles across her nose, seemed more vivid. Henry paused to compose himself. She was breathtaking. Leah stood still somewhat demurely, not wanting to intrude on his reunion with his family, and that made her seem even more irresistible. The intervening years since their last meeting had taken the edge off of the painful memory of their parting, but seeing her now only re-ignited some faint hope that perhaps she had reconsidered his offer. Perhaps the sting he had been carrying with him for all this time was for naught.

"Milady," he said formally. "I thank you for troubling yourself over such a trivial matter as this." He took her hand and kissed it.

"I would not have missed it, Sir Henry," She said in her customary guileless manner. Henry could not fathom this woman. If their roles had been reversed, he would not have set foot anywhere near Dawning Castle. But here she was, and she seemed just as happy to be here as if nothing untoward had ever passed between them. Perhaps this was a sign after all, he thought.

"Trivial thing?" Thomas interrupted. "And what about all the time and trouble of those assembled here do you consider trivial?"

"Very nice, brother," Henry said to him sardonically.

"I'll tell you what had better not be trivial," he said. "The food." He rubbed his hands together as he surveyed the room full of servants piling the tables high with all manner of fruits and meats. "Mother, I am wasting away to nothing. Did you intend on eating that food or only looking at it?" he called to her.

***

"... I thought Henry was going to have to change his leggings!" Thomas said, and the table roared with laughter. Henry colored in embarrassment but tried to appear unruffled. The feast at Dawning Court in Henry's honor passed off smoothly. Most of the nobles and knights of Dawning Court were in attendance. Thomas, as usual, played a prominent part in the entertainment of the evening with his boisterous jests and his larger than life personality. Henry often wished he were more like Thomas. He could so easily make people laugh. Henry had tried on occasion to carry that same flippant attitude about life, but it was just not him, and invariably he ended up offending. Thomas also tended to get too carried away, but somehow family gatherings never seemed to be complete without him.

Henry enjoyed watching his old friends and family back together. Sitting in the warmth of the company, he told himself that the nightmares that haunted him for the last few months were just that, nightmares and nothing more. But it was one particular figure half way down the central table that kept his attention for most of the night. Why was she here? Of course, where else *would* she be? Surely she could not be that good and kind. Only a devil could seem so angelic. She was captivating. Every movement, every word, every note of her light, musical laugh stirred his heart.

As the evening wore on, most of the friends, family, and well-wishers began to make their way out. Eventually, even Martha Dawning, having said farewells to the last of the guests, had retired for the evening with a kiss on Henry's forehead. Henry sat in the mostly empty dining hall watching the servants scurrying about, cleaning up the remnants of the repast. He noted that Edith, Leah's handmaid, had momentarily disappeared. Leah rose to go also. "Uhmm, milady," Henry said formally, standing to address her. "I wonder if you would not tarry for a moment."

"Of course, Sir Henry," she said, betraying no hint of what thoughts she might be hiding behind her beautiful eyes. She dutifully took the seat to the right of the head of the table where Henry again seated himself.

"I trust the intervening years have kept you well," Henry started awkwardly. It was maddening to be so formal with the one person in the world he most wanted to be close to.

"I have been very well. Although," she said sweetly, "it has been rather quiet with the Dawning men all but absent." Henry searched her words for some sign of something other than plain good breeding—some indication of some deference to him.

"Yes, well, such is the life of a knight. His destiny is not his own." He tried to sound dismissive.

"Oh, please do not take my own selfish expressions as reproof. My pleasure in your noble family's willingness to serve the Pope's divine cause is equaled only by my joy at your safe return."

Was that it? Henry wondered urgently. Was she showing him deference with that remark or merely being her sweet, thoughtful self? He chewed his lip thoughtfully as he tried to work out how best to proceed.

"Sir Henry?" Leah prodded him gently.

"Hmm? Oh, sorry, I was just reflecting on my own time serving the Pope's divine cause." He could not entirely keep the bitterness out of his voice as he echoed her expression.

Leah hesitated for a moment. "Are you quite well?"

He was not well at all, but he could not tell her the real reason for it, at least not yet. "It's just that phrase, 'the Pope's divine cause,' that gave me pause," he admitted. While this was not the matter on his mind, they were real doubts that had been plaguing him since that day of his defeat on the battle field.

"When you left, I had never known a more fervent desire in any man to do the Lord's will," Leah said gently. "Has something happened to hood your noble desire?"

Henry snorted. "Has something happened? Nothing at all except being abandoned by the Lord while I watched my men be slaughtered around me." Leah's hand came to her mouth.

"Surely you still believe in the divine nature of your calling to serve in the Crusades?" She said. "You must know there was a reason for the work you were undertaking."

"What was the reason for my entire company being wiped out in Persia?" Henry was suddenly heated as the terrible mass of fear, resentment, and guilt was tapped into for the first time since that fateful day.

Leah was surprised by such vehemence and unsure how to respond. "I imagine the reason was superior numbers. As I understand it, your men were outnumbered. Is that correct?"

"Why should that matter? If I was on God's errand, why wasn't He with me? Why wasn't He with us when we needed him most? Like ancient Israel defeating Canaan with three hundred soldiers? If those old legends are true, where was He when we needed Him?"

"I think perhaps you are confusing God's condoning an act with destiny," she said gently. "God wants us to reclaim the

Holy Land from the Saracens, but if I were to try to take it alone, I would not prevail." Leah hesitated again, afraid she would sound like she was accusing Henry of some miscalculation or wrongdoing. "It is incumbent upon us to be adequately prepared for the challenge at hand. And if the Lord wants to use us to make a point as he did in Jericho, so be it. But it is far more common in scripture that the blood of the righteous makes the more poignant point."

"Well that may be, but I am certain that my men died for nothing. Though they were acting in the service of God, they are just as dead as they would have been if they were acting on selfish or evil designs. We lost every bit of ground we had fought for, and their bodies were burned on a foreign land by unclean hands. Their lives were wasted."

"It saddens me to hear you speak of your sacrifice as wasted," Leah said with genuine emotion in her voice. "No life given in the service of the Lord is ever wasted. And we expect that those soldiers were received to the bosom of the Lord for their willingness to sacrifice."

"You are aware, I trust, that the Moors use that same language to justify themselves. They are saying that they are being received to the bosom of Allah for their service and defeat in battle. So, who is right?"

"Who is right?" Leah asked incredulously. "Sir Henry, the Lord has seen fit to spare your life. I, for one, am very grateful for that, but instead of your experiences heightening your gratitude and greater devotion for God, as one might expect, you seem to be angry and embittered. How can that be?"

"Are you so certain I was spared by divine intervention?" Henry challenged. "Were you present? Was I carried to safety in a heavenly cloud blown by a divine wind? Or did I fight through the day and only when my last men were being cut down did I flee from the field like a cowardly dog? What is divine about that?" He slammed the table with his fist and jumped to his feet. He walked a few paces away and stood brooding. The silence was palpable.

"Is it the loss of your men and the defeat that is gnawing at your soul?" Leah asked softly. "Or is it the fact that you were forced to flee?"

"It is everything! We were supposed to be divine warriors that swept off the enemy before us, but instead we were like lambs at the slaughter."

"Do you believe your call to crusade was divine?" Leah asked again.

"No, I don't believe it was divine!" Henry yelled in exasperation. "Nothing about the experience was sacred. It was abysmal, dark, and horrible. I would never go back and I would never do it again."

Leah did not respond. As Henry's emotion cooled, he realized that he had just accomplished the opposite of what he had set out to do. Instead of letting this sweet, beautiful creature know that he still cherished feelings for her, he was using her as an outlet for his most lurid thoughts. He dropped his eyes, unable to meet her gaze. He had surprised himself with the vocalization of the doubts of the divinity of the Church and the correctness of the Crusades that had been swimming in his mind since that day. But he did not regret saying them. Expressing the pain he was in and the horror of that day was cathartic for Henry. He felt justified in lashing out against the organization that had put him in that situation but realized that Leah may take it as lashing out against her. "Forgive me, milady," he said, seating himself again. It seemed to him there was a space between the two of them suddenly, and he rushed to try to remove the discomfort. "I guess I did not realize how hard on me the ordeal had been."

Leah was silent a moment. "It must have been truly terrible."

Henry only nodded as Edith reappeared through the doors that led to the kitchen and servants' side of the house. Henry realized his opportunity had passed and he had wasted it. He stood formally as Edith approached to remove the appearance of any impropriety. "I do hope it will not be long before I see you again," he said loudly enough for Edith to overhear.

Leah also stood as Edith approached. "Oh, Sir Henry, I am sure we will see each other frequently," she said sweetly. There was no indication in her voice or manner that their conversation had been anything but a pleasant discussion of the weather. He marveled at her as Edith encouraged her to return with her. "It has gotten quite late, Leah." Henry could not help scowling at Edith. He felt that she was a constant wedge between Leah and himself, as though she were trying to keep them apart. He wondered if she knew of his erstwhile professions of love to Leah and her sound rejection of him. As she was Leah's closest confidant, he had to assume that she did. How mortifying to know that she was discussing his most personal humiliations with anyone she saw fit. He found himself really disliking the small blond girl.

"My goodness! You are correct, Edith. We should be off at once."

She said her farewells to Henry, and they departed through the main doors. Henry sat down again, drinking long into the night, thinking about all that had happened, all that he had become, marveling that after three years in grisly combat he could be exactly where he was prior to his departure from Dawning Court—stewing over a woman. Henry needed to rest. He was exhausted, but he was too afraid to sleep.

CHAPTER NINE

"I was very grateful to see you," Henry said to Roland as they walked through the gates of Dawning Castle toward Dawning Court's outer wall. The memories poured in as Henry and Roland meandered past the estates and cottages that dotted the land, through the vast fields of grain interspersed among the cottages, estates, and roads. It seemed that every inch of this place was tied to a memory for Henry. Closer to the castle there was a fifty-foot wall that surrounded Dawning castle and courtyard. This was intended to be the primary defense of Dawning castle. In the event of an attack, most of the local residents could take refuge within these walls for safety. In times of relative peace, however, both the gates on the inner and outer walls remained open most of the time. Within the inner wall only those closest to the Dawnings resided. Certain nobles, knights, and servants as well as the church were here. Leah's family was one of the prosperous families of Thanes that lived here.

The outer wall of Dawning Court, which surrounded a vast tract of land immediately around the castle wall, was built a generation before, and because of the scope of the project, it had been built only fifteen feet high and offered only marginal protection to those that took residence around Dawning Court. The area within this wall was populated by the tenants of Dawning Court: yeomen, villeins, and serfs who worked the land in exchange for food, shelter, and protection. Minor nobles and knights that were pledged to the barony also resided within the outer walls. Outside the walls was another large group of tenants who had spilled over the usable land within the walls during the Dawnings' more prosperous times under the reign of Braden Dawning, Henry's father. Around this population a town of sorts had sprung up, with a small market square occupied by permanent shops.

"I was very glad to see you, but I must confess, I had expected to see more than just you upon my return. Shall we not call upon Adler, Colin, and the others?" Henry's lanky friend was lean like himself and a head taller. And though Henry had never felt himself particularly agile or dexterous, Roland's coordination was even more challenged. He was thoroughly awkward in manner and speech, and any discomfort felt in a given situation only served to exacerbate this awkwardness; but he had proved a faithful friend to Henry, and Henry felt deeply the absence of friends at the moment.

"Oh—Umm…" Roland hesitated.

"Roland, what is it?" Henry asked, amused by his friend's discomfort.

"It's just that…" Roland stopped and scratched the back of his corn silk hair.

"What are you are trying to say?"

"I assumed you would have already been made aware."

"Made aware of what?" Henry snapped impatiently.

"Well, Adler is dead."

"What?" Henry stopped and looked at his friend, searching for some sign that this was an ill-judged jest. Roland fidgeted nervously under the scrutiny. "I had no idea!"

Roland nodded. "He never returned from the Crusades."

Henry resumed walking again to combat the nauseous feeling in his stomach. "What of Colin, and Zachary, and the others? Are they dead too?"

"No, no," Roland assured his friend. "They are not dead. At least, not so far as I know."

"So where are they? Are you the only friend I have left?" An uncomfortable silence followed. "That was a jest!" Henry protested in dismay.

"No, no, I am certain their friendship is as true and abiding as it ever was," Roland said placatingly.

"So where are they?" Henry asked, suddenly in a sour mood.

"They are gone, Henry. They have all moved on. Dawning Court's economy has been struggling, and they have been forced to offer their swords elsewhere."

"Are they so mercenary that they sell their allegiance to the highest bidder?" Henry growled.

"Well, Henry, they came back from the Holy Land ready to be knighted and take an oath of fealty, but Dawning Court would not offer them anything. They would have had to stay on out of goodwill, and that is difficult to live on."

"That doesn't sound right," Henry said defensively. "My father is reputed for his generous nature almost as much as his thundering hand."

"Yes, well . . ." Roland said awkwardly, scratching the back of his head again and averting his gaze from Henry.

"Well what?" Henry demanded.

"Your father is not in charge any longer, is he?"

"Just what are you implying?"

Roland held his hands up defensively. "Whether real or imagined, it is taken for granted by the locals that the Dawning largess ended with the death of your father."

"Are you suggesting that my mother—" he sputtered on the words.

"I am not suggesting anything or accusing anyone of anything," Roland said quickly. "I am only saying that the local economy is depressed and that there is very little remuneration offered to knights that would otherwise willingly align themselves with Dawning Court."

"You seem to be doing well enough," Henry accused him.

Roland only shrugged. "That is incident to my family's prosperity more than my own choice of benefactors."

Henry opened his mouth to argue again but closed it without saying anything. Nothing he was hearing made sense to him, but Roland had no reason to lie. There must be more afoot than he realized. He could not imagine his mother selfishly depriving the chivalry their just rewards.

"It's not the same, is it?" Roland asked knowingly as he again fell into step with his old friend. "Coming back, I mean. I remember when I came back. I felt like I had learned a great many things and changed as a person, but everyone here wanted me to be the same person that had left, and they weren't happy when I wasn't. I couldn't be me, but I wasn't the person that had left here any longer either. I wasn't happy, and they weren't happy. It was rough for a while."

"I guess that's it," Henry acknowledged, grateful for his friend's empathy. "I just never imagined it being so different when I came home. It is like I am a stranger here and nobody really knows me. What did you finally do?"

"You run away and never come back," Roland grinned, but seeing that Henry did not appreciate the jest, shrugged and said, "You get through it. Once you are back in a routine, everyone will realize that you are not the person that left and you will realize that you are still the person that left and everything will be fine."

Henry sighed, "I hope so. It just seems so foreign. It makes me want to be back on the battlefield. At least there I understood the rules."

"Yes, well, don't run off just yet." They walked for a time in silence, each thinking his own thoughts, until finally Roland said, "Well, this is where our roads diverge."

Henry was surprised that they had arrived so quickly. He was attempting to repay a visit Thomas had made to him when he was away. He had been directed to a tavern in the square, and Roland was destined for home.

"Roland, I apologize for my outburst at you. I was affected by the news of Adler. But I am thankful for your friendship."

Roland smiled awkwardly and with a wave started down the adjacent road.

***

Henry approached the tavern down a dirt road and into the cobbled streets of the town square. He had been directed there by Lindsay Dawning, John's wife, after returning Thomas' visit only to be told by Annie, Thomas' wife, that Thomas was probably with John. Lindsay had indicated with obvious distaste that John had been frequenting this tavern. The tavern was a small cottage that was patronized mostly by the local farmers and tenants of Dawning Court. It was not a nice place by any standard, and Henry was sure there was some mistake. This was certainly no place for a nobleman. As he approached the door, he heard raucous laughter coming from inside. He hesitated a moment, his hand half-way to the knob on the door. Henry was certain this was not the setting in which he wanted to have a reunion with his brothers, but he was here now. Taking a deep breath and steeling himself, he swung the door open.

The inside of the pub matched the outside. It was dark and dirty. There were a few tables placed haphazardly about the room and a bar along the back wall tended by a fat bartender in a filthy apron that looked to be part of the elaborate tapestry of dirt. He was absently wiping down the counter with a rag that could only have been making the less than clean surface even more questionable. It was early afternoon and there were only a couple of locals present. They were slouched over the bar in a drunken stupor.

Henry was disappointed to see Thomas and John at a table in the center of the room. John had not turned out to greet Henry on his return, and now seeing him for the first time, Henry was struck by his altered appearance. He had put on a great deal of weight that was visible in his belly and face. His skin was splotchy and his brow darkened. Clearly the intervening years had not been good to him.

Thomas and John were not alone at their table. They were joined by two women that were as filthy as the pub itself. They were probably fixtures of the place. The 'ladies' sat side by side on one side of the table.

There was an empty pitcher of wine lying down on the table and another mostly empty pitcher between them. The two men were talking very loudly and laughing even more loudly at each successive comment either of them made. The clamor they were making was accentuated by the shrill laughter of the harpies that accompanied them. They were clearly well on their way to complete stupefaction. Henry turned to walk from the filthy establishment when John spotted him.

"Hey, if it's not the hero of Persia." His words were slightly slurred, and he was squinting through blurry eyes. "Have you come to rescue us, hero?" It unsettled Henry greatly to see his brothers sitting here like this, uninhibited, without a trace of shame, as it was an indicator that this was far more than a rare lapse in judgment but instead an indication of life choices they were making for themselves. No one had prepared him for this.

Henry approached the table. "It doesn't look like you need saving, as both of you are doing an excellent job of running away on your own," he said lightly, but with an air of disgust in his voice.

"To running away," John said, holding up his cup of wine with some of the cheap dark liquid sloshing over the side.

Thomas held his cup up as well. "He who drinks to run away, lives to drink another day," he added, and they all laughed heartily before draining the contents, with much of the beverage spilling down their chins.

"Sit down, sit down," Thomas ordered, indicating an unused chair on the opposite side of the table from their company. Henry pulled the chair back and inspected its dirty surface for a moment before sitting down. He sat upright in the chair that was pushed back from the table a ways with his legs crossed in order to remain aloof from his brothers' activities and to make it clear he did not plan to stay long.

"So what brings Dawning Court's golden boy to a cruddy little place like this?" Thomas asked, refilling both their cups.

"I came to see my brothers for the first time in three years," Henry said pointedly, hoping they would understand. They did not. "I had no idea they had turned into lushes in my absence."

"Lushes? Why, because we decided to have a drink today?" Thomas said, suddenly angry.

Henry indicated the empty pitcher already lying on the table. "This was just a casual drink on the spur of the moment? It takes a lot of practice to imbibe that much."

"Well, we had some help," Thomas said, evoking a shrill squeal from one of the ladies with a pinch. It was inconceivable to Henry that this gaudy, filthy, crass, and appalling creature could in any sense be of the same fairer sex that he so worshiped in the form of Leah. These persons with matted hair, cloying amounts of make-up, and a generous amount of cleavage exposed could not be the same species as his fair one.

"Hmmm, and how do Lindsay and Annie feel about that help?"

"Don't mention those names in here!" John ordered. "If we were not married, we would not have to drink."

"You're married?" The woman closest to John squealed in a thick Irish brogue. "If we had known that we would have charged extra." And she let out a great shrieking laugh that hurt Henry's ears.

"No wonder you're Martha's golden boy," John said. "You're exactly like her. A person does one little thing you don't like and they are trash, good for nothing but to be ground under your heel."

"To the golden boy of Dawning Court," Thomas said, holding up his mug again. The others followed suit, and they all drained their cups simultaneously.

"Maybe Martha would be a better person if she had a drink occasionally," John suggested as Thomas stared into the bottom of the now-empty second pitcher, trying to grasp what he was seeing.

"Of course; look how much good it has done you two."

"What do you mean?" John said, his blurry eyes narrowing at Henry. "We are just having a little fun. This isn't hurting us, but our mother definitely needs something, because she has a whole lot of problems."

"Wine!" Thomas called, crashing the pitcher down on the table. Henry winced from the noise. "You wanna drink?" he asked, glancing at Henry and crashing the pitcher down again.

"No, thank you," Henry replied with disdain, then turning back to John, "The only thing I can see that our mother lacks is noble sons. You should be tending to Dawning Court and ensuring that her final years are spent in comfort rather than anxiety over her useless children."

The bartender arrived with another pitcher of wine. "It is on that fellow's tab of course," John indicated a tall, lean Saracen merchant that was hunched over the bar, ready to pass out. As the bartender nodded and retreated, the conversation continued.

"So what are you doing to take care of her? You are her golden boy, the one she loves best. It escapes me how much her life has improved under your loving protection."

"You are correct, of course," Henry assented. "I have been back for nearly three days; I should have a lot more to show for myself than you do after 11 years." Henry leaned forward. "You are her eldest son; the birthright, the inheritance and, yes, all the responsibility goes to you. So much depended on you and your good decisions, and yet you have consistently failed."

"Oh, you're so righteous?" Thomas jumped in after refilling all their mugs from the fresh pitcher. "What happened to that young man that we grew up with that was into everything bad that came along? I never did the things you did when I was young, so we indulge a little now and you are so much better than us?"

"That would be William," Henry sat back, surprised by the unpleasant reminder of his younger brother's misspent youth. He had been a very angry young man and had lashed out at most everything. He defied every authority that was placed over him except one, Jurou.

"Oh that's right!" John said. "William was the malefactor. You were not bad, nor were you good. You did nothing. You did not live at all."

"So we drink," Thomas continued. "We drink to forget. We drink to take our minds off of the terrible things that happened to us."

"What terrible things?" Henry asked quizzically.

Thomas looked at John for support. "Our wives," John said, raising his mug.

"Yes," Thomas confirmed. "To our wives, the plagues sent from the underworld to scourge us for our sins."

"And to cause us to sin more," John added.

"Oh that's right," they both laughed and noisily drained their cups.

"So you have made a lot of bad decisions in life that have left you unhappy—"

"And have your good decisions made you happy, Henry?" Thomas interrupted him. Henry was disconcerted by the question. What had his desire to always be on the side of right brought him? Did he have the company of the woman he loved? Did he enjoy the pleasure of the reputation he had always dreamed of? All he really had were a bunch of painful memories and nightmares that would not let him escape even in slumber.

"Well, if you are looking for happiness," said one of the women, rising from her seat suggestively. The whole table laughed.

"So you have made a lot of bad decisions in life that have left you unhappy," Henry repeated. "I'm sure the choice to forget your troubles by becoming useless sots will bring you the self-respect you have failed to achieve thus far. That seems reasonable."

"Go to Hell, golden boy!" Thomas said. John raised his mug and they both drank to that. The trollop, encouraged by their laughter, continued around the table and leaned against Henry, her ample bosom pressed very near his face. Henry tried to avoid acknowledging her at all. "If it is experience you are looking for," she breathed into his ear, "I will make sure you never forget this." She stuck her tongue in his ear.

Henry shot up out of his seat, dumping the harlot to the floor in the process. He was blushing furiously. "I came here hoping to find my brothers, but I see they are not here. I hope for your sakes you have no recollection of this tomorrow." He slid his chair into the table to hide any evidence of the fact that he had been there. "I can't tell you two how sad I am to see how you have fallen."

"We didn't fall," John said, looking at Thomas.

"No," Thomas added. "We walked arm in arm down here." They both laughed and drank again.

"You two do bring out the best in each other."

Henry exited the pub to cries of "to the golden boy of Dawning Court. May you never lose your luster," and loud, drunken laughter.

Henry felt very much alone as he made the trek back home.

CHAPTER TEN

The Dawning courtyard was in full tournament regalia on this beautiful summer day. There were banners fluttering in the gentle breeze. There were streamers of every color decorating the stands, the walls, and the castle itself. Along one side of the courtyard were pavilions set up for each champion and his retainers, the two largest, of course, being that of the Dawnings and the Braddocks. All were in attendance. The villeins and serfs were crowded into an area with no seats other than the makeshift places of rest they were able to elbow out in the press of bodies. The nobility were seated comfortably above the rabble on an adjacent side that abutted both the pavilions of the champions and the area cordoned off for the peasants. There was a general air of excitement that pervaded everything.

This was an annual tournament that was staged alternately between the Dawnings and the Braddocks. Many knights would travel great distances to participate in it, but the real excitement came from the intense rivalries of the two families. The Dawning men were invariably pitted against the Braddock men of similar status, and the competition was fierce.

Leah did not particularly care for the violence of the tournaments, but these so-called "tournaments of sport" were usually fairly mild, although they could and frequently did get out of control. The long-standing rivalry between the two families often fanned the embers of the competitive game into something more fierce. But today she had a special interest in

96   The Knights Dawning

arriving early and sitting close to the yard. Today was William's first tournament. There was an unmistakable air of excitement to it all. Leah was nervous and excited for him all at once.

"Milady," *said a familiar voice. She turned, and there was William in his beautiful white armor with blue and gold embroidery. She had never seen anything quite like it, and she thought if very striking and William particularly handsome in it.* "I hope this day finds you well," *he said with a slight bow. He could not suppress his grin.*

"It does indeed," *she replied, smiling back at him.* "And how is your arm today? The competition is said to be fierce."

"Fear not, milady," *he said with mock humility.* "I am spared the anxiety of the heated battle as I have not yet had the honor of being knighted. Therefore I am good for nothing but periphery exhibition before the real entertainment commences."

Leah leaned forward over the rail until her mouth was close to his ear. "I await your match with earnestness. I have no doubt you will be victorious."

"The lady does me too much honor," *William said, bowing again to try to hide his smile at her compliment.*

"When you are finished fawning over the lady, Dawning," *a mocking voice interrupted them,* "clear the lists to make room for the real knights." *They both turned to see Vincent Braddock, the youngest son of the neighboring baron, approaching in his new suit of armor. Vincent was Leah's age and therefore a couple of years older than William. He had been knighted in order to participate in this tournament, and his armor was a little large on his frame.*

"Terribly sorry, Vincent," *William said, still looking at Leah.* "I did not see you hiding there in that suit of your father's armor." *Leah quickly dropped her head to hide her smile.*

"This armor was made for me by the finest armorer in all of England," *Vincent retorted haughtily.*

"The finest armorer he may be, but he needs a new ruler," *William continued in his mock serious tone.*

"At least I don't look like a peacock," Vincent shot back, making reference to William's own unusual armor. William had five older brothers that had been teasing him about his choice of armor and weapons for as long as he could remember; Vincent's remark did not faze him.

"Ah, but how much better to be a peacock that knows he's a peacock than a lamb that thinks he's a lion," William tittered.

Vincent's face crimsoned. He was keenly aware that William was getting the better of him in front of Leah. "What would you know about it? You are not even close to becoming a knight. You cannot possibly understand the importance of a good suit of armor."

"I should hope it is not to make one look noble, as the greatest armorer in England was clearly unable to manage that on your person," William replied, still watching Leah, who was still studiously pretending not to hear any of it but not entirely successful at covering up her reactions. She did not care for Vincent Braddock or his brazen overtures toward her, of which he took every opportunity of availing himself. He was handsome with a thin, refined face, delicate nose, and brown hair that swept back from his forehead in flowing locks; but he was presumptuous that she would be flattered by his advances, and that irritated her to no end.

Turning abruptly from William to Leah, Vincent addressed himself to her. "Milady, I trust you will be selected the Queen of Honor and of Love for this tournament," he said formally to Leah with all the chivalry of a full knight. "For there is certainly no one more fair than you are in all of England."

It was William's turn to color with jealousy at this. "She is too young, fool," William spat.

This flustered Vincent for but a moment before he continued, "Nonsense! I assure you, milady, if I have the fortune of making the selection for the Queen of the Lists, there is no other before you."

"You do me too much honor, Sir Knight," Leah replied demurely, "but I should be mean indeed to accept an honor to which I am not entitled. Surely your affections and your gallant eye would more suitably and more deservedly fall upon one of the many beauties in attendance rather than on a mere child such as myself."

"Nonsense," Vincent said again, more determined than ever by her objection. "I will settle the crown of Queen of the Lists on you in anticipation that I will be rewarded by your fair kiss at the end of the tournament." The tournament was a two-day affair with the victor of the first day receiving the honor of selecting the most lovely maiden in attendance to bear the coronet and sit in the place of honor for the remainder of the tournament.

"That is perfect," William uttered caustically. "The only thing stopping you from carrying out that promise is your lack of skill and your cowardly heart."

"Saxon Dog!" Vincent turned and shoved William who stumbled and fell backward." I will kill you for insulting my honor." He ripped his long sword from its sheath and leveled the tip at William, who was just pushing himself up on his hands.

Leah leapt up in alarm. "Sir Knight, you would attack an unarmed man?"

"He should have armed himself before insulting my honor," Vincent said darkly, not moving his sword.

"How can one be insulted about something one does not possess?"

Vincent roared and started forward. William rolled back over his shoulder and was on his feet again.

"If this truly is a matter of honor," Leah said, thinking quickly, "should it not be settled in noble combat on the lists, as knights do?" Vincent hesitated, and the marshals of the field were there.

"What is the meaning of this?" Jean de Wycliffe demanded. "Fighting outside of the sanctioned event is grounds for ejection from the tournament."

Vincent sheepishly sheathed his weapon. "I have insulted his honor," William said boldly. "Sir Vincent was just challenging me to a duel, is that not so?"

Wycliffe looked between them. "He is not a knight," he said to Vincent. "This is not appropriate for a tournament and cannot be held in conjunction with the other battles." One of the two marshals of the field was provided by the Dawnings and the other by the Braddocks. Jean de Wycliffe was closely associated with the Braddock family and had been so for as many years as the aging but still powerful Martin de Boutillier had been with the Dawnings.

Vincent nodded. *"Very well, we will match now as part of the exhibition. My honor is more important than some silly tournament,"* he declared heartily to Jean's skeptical look.

"You know he is not a knight; he has nothing to lose," Jean said confidentially to Vincent. *"But you have everything to lose in your first tournament with your father looking on. This is not worth the risk."*

"My honor is not worth the risk of defeat?" Vincent glowered at him. *"Then what is it worth?"* he demanded. *"I am not some silly child playing at being a knight. I have been insulted and I will receive satisfaction."*

Jean looked at Martin de Boutillier. The other marshal only shrugged.

"Very well," Jean said, stepping back. *"Prepare yourselves, gentlemen, as you are up next. I will announce you."* The marshals returned to their posts on opposite sides of the yard.

"Now, Dawning," Vincent said with a malicious grin, *"you are about to feel firsthand what it means to be a real knight.*

"I already know what it is like to have a parent that is at a loss for a birthday gift. Perhaps I will ask for a knighthood for my next one as you have done."

"Keep laughing, Saxon. Keep laughing while I run my Norman lance through your Saxon heart."

William's jaw tightened at his insult. It was one that he had heard often as his mother was, in fact, a Saxon. *"How much more the insult then, when you not only lose your honor to a simple, unknighted nobody, but to a lowly Saxon. Will there be anywhere you can travel in all of England that you will not be laughed at for more than your oversized armor?"* Vincent *looked as though he would take another swing at William but only turned and stalked away, pausing just long enough to make a curt bow to Leah.*

Leah, who had stood tensely, watching this whole ordeal unfold, called to William as soon as Vincent had gone. "William, please don't do this," she said. "I have a sense of foreboding about this."

William smiled at her. "Why concern yourself, milady? This is the hero of Dawning Court you are talking to."

"William, please, no jokes. I cannot tell why, but please make an excuse, apologize to Vincent, anything." She looked very earnestly into his eyes.

"Leah, I find your confidence in me very moving," he said caustically. "But I can beat this fool. These silly games the knights play are dependent upon everyone playing by the same rules; otherwise it is not fair and they are easily put down. I will put Vincent down."

"William, what are you trying to prove?" she whispered urgently. "You berate the chivalry for their vain pride and stupidity and yet here you are being led by the same impulses. He is a knight!" she said desperately and immediately wished she had not.

William's jaw tightened and his eyes narrowed at the insinuation. "He started this, not me," he said stiffly.

"Win or lose, do you think that would change my affections? Would I be less inclined to one man who holds my affections because he beat or was beaten by another? Is that important to me?" she demanded.

"He started this, and I will finish it." William turned to leave, but Leah pursued him, stepping over the other spectators as she followed him on the other side of the railing that separated the stands from the field.

"William will you tilt with him when you know nothing of such things?" Her pleas were taking on an air of frustrated anger at his obstinance. "You have a great many talents, and I have no doubt that you could best him in hand to hand combat, but you know nothing of such sports as this." He did not slow *his pace or give any indication that he had heard her at all. "William, people get killed for such trivials as this," she said desperately.*

He whirled to face her and stopped with his face very close to hers. His eyes were hard. "There is only one thing I am bred for. There is only one thing that I was trained to do, and this fool has chosen this thing in which to test me! If there is blood spilled today, it will be Braddock blood!" He roared the last at her with a murderous look in his eye. Leah watched him storm off in a stunned silence. What was happening? How could what had been a perfectly pleasant day only moments before spiral out of control so quickly? She wanted to run after William to make him see, but there was no point. Men and their stupid vanity! All she could do was wait to see and pray for the best. She fidgeted and squirmed and sat tensely in her seat with a presentiment of evil that she could not shake.

***

They faced each other across the lists. William was on a borrowed destrier that would not seem to hold still, sensing the excitement of the crowd and the tension of its rider. It stamped nervously and cantered slightly in this direction and that.

Meanwhile, Vincent looked every bit the noble knight in his new jousting armor with a reinforced, oversized left shoulder plate. His shield had a lion's head emblazoned on it crossed by two swords underneath and the motto "Lion Hearted" engraved beneath it in a childish emulation of England's late great king, Richard, Cur Du Lion. William smiled to recall his unwitting insult of this earlier when he had compared Vincent to a lamb that thought himself a lion.

For all his jabs at Vincent's skills, Vincent was bigger than William, and he was from a strong family. William was not at all sure of himself. But he had been unable to resist. He hated that Vincent had such an obvious design on Leah, and he was even more uneasy with the fact that Vincent was very close to the age where he could make an actual suit for Leah's hand. Then to be humiliated by him in front of Leah was more than he could bear.

William began to feel nervous. He knew well what he planned to do, but he had scarcely trained in the knights' arts of chivalry. Jurou's instruction had been far more pragmatic and devoted little time to "silly games," as Jurou called them. "I'm teaching you to stay alive, not win a silly contest," he would say whenever William asked about it. Nevertheless as a consequence of this training, William could see a hundred weaknesses in the mode of attack Vincent was guaranteed to employ on this occasion. There was no cunning or strategy at all involved, it was simply a test of who could take a hit better, and William had no intention of taking a hit from Vincent. In fact, he would unseat Vincent so dramatically that no onlooker would have any choice but to acknowledge the folly of such foolish games as any real test of prowess in battle. His mind was made up, but even as he contemplated his course of action, his resolve waivered. William suspected that his actions would be frowned upon for his unconventional method. "And what do you care for the approval of these people who have so long made you the object of their scorn?" he demanded of himself. "You have been trained for one thing and one thing only: to win. Jurou did not waste time with pretended nobility or vanity. He trained to keep you alive, and that is exactly what you are about to do. You can see how easy it will be to crush this dolt who has challenged you and who sets his lustful eyes on Leah; why then do you hesitate?" Jurou's words echoed in his ears: "It is too late to turn back now. This is your life! The time for fair play is before the battle has begun. If you should not be at odds with an opponent, you halt the situation before it deteriorates to combat. But once the battle is joined, there is only the living and the dead!"

Yet even as he contemplated all this, something else was eating at him. "Anger is not your ally," Jurou had said a *thousand times to William, who had come to him as an angry young man. "Anger robs you of your strength prematurely; it puts blinders on you so all you see is what's in front of you, not what's around you. And it robs you of your most important weapon," he said, poking William in the forehead. "Your mind. Great warriors are not emotional warriors but calculating, detached intellectuals! This is the most important lesson for you." William had long struggled to control his rage; although Jurou had said this was his most important lesson, it had also proved to be the hardest of all Jurou's lessons.*

When he remained in control of his emotions, he was amazed by the almost transcendent power he seemed to have over the battle. But he loved the cathartic release of focusing his anger on a single target and destroying it. It was how he had always dealt with his emotions and the only way he really knew to release them. Jurou's method taught him to not let himself get worked up, but that was easy for one as naturally calm as Jurou. For William it was a daily fight. He knew that anger was controlling him now, but he didn't care. He wanted this. He had always wanted this, and the pleasure of the kill was so much richer in the moment when he surrendered to the rage that fueled him.

His eyes fell on Leah, anxiously watching from the stands. He made a mental note to apologize to her when this was all over. Leah was exceedingly soft-hearted, and he worried that he often injured her with his coarse manners. She was only concerned for his well-being, and she was perhaps the only person who did care about that at this point. William tore the cumbersome helmet from his head. He had been trained to use every sense, and he could not tolerate the restricted visibility and hearing the helmet brought with it. The added protection was not worth the sacrifice. The marshals of the field had insisted on it as a well-placed lance to an unprotected head would be the end of any that were so met, but again William had no intention of being there when Vincent's lance crossed his path.

He and Vincent stared each other down across the lists, and William felt very out of place sitting astride a strange horse, holding his spear instead of a lance.

He could almost see Vincent's smirk as he considered William's unprotected head. William felt every eye on him. The blood coursed in his ears, and his anger flowed into him and tensed his muscles.

As if sensing his thoughts, Vincent dropped his visor and spurred his horse into a charge. William did likewise. Those assembled drew a collective breath. Though they were only boys, it was to the inexperienced that the most grievous injuries were often dealt, the victor not being able to judge the force of his strikes and the loser not being able to absorb them safely. This was even more the interesting battle as it was the only Braddock - Dawning contest that would take place that day and symbolized the next generation of Braddocks and Dawnings crossing swords in bitter rivalry. Today's was a joust that no one would soon forget. The lines were clearly drawn between the two sides, and that was typically the biggest draw for all the locals. John Dawning had been good, as he rarely but occasionally lost in such contests. Richard was an old favorite as he never lost, and now the two youngest sons of each of the powerful barons were facing off for the first time. William Dawning had taken a dramatic turn indeed from the upbringing and chivalry of his father and siblings, but no one assembled there could have known just how far from his father's legacy this son had grown; they were now about to find out.

The two young nobles galloped across the meadow, their horses' hooves churning up the earth with each thundering step. Vincent's armor was slightly oversized for the young man, and William's something outlandish that none assembled had ever seen before, much more sleek and oriental in design. It was at that moment that they saw the function of its design. When the two combatants were only a few paces from each other and a collision imminent, William rolled to his left out of his saddle and onto the soft turf with a fluidity and grace that was inconceivable in the bulky iron suits his contemporaries wore.

He came to his feet with his spear in hand. Vincent could only watch in confusion as he charged past the riderless steed. He was unable to rein in his mount in time even as he understood what was happening. William was swinging his spear with both hands at Vincent's mount's forelegs as if he were swinging an axe at the trunk of a tree. He was in a full gallop and there was nothing to be done. The horse's legs were torn from beneath it. With a piercing whinny it pitched forward, catapulting the young knight face first into the dirt. He hit the ground hard and his back arched unnaturally, his mailed boots snapping up almost to the back of his helmeted head. His lance tip stuck into the ground and stayed standing there at the angle in which it had fallen. There was a terrible crash of armor and barding followed by a profound silence. Astonishment struck the assembly dumb for a moment as no one had ever witnessed anything like this.

Vincent struggled to his hands and knees and crawled forward in a daze. William stepped up to him with disdain and put his foot on the mailed side of the severely injured competitor. "You lose, Sir Knight." His words dripping with contempt, he shoved Vincent down into the dirt.

As if this was the signal, the shock of the moment wore off all at once and the crowd was on its feet, howling its displeasure. The marshals spurred their horses forward and raced out to the competitors.

"Surrender your weapon!" Jean ordered of William while Martin tended to Vincent.

William looked up at Jean in mild surprise. "Since when is it a custom to demand the weapon of the victor?"

"How dare you claim victory for such an unchivalrous, unbecoming—" The marshal's words failed him as he sputtered in rage. "How dare you speak in such a way! Shame, William Dawning, shame! Now surrender your weapon!" He took a menacing step forward and William's spear fired out of his right hand. He let it slide through his hand until the point was only a few inches from the throat of the marshal before tightening his grip to halt its progress. The marshal instantly

froze, looking down at the point of the weapon uncomfortably close to his unprotected throat.

"I take such actions as this to be threatening. And I will only surrender my weapon when it has been struck from me. Do you believe that you are the warrior to do that?" His spear was steady and his gaze leveled at Jean. "I await your decision, Sir Knight." William said the last to the aging marshal with the same derision he had said it to his young counterpart, who by now had his helmet removed to reveal a face that had been crushed on the inside of the helmet. Vincent's nose was broken, his jaw was twisted, and there were lacerations running across all visible parts of his face. His eyes were rolled back in his head and there was such an effusion of blood that William's resolve waivered slightly to see the damage he had inflicted.

The marshal looked for help from his comrade, but Martin was already racing toward the stands yelling for help. Feeling helpless, Jean only repeated with all the force of passion he could muster. "Your coat of arms shall be reversed and subject to derision for your misdeeds. You shall be known as a coward and as unchivalrous. How dare you? How dare you? Oh shame, shame, William Dawning!"

At the sight of Vincent's condition, William began to feel the moment of the marshal's words, but the hissing, booing crowd strengthened his resolve to behave as if this were what he had intended all along.

Baron Braddock and his entourage were running across the field toward Vincent. William felt this was a timely moment for his departure. Wordlessly, he whirled his spear back under his shoulder with a flourish and stood upright from his guard position. "Do as you like. I am not a knight, and your threats are meaningless to me."

William mounted his horse, trying not to show that he was in a hurry, though he felt any moment he would be seized from behind. He turned his mount to leave the field. As he did so, he had to pass the gallery of the nobles where his mother was seated, as well as Leah and Vincent Braddock's family. One by one, each spectator in the stands of the nobles turned their backs to him, disavowing any connection with him. Everyone in turn followed suit in the general crowd, taking their cue from the nobles. All at once the field was silent save for the exertions of those laboring to assist Vincent. Only Martha and Leah had not turned their backs on him, but his mother had her eyes fixed on the ground.

Leah's eyes were wide and full of emotion as she watched him. William stopped and looked at her for a long moment, he saw in her face concern and disappointment. It was in her fervent gaze that William found the shame that he had refused to feel up to that point. She looked as if she would go to him, but some unseen hand would not permit it.

Instead he continued his solemn ride from the lists, refusing to flee from the palpable scorn of those assembled as he so desperately wanted to do. But to do so would have been a sign of weakness, and all his actions today had been to project strength, to prove himself. There was extra commotion around Vincent that caught William's attention. William's eyes locked with Daniel Braddock, who was cradling the body of his son, which hung in an unnaturally limp position. Daniel set his son down gently and stood and roared across the lists to William: "I will avenge this insult that has been done to my family! I swear to drink your blood, William Dawning. You and I are enemies, and I will consider any who aid you as an enemy to the Braddocks also." William did not respond. He did not show any emotion. He was terrified that he could have turned so many people against him in an instant. Even Daniel Braddock, who had known him since birth, not only hated him but had sworn a blood feud against him. Braddock took his silence as disdain and only grew angrier. "I would challenge your honor if you had any honor to challenge. You are a fool and a coward!" he screamed at William's retreating back.

William forced his pace to remain steady. He knew the epithets that Daniel Braddock was hurling at him now were intended to goad him into a duel, but he was fearful of the anger of this large, seasoned warrior. Still, William's pride would not permit him to be seen as fleeing. He snorted at Braddock and withdrew, praying they were not riding after him.

***

William felt the injustice of this day very acutely. He had been wronged and it was he who had been challenged, and when he chose to defend himself in the way he knew best, he was scorned and despised. He rode his horse through the forests in isolation for some time before finding himself at the lodging of the one person that should understand what happened. He walked into the small training building in which he had spent so many years. The floor was made of tatami, a traditional Asian straw that was tightly woven into mats that were softer than wood or dirt but still strong enough to withstand the abuse they were subjected to. The interior walls were made of paper. William had never realized how divergent his educations was from that of his brothers—never until that day. While his friends and brothers were learning to be knights, he was learning something else entirely in this room with the paper walls and tatami floors. He was totally unprepared to participate in their shows of gallantry and chivalry, and obviously they were as equally unprepared to withstand him. He walked through the main room, whose walls were liberally covered with racks of weapons of every description. He entered a small, single-room antechamber that Jurou had made his home for all the time William had known him.

There were few decorations and even fewer mementos of Jurou's past. His history had always been something of a mystery to William. He spoke little of it. On a few occasions Jurou had alluded to the fact that he had left his own land because of much oppression. William had gathered that his exodus was an extremely bloody affair, but Jurou had never volunteered more and William had never felt it appropriate to pry into something that his instructor clearly did not want to speak about.

Jurou slept on a mat on the floor, and there was a small tokatsu: a short table for kneeling around, with a small brazier set in the middle for warming the room and heating a small tea kettle. Jurou had always lived this way, neither asking for luxuries, nor accepting them when offered. He seemed eminently content in his surroundings, but his real motives for staying on at Dawning Court after the death of Braden Dawning had always been inscrutable to William. He kept little society with the locals and trained few apart from William, and even then the training was only casual.

William tapped softly on the wood frame of the thin paper door. "Shitsurai shimasu," he said to announce his presence and slid back the panel. Jurou was inside, loading his scant belongings into a trunk.

"What is this?" William said in shock. "You are leaving?"

"You leave me little choice, William," he said in his proficient but accented English.

"I leave you little choice?" William demanded. He was already sensing that he would find no comfort for the day's deeds here. "What does that mean?" Jurou continued what he was doing without a word. "Is this about today, about the tournament?" Jurou made no reply. "This has nothing to do with you! This was what I did of my own free will and choice, and I would do it again."

"You have disgraced me, William," Jurou barked, standing up suddenly.

"Disgraced you? I did exactly what you taught me. You taught me to fight to win. I do not know all the ridiculous rules of their games. Because of your training, all I can see is the many weaknesses they throw open to those who do not obey their rules. He challenged me, he lost."

"You were participating in their games, you were obliged to obey their rules. If you were unwilling to do that, you should never have agreed to it." Jurou had resumed loading his belongings into a trunk.

"He insulted me in front of Leah and then he challenged me!" William protested.

"And you allowed him that control over you? You allowed yourself to be put into that situation where your foolish pride dictated your actions— not your sense, not your brain, but your pride? Yes, you beat him, and where is your pride now? Is this a victory in your heart?" Jurou said all this without looking up from his preparations.

"I thought you would understand," William said, deflated. "I thought you would..." he trailed off, unwilling to open himself up for another scathing rebuke.

"Thought I would what? Approve?" Jurou paused for a moment to face his pupil in the yellow light of the small, clean room. "Then you have understood nothing of what I have tried to teach you. Of all the people I have trained, you were my best, my brightest pupil. To do yourself honor was to do me honor, but you have disgraced yourself and disgraced me."

"You do not have to leave!"

"I have no choice. I made you what you are. I took a child haunted with demons and thought to tame those demons, to make him a man. Instead, I have made a remorseless weapon that cannot tell the difference between right and wrong. How can I live under the good graces of those who trusted your development to me when this is the result?" His words stung William like no one else's could have. He felt the disappointment he had seen on his mother's face in Jurou's words. "My ways are strange to your people, but your father and mother gave me a sacred trust. A trust in which I have failed. That was never so plain as it was today. And someday, those demons are going to get loose again, and then wo be unto all who are in your way."

"You want me to apologize to that buffoon?" William remonstrated. "Very well, I will do that now. I will degrade myself in front of everyone and beg the forgiveness of a lesser man for besting him in his own contest. Will that satisfy your 'honor'?" William spat the last word in disgust.

Jurou stopped suddenly and looked at him. "William... Vincent is dead!" Jurou barked. "How do you apologize for that?" He had raised his voice, something he only did on occasions when he felt he was not getting through to his pupil. "How do you undo that? Shame, William, for shame." He unknowingly repeated the reproach of the marshal of the field.

William leaned against the frame of the door, stunned. "I don't understand what I did wrong!" William protested in a weak voice. He felt that his whole world was collapsing around him.

"And that is the problem," Jurou finished simply. Neither of them spoke for a long moment. Jurou paused and looked at the floor, ruminating. At last he sighed and placed both hands on William's shoulders. "You are the most talented pupil I have ever trained," he said. "But your fear and anger have robbed you of your humanity. I thought I could quell that in you. I believed that with patience and care I could channel that, but I have failed. You felt the power of emotionally distancing yourself while in the training yard. Yet as soon as it mattered, you let your anger rule you." He sighed. "You don't understand. At least had I instilled in you your country's rules of chivalry, valor, and honor, you would have had some guidelines by which to govern your behavior; but I have robbed you of even that."

"Is there no hope for me, then? Am I so lost that even my old friend and teacher cannot abide with me?" William's voice cracked with emotion.

"There are noble and good things in you, William, but like once-hewn grass that is now overgrown with weeds, the fruits of fear, anger, hatred, and pride have cast a shadow over them until they are all but invisible. You have demons that rest upon your shoulders, and until you cast them off, they are in control. Now," he said straightening, "I must beg redress for my failings at your mother's hands." He walked around William to leave his chamber.

"Won't you stay? Won't you help me?" William pleaded, unable to look at him. "I don't have anyone else."

Jurou paused when they were shoulder to shoulder, also not looking at his young ward, not wanting to show the emotion in his own eye. "My staying would avail you little as you will no longer be at Dawning Court." William looked at him sharply, wondering what worse fate was presently to befall him. "Braddock's last son is dead because of your actions. If you wish to survive the night, you will not be here when the sun sets."

"What?" William suddenly felt fear grip him. "I—" his words were lost in his stunned mind.

"There is a contingent of soldiers passing by Dawning Court this evening on their way for the Holy Land . You best be with them." William fell back against the door frame. "And William," Jurou said meaningfully. "Not a word to anyone. Your very life depends on your anonymity in this." Jurou made as if to leave and then stopped. "May God take you to His bosom, my son," he said, still not looking at his erstwhile pupil ,and left the room.

William remained in stunned silence, unable to comprehend how quickly his life had been destroyed. It was as if all his past deeds that had gone unpunished caught up to him at this moment and all the injury he had done was being returned upon his own head. He remained in this attitude for a long while until the overwhelming impulse struck him that he had to be with the men leaving for the Holy Land. He raced out of Jurou's room. He would be with them.

***

The moon was high as Leah rode up the path that ran along the stream into the woods. It was too dangerous for a loan female to enter the woods after dark, but if she was right, she would not have to. She crested the small hill and looked over the moonlit clearing where she had spent so many carefree hours as a girl with William. If he had intended to see her, this is where he would be, and oh, how she needed him to be here.

She needed to know that he spared a thought for her as their lives were being suddenly and dramatically torn apart.

There was a gnarled old tree not far from the tree line that they had shaded under on a thousand warm afternoons, and that is where she was headed. She rode slowly now. Though the moon was high, the shadows it cast made this old familiar place seem very foreign indeed. The sounds seemed unnatural, and the shapes looked ominous. More than once she almost lost her nerve and thought to turn back, but of all nights, this was not the night to be frightened of shadows. There was too much at stake.

She rode up to the large willow trunk and reined in sharply. A figure was before her, spear dramatically whirling overhead. It was only after she identified herself that William relaxed.

He stood from the tense crouch he was in. "I was wondering if you would come," *William said with relief plain in his voice. She slid out of the saddle and followed him behind the trunk of the old willow tree where they were hidden from view of anyone not coming from the forest itself.*

"I had to come," *she said in an earnest whisper. She was not sure why she was whispering, but it seemed appropriate.*

"And I had to see you."

"William," *she started anxiously but could not say what was in her heart. He looked up expectantly from where he dropped to the dirt and slumped against the trunk of the tree, but she only dropped her eyes.* "I am sorry... about all of this."

He snorted and shook his head. "It is so strange to think that I have forever altered the course of my life. Everything I ever wanted, that I ever thought I would be, has just changed forever. I have changed it forever."

"It doesn't have to be that way," *she protested.* "We can fix this, we can talk to Baron Braddock. We—"

"It cannot be fixed," *William cut her off heatedly.* "His son is dead! He is not going to forget that. He is not going to forgive me because I say I am sorry. Vincent is dead and nothing will change that." *Leah dropped her eyes. William chortled a mirthless sound.* "You know what I have been sitting here thinking about all night?" She shook her head. "I have been wondering if I should give myself up. If I should go to Braddock and let him have me."

Leah looked confused. "Why would..."

"Don't you see, Leah? Everything has now changed because of this. If I stay, my mother will protect me and we will go to war with the Braddocks over this. Instead of one life being lost, hundreds will be slaughtered. And my family could lose everything. Because of me!" His voice cracked at this last statement. "But I cannot seem to bring myself to that point. Whether by fear, pride, or something else, I cannot imagine myself submitting to my doom over this." Leah said nothing. She wanted to comfort him, but he obviously needed to speak his mind. "I suppose there was nowhere else my road could lead. It seems inevitable that I be sitting right here one day. I can see that now. Yet somehow, I never saw myself as the villain before today. I always believed that I was the good guy and everything would work out because deep down I never really meant any harm. What a naive fool I was—am." He shook his head in disgust. "But..." he said hesitantly, looking at the ground as he spoke. "You tried to warn me. Had I listened to you, none of this would be happening," he trailed off, and they sat in silence for a long time.

"What will you do?" Leah asked at last.

William shrugged. "I will leave. If I run, I will be branded an honorless coward, but it would avail Braddock little to exact revenge on my family, as he will not get what he wants. If only my father were still alive, Braddock would not even consider going against the Dawnings. Yet my father is the reason that I know there is no forgiveness to be had. He would not let this stand, and Braddock is cut from the same cloth." He chuckled the same mirthless laugh as before and shook his head.

Leah went down on her knees beside him and took his hand in both of hers and pulled it close to her. "You will always have a friend here." There were tears in his eyes as he considered his next words to her.

"Leah, will you make me a promise?" he asked, sitting up close to her. "Something that I have no right to ask but must anyway."

Her eyes widened slightly and her pulse quickened. "Anything," she said breathlessly. Impulsively.

"Will you promise me that you will always remember this? That I meant no harm. That there were true and noble things in my heart."

"Oh." Leah's countenance fell. "Of course."

"Even should Braddock sweep down in his wrath and those you love are killed and your family is forced to flee, will you remember this? Will you recall that I gave up everything I could in order to fix this? Will you remember that?" He was very earnest as he sought the answer from her lips and confirmation in her eyes.

Leah took a deep breath to gain control of her emotions again and forced herself to meet his gaze. "Of course, William. I have always known that about you, and this has not diminished my esteem for you. I would give anything to undo it, but what's done is done."

William was on his feet again. "I must be on my way. It will not be long before Braddock discovers I have fled, and he will pursue me." He looked from her as she rose. "I would that I had listened to you, my good angel. It was only after it was over that I could see so clearly that is what you are to me. If only I had had the wisdom to see it before, how much happier would I be now?"

"And I, William," she said softly. He stared at her a moment longer as if trying to burn her image into his brain. "I must not delay any longer." He started for the trees to retrieve his horse only to slow and come to a stop again a few paces from her. He dropped his spear but did not move for a long moment. "William?" Leah took a step forward. "Are you all right?" Without a word, he spun and crossed the distance to her with a few long strides and pulled her to him. His lips found her ready to receive him, and for the first time they shared a passionate kiss that did more to express their emotions than their words *ever could. Leah lost herself in that moment as warmth flooded over her body. Their passion mingled with their tears as they showed the first signs of anything more than friendship on the eve of being separated perhaps forever.*

William held her close to him for a long time while she wept silently. "If there were one thing I could change, one thing I could undo..." he trailed off, not bothering to articulate what Leah could feel so clearly. She held onto him and wished there was some other alternative.

"Where will you go?" she asked when he finally stepped back.

"I suppose I will join the Crusades. They can always use a good spear there." He wiped her tear-stained cheeks and brushed his own away. "I must go." She nodded mutely and reluctantly released him. He disappeared into the dark mass of the forest and emerged a few moments later leading his heavily laden mount by the bridle.

"William—" Leah started and again stopped herself when she met his eyes. "Please be careful," she said simply.

"Leah, I don't know what to say," he was fiddling idly with the ties he used to secure his weapon. "Thank you... Thank you for everything you are and have always been to me." With that he climbed into the saddle, and taking one last lingering look at her, he spurred his horse into a gallop.

Leah watched him ride away into the darkness. As he reach the crest of the hill, he stopped once more and looked back for a long time before disappearing into the black mass of the landscape.

CHAPTER ELEVEN

"**H**is majesty wishes to inform the Lady Dawning that she is seriously delinquent on her duties to the crown," the tall, thin man, draped in brightly colored livery that distinguished him as one of the king's personal messengers, informed Martha Dawning haughtily. "Knights from Dawning Court have failed to accompany his majesty on either of his last two campaigns-"

"And which campaigns were those?" Martha interrupted caustically, "The Welsh uprising at King John's questionable claim on the throne, or his defeat at the hands of the French, losing most of Normandy?"

"And while you have chosen to invoke your right of scutage," the messenger continued as if she had not spoken at all, "which his Majesty has so generously offered to relieve the burden the demand for knights may create on some of the less fortunate barons, you have failed to show any intent to such payment." He finished with his hand on his hip, his half cloak hanging fashionably over his extended elbow and the tips of his shoes turning up on themselves, looking every bit the smug messenger that could act with impunity under the auspices of the throne. The main chamber of Dawning Castle was set below the dais, causing those addressing the baron—or in this case Martha Dawning, with Henry standing behind her right shoulder—to have to stand in the middle of the largest room in the palace and look up to the dais. This tended to intimidate most guests. It made them feel small and powerless; but the messenger was completely self-possessed and showed no inkling of being self-conscious if, indeed, he harbored any such feelings.

All of this conversation was coming as a surprise to Henry, who was only there at his mother's insistence. He had no notion that Dawning Court was delinquent on taxes to the crown. He was further surprised at his mother's knowledge and low opinion of the king's movements, but what happened next took him completely by surprise.

Martha looked at her interlocutor seriously for a time before speaking. When she did speak, she ordered all the servants from the room and said nothing further until her command had been obeyed and the door shut behind the last. "There is nothing left," she confided to the messenger. "The coffers are nearly empty and there is no new income to speak of. I have only managed by cutting expenses and borrowing. These days I can scarcely scrape together enough to pay the interest on the loans I have taken to maintain King John's misadventures. There is nothing left." Henry wanted to stop her from saying any more but could only stand there in shock. In these times of feudal strife, such an admission of vulnerability could spell the end of their barony. She must be very desperate indeed.

The messenger was unmoved. He merely raised an eyebrow at the bold declaration. "And the tenants?" he asked, referring to those who farmed their land.

"Three years of crop failures," she explained. "The meager surplus they produce is what we have been living on. I have had to sell off much of the tenanted land. That left little to go around. My husband won the Dawning fortune through war, but on the Crusades in which my sons serve, all the spoils go to the Church or the king." She stood up and continued in earnest. "These are tumultuous times. We have very few knights left that are pledged to Dawning Court, and most of those are remnants from my husband's legacy: knights who only remain with us because their fathers fought beside Braden and who have grown up with a loyalty to our family. And I don't know how much longer that loyalty will last if we cannot pay them better. We may keep them, but we certainly will not keep their children." She sighed. "Now King John is demanding more knights from all the nobles in order to lose more land to France. We don't have any to send, so we pay the scutage tax with money we do not have. His exploits demand heavy taxes of us. We are contributing to the Church and the Crusades, not to mention the cost of sending each of my children into the field to serve."

"Why does his Majesty think the barons are pressing him with such unprecedented vigor for this Great Charter?" she asked of the messenger, whose countenance had not softened in the least degree. "He heaps burdens on us that are grievous to bear."

"Lady Dawning," The messenger resumed in his same haughty tone, "I fear you have spoken very much, and very freely, and I have lost the thread. Which part of what you have said would you have me relate back to our noble king? That the Dawnings believe him to be an inept and unjust ruler? That you are a weak barony on the brink of collapse? Or that you have no intention of paying the required taxes to the crown and are fomenting a rebellion?" He paused for a moment to let his words have the desired effect. Henry for his part was amazed at this messenger's self-possession. This man conversed with the most powerful people in the land and did not have the faintest air of insecurity. Henry knew much of that came from being on the king's errand, but a lot of it was presentation. Henry wanted to be more like that.

"Fomenting a rebellion?" Martha Dawning repeated incredulously, clearly not sharing in Henry's silent admiration of this bearer of bad news. But, Henry admitted to himself, his mother had spoken too freely. What did she expect would come of such admissions? She should have known better.

"Certainly it is not necessary to remind her ladyship that the crown considers any barony supporting such treasonous notions as this 'Great Charter' to be in rebellion."

"I was merely suggesting—" Martha began in a tone of forced calm but was interrupted by the audacious messenger.

"His majesty urges you to remember that the cherished friendship his predecessor shared with your late husband is in no way shared or valued by King John and should not be relied upon to absolve you of your pecuniary obligations." Martha's mouth tightened into an angry line as she contemplated the messenger. She could almost hear King John's ridiculous mouth uttering these very words. Oh, how she longed to have Braden back. These things did not happen when he was here. When he was here, the Dawnings were powerful and everyone, even the king, showed the appropriate respect. "I have not, at this time, pledged my lances to the barons' cause," she said. But you would do well to remind *Prince* John to remember who his friends are in these tumultuous times. It would seem he has fewer and fewer with each passing day."

"His Majesty well knows that you have not aligned yourself with the rebels, else it should not be a simple messenger but the king's own guard standing before you. As you have failed to offer any acceptable reason for failure to pay, and as you have indicated that you are still King John's loyal subject, His Majesty will expect payment no later than a fortnight from now."

Martha Dawning looked like she was on the verge of ordering his imprisonment when Henry stepped up beside his mother. "Very well," he said in a conciliatory tone. "Tell his majesty that he will have his tax," he assured the messenger. He had no inkling of how they might pay it, but he could see this man was not going to take "no" for an answer.

"Though it be paid in the very bricks from the castle walls," Martha muttered angrily. The messenger hesitated a moment and then assumed a decidedly different tone.

"Do I have the privilege of addressing Sir Henry Dawning?" he asked diffidently. Henry puffed up slightly.

"I am Henry Dawning," he replied, not wanting to concede that the messenger had "the privilege" of addressing him.

"His Majesty desires your expertise in London."

"Wha— Why?" Henry stammered. "I mean, why me?"

"His Majesty is assembling a team of learned scholars to decipher a number of scrolls that were returned from the Holy Land."

"Well, I am not very learned—" Henry started and stopped, flustered. "The King knows who I am?" He asked again.

"You have come very highly recommended for your knowledge of the various tongues of the Middle East."

"I do know—That is, I—"

"Do I understand you correctly?" Martha interrupted. "That you have come here to extort silver from the blood of the oppressed in one breath and in your next request the assistance of a Dawning?"

"Your husband, and your husband's father, and his father before him have all paid customs to the sitting king in fine Norman tradition," the messenger said pointedly, reminding her that she was both a woman and a Saxon and therefore lucky that she was being recognized to hold control of the barony at all. "They would have been proud to serve his Majesty and the Church in such an undertaking and recognized it for the honor it was." The messenger resumed his same haughty tone when addressing her.

"Very well, then there is no harm in my refusing it," she said spitefully. Henry turned to her to protest, but she held up a hand to forestall his objection.

"He is still a knight of Dawning Court, and he is much needed here." She calmly reminded the messenger that though the king may recognize her authority only grudgingly, he had just acknowledged that he did, in fact, recognize it, and a baron had the right to order his—or her—knights wherever and whenever he or she may.

Henry fumed but saw from the steel in his mother's eyes that now would be a very inopportune time to challenge her authority. Of course he could ignore her and do as he chose, but he carried pride in being the only faithful Dawning male. He turned back to the messenger, trying to make his face stony. He thought he should again step behind his mother to show his full support of her but could not bring himself to do so. Instead he stayed rooted in place between them.

The messenger sighed. "His Majesty has granted through his goodness and generosity that in order to alleviate the hardship of losing the services of Sir Henry, if he would agree to accompany me on my return trip to London on the morrow, all the arrearages on the Dawning register might be forgiven."

Martha Dawning's eyebrows arched skyward in surprise. She considered the messenger, whose contemptuous posture had not altered in the least degree throughout the course of the interview. "Very well," she said. "I accept your terms and grant Henry leave to do as he may wish. But," she added, looking at Henry meaningfully, "I leave it up to him to decide whether or not he will attend you."

Henry could not hide his excitement. His mind was already racing over all he must do to be ready to leave the following day. He feigned a thoughtful posture of consideration and hesitated as long as he could before nodding. "I would be honored to accompany you." The messenger nodded mutely and withdrew.

Henry rounded on his mother. "Why would you deny me the opportunity to win the king's good graces?" he demanded. "That is not only good for me, that is good for Dawning Court!" Martha did not respond but chewed her thumbnail thoughtfully.

"That is a disgusting habit," Henry chided her in annoyance for failing to respond to him. "Mother, what is it?"

"Prince John was willing to give up a large sum of money in order to have you look at some dusty old scrolls. Why would he do that when he needs money so desperately at the moment?"

Henry was insulted. "I'm sorry that you do not value my education as others do," he said sulkily.

"Oh, that is enough of that," she waved her hand dismissively. She refused to coddle him on this occasion. "You know perfectly well that I have a great respect for your intellect. So," she fixed her attention on her son, "what is the one thing that Prince John needs even more than money?"

Henry was still feeling hurt but could not help perking up at the challenge his mother presented to him. "Friends, I suppose," Henry shrugged. "Respect."

"Correct," she agreed.

Henry was suddenly intrigued. "A few years ago when King John was at odds with Pope Innocent III over the new Archbishop of Canterbury—you remember when Archbishop Hubert Walter died," he reminded his mother.

She looked at him in surprise. "I remember, but why do you? You must have been about fifteen then." Henry ignored her and continued.

"King John wanted John de Gray in that role to give him more sway with the Church. But the Canterbury Cathedral chapter held a secret election and elected their own candidate for the post. When both candidates appeared in Rome, Innocent disavowed them both and pushed his man, Stephen Langton, into being elected to the position." Henry began pacing. His feet always seemed to move reflexively when he was excited.

"Yes," Martha added. "Most of the barons supported John in that. We thought it would increase our clout as well with the Church."

"Right, but things only escalated when King John reacted by expelling the Canterbury Cathedral chapter. Pope Innocent, not one to bow easily to political pressure, retaliated by placing an interdict on all of England. No marriages, confessions, or the Eucharist could be performed in England."

"That's right. And then John closed down all the churches completely and confiscated the churches' possessions." I even recall them showing up here, but Father Garand would have none of that nonsense. He might have been the one church in all of England that continued an open door service in defiance of both the King and the Pope." She chuckled to think back on the feisty overweight father literally bullying the king's men out of his church.

"The interdict did not result in a general revolt against King John as the Pope had anticipated, did it?" Henry asked to confirm what he already knew. "In fact, about all that did happen was that the Church lost a lot of money and Innocent realized he was in danger of losing his congregation altogether. He escalated again by excommunicating King John entirely a few years ago. John is now at odds with the barons *and* the Church in a time when he really needs a friend. He probably feels he will give up less by making conciliatory overtures to the Church than in submitting to the barons' 'Great Charter'."

Martha was nodding, having seen the implications of it all quite a while before hand. "I think you are onto it. Using John's excommunication as an excuse, Prince Llywelyn of Wales rose up, with Innocent's blessing, and burned John's castle at Ystwyth. The Welsh lords chose Llywelyn as their leader instead of Prince John. They recaptured land John had taken from them. Meanwhile King Philip II of France, whom John was preparing to invade when the Welsh uprising took place, allied with Llywelyn. "

"I heard about that," Henry nodded. "Then John did not exactly make any friends when he hung all of his Welsh hostages. Many of the nobles have sided overtly or secretly with Llywelyn, and John has now led a desperate campaign to reconquer Normandy from France."

"And he wants me to fund his silly feuds so he can continue behaving like a headstrong jackass and never have to admit he is a fool." Martha Dawning shook her head in disgust, and Henry looked back to ensure the king's messenger was nowhere to be seen. People had been hung for uttering less than his mother was saying. "He is currently faced with enemies on every side," she continued. "He has neither the support of the barons at home nor the Church abroad. He needs friends, and he does not have any."

"Well, he is really the perfect monarch," Henry said somewhat quietly, afraid of being overheard. "If he is not hated because of his heavy taxes, he is hated for his excommunication. If he is not hated for that, he is hated for the ridiculous wars he keeps getting embroiled in and losing. And if one does not hate him for all that, he has not a shred of personal character with which to ingratiate himself to his people." He laughed ruefully. "Oh, how I do miss King Richard."

"The one thing that Prince John needs more than money is respect. If he can win favor with the Church, he may have an ally against the barons. Given all that, are you quite certain you wish to participate in this venture of his, to be a pawn of the king?" Martha asked her son seriously.

Henry spread his hands in front of him. "I do not see how that changes anything. Like it or not, King John *is* England. His decisions are often ill-advised, but if he falls, would you have a French Monarch bleeding us dry?" he asked rhetorically. "Furthermore, whatever happens with this venture benefits us. If John stays in power, getting in his good graces can only help us. And if he is dethroned, so much the better to be in the Pope's favor. And…" he hesitated. "If you spoke candidly to the messenger, we need the financial relief… How did it get to be so bad?" he asked when Martha made no effort to deny her previous assertions of pecuniary hardship.

Martha was rubbing her temples now. "It happened much as I indicated to that insufferable messenger. Richard also took a healthy share when he left," she continued. "Then outfitting you was costly, of course. About the only child that has not taken a substantial portion of his own inheritance was William." She trailed off at the mention of her youngest son's name and then abruptly snapped out of it. "Meanwhile the barons are pressing the king for this 'Great Charter' that will limit his official power and are requiring a show of force to make their point."

Henry shrugged that off. "Why does that matter? Simply ignore them. The nobles of this country are constantly getting crosswise with the king—particularly this king."

"We cannot afford to be left out of this. This 'Great Charter' is possibly the most significant piece of legislation to come under the royal quill in a thousand years."

"Then it will never be ratified," Henry dismissed it. "Or it will be so diluted it will not have any actual power. Every few years some radical movement makes its way to London before being put down."

Martha shook her head. "This one is different. Consider the situation for a moment. John is so desperate for support, he is even willing to swallow his pride and attempt to make amends with the Church rather than submit to this Great Charter. He is overextended, and his opposition is coalescing into one force. I have been around a long time, and I have never seen such a concerted effort from all the nobles. Usually they are fighting amongst themselves, and some use it as a chance to ingratiate themselves with the sitting monarch. But this time it is not like that. Other than those barons near London who directly and regularly benefit from the king's largess, I have never seen a division so clearly drawn between the nobility and the king. We dare not be left out of this one. But neither can we be seen to be openly supporting it." She sat back, looking haggard. "And quite frankly, I believe that your father, were he still with us, would be at the forefront of this movement against this incompetent, semi-legitimate king." Henry did not argue further. He did not fully trust his mother's instincts over his own, but he knew that argument would be fruitless. She had years of experience in politics that she neither sought nor desired but that had imbued her with a certain stubborn cleverness. She would act as she saw fit.

"Do the others know about this?" Henry asked suddenly. "Our pecuniary situation, I mean."

She shook her head. "Dawning Court's reputation depends on its power and prestige, which is diminishing every day with each passing son. If it gets out that we are financially weak also, then we will have a fight at our gates for which we are not prepared."

"But surely my brothers should know so we can help—"

"They do not need to know and you are not to tell them," she interrupted him. "Trusting my sons has only brought me heartache and trouble," she said bitterly. "For all I know they would be the first ones breaking down the gates if they knew we were vulnerable."

Her words stung as Henry felt he was being unfairly lumped in with his wayward brothers. "Now don't you have a trip to prepare for?" she reminded him.

"Yes, at once!" He jumped up. "I had very nearly forgotten." He quickly strode toward the exit and ordered the nearest servant to send for the tailor. He was traveling to London, and he had to look the part.

"Henry," Martha called lightly.

"Yes, Mother?" He turned to face her, his mind still occupied with his preparations.

"In all your rushing about, do not forget that your presence will be required at this evening's repast."

"What? I don't—" He started to protest but realized there was no getting out of it. "I haven't forgotten, Mother," he assured her. "I will be there."

CHAPTER TWELVE

Richard started awake in the darkness. The rat was back, gnawing on his foot again. It was pitch black other than some ambient light that must have been coming from somewhere down the hall outside his cell door. The rats had gotten more aggressive as he had become increasingly weak.

He resisted the urge to kick at it and send it scurrying back into the wall as he usually did, for he knew it would just return to try again later. It was not the darkness that had taxed Richard to the core when his captors had first thrown him in here. It was not the cold stone floor, the dank smell of mold and urine. It was not even the silence punctuated only by the screams of the tortured that tried Richard; it was the rats—little parasites that ruled the darkness. They ran free, they spread disease, and there was no end to them.

These rats were hungry and seemed to think Richard would make an excellent meal. They were persistent in their attempts to turn him into just that. They tried again and again until they got what they wanted. They were persistent creatures. Unable to get what they wanted by force, they simply nibbled and tested until their victims had no more strength to fight. The rats had almost pushed him over the edge of sanity. But as much as they continued to disgust him, much like the rest of his surroundings, he was getting used to these, too.

He waited, biting back on the exclamation of pain as the rodent bit into his flesh. Without warning, Richard slammed his foot down on the creature. The rat flinched at the last moment and avoided the crushing foot fall, but he trapped its tale under his bare foot. Seizing it in his hand, he hurled it against the stone wall. It squeaked loudly, he heard it hit the floor, and all was silent. He was gratified that he did not hear the sound of the little claws scurrying away. A small victory, but a victory nonetheless. "One down, only a million more to go," he thought to himself.

Physically, Richard was just a shell of his former self. At first, when he was stripped naked and thrown in here, his captors had paraded people past his cell to mock and laugh at him. The mighty terror of the Moors, the Christian Curse, was nothing but a filthy, naked slab of meat. He smiled vaguely to remember the first time they came in to torture him. They sent three men in to get him, thinking the fear of the armed men would be enough to control him. Richard did not fear death, particularly since he knew that was his inevitable fate at the hands of these barbarians. One had held a sword point at his chest while the other two tried to bind him. He knocked the sword aside and slammed his elbow into the face of the sword-wielding guard, crushing his nose and knocking teeth out. He kicked backwards, knocking the guard trying to bind his wrists behind him into the wall, and then turned and slammed the body of the first guard into his friend. They both hit the ground in a heap, and he turned on the third one only to find he was already barring the cell door from the outside. After that they had starved him until he was too weak to resist. Then they came to get him in force and dragged him out of the relative safety of his cell to perform their foul deeds.

His food, now that they had begun feeding him, again consisted of old rotted cabbage and fetid stinking meat about every other day. He had lost a lot of weight and was very skinny now. His skin hung off him in saggy, loose folds. His fingernails had fallen off from the bamboo shoots. Many of his fingers and toes were broken. He had been burned, been stretched on the rack, and had a hundred other unspeakable things inflicted upon him out of pure hatred. There was nothing the Moors wanted—they never asked him any questions—it was out of plain and simple hateful vindictiveness that they did what they did.

He wondered how long he would exist here until they tired of him and finished him off. Early on he had maintained the hope that his men would come for him, but they had not. "Perhaps your family?" the voice suggested. The voice had appeared a few weeks after he had been in here. At first he had just thought it part of his own inner conversation, but now he found that he was responding to it vocally.

"My family? I'm sure they think I'm dead."

"Would they not come on the chance?" Suddenly Richard was standing in Dawning Court on a grey spring day.

"You can't do this," his mother said. Richard had taken a large percentage of the treasury to finance his own personal crusade. "Crusades have to be ordained of God and sanctioned by The Pope. You may not take this upon yourself."

Richard was saddling his horse and had servants saddling mules with supplies and money for mercenaries. "The Pope? Be serious," he spat, disgusted. "Why would you believe in some doddering old fool more than your own son?"

"Because I see you are making a mistake."

"Why do you doubt me?" he demanded loudly. "On the battlefield I am treated like a God, only to return here and have you try to control me like a child."

"What about your brothers? Don't you think they need you? Don't you think John could use your help running Dawning Court?" she pleaded with him.

"My brothers are worthless fools. John is useless as a warrior and will be even more worthless as a baron. Edward is such a coward that he could not even meet his most basic responsibilities as a man. Thomas just takes up space but will never have anything to show for his life. Henry has no mind of his own. He can't figure out what he wants and vacillates constantly based on what he thinks will win him respect; and he will continue to do so all the days of his life. And your baby, William, for all the extra time and attention that you have

lavished on him over any of the rest of us, is just a little Caligula. I am the one who was meant to be great, and I will not find greatness here. And I certainly won't wait for the Pope's permission to do it. I will go out and take what is rightfully mine!"

"I should be very sad if your brothers heard you say this."

"They already did. I told each of them what I thought of them." *He finished cinching up the saddle straps and turned to find his mother standing very close to him.*

"I will not permit you take that money from our family. Not for this."

"Permit? Why don't you try and take it from me?" he sneered at her. "When I have returned this gold to you a hundredfold, you will see that I was right."

She shook her head sadly. "No. Even if you return it to me, what you are doing is still wrong, and it will always be wrong. What you do, you do on your own and you go without God; you trust to the strength of your own arm."

"I wouldn't have it any other way," he said, climbing into the saddle of his warhorse. "The weak need God. I make my own destiny instead of waiting for it to be delivered to me." With that he drove his heels into the sides of his steed and led the procession of supply-laden mules out of Dawning Court.

"No," he said to the voice, now back in the blackness of his cold, miserable cell. "Why would my family come for me?" He took it for granted that the voice had been at Dawning Court with him just now.

"Don't you think your family still loves you?"

"Why would they? I would not forgive someone who had done what I have done... Besides, how could I face them again? How could I face them after everything I have taken and all I was supposed to do but did not? I think that would be worse than being here."

"So rather than support your own family, you ran off in search of personal glory?" The voice was exceedingly soft, but always struck him at moments like this as being very loud.

"You know I did. Why must you keep rubbing my face in it?"

"And now that you have failed, you would rather die here than go back and right the wrongs you have left behind?"

CHAPTER THIRTEEN

Henry struggled within himself. He did not dare open his heart again without some assurance that it would not be ripped out of his chest once more. But he needed to know if she shared his affection.

"Leah, I am leaving on the morrow." She looked surprised.

"But you have only just returned," she said. She was seated in the Dawnings' private garden amongst the plants and flowers in full summer bloom and looked to be in her natural surroundings in this picturesque scene. Henry had called upon Leah and taken a walk back here where he knew Edith would be enticed away for as yet undiscovered reasons, and he could speak to her privately.

"I would tarry longer, but King John has requested my assistance in an intellectual endeavor." He tried to sound nonchalant, as if the king were always consulting him on something or other.

"Well, his Majesty could not have chosen better than you, Sir Knight. I know of no one who surpasses you in intellect." Henry gritted his teeth in frustration. She seemed genuinely pleased for him. Did that mean she cared for him, or that she did not care, since she was not concerned that he was leaving her again?

"I do not know how long I will be gone," he blurted.

"Well, you must go with all speed and return to us as soon as his Majesty can spare you." Henry was bursting with frustration. He wanted so badly to simply blurt out what he was feeling. He was, after all, leaving the next day, but that was the exact thinking that led him to his rash profession of love for her in the past and resulted in his most humiliating memory to date. He decided to take a more roundabout way to the point.

"Why do you still cherish feelings for William?"

Leah drew back in surprise. "Sir Henry, I—"

"Is it because of his first battle when we were kids? Because he was a hero?" he demanded. "He was no hero. We told everyone that to protect him."

"Sir Henry, I am sure I do not know where this is coming from."

"Oh, come now, milady, confess it. You still cherish feelings for my buffoon of a brother."

"Sir Henry..." Leah was at a loss for words.

"He is never coming back! Do you understand that you are wasting your life on a phantom that was no match for you even before he dishonored his family?"

"Sir Henry, what are you saying? How can you speak so against your own brother who has never done you any wrong?"

"He has wronged all of us!" Henry said angrily. "Every resident of Dawning Court has been tainted by his cowardice."

Leah stood. "I do not consider that my reputation was harmed, nor that your brother's actions were the actions of a coward, and I am quite sure I do not know why you felt it was appropriate to address yourself so to me. I consider myself to be a staunch friend of the Dawnings and will remain so." She hailed one of the gardeners, who was inconspicuously pruning a rose bush at the edge of the garden. "Please tell Edith that I will be departing shortly." He bowed slightly and departed. Leah turned back to Henry, who sat fuming. "Sir Henry, I wish you all the best on your travels to London. I hope to see you again soon." She turned to go and stopped when Henry called to her.

"Leah! Leah, I regret speaking so rashly." He walked quickly after her. "Have I lost your friendship?"

She looked at him as someone deserving her pity, which Henry did not like, but it was infinitely better than her stinging anger that he had felt a moment before. "Henry, I know what a good and noble person you are. It is those feelings that have earned my respect and friendship. And that is still who you are to me."

Henry collapsed onto the bench where she had been sitting a moment before, and slumped. "What, then, is required of me?" he said weakly. "I have done all that I know to do, and the person I admire most in the world values her memories of a misguided boy over my loyalty here, now, and forever."

"Dear Henry," Leah said, putting her hand on his shoulder. "We are kindred spirits and shall always be, but that is not the same as romantic love. We were simply not meant to be. Do not waste your strength on me. I am no match for your wit and intellect. Someone far more challenging awaits you," she said with a smile.

He smiled sadly up at her as a tear spilled from one eye. "You did not deny having feelings for him. Only tell me how he has done it. Tell me how a brash young man could snare the heart of the fairest, most wonderful maid in all of England. Then I will believe I can find someone like you.

Edith glided into the garden looking flushed. A slight, blond girl who was pretty, though not as pretty as her mistress, kind but not so much as Leah, Edith was the perfect lady in waiting. She possessed all of the qualities of a noblewoman but not so much so that she would ever outshine her mistress.

Leah looked vexed at being cut short, but whatever she might have said, Henry would never know. Instead she squeezed his shoulder and said softly, "I am forever your truest friend. Everything will work out for you, but you must trust to the Lord."

Her words did little to comfort Henry, but he forced himself to smile in acknowledgment of her kindness. He did not move for a long time after the ladies had departed. Part of him hoped Leah would come rushing back, but he knew just as well that she would not come for him now or ever. He felt he had lost her, but he was forced to acknowledge he had only lost the idea of her that he had enjoyed for so many years: the girl—the woman had never been his to lose. He felt an overwhelming sense of emptiness, that he truly had nothing in his life.

CHAPTER FOURTEEN

"You look scared, boy," John said to William.

"Hmm? Scared? No, just thinking," William tried to dismiss his eldest brother's comment. In truth his heart was pounding so hard he could hear it, but he was not going to admit that to his brothers.

"Don't worry about it, boy," John said. He always called him boy, probably because of the age difference between the two of them. John was not old enough to be William's father, but he did have twelve years on him. "A little fear will keep you alive. It's good for you."

"That's true," Richard chimed in. "That's why John always does so well in battles: because he's such a coward."

William smiled at his brothers as they roared with laughter. He could see Henry sharing an expression not too dissimilar from his own as he pretended to be calm and collected like his older siblings, though he, too, had very little time on the battlefield.

"Next time we were thinking of leaving John home and bringing Mother. At least she is only physically feeble; she's not weak on the inside," Richard continued to prod John. Though they were all laughing as John swung a heavy blow toward Richard, this was a bit of a sore spot between the two. Both of the eldest brothers were massive in stature and naturally gifted warriors, but Richard had always shown more dedication to his studying and training than John did and had excelled at every physical endeavor he had set his mind to. Richard was driven *and disciplined, whereas John's primary motivation seemed to be to try to keep pace with his younger brother. This dynamic between them in many ways made Richard seem like he was the elder of the two.*

The group passed Dawning Court's outer gate and proceeded to the nearby town. They met up with the local guardsmen there. This was a group of local militiamen and retired soldiers that were employed to keep peace in the area. They mostly watched the town square during business hours and escorted the occasional drunk home safely. A full scale uprising was far beyond the scope of their duties.

William watched as the head of the local detachment came to report to William's knighted older brothers, a consequence of good and faithful service on their crusades. Of his older brothers, only Edward and Henry had not been knighted, and Henry had yet to serve.

The guardsmen briefly explained that the rebellion consisted of the local townsmen, who had since fled to a nearby forest for cover. He indicated a tree line that was adjacent to a disused field about a hundred yards long that backed up to a group of cottages occupied by the townspeople. "While they are in there, it is impossible to mount a straightforward assault," the guardsman explained to justify why the knights had been sent for.

"Fine, Captain," John said, looking at the tree line. "We will handle it from here. Hold your men in readiness." John turned to his brothers. "We must draw them out," he said, looking around for ideas.

Without a word, Richard dismounted and walked over to a nearby fire pit the guardsmen had lit. He snatched the end of a burning log from the fire and walked to the nearest thatched cottage of the town. He held the burning log aloft until the flame caught the thatching on the roof, which was immediately consumed. Then he walked to the next one and did the same thing.

John jumped down from his saddle and hurried over to him. "You can't do this," he said quietly. "These are our subjects.

We are sworn to protect them." An old man came running from the burning cottage, shouting in surprise and fear. He stopped short when he saw the massive, iron-clad knights standing before him, evacuated his wife and grandchildren from the cottage, and ran for the other edge of town as quickly as possible.

Richard watched them flee. "These are our subjects and they are in rebellion. Whatever consequences their families suffer because of their actions are up to them, not us." With that he turned and flung the still burning log onto the roof of a third cottage across the lane, igniting it. The second cottage, which the old man had fled from with his family, was now well consumed by the flames. It shortly toppled, throwing burning embers onto the one next to it and igniting that one as well. There was a large plume of smoke rising from the village that would have been unmistakable for leagues around.

"Assemble the guardsmen here!" Richard ordered to the brothers, indicating the field on the edge of town between them and the tree line. Richard strode purposefully across the field toward the tree line, his sword still sheathed and his head bare.

He stopped twenty yards in and shouted, "Attention, rebellious subjects of Dawning Court. I know you can hear me, and I know that you are watching your village go up in smoke. You have three options. You can surrender, submit to being arrested, and pay the penalty for your treacherous behavior; you may stand and fight like men and die like dogs as my brothers and I slaughter each and every one of you for your villainy; or you can stay hidden and watch the rest of your village burn. Your families will be arrested for complicity in this conspiracy, and then my brothers and I will hunt you down one by one like the cowardly dogs you are. Once you are dead, your families will serve the time in the dungeon that you should have served for your crimes. You have an hundred count to decide."

With that he turned and strode unconcerned back toward the brothers. The guardsmen had fallen into a line standing shoulder to shoulder. They were a ragtag group of men dressed in mismatched pieces of leather and armor, wielding a myriad of weapons in various stages of disrepair. They were about fifty strong. For most of them this was a part time job, and they would go back to their fields, or butcher shops, or farms when this was over. About the only thing that set their appearance apart from the men they were facing was a red arm band each of them wore around his left bicep bearing the Dawning family crest. The crest depicted a helmet above a square shield with a blue stripe running from the top left to the bottom right of the shield. To the right of the stripe were two butterflies, and on the left a single one. It was all set over an elaborate plumage of blue surrounding the helmet and grey around the shield.

The brothers assembled in front of the line of guardsmen. "Remember one thing," Henry leaned over to William quietly. "Though untrained, if these men choose to fight, they are now fighting for their very lives and will do anything necessary to maintain a grip on it."

It was difficult to see much past the tree line, but there was definitely movement among the shadows. They were there, and they would respond. Slowly the shadows of the individuals began to emerge from the murky shadows of the trees and resolve into distinct figures as they stepped into the clearing to face the knights. They formed a line opposite the knights, clearly intending to fight rather than surrender.

William's heart stopped. There were at least a hundred of them that he could see and maybe more still lurking in the trees. They were outnumbered at least two to one. He looked to his ironclad brothers for reassurance. John and Richard were encased in full plate armor from head to toe now that Richard had donned his helmet. Thomas, the most rotund of the brothers, was protected on this occasion by his customary long shirt of chain mail with plate reinforcements sewn into it at critical places. His large girth managed this better than the restrictive suits of plate armor. Henry tended to favor a lighter suit of armor to John and Richard because of his slight build.

Though stocky, William had learned early on that strength was not going to be his edge on the battlefield. There were too many others as strong or stronger than he was, as Richard and John so clearly demonstrated. As such, William's custom-made suit of armor was designed to maximize his mobility and let him use his speed to full advantage. His new suit of white and gold armor of interlocking plates shown in the sun this morning with pristine radiance.

Each brother wielded a unique weapon as well. John's weapon of choice was a heavy broadsword, while Richard favored a massive Scottish claymore that ordinarily required both hands of a strong man to wield. Richard, however, seemed comfortable with it in one hand. Thomas opted for a sinister looking mace, a spiked ball connected to a chain that was attached to an eighteen-inch handle. It was a thoroughly nasty weapon that required a great deal of skill by the wielder to prevent harm to himself.

Henry was still trying to find himself. He was constantly vacillating between the heavier swords like those preferred by John and Richard, and the finer European blades like the rapier that Edward had favored for the brief period he fought side by side with his family.

As for William, he had chosen an entirely different path here, too, largely because of his mentor. His family had brought on an oriental teacher when he was just a young man. This teacher, Jurou, fought in a manner they had never before beheld. He was proficient with any standard weapon but also seemed to be able to turn any ordinary object into a weapon. He, too, was small in stature as was common to his people but was widely regarded as the most fearsome fighter in all the land roundabout.

His ways intrigued the whole family, particularly Braden, the knights' father, who made Jurou a fixture at Court. But it was only William who had really responded to these foreign ideas. All the brothers except Henry and William were well indoctrinated into traditional combat rules by the time Jurou made his appearance, and Henry was simply more comfortable following the traditional route of study.

Jurou became a mentor to William in the absence of his father. He taught him more than just combat, he taught him about self-control and discipline. It was a direct consequence of his influence that William's armor deviated so markedly from the norm. His weapon, too, was unlike any of the other brothers' steel. His sword of choice was a katana. It enhanced his speed over the heavier English blades, but the long, slight, curved blade was not limited like the flimsy rapier that was primarily a stabbing weapon. The katana was very strong and could be employed for both stabbing and cutting as the situation warranted.

"Well, it's time to see if that pig sticker of yours is worth anything," Richard said to William. "I wager ten pounds it snaps off at the hilt on the first bit of metal it hits." His brothers continued to tease him about it because a katana was a weapon not seen around Europe and certainly not on a knight or one who aspired to become a knight. His brother's playful jabs did nothing to lighten William's mood or quell the sickly fear that was coursing through his veins at that moment. Usually this did not bother William because he was very comfortable with this weapon, but moments before his first real battle was not the time to be undermining his confidence. It was only with a conscious effort that he was keeping his knees from trembling as he watched the enemy line form opposite them. He did not dare open his mouth to respond to the ribbing for fear that his cowardice would betray him in a trembling or cracking voice. It was pride alone that kept him from fleeing at that moment. Pride, and the recognition that he had to face this moment at some point. It was his destiny.

John pulled his mount in next to William and leaned over to him. "Remember, you are a trained, skilled warrior and these are farmers. They have likely never held a sword before today. Keep on your guard and you have nothing to fear. This is who you are, who you were meant to be, and who you will become. The blood of a thousand great warriors courses through your viens. Trust in yourself."

William nodded mutely. He was very glad his brothers were there. He believed in their abilities, though he was not at all sure about his own.

"It does not seem that they intend to surrender," Richard said casually, then raising his voice and calling across the distance to the other line, "This is your last chance to surrender. Expect no quarter if you insist upon a battle."

A very large man from the other line yelled back in ever so slightly accented English, "Since we far outnumber you, we will give you one chance to surrender." There was a smattering of nervous laughter through his line of rebels.

William squinted across the line at the speaker. He did not belong here. Nothing about him made sense. The farmers were eye level with this man's belly. He was a veritable giant. His hair was long and black, his skin was a light brown, and he wore real armor. There was a nasty scar that ran down his left cheek that was visible even from this distance. This was no farmer. William leaned over to John to point that out, but at that moment Richard wordlessly began to close the distance between them, motioning for everyone to follow. It was again only with a concerted effort that William was able to spur his horse into advancing with the others, but advance he did.

The enemy line started toward them, albeit more hesitantly, the farmers clearly taking their direction from the giant. They did outnumber the guardsmen but nobody, no matter how foolhardy, willingly took on full knights. One did not get the title of "Knight of Dawning Court" for his lovely singing voice or enchanting wit. One got it for combat, terrible and brutal combat, and even the lowliest serf knew that. Nevertheless, there were only a few knights and the rest were ordinary farmers the same as them. So if they could just dispatch the knights, the rest should fall easily.

Richard led out with a measured pace intended to draw the rebels away from the tree line. He did not want them fleeing back into the trees at the first clash and have to spend the next week rooting them out. Richard brought his horse up and casually pulled his massive sword from its sheath and held it *aloft. The brothers and guardsmen all followed suit. Then as one they yelled, "For God and country!" except for Richard, who shouted, "For glory!" and jabbed his gilded spurs into his warhorse's side. His mount leapt forward and charged the rebel line.*

The unmounted guardsmen's line broke as they sprinted to catch up to the knights, and soon the battle was well joined. Richard, John, and Thomas began to cut their way through the ranks of ill-prepared farmers like explorers through a thick jungle: cleaving enemy weapons in twain, piercing the makeshift armor, and smashing the bones underneath the antique shields.

William tried to clear his mind of the fear and emotions of the moment in order to let the training take over. It wasn't easy to close out all the distractions, but he tried. He came upon the first of the farmers who had just turned to take a swing at John as John rode by. The farmer was wearing virtually no armor and had left his left flank completely exposed.

William swung his blade in an underhand arc and pierced the farmer's side. The farmer's body crumpled instantly as his major organs were skewered. As William wrenched his sword free he slammed his boot into the unprotected head of another man standing a few feet away. The peasant dropped to his knees in surprise and pain.

William reversed the momentum of his katana to swing it around and down in a strong overhand swing toward the same unprotected head. His blade connected with the top of the rebel's head as he was just regaining his feet. His eyes rolled back in his head as he collapsed and blood ran through his hair.

William paused for a moment as the rush of the moment passed and the magnitude of what he had just done sunk in. He did not feel proud or happy, as he always imagined, but disturbed and slightly nauseous as he contemplated the farmers' bodies on the ground around his horse, one dead and the other dying. Did the punishment meted out to them fit the crime, he wondered? Of course, they would have killed him if he had given them the chance. Was what they were fighting for worth their lives? What were they fighting for? How strange no one bothered to ask.

***

    Charles watched in disbelief as the knights of Dawning Court rode through the line of his friends, turned, and made another pass into his ranks. He had lived on the Dawnings' land all his life and had a certain pride in the exploits of Braden Dawning. He used to watch the Dawning boys in tournaments with amazement, dreaming that one day he would be called on to fight alongside them. He could not imagine how they ever came to be facing him and his family on opposite sides of the line.

    Being a lowly villein on the Dawnings' land was all Charles had ever known and all he had ever wanted. He had been content enough with his little family and his life until the foreigner that now stood at their head had appeared and started filling their heads with stories about the luxury the Dawnings lived in; about the abuse they heaped upon those beneath them and how their children, as villeins, were doomed to be subjects of the Dawnings forever. They would never have a better life.

    Charles was not convinced, but his brother had been and persuaded Charles to go along on a few raids of Dawning supply trains. No one had been hurt and it all seemed like childish fun at first, but somehow now they were being cut down by the very people he had long admired. This could not be right. This was just a misunderstanding.

    Charles turned to his brother not far from where he was and called to him. He had to bring him back to reality. Together they might be able to put a stop to this. He located his brother just in time to see a young man that he did not recognize ride into their line a few paces behind the others. He was strangely dressed, but the Dawning coat of arms was clearly visible on his armor. His bare head revealed that he was only a boy. This was way out of hand. Charles got his brother's attention just as this Dawning boy cut one of the others down. Charles' brother was still looking at him, trying to understand his message when the young Dawning kicked him in the head.

Charles watched his brother stumble and fall. As he tried to stand to defend himself, the Dawning boy brought his sword down on his unprotected head.

Charles knew instantly his brother was dead. His disbelief turned to horror at what he had just seen. The Dawning boy stopped to survey what he had done and Charles' shock turned to rage. It was his fault his own brother lay dead instead of this child. Had Charles not distracted him when he did—Charles cried out in anguish and charged the back of the Dawning boy.

The Dawning boy twisted around in his saddle and spotted Charles charging him with his massive cleaver raised over his head. The boy saw what was coming but could not wheel his mount fast enough to defend himself properly.

Charles aimed his blow at the kidney, but instead of soft flesh, his cleaver found only the hard leather of the back of his saddle as the young Dawning rolled off of the horse just in time to avoid the blow. Charles' cleaver whizzed by William's retreating foot, cut through the back of the saddle, and into his horse's flesh. With a loud whinny, his horse galloped off the field.

In one smooth motion the youth hit the ground and rolled to regain his feet. He came up facing Charles. They stood rooted in place for a few moments, sizing each other up. Charles suddenly felt somewhat foolish in his green hunter's outfit. It was evident from the boy's elaborate armor and weapons that no expense had been spared in training and equipping him. There were obviously very powerful people interested in his safe return. Almost everyone interested in Charles's return was on the field with him at that moment. He suddenly sensed that this fight was much bigger than some farmers' living conditions. He realized at that moment that he was merely a pawn in a bigger game that he did not understand. He knew he could not win. Even if they managed to vanquish these knights, *the same powers that trained and equipped this young man would pour their wrath out upon any that were to do him harm.*

Nevertheless, he had no choice but to fight or be killed now. Still, Charles did not know what to make of this young warrior. Though Charles was half again the boy's size, he knew this young man had far more combat training than he did. But what options did he have? This same boy had moments before murdered his only brother. Charles took a hesitant step forward to test the young warrior's reaction. That seemed a safe enough move. It was not.

Instead of backing away defensively as Charles had expected, the young man swung his back leg out and kicked the exposed side of Charles' weight-bearing thigh with his iron-covered right shin.

Charles had been so intently watching the Dawning's sword that he had not seen it coming until it was too late. He exclaimed in surprise and pain as his leg buckled involuntarily beneath him. The boy's sword was instantly there to finish the job. With his other foot he kicked Charles in the side of the head, dropping the man to the turf to finish bleeding out from his gaping neck wound.

***

William gazed down at the twitching body and felt nauseous. There was no glory here. Cutting down a bunch of foolish peasants is something for which he would never be proud.

He heard the rapid footsteps at his back. He sidestepped the blow that dropped just to his left but was taken between the shoulder blades by this latest charging enemy. The force of the collision snapped his head back and sent him sprawling in the dirt. A voice in his head shrieked that he had lost control of the situation and he had to regain his feet immediately before this ogre was on him again. William rolled completely over his shoulders in a series of rolls that he hoped would remove him from danger. He swung his katana in a wide arc blindly as he was trying to break loose from the glimpses of the rebel fast approaching. William knew he was incredibly vulnerable right now but hoped the wild, unpredictable sword swings would keep his opponent at bay. He could only imagine Jurou's expression if he were watching this pathetic display. Nevertheless, the blow that should have been his undoing did not come. William rolled a final time and leapt to his feet. Standing not far from him was a massive, menacing form. William held his weapon at the ready as a slight wave of dizziness passed over him. It was only then that he recognized the form of Thomas, who was standing over the crumpled heap of his assailant, his ugly mace smattered with blood.

"Taking a rest so early in the battle, are you, little brother?" Thomas grinned at him. "We'll have no gold bricking here." He caught the blow of a nasty looking club on his shield and smashed his mace back at his assailant.

William was shaken up. He did not know what had happened exactly, but he felt that he had been very close to the end. He had not been prepared for the massive chaos of the battle. In the training yard he could take his time and control the situation. Even if there were multiple opponents, he knew he just needed to strike a "killing" blow to remove them from the battle and restore order. But here the onslaught did not stop. It was one opponent after another after another, with no respite between to collect oneself or reassess the situation.

Then the chaos enfolded him again. He caught the blade of a sword on the side of his own blade. He swiped the weapon aside and stabbed violently at the face of its owner. The blow sent the swordsman reeling, but before William could finish him off another rebel was upon him, and another and another. He was shortly surrounded by several enemies in waiting. Time seemed to slow down for just an instant, where nobody dared move. William's peripheral vision seemed to open up and take in far more than he ordinarily saw, sizing up each opponent, wounded shoulder here, torn leather armor there, a hobbled leg on this person, a blind side on that person. He saw it all, just like the *training exercises back home. There was no fear, but a clear understanding of what was required of him.*

William would have to strike first. He would need that small advantage to extricate himself from this circle. Enemies on every side was the worst scenario for a warrior to be in. But if he cut his way out of the circle he could turn on them and they would all be on one side of him, a much more controllable scenario. Without warning he struck, stabbing his katana point hard at the man in front of him. The farmer lurched back to avoid the blow and William spun the end of his weapon down and underneath his shoulder to catch the assailant he felt more than saw moving in behind him. He felt the knees buckle from the force of the thrust. Next his blade swung out in a wide overhead circle toward the heads and necks of all those closing in on him. They jumped back in an automatic reaction to the threat. William spun with it and brought the end of the weapon down sharply on the head of an assailant that had ventured too close. William immediately swung the end back under his shoulder to hold the opponent to his rear at bay. Hitting nothing, he swung it up in front of him, catching a rebel to his right in the chin and dropping him sharply. He then spun the weapon sharply to the right, catching another charging assailant in the temple.

William spun still again in an endless loop to keep his opponents off guard and field the many attacks that were coming from all sides. He then whirled out of the circle of chaos. Facing the remaining enemies, he caught the blade of a third man on his own sword. He rolled his katana over the blade, turning his back to his opponent, and caught his attacker's sword arm under his right arm, trapping it against his body. He then reversed his grip on his sword and drove the point into the body of his hapless victim.

William took position with his sword point leveled at the chest of the remaining opponent. It had all happened so quickly that some of the rebels had not yet finished collapsing, a fact mostly lost on William, who was now completely focused on his next victim. The farmer, however, was acutely aware that his *band of men had been cut from around him in what seemed an instant. He faced William who was standing, sword leveled at his chest, panting from his exertion but looking none the worse for wear. The rebel farmer suddenly thought better of this particular challenge and retreated into the fray to find more appropriate opponents.*

William was just starting to chase after him when he was hit solidly in the side of the head. Stars exploded before his eyes and he staggered in a daze. His feet felt unsteady, but he knew to fall would be certain death. He vaguely saw a huge form in front of him as he stumbled away and swung a wild blow at the large form which was easily deflected.

His assailant came into focus a moment later. It was the large, long-haired man that had been taunting them from the enemy line. He really did look like a giant up close. The giant swung at William, who parried with his blade and trapped the giant's arm as he had done to his previous victim. He started to reverse the grip of his sword but the giant pulled sharply back. It took all William's strength to maintain control of him, and his katana slipped from his hand. In desperation, William tried to break the giant's trapped arm at the elbow. He held the larger man's wrist in his left hand. William slipped his right arm under the giant's elbow, and locked onto his own left forearm. He slammed down on the giant's massive wrist, straining the giant elbow backward. William felt very vulnerable with the giant still at his back and jammed down as hard as he could, hoping to hear the pop of the bone and scream of pain from his opponent. But the giant was huge. He resisted, and for a moment they were locked in a contest of might over the giant's arm. William's eyes widened as this man began to curl his arm up against all the force William could muster to counter him. William re-exerted himself with everything he had, forced the huge arm straight again, and tried to force it to the breaking point. He could feel the giant's back start to arch in pain and knew he was getting close when stars again exploded in William's eyes as the giant punched him in the back of the head with his gauntleted left hand.

William released his grip on the giant's right arm and jumped forward to avoid the next punch that was already on its way. The next punch glanced off William's shoulder, doing little damage, but William had no idea what to do next. He was very disturbed by this oversized man simply out-muscling him despite his most valiant exertions. This was no farmer. One more poorly chosen attack against this opponent may spell the end for him. William stood in a half crouch waiting for the giant's next move. He glanced down and saw his sword on the ground halfway between himself and the giant. He would expose himself too much if he tried to retrieve it, but he was very seriously doubting his hand to hand combat edge against this man.

William went for his weapon. Taking a few steps, he bent over to make a grab for his sword. The giant got there first and trapped it under the thick heel of his right boot while the toe of his left boot planted itself squarely in William's ribs. William sprawled backwards but quickly rolled to his feet again, trying to ignore the pain that was spreading quickly out from his ribs to the rest of his body. The giant was instantly standing over him and swung his sword hard at William to finish him off.

At the last moment William lurched to the side. Instead of the blow to his head that certainly would have been his demise, the blade cut a deep gash in his arm. The giant had the advantage now. He followed up instantly with another kick, catching William, who was already partially doubled over, in the upper stomach just under his chest. The wind exploded from his lungs and the shock made his legs go involuntarily limp. He dropped to all fours, gasping for breath. He knew another strike must be coming and pushed himself backward in desperation.

The blade whistled by his head and cut into the soft soil. He had narrowly avoided death again but was now on his back. He was helpless. This was the end. He knew it, and his opponent knew it. The giant sneered as he raised his blade over his head. "The head of a Dawning will make an excellent trophy," he said and brought the sword down with both hands.

CHAPTER FIFTEEN

"Henry Dawning?" said a cheerful female voice from beside Henry. He turned to see a short, dark-haired girl with fair skin, a wide face, and a beaming smile walk up beside him and interlock her arm with his. "I might have known you would not remember me," she continued when he did not respond.

"Please forgive my insolence, milady, but I am sure I have not had the pleasure of making your acquaintance, for I surely would remember." She was broad of build without being manly. Her slightly oversized chest added to this impression, but as Henry regarded her, he became aware that she was not at all unpleasant to look at.

"I am from Mayfield," she said and waited for it to sink in.

"Mary of Mayfield?" Henry asked, shocked. "That little obnoxio—sweet girl that used to visit Dawning Court when we were children?" The memories came flooding back to him as he recalled that her father was often campaigning with his own, and the baroness and her spoiled little daughter were often hanging about Dawning Court for weeks at a time.

"The very same, you big bully," she said light-heartedly.

"How ever did you recognize me?" Henry asked, embarrassed.

"In truth, I was in Devonshire visiting an old friend when your party arrived. When I heard your name, I knew I positively must find my old friend and become reacquainted. Now, you must tell me absolutely everything that has become of your family since I have seen them last. Omit no detail."

"In truth, milady, I am ignorant of such details to a great degree myself as I have only returned from Persia some few days prior," he admitted. Then, realizing she might be impressed with this addition, he added, "I have just returned from the Crusades."

"I might have known!" she said, looking suitably impressed. "When I first laid eyes upon your person, I could not believe the man that stood before me compared to the little boy that used to tease me and pull my hair." Henry blushed at the compliment. "Of course you are a mighty warrior. Tales of your valor precede you, Sir Knight, as they do all your family." Henry was not certain how true the "valor" part of that was but decided she was being sincere at least where he was concerned.

"It appears the years have been kind to you as well," Henry said abruptly, fearing he was being outstripped in the compliments.

She smiled up at him. "Neither have your charms withered in the intervening years."

"Perhaps you have me confused with one of my brothers."

She chuckled at that, a light musical sound that was quite charming. "Your brothers are all great warriors, I'm sure, but that is not enough. A man is destined to come to naught if the strength of his intellect does not match the strength of his sword arm." Henry liked that sentiment very much.

"Lady Mary?" Another finely dressed woman called from an adjacent walkway. "Will you be joining us?"

Mary rolled her eyes. "I'm afraid I must go. Henry, will you call on me? I really must hear all about the Dawnings. It has been too long."

Henry promised he would and watched her walk away with a spring in her step that he very much admired. He wondered if her forthright personality affected everyone the way it was affecting him. Whatever the case, he would definitely see her again.

CHAPTER SIXTEEN

The darkness drew out for Richard. It seemed endless. He no longer knew how long he had been there. He did not know when the days changed to night or back again...

"Why am I still alive?" he shouted in anguish, but he could not be certain if he had done so only in his head.

"Would you prefer to be dead?" The voice returned to answer him as it often did.

"Compared to this? Of course I would prefer death!" he said angrily. "Why couldn't they have killed me on the battlefield? There is honor in that. This is nothing but degradation and shame."

"Don't you think that is what they want you to feel?"

"Why? Toward what end?"

"You have killed many of their people. You have done much damage. In some measure they are trying to exact payment from you... or at least punish you appropriately."

"*Shouldn't* I have done those things?" Richard was still angry. "These are strangers in our land. They forced their way in, killed our people, and took over. They are the enemy."

"And as the enemy, how would you expect them to treat you?"

"I expect them to execute me with dignity!" Richard shouted at the voice, who he always felt was somehow patronizing him.

"There is no dignity in execution, there is only finality. Isn't that what you really want? To be released from this?" The soft voice was always calm, never harsh or angry, but quiet and rational no matter how heated Richard became.

"So I want to be released, what about it? If I cannot be freed physically, so much the better that my soul should be free in death."

"No, you have come too far for that. You are not a simple soldier on a battlefield. You are a powerful warrior that used your influence and talents to inflict vast amounts of damage. You are now reaping what you have sown."

"You keep talking like I am a villain! These people are the enemy! What I did, I did for God and country. What is wrong with that? And if I hadn't relied on that mercenary scum, I would still be waging that war."

"You did it for God and country?"

"Why else would I do it?" Richard challenged. There was no response. "What? You think I did this for my family, is that it? To spread the fear and awe of the Dawning name?" Still no response. Richard was getting angrier. "You think I did this for myself? You think this whole thing was about self-aggrandizement? Why would I do that? Look at what I got out of this! Misery, sickness, and insanity!" He was shouting now. "Robbed of even the dignity of death! I got nothing out of this! Nothing! Everything I did I did for God, country, and family! And they all forgot about me! They have all forsaken me." The voice was gone now. It always tended to disappear when he went on his tirades, but at that moment Richard did not care. "They all forgot about me. If I ever get out of here, I will have my revenge." Richard was ranting now. "I will have my revenge on these miserable dogs, then I will have my revenge on everyone else for not appreciating the sacrifices I made for them. I gave up everything for them! Everything!"

CHAPTER SEVENTEEN

Bashir cast his eyes on the low, dark clouds rolling overhead and spat. "Does the rain ever stop in this cursed country?" His companion only grunted in reply. This was Bashir's maiden voyage to the shores of Britain, and it was not agreeing with him. The humidity caused him to sweat incessantly, and the rain was relentless. In his three days in country they had seen more rain than they might see in an entire year in their homeland. The muddy roads were frequently impassable, and the thick foliage that lined the roads robbed him of his sense of direction and made him feel trapped. "I could not point north in this forest prison to save my very soul," Bashir groused. They were riding on a road so tightly shouldered by trees that a horse could not make it through the tangle of undergrowth on either side. "I never realized this island could persevere so many times over the horizon, and still it does not end." Bashir's ordinarily sour disposition had continued to darken each day they had been out of their own land.

Ibrahim for his part was relieved by the relative ease of this assignment. To be sure, there would be some danger as they approached their destination, and there was always some amount of danger for two unescorted Saracens in such an unholy land at times such as these. But the lion's share of their assignment consisted simply of riding through beautiful country. No fighting, no killing at all, in fact, as they were intent on keeping a low profile. Anonymity was their greatest ally here, and they would go unnoticed as far as possible.

Nevertheless, Ibrahim knew well his companion's disposition after so many years of serving Allah by his side. And to point out the many positive things while Bashir was bent on being unhappy would only give this perverse man more cause to complain; Ibrahim held his peace while Bashir continued to complain. Thus was each absorbed in his separate thoughts until Bashir suddenly perked up. "What is it?" Ibrahim asked, growing uneasy. "Is ther—"

"Be still!" Bashir barked, and they listened in silence until the sound came again.

From somewhere in front of them, they heard it. Softly at first, but it grew louder as they progressed.

"Is that... singing?" Ibrahim asked in disbelief. They continued on, and the voice grew louder still. Yes, it was definitely singing. Somewhere up ahead a man was singing very loudly off key. They looked at each other in surprise and confusion, but assuming this was not the war cry of a vicious crusader, they continued toward the sound. As they rounded the bend, they saw the source of the singing. There was a lone figure in a large bulky brown robe astride a modest but not unhealthy palfrey ambling along as if he had nowhere at all to be. He did not seem to notice their approach. Bashir and Ibrahim exchanged glances as he launched into another verse.

"Oh, I gave my love a sweetheart. So my sweetheart she would be."

Satisfied that this was no threat, they thought it more suspicious to ride past without a word than to greet this curious stranger. They reined their mounts in to match his plodding pace. "Hail, good sir," said Ibrahim hesitantly in heavily accented French, which both spoke passably well, though neither cared to speak the languages of their oppressors.

The rider gave them a sidelong glance from under his long, sun-bleached bangs but continued the verse he was in:

"If I can't have my sweetheart, I shan't go home again."

Ibrahim and Bashir exchanged another puzzled glance. The rider sighed and turned his attention to the two Saracens. He studied them for a moment and then addressed them grandly. "Greetings, fellow travelers on the road of life."

"Is this the road of life?" Ibrahim stuttered, not understanding the meaning. "We had thought this to be the King's highway."

"And so it is, gentle sir. So it is." He wore a smirk on his suntanned face. Ibrahim looked slightly confused but did not press the matter.

"Forgive us, we are slow to understand your tongue and are clumsier still in speaking it, Sir Knight."

"Oh, I am no knight." The stranger replied in deft but somewhat careless Arabic.

"You speak our tongue?" Ibrahim rejoined with surprise as well as suspicion. "We must beg your forgiveness if we were too abrupt." They were suspicious not only because everyone they met at best disdained and refused to interact with them and at worst were downright hostile toward them, but also because the fact that he spoke their language suggested he had been to their land; and that usually meant a godless, bloodthirsty crusader. But this man did not look like a crusader. His hair was cropped short in the back, and the bangs had gotten long over his brown skin, tanned deeply from many days in the sun. He wore a large, brown robe that bunched up everywhere, and the folds made him seem unusually large. The robe was slit up the middle to accommodate equestrian activities. "Is it wise to be drawing attention to yourself in the woods?"

"Drawing attention to myself?"

"With the singing. I understand these woods are full of highwaymen and brigands," he explained.

"Oh... I'm more worried about bears."

"Bears, sir?" Ibrahim looked around nervously." Are there bears in these woods?"

"I don't know, but it never hurts to be safe. So tell me what brings you to this foreign land in times such as these."

"We are but humble pilgrims from the Holy Land," Ibrahim provided their cover story. "We are traveling the world in search of religious enlightenment."

"I pray you God speed in your quest then," he said with a wry smile. "If you do rush, perhaps you can catch the last glimmer of spiritual enlightenment setting on this land like the sun going down."

"You are not a believer then?" Ibrahim asked, thinking that this put this man far from the religious zealots of the Crusades.

"These are times when the blood flows in the streets in the name of religious fervor, and yet I cannot conceive of a time when men's minds have been so shadowed from the light of the Lord." He smiled again. "You will allow some license on this subject, however. I fear I have been jaded as my father impregnated my mother in a fit of passion and left because of the shame that the Church would have rained down on his head. My mother, then fearing ostracism for giving birth to a bastard child, had me in secrecy and left me to the monks. I spent my young life among holy men who loved nothing better than a good drink. Excepting perhaps a woman." The Saracens stared at him in amazement. To betray so many shameful secrets to two perfect strangers was unheard of. "Then, when the monastery fell on hard times," the stranger continued in a forlorn tone, "they traded me to a Frenchman for a hogshead of cheap ale. The Frenchman promptly forgot me on the side of the road near a brothel he had stopped at for refreshment. I owe my very life to the tender mercies of those ladies of ill repute. They alone would accept my society, which could not be brooked among good, god-fearing people." They stared at him in silence for a moment before erupting in laughter.

"You are a fool," Bashir said, barking a loud, harsh laugh. "A jester."

"Alas," the stranger replied in an even more forlorn attitude. "Such was my fondest wish, but my mind is too feeble. I haven't the wit for it."

"But you speak our tongue?" Ibrahim inquired, still surprised and not yet satisfied on this point.

"My head does not rest long in any one place."

"What brings you to this highway on this day, then?" Ibrahim asked.

"Why, the most miraculous turn of events brings me thus. But I would not distract contemplative pilgrims with such sordid tales."

"Please, it would do us good to have our minds relieved of our heavy pursuits if only for a moment."

"Well, all right," he conceded hastily with the air of a man that really did want to share his tale. "I had embarked on a pilgrimage. It has indeed always been my life's ambition, my destiny if I may call it such, to see the grass of the Holy Roman Empire in person. Nay, not just see it, but touch and smell it. Surely the grass of a place which the dew of heaven so lavishly rains down upon must be more wonderful than anything in all the world, but I wanted to know for myself," he said with some passion, sniffing at his hand as if he were taking a whiff of the imaginary grass in his fist.

"And what befell you there?" Ibrahim pressed with an expression indicating he expected to be amused by the answer.

"I fear I shall never know. For I was on my way to the boat, a few leagues from my own humble cottage, when perchance I passed lands that were even then being worked by the local serfs. And there, taking water to the hands that toiled in the fields, was what I believed to be an angel descended straight from heaven. I now know that the very devil himself put her in my way to try my resolve, a fair-haired beauty in her simple serf's gown, the likes of which I had never beheld," he expounded dramatically. "I submit to you good pilgrims that I was in love. Cupid's arrow had found me, and I am as mortal as any man."

"I say," Ibrahim feigned surprise, "were you so easily moved from your resolve?"

"What excuse may I make you? When the Lord made beauty, he did not discriminate between nobility and serfs." The pilgrims noted the faintest of smirks playing across his countenance that did not disappear when his face darkened as he said his next piece. "And I say to you that prejudices against other classes of men run as deep in the lower classes as ever they did in the nobility. I had at once addressed myself to this fair maiden when her father appeared and interposed himself between us. He demanded to know what business I had with his daughter. I informed him that I was merely remarking on the weather to her. But he would have none of it and banished her from the fields to her own lodgings."

"Why? Whatever did you do?" Ibrahim inquired.

The jester leaned in his saddle to be closer to the pilgrims and spoke confidentially. "I surreptitiously watched whither she retired, that I might discover her lodgings."

"Against her father's wishes?" Ibrahim again feigned surprise.

"What excuse can I make for my actions but that I was overcome with love? I was thus overcome, and I did not even know the maid's name. I confess to my indiscretion, but I trust Saint Peter will forgive me as I was only doing that which, though unseemly sounding in purpose, was what one of my sex was bound to do for such a creature as this. I waited until nightfall, and under cover of darkness, I stole up to her window and knocked gently on the shutters. When I heard a stirring inside, I slipped a map through the slats with a place where she should meet me. I had my seal upon it that she might know from whom it was given. I then retired to that secret meeting place and arranged a safe haven wherein I could bespeak my true and everlasting love for this maiden and entreat for her hand to be joined to my mine until the icy claw of death alone could separate me from her."

"Did she meet you?" Bashir asked, faintly amused that he was actually curious about the outcome of this tale.

"Would you believe it?" the jester said expansively. "I stole to the edge of the trees from whence I had been hiding lest I be seen by unfriendly eyes. I knelt behind the hedge and took my love's fair hand in the darkness through the undergrowth. I poured my heart out to her and exclaimed that if she would but have me, I should forever strive to repay to her the honor she would do me. She told me emphatically that she would, and I burst forth from the hedge in exultation only to find that I was face to face with her portly, aged grandmother. It seems I had knocked on the wrong shutters, as the comely daughter was housed on the opposite side of the cottage and I had rather roused the grandmother, who was now determined to be wed according to my word."

Bashir barked a loud, gruff laugh while Ibrahim roared with laughter. "Did you keep your promise to the 'fair maiden'?" Ibrahim asked.

"Alas, what choice did I have? I had pledged my love, even if mistakenly. I had promised my hand. What recourse had I save one?" They looked at him expectantly. Sitting up in his saddle to appear as proud as possible, he proclaimed, "I fled."

"You fled?" Ibrahim repeated.

"You ran like a filthy dog?" Bashir said with some bite.

"Oh, I ran faster than the filthiest dog. The elderly lady roused the whole village and proclaimed what dishonor I had done her and her family, and they all came after me. You may think it humorous," he said, seeing their smirks, "but thirty men armed with pitchforks, knives, and clubs bent on having my head is an altogether new experience for me and more than my delicate fortitude could take. Alas, I have since been wandering these strange paths, unsure of where I am or where I go. But in my broken-heartedness, I care little for my own safety," he said with an air of melancholy that would have done the most skilled troubadour proud.

"I suppose that is why you are armed thus?" Bashir suggested skeptically, nodding at his spear tied loosely along the length of his horse. "Perchance you should round a corner and there be a group of angry serfs waiting to force your nuptials with that unhappy woman?"

"Precisely, gentle pilgrims," he grinned and leaned toward them in his saddle. "Truth be told, I can hardly tell a spear from a sword, so I pray I will never need to draw it, for by then it may already be too late," he told them confidentially. Then, sitting upright in his saddle again he declared, "We are not so different. We are all pilgrims. Yet I pray your hearts will not be distracted from your higher purposes as mine was. If I had been faithful to my pious aims, the woes with which I have regaled you would be nothing but fanciful tales."

"And were these not just that?" asked Ibrahim incredulously, his laughter diminishing. "Fanciful tales?"

"I swear by the holy belt of Saint—"he was saying as they rounded a bend on the road. Up ahead was a man with a wagon, struggling vainly to repair the wheel by himself. It had collapsed such that the wagon was blocking the whole road at a point where the trees pressed in upon the road, making it impossible to pass. "I swear by the holy belt of Saint Benedict that if you do value your life, you will flee now." He had not taken his eyes from the unfortunate wagoner in front of them and finished the last in the same conversational tone so that the pilgrims did not immediately understand what he said.

"What was that?" Abdul doubted he had heard correctly.

"Flee." They stared at him, trying to ascertain if this was another jest or not.

"Now, gentle sirs, you would do better not to flee from us," said a tall, dark-haired man that stepped out of the trees wearing a long, green jerkin with no crest. His simple woodsman attire was matched by the man that stepped out of the trees beside him. The wagoner feigning to work on the cart now stood to take his place on the opposite side of the speaker. The speaker brandished a short sword while his two cohorts had long bows drawn on the travelers.

"What is the meaning of this?" Bashir demanded.

"You are traveling on the king's highway and have been for some time. As the king's loyal subjects, we are required to exact payment."

"Use of the king's highway is free and is protected under the law of the land," Ibrahim argued. "You may not extort money for its use."

"These are trying times for poor King John. With so many of his affairs domestic and abroad going so wrong, he seeks new sources of revenue," he explained cheerfully.

"You are not part of the king's guard," Ibrahim said narrowly.

The bandit only rolled his eyes and turned to the stranger. "And what of you, sir?" he asked. "You are surely hiding something in that oversized robe."

"I fear I am but a humble fool and could offer you little by way of monetary compensation."

"A fool, eh? And where is your hat?"

The stranger touched his bare head as if embarrassed. "I fear I matched wits with a better fool, and he has taken it from me as a symbol of my unworthiness to be among his ranks."

The highwayman laughed heartily. "Unworthy to be a fool? My heart bleeds for you, for what could be left to you now?" he grinned.

"I fear only ruin and death," said the stranger. "As I have no quarrel with you, I pray you to let me be on my way and impede me no longer. I have a serious death to contemplate."

The rogue laughed again. "Forgive the inconvenience, but we must detain you a bit longer yet until we have relieved you of your valuables. But since you face nothing but grim death, you surely will not miss them," he said in a conciliatory tone.

"But what might I possess that you would deprive a doomed man of in peril of your everlasting soul? I have no quarrel with you; let us not create one," he replied in the same lighthearted tone.

"I pray do not hold it against me that I execute my necessary duties. Were it up to me, I would never dream of disturbing your pleasant journey; but the choice lies not with me." While they were thus engaged, men leapt into the road directly behind each rider and horse and dragged Bashir and Ibrahim out of their saddles. The third man, however, met with misfortune as the Englishman was warned of his approach by Bashir and Ibrahim being seized only a moment before, and he jerked his elbow sharply backward, catching his would-be assailant in the nose. The rogue's head snapped back and blood erupted from his face. The jester tore his spear from the loose ties that bound it, leapt from his saddle, and charged the three men in front of him.

The spokesman for the highwaymen was instantly on his guard, his sword held high. "Stop, or your friends die," he commanded.

The Englishman stopped and looked back at the Moorish pilgrims. He only shrugged. "Do what you must; they are not my friends." He advanced another step. Ibrahim and Bashir were dragged forward with knives to their throats. "I am warning you."

"Warning me of what?" he smiled. "I already indicated I care not what becomes of them. So what is it you were warning me of: the fact that you and your cohorts are about to be cut down for your poor choice in occupations?" He seemed genuinely amused by the whole intercourse. As if to accentuate his point, he flicked his spear suddenly with blinding speed at the face of the wagoner and cut a deep gash under his eye before he even had a chance to wince. He shook his head and pulled the string of his bow taut, preparing to let fly at the jester.

"Hold," the leader barked. "They will die unless you surrender your purse to the protectors of the king's highway now!" he demanded of the jester.

The jester looked coolly at the leader and said in deadly quiet voice, the butt of his spear once again resting on the ground and a blue flag with a crest embroidered on it billowing from just beneath the point of his weapon. "I am your angel of death, and you will not escape me. Your life was forfeit from the moment you refused to let me pass in peace!"

Their leader looked back and forth between his men and the armed stranger, suddenly unsure of himself. "Kill them!" he roared to his men restraining the Moors. The jester's spear whirled overhead in an instant and struck past the first man restraining Ibrahim, causing him to flinch back enough that Ibrahim was able to knock him back with a kick to the chest and regain his feet. The heavy spearhead then slammed into the side of the head of the man holding Bashir and knocked him to the ground.

It was only an instant and the spear was back around, knocking the bow of the wagoner just as he released his string, causing his arrow to embed itself high in a tree off the side of the road. The spear was on its way to the next bowman, but the jester was not fast enough. The archer let fly, and with a whizzing noise the fletching cut through the air and hit the jester in the chest, knocking him backward.

The highwaymen charged the jester but stopped short when he did not fall. He righted himself, and the arrow fell to the ground, broken. If they had not already realized this was no mere jester, the fact that he was wearing armor under his robe clued them in. They hesitated, and the jester turned and leveled the point of his weapon, held securely in both hands now, at their leader. "I wouldn't do that," he said to the men reaching for arrows. They froze in place but did not lower their hands from their quivers.

Bashir and Ibrahim were on their feet again. Both had taken up the rogues' fallen short swords, but they were still several paces behind the jester. Ibrahim was talking quietly but rapidly to Bashir, gesturing frantically toward the jester's crest.

"I'm telling you, that is him!" Ibrahim insisted to Bashir.

"How can you be so sure?" Bashir growled, still breathing hard from the exertion of dispatching a man only a moment before.

"The crest on his spear is the Dawning Crest!"

"What if it is not him?"

"I tell you, it is him! The descriptions, the spear, the stories we have heard, all of it fits."

Bashir calmly considered this as if there were not men fighting for their very lives only a few feet away."

"Now's our chance!" Ibrahim insisted desperately.

"But what if it is not a Dawning?" Bashir demanded.

"That man is pledged to the Dawnings regardless. If we leave it with him, they will receive it!" Ibrahim assured him, desperate for this chance to relieve themselves of their burden and escape this country.

"We cannot take any chances," Bashir growled. "Dawning!" He yelled out to the jester. The jester pivoted to look back at the Moors.

The highwaymen did not miss the opportunity, and the leader rushed at him as the two on his flanks snatched arrows from their quivers and knocked them. The jester thrust his spear straight ahead. The lead rogue jumped aside, and the jester did a shoulder roll past the advancing man, just avoiding his counter strike. He regained his feet still facing away from his assailants and without taking the time to turn rammed his weapon straight back. He felt the satisfying resistance as his fine blade met soft flesh, and he heard the sharp intake of breath being cut short. The jester spun now and brought the back of the shaft up to catch the chin of the wagoner, who again lost his aim and sent another arrow into the woods as he blacked out from the force of the strike.

The limited length of their short swords, though ideal among the thick of the trees, was proving a disadvantage on the open road as they were forced to move in close to their opponent to strike, and their opponent was not allowing that.

It was now only the jester and the leader of the band of rogues, who was now standing in a low crouch, his sword held high. Behind the highwayman, the jester was dimly aware of the Moors rifling in the saddlebags of his mount, but he was so engaged that he hardly noticed when they alighted on their fleet-footed Arabian steeds and flew back in the direction they had come. "You see now that I spoke the truth," he addressed the rogue captain in a calm voice through the sudden silence of the lonely forest. "Had you heeded my warning and fled as befits a coward such as you are, you might have been spared. But now nothing can alter your fate." The jester grinned a friendly grin at him as if he were having a perfectly pleasant conversation.

"What manner of fiend are you that cares for no life and deals death with relish?" The rogue was trembling now, seeing the likelihood of the jester's words coming to pass. He knew his only chance lay in the forest.

"I am merely the sum of your miserable life. Only think, the moment you had determined to rob my little party, your life was forfeit," he pontificated as if he were not speaking of the rogue's imminent demise. "Indeed, it might be said the moment you forsook honest society and went into this trade you were a dead man."

"Honest society?" the rogue spat. "What is that to me? I merely relieve you fat nobles of your purses," he said, dropping all pretenses of politeness. "I do not rob you of your dignity, plunder your women, and murder you. My occupation may indeed be dishonest, but at least that is all it is, an occupation, and that I can change as a suit of clothing. The sins of the nobility are stains that pierce to the core, that cannot be washed from you. Strike me down then, oh noble knight. What can one more black deed do to soil the soul of a soulless, black-hearted noble?" At this the rogue dropped his sword to his side and stood upright as if to accept his fate.

"That was quite a speech," the jester said, relaxing against his spear that was now resting on the ground. "Your castigation of nobles is just and true, but you do err in your assumptions where I am concerned," he said smirking wryly to himself.

"Why is that, good sir?" he applied the title with much sarcasm. "Am I to believe that you are different from that of your class? That you are a charitable Christian man as I stand in the gore of my friends that you have cut to pieces right before my eyes? You have spilled Christian blood to save heathen blood. And for what? Your friends have robbed you and fled, leaving you to your fate. You have spilled the blood of my men to gratify your own pride! To prove you were better than common highwaymen! And you are about to tell me you are a better sort than they?"

"Oh, I did not say I was better, I just said you were mistaken," the jester said, not the least bit perturbed by the rogue's scathing reproof of the class he assumed him to belong to.

"And how, may I ask, are you different from the others of your ilk?"

"I am not a knight," he smirked broadly at the thief, and with that he swung his spear in an overhand arch to finish off the rogue, but he struck only air. The rogue darted to his left, his last hope in the trees. The jester took a step forward and spun in the opposite direction to give himself momentum and hurled his spear with all his force at the retreating back, but the fleet-footed rogue dodged behind a tree and the spear imbedded itself deep in the trunk of a large oak tree and stayed there.

The jester raced after the rogue without hesitation. He dodged around trees and leapt over fallen logs and brush. The rogue was fast and familiar with the forest, but his pursuer was determined, and shortly he was almost within arm's reach of his objective.

The rogue looked over his shoulder and squealed slightly in consternation to see his pursuer directly on his heels. In a panic he swung a wild swing behind him with the sword he still carried. The jester, having nothing with which to defend himself, was forced to jump aside and had to throw his hands out to catch himself from running into the trunk of a large tree. He bounced off unharmed and whirled around the far side of it and continued the pursuit. The rogue, now ten paces ahead, turned sharply to avoid a large patch of heavy undergrowth, and the jester saw his chance. Racing out ahead to intercept the rogue, he got to a small clearing just a pace ahead of him. The rogue could not believe his fortune. He drew back to strike this foolish jester down from behind. But the jester did not stop as expected. Instead he ran two steps up the trunk, leapt into the air spinning, and delivered a devastating blow with his armored shin to the side of the rogue's head. The rogue's own determination propelled him straight into the blow, taking the full impact in the head.

Light exploded before his eyes as he was struck, and a dull thud from hitting the ground shot pain through his head. He instinctively curled up protectively in pain and terror, holding his head. "What pit of Hell did such a devil spring from? Why are you doing this to me? Why are you so determined to destroy my life?" he pleaded.

The jester stood over him and slowly drew a curved sword from under his robe. It was rippled with stripes all up and down the blade that made it seem somehow even more sinister than a highly polished blade would have seemed. "Destruction is all I know. It is the only thing I'm good at."

"I don't deserve this," the rogue whined.

The jester cocked his head in confusion. "Everyone deserves this," he said, and he raised his sword to finish off the now pathetic figure that only minutes before had been so self-possessed. But as he did so a memory stirred, a memory from long ago of his own father standing over a cowering peasant. On an impulse that he himself could not have explained, he reversed his swing and struck a blow with the hilt of his weapon to the rogue's head, rendering him unconscious, and walked away leaving him injured but alive.

He was very perturbed by this incident. It was not his habit to leave those that crossed him alive in his wake. It was a dangerous practice. But he was ever the more perturbed as he could not explain why he was suddenly and deeply so out of sorts. Little did he know that he was about to become far more vexed. He was returning to his mount grazing by the side of the road as the well-trained animal should have been when he recalled the Saracens rooting through his things. The singularity of this act had not registered in the heat of the battle. Were they such lowly opportunists that they had robbed him even as he was fighting the men who would have taken their lives? But if such was the case, why not take his horse, too? He threw the leather flap back from the bag and his heart stopped. Lying on top of his gear was an emblem he had not seen in many years. But he knew instantly what it was and could have guessed at its meaning even had he not seen the sealed letter underneath it. The letter was written on parchment and closed with a seal he did not recognize.

He cracked the seal and read the letter. He was sick to his stomach. His first impulse was to ride after the Moor 'pilgrims'. There were very few roads they could turn off on in this heavily forested part of the country, and he might just catch them. But that was unlikely on his English palfrey. Their Arabian animals could run faster and longer than his New Market steed that was bred for an entirely different purpose. But it really did not matter; catching the messengers could yield but little. This was much bigger than those two, and he alone could not handle it. But how had they known who he was? He looked at the pennant attached to his spear. What foolish impulse had prompted him to affix that? "No one will see it," he had told himself. "But you must have wanted people to see it, else why attach it at all? Of all the stupid, vain—" He stopped himself, realizing the futility of this line of thought, and climbed into his saddle. With a heavy-hearted sigh, he turned the nose of his animal toward the home to which he had sworn never to return.

CHAPTER EIGHTEEN

"I will drink the blood of William Dawning while sitting on the throne of Dawning Court!" Baron Braddock roared and swung the sword in his right hand wildly in the air, sloshing the contents of the mug of ale in his left hand over the sides.

"Of course," Rafiq had seen enough of Baron Braddock's drunken rages to know better than to get excited about anything he said while in this state.

"You doubt me?" Braddock glared at him on unsteady feet.

"Of course I support my lord," Rafiq said with easy obsequiousness. "I would encourage you in such an endeavor. With Richard Dawning a continent away and John Dawning disgraced, now is the perfect time to move against them.

Braddock continued to stare at him. "But no William?"

"William has not returned," Rafiq admitted.

"William is the one I want!" Braddock swung a wild blow at Rafiq, which he easily avoided, and hit the coat of arms hung over the shield on the wall, sending it crashing to the floor with a terrible clatter. "He is the one that robbed me of my most beloved son." His attitude instantly went from violence to tearful melancholy in his inebriated condition.

"But have you lost sight of what the real goal was?" Rafiq reminded him. "The goal has always been to control the Dawnings' lands also. If you were to act now, that can happen. The Dawnings are weaker than they have ever been."

"I don't care about lands anymore. I only care about vengeance!" He turned and cleaved a chair in half with his aging but still powerful arms.

"Is everything all right?" Hans, Braddock's second son, came running in upon hearing the commotion.

Rafiq began to make excuses for his master but was interrupted by the baron. "No, everything is not all right!" he shouted at his son. "My best son is dead, and those who are responsible still remain unpunished; and all I am left with as a reminder of him is this," he gestured in disgust at Hans. "If you were any kind of real warrior, you would have already avenged him and taken Dawning Court for your own! Collin will do my bidding. Where is Collin?" He said looking around for his eldest son. "Collin!"

"Your Lordship's eldest son is leading your armies overseas," Rafiq reminded him quietly.

Hans flushed at the tirade. He was used to it, having heard them from his father all his life, but they had grown even more frequent since Vincent's death. Still, it shamed him each time. "Father, I assure you, if I knew where to find William Dawning, he would be a dead man."

"Everyone knows where to find William Dawning! It is the worst-kept secret since you were born a bastard to a serving wench. Can there be any doubt he is this William of York?"

"So you would have me travel a thousand leagues to discover if a person who may or may not be a legend is the boy who killed your son in a joust almost five years ago?"

"I would have you," Braddock said in a quiet voice and then suddenly shouted, "die! You are not fit to be in a world where Vincent is not!" He dropped his ale cup and drew back his sword in an overhand swing, but the remnants of the chair clung to it, and he began wrestling with it in a mad rage to tear it free.

"Father, what can I do? If you would have me ride to Egypt, I will do so."

"You can die!" Braddock was still swinging his weapon wildly, but the last piece of wood was too light and would not dislodge from his blade.

"Baron, why not have Hans ride at the head of your remaining army to destroy Dawning Court!" Rafiq suggested.

"I will ride, father," Hans added quickly, stepping toward his father. "Is that what you desire? I will take Dawning Court and burn it to the earth! Not a stone will be left standing when I am finished."

Braddock dropped his weapon as his dizziness got the better of him, and he fell on the step of the dais. "I only want my boy back!" He broke down into sobs, and Rafiq motioned for Hans to steal away while Braddock was distracted.

Rafiq waited patiently for the old fool's sobs to surrender to unconsciousness, and he had the baron placed in his chambers on his bed.

CHAPTER NINETEEN

"I'm not going to do that anymore. The knight's life is the refuge of thugs and murderers. It's couched in terms of nobility and valor to justify the things they do, but it just makes them feel good about being another's lapdog," Henry blurted at Mary's insinuations that she was not impressed with the chivalry of the country as she had seen it.

She smirked slightly at him as they strolled together through the garden on the grounds near her lodgings. "I'm surprised to hear one of the order make such professions," she said. Henry had called on her as promised and had rapidly been taken with her seemingly insatiable interest in him and his stories. He expected she would grow bored shortly, but she never seemed to; she just kept probing deeper and further, and Henry found he was looking forward with more excitement to each successive visit with her. There were few people that were interested in exploring the intellectual mysteries as he was, and though Mary did not participate much in these philosophical discussions, she did seem to understand him and seemed to be interested in his insights.

"My knighthood is by default, not by choice. There were certain things I had to do being a Dawning because of my family's religious traditions. The knighthood was conferred as a result of those things."

"You would turn your back on those traditions that have made your family great?" she asked with a seemingly detached interest.

"If they are foolish and silly traditions, it is folly to continue with them at any cost, would you not agree?"

Mary shrugged casually. "It is easy to disdain established tradition but much harder to distinguish oneself while charting a new course of your own."

"I am sure that is true."

"One would need a good woman by his side to make such a mark," she said again with a detachment that made it seem as though they were casually discussing some unrelated person rather than Henry himself."

"How so?" Henry asked and immediately wished he could take it back. But Mary took it all in stride as if he had said nothing amiss.

"I suppose having the father you have described to me, who placed little value on his family, it would be easy for you to miss this, but can you not see that a smart and clever woman is instrumental in re-establishing a different order? Her charms will avail where his steel may not. She keeps company that he would or could not and has the ears of other influential women. If one truly wanted to dislodge an entrenched evil from a community, say a barony, a good woman is a necessity."

"Ah, yes," Henry said placatingly. "You are correct, of course. I fear I simply had not considered all the sides of such a quandary well enough." He had no intention of admitting to this charming little woman—for fear of seeming a coward—that he never planned on trying to get anyone else to change; he was simply planning to retire quietly to lead a life of intellectual and scholarly pursuits."

"If you want the mind of a lady," Mary segued into a new subject, "I could never be wed to anyone who was simply content to be a knight. A woman needs a certain amount of virility to be certain that she could be... satisfied. Such virility is often coupled with ambition."

Henry was startled by the boldness of this statement. Was she saying she wanted to marry him? Or was she implying that she believed he wanted to marry her and was setting down the conditions? Or was she actually suggesting he not bother to pursue her because he was not ambitious enough? He had scarcely given the idea much consideration as he had only known this girl—lady—a few short weeks. She was pretty enough, and she was quite clever. But he had only really imagined himself with one woman by his side for years. But that woman had rejected him outright twice. He could not suppress a smirk when he imagined returning back to Dawning Court with a wife, showing her that he had put her behind him and moved on. She would not be able to toy with his affections any longer. He would be insulated from that—from her. Mary would be a suitable match. Martha could not complain of her station, and she would surely make as favorable an impression on everyone in the family as she had on him. He grinned wider as he considered showing her off to his brothers and their jealousy over her. For her beauty far exceeded that of either Annie or Lindsay, and he had watched with disgust the way they fawned over Leah, often right in William's presence. All at once this wild idea excited him. And she had approached him? How fortuitous was this for someone that did not have a great deal of success with the opposite sex thus far in his career.

"Henry?" Mary broke him from his reverie. "Are you listening?"

"What?" he asked, startled. "Oh yes. I was only considering the portent of your words."

"And what do my words portend?" she asked, a little more sharply than before.

"Uh, perhaps portend is the wrong word. Perhaps, implications of your words."

"Humph," she pouted in an adorable way. "You are making fun of me."

"What? I would never dream of it!" he insisted a bit too forcefully. "I hold your person in the highest reverence, milady, and I could never be anything other than candid with you," he gushed, in fear of displeasing her when he was on the verge of something momentous. Henry's heart was beating fast, and his hands were sweating. A wild idea had occurred to him, and he was quite uncertain of whether he should act on it.

"Well then," Mary said, suddenly perking up again and hugging his arm to her as they walked. "All is forgiven."

He loved it when she did that. He loved how much easier she was to read than Leah. She was bold and straightforward, and it was refreshing. Henry tried to say something, but the words caught in his throat and he walked stiffly along beside her. He was excited, but what if he was wrong? What if he was about to make another miscalculation as he had made with Leah? What if he was about to be humiliated? Forevermore this woman would be laughing at Henry Dawning. Any time he or his family was mentioned within earshot, she would laugh and relay the story to all about her. Could he take such mockery? Henry forced himself to push those thoughts aside.

"Why do you not speak?" Mary asked, looking up at him with her dark eyes. "Have I said something to displease you?"

Henry swallowed hard and made up his mind. "If I don't speak, milady, it is only because I fear words will fail me." His voice cracked on the word 'fail' and he cursed himself. Mary looked up at him, but said nothing. "Milady," he stopped walking and turned to face her. "Though I have only known you a short time, I can think of no one that I so admire as I have come to admire you. Your beauty, your wit, your charm are not to be equaled by any I have ever known. Will you accompany me to Dawning Court?"

CHAPTER TWENTY

William was flat on his back with the giant standing over him, sword poised. He knew this was the end. *"The head of a Dawning will make an excellent trophy,"* the giant roared exultantly and brought his blade down with both hands. William involuntary closed his eyes as he awaited death. But the death blow never came. Instead he heard clamoring and swearing in two languages in front of him.

William opened his eyes slowly to see John rolling on the ground, grappling with the assassin. The giant threw him off and they both regained their feet, facing off, circling each other. William looked desperately for his weapon, but could not see where the giant had kicked it. He looked for anything with which to defend himself, but before his search yielded any means of defense, his plight was noted by others on the battlefield. A small group of farmers began to push through the melee in order to reach William while he was vulnerable. John saw what was happening even before William was aware of just how dire the situation was about to become. John wanted to rush to his aid, but was locked in a heated dual with this man whose size was proving to be a problem, as he was even bigger than John.

"Richard!" he shouted, his voice cracking with the force of the sound, *"Thomas, get William! Get William!"*

Hearing this, William, who was still on his hands and knees in search of a weapon, looked up to discover that he was being closed in on while still completely defenseless. He searched *desperately for anything he could use to defend himself but to no avail. Though this once-peaceful fallow field was now littered with bodies, weapons, and armor of all shapes and sizes, this particular patch of ground was barren. William cursed his luck. A hundred dead men on the field and not one of them had dropped a weapon within his reach.*

Still on the ground, William began frantically looking for an escape. But he could not risk getting too close to any enemy soldiers, for if he was attacked, he would be helpless. What are you even doing here? He found himself wondering. In the training yard war was a sport, a game where he always tried to be faster and better than the other opponents that he repeatedly challenged until he learned their weaknesses. He could afford to attempt overly elaborate moves, for if he failed it only cost him a match and a tongue lashing. But this was no sport. It was not fun, and William knew fear he had never imagined in the safety of the training yard.

Three angry-looking rebels were striding purposefully toward him, weapons ready. John had his hands full with the giant, and neither seemed to be gaining the advantage at the moment.

William climbed slowly to his feet to face his destiny. He was not sure what he was going to do, but if he was going to die, it was not going to be crawling around in the dirt like a dog.

He felt faint as he got to his feet and noticed his whole left arm was covered in blood from the gash the giant had inflicted. The world swam before him, and he felt nauseous. He wanted to lie down, but instead assumed a fighting stance, standing in profile to the approaching foe to create a smaller target. He spread his feet wide, knees bent slightly and tried to exude a strength and a confidence he did not feel.

The first of the three farmers came into range, and William leapt forward and slammed his foot into the farmer's unsuspecting stomach, taking the rebel off-guard. He doubled over and stumbled backward. But the exertion of the strike sent the world swimming for William even worse than before. His knees gave way and the ground came up and hit him in the face. He could feel darkness closing in as the farmer he had just hit straightened up, angrier than before. The farmer's two friends caught up to him and advanced into William's dimming peripheral vision.

Then Richard was there, hamstringing one of them as he ran from behind to interpose himself between William and the enemy. Unfortunately, with him came another complement of men that he had been engaged with when he was called to come to William's aid. He was also now in the very disadvantageous position of being limited in how far he could move about the field lest he leave his younger brother vulnerable. If he stepped aside too far, he would expose William to danger, but if he stayed put, he was trapped.

The first person that ventured too close to him got a section of his neck cut out and collapsed in a bloody mess. Recognizing their advantage, the seven men began to coordinate their movements with each other. They reasoned that he could not defend against them all at once.

William's vision was blurring and the blackness was pressing in around him. He blinked and could scarcely open his eyes again. Then Thomas and Henry were there, standing shoulder to shoulder with Richard, and now John appeared and they formed a protective ring around their fallen brother. If anyone was going to get to him they would have to cut through all of the brothers first.

The greater portion of the remaining rebels concentrated their force on this small cluster of brothers. They rushed them, and there was a great clashing of steel as blackness closed in on William...

CHAPTER TWENTY-ONE

"When will I meet these friends of yours?" John asked, not quite suspiciously, but annoyed that he was obviously being put off.

Anisa smiled at him and patted his hand. "Why John," she said. "If I did not know better, I might think you jealous."

"Why would I be jealous?" he demanded, sounding more defensive than he meant to. Anisa made her face appear slightly injured, and John quickly backpedaled. "I only mean that if I am to rely on others for my ascension to power, I would like to know them and know what their interest is in my success."

Anisa's hurt expression only deepened. "Do you consider my motives suspect as well?"

"No. I know you are a true friend to me," he said quickly. "The only friend I have left," he muttered to himself, but Anisa caught it.

"Then you think me incapable of looking after your interests?"

"Of course not!"

"Then you intrinsically do not trust us, as we are Saracens?"

"Now you know I do not share in my countrymen's prejudices," he said defensively.

"So you do trust me, then?"

"Of course I do!" John assured her, sounding not entirely convinced himself.

"Then trust me when I say you will meet them soon enough, Sir Knight."

"It matters not, lady," John said gallantly. In truth, he was so relieved to not be the object of her anger that he swung to the opposite extreme. "I know that you are a better custodian of my welfare than I myself am." .

She gave him a warm smile and touched his face. It thrilled John when she touched him, and she had been touching him with increasing frequency. "Where did you get this scar?" she asked, touching the jagged line on his chin that he had received at the hands of his brother so many years before.

"You know," he said looking into her eyes, "I don't really remember." John's heart was beating fast at being so close to her.

Anisa shrugged and started to depart. On impulse, John pulled her to him and kissed her solidly. Anisa resisted at first, but then melted into his embrace and returned his kiss passionately. After a long time, she disentangled herself and stepped back with a mischievous smile.

Wordlessly she disappeared into the trees to meet her friends. John resisted the powerful urge to go after her as he watched her disappear into the night the way he had so many nights before. But now he knew. He knew that her affection for him was not simply platonic. She was interested in him as a man, too, and that changed everything.

CHAPTER TWENTY-TWO

Anisa snatched a sprig of pine from a tree and began nibbling on it. She was desperate to get the taste of swine out of her mouth. She had made many sacrifices for her people: she had forgone all chance for a normal life, she had done many things she preferred not to remember; but of all of them, this was testing her the most. This was trying her not just physically and mentally, but emotionally as well. But, she reminded herself, that is why this would be the most rewarding of all.

"How long can you keep that up?" a voice came to her in the darkness.

"As long as it takes, Khalid," she said, not the least bit surprised as a tall, dark-robed and hooded figure fell into step beside her.

"I cannot stand to see his hands on you. My blood boils to dispatch that miserable Christian!"

"And destroy all we have worked for?" Anisa rounded on him, her eyes blazing in the moonlight.

The corners of Khalid's thin lips turned up behind his black beard as he looked down at the beautiful woman. "Would you put a dagger in my heart?" he asked.

"If you hurt John Dawning," Anisa said neutrally. "You best pray that I finish you off before Amir finds you."

"Speaking of Amir," Khalid said, changing the subject abruptly and resuming his walk toward the cave they had been using for their meeting place. "We have received word from him."

Anisa breathed a sigh of relief and was surprised at how tense these meetings with John were actually making her. "It's about time!" she said. "What word?"

Khalid, gliding silently beside her, like death himself in his dark merchant robe, was silent for a moment. "He says the message has been delivered and we should do nothing until the Dawnings have departed."

"Nothing until the Dawnings have departed?" Anisa demanded. "And what do we know except that John Dawning will accompany them?"

Khalid looked down at her, his hood a mask of shadow in the darkness. "I'm sure someone with your unique... charms will find a way to convince him to remain behind."

They reached the cave, and Anisa looked around at the four other men present in the dim light of a single-hooded lantern. Each of them was stationed around the countryside, acting as various merchants, servants to nobles, and even vagrants. They were all united in their efforts and were focused on the same single goal. "What news?" she asked simply.

"Nothing from Braddock," said Rafiq, the personal servant of Baron Braddock. "The fool continues to bluster incessantly about the Dawnings and how he cannot wait to cross swords with them; but then he refuses to act."

"Mmm, that was Amir's report as well," Anisa confirmed. "What do you think it will take for him to be convinced to move against them?"

"A sure thing," Rafiq shrugged. "For all that fool's blustering, I believe he is genuinely afraid of these ridiculous Dawnings." There was a ripple of laughter through the cave.

"Enough!" Anisa barked suddenly, and the laughter died away. "Make no mistake about this, the Dawnings are men to be feared. Their father rode at will through all of Damascus and the Holy Land. Each of them is cut from that stock, and each of them in his turn has proved himself worthy to be called a Dawning."

"If they are such men of power," Rafiq challenged, "why choose this family on which to execute this plan?"

"Though fierce warriors, the Dawnings are replete with vices and weakness that make them easy to exploit. Each one is stubborn and proud, and a great rift has opened in the family. That is the weakness we are here to exploit. Do not make the mistake of underestimating the wrath of these men should they unite against us."

"Isn't that exactly what Amir is laboring to prevent? Their galvanizing against us?" Najid asked. Najid was employed as a servant in Dawning Castle and was frequently privy to sensitive pieces of information.

Anisa nodded. "That is why we must do our part to ensure they do not realize their plight until it is too late. If we can keep them divided long enough, Amir will dispatch half the family, including Richard, who is our biggest threat to John becoming baron. Any leftovers that may arise at that point will be easily dealt with."

"We would like to believe you, of course," Khalid assured her in his easy, deep voice. He looked every inch the Saracen merchant that he portrayed to the locals. This cover allowed him to move from place to place as needed, interact with the locals, and hear many things. Anisa wondered how many of the locals who frequented his mobile stand of exotics would have any idea that he was a ruthless assassin. "It is only that we are not comfortable with a plan that places so many important pieces out of our control."

"You want assurances of success?" Anisa demanded. "Then do your jobs! Najid, they have received the message, that means they will be in council shortly. Find out what they are planning and get word to Khalid or me. Rafiq, push that great cowardly mass of a baron into action. Even if he will not directly attack the Dawnings, any disturbance he makes during this critical time will work to our advantage. The rest of you get out there and be ready to be called on at any time. When the moment comes, we may have to act quickly to capitalize on an opportunity."

With that they all dispersed into the trees going their separate directions. Anisa watched from the cave entrance as they all departed, wending their separate paths through the forest as they could not risk being seen together. When each had disappeared from view, she found her way to a nearby trapper's hut that she used for shelter. There she built up a fire and removed her bulky robe that was damp from the forest. She was hanging it up to dry when a dark figure appeared in the doorway.

"You made it," she smiled slightly without turning around. "I feared you would not."

"I could not risk the others' seeing me; I had to wait until there was no chance of my being observed," the deep voice said from the behind her. He spun her around and pulled her to him with a passion that threatened to consume her. It took a moment for Anisa's natural strength to surrender to Khalid's commanding presence. But it did now as it always had in the past. And she let him take her, excited by his strength and by the danger this forbidden liaison represented.

CHAPTER TWENTY-THREE

"*I* knew he was too young, I knew he should not have been out there yet." Martha Dawning's voice broke through the darkness. William cracked his heavy eyelids to see John setting him in his bed with his worried mother looking over him in the lamp light.

"Mother, he is fine. He just lost some blood, but he will be fine in a few days," John assured her, only slightly trying to hide his smile at her overreaction.

"He wasn't ready," she reiterated, looking down at William, whose eyes were closed again. "He is so much smaller than the rest of you. I knew it was not ti—"

"He did great. He fought like a lion! He was just unlucky, that's all. He was...."

William drifted off into oblivion again. When next he opened his eyes, his room was lit up with the afternoon sun. The chair next to his bed was vacant, but there was a tray of food sitting next his bed that was still warm, indicating the chair could not have long been empty.

William felt very weak, and his stomach was unsettled. He sat up in bed and picked up the bread next to the bowl of soup laid out on the tray, took a small bite, and set it back down. The emotions of the battle came flooding back in: the rush of excitement and fear, the helplessness of having to be rescued like a child. The shame of it weighed him down. His first battle was supposed to be glorious, but he was miserable. He had *studied all his life to be a warrior, and yet he had to be rescued from farmers with rusty swords.*

"You're up. How are you feeling?" His mother walked into the room wearing a grey dress with black lapels and cuffs, her dark widow's cap in place over her once dark brown hair. She had always worn very drab colors for as long as William could remember. He had only one vague memory of her in a vibrant red dress, and he could not even remember the occasion.

William managed a weak smile for her. "You need to eat something; you have to regain your strength."

William didn't move as his mother took the tray from the bedside table and set it on his lap. Despite his disinclination to food at the moment, William did not want to worry her. He slowly raised his head from his hands and started to nibble on the proffered food.

"All of Dawning Court is talking about the mighty warrior prince, you know. So when you feel up to it, you will need to appear in public." There was no trace of the worry that filled her voice the night before.

William swallowed the bite he was working on. "The warrior prince?" he asked, then not waiting for a response, "Is everyone all right?"

"Your brothers? Of course. They have been telling everyone what a hero you were. How you were cornered by twenty men and single-handedly fought your way out of them." She gave him a sidelong glance as she folded some bed clothes across the foot of his bed. She was watching his reaction.

"Some hero," he said, dropping his head back into his hands. "They had to carry me off the field like a child. I don't even know what day it is."

His mother resisted the urge to remind him he was a child and instead said, "What? You think heroes never get hurt? Heroes never lose? You think your father was never carried off of a battlefield?" When he didn't respond, she continued. "A hero is someone who gets out there and fights despite the fear and pain. Your father was often wounded, often outnumbered, but he did what he had to do, regardless of the consequences.

He did not think of himself, only what had to be done. That is a hero."

William's father had been a great warrior in the Crusades, leading many of them for the Pope himself. He was widely regarded as a hero. He was even declared a saint after his death for his service to the Church and his many great victories.

His family had a much different opinion of him than the public at large, however. At Dawning Court he was a harsh taskmaster, short-tempered, and occasionally even violent towards his older children. But Braden Dawning loved little children, and because William had been so young when he died, images of his father shared two places in William's memory. One was of feeling his father's thundering hand for some wrongful deed and the other was of being bounced on his knee.

Eventually his memories of his father had resolved themselves into an amalgam of his vague firsthand recollections and the stories he had heard from family, friends, and even strangers everywhere he went since he was young. He had even studied his father as a historical figure with his tutor, which was very strange to try to relegate the legend of the man his tutor spoke of to the memories he had.

He forced a smile for his mother again. "Thank you," he said weakly.

She kissed his forehead. "Now if you ever scare me like that again, I will have your head."

"I guess you were right," he said, remembering her oft-repeated words that she had uttered again last night. "I guess I am too small."

She looked at him for a long moment. "I hope you do not equate small with weak. You simply take after my side of the family. Richard and John take after their father, and the others seem to be a mix of the two. My father was not built like your brothers. He was shorter than you, but he was massively strong."

She sat back in reflection as she spoke. "I remember when we were little, he used to hold his arm out and we would swing on it like a tree branch. My family were woodsmen, and one has to be strong to make a living that way." She looked dreamy for a moment. "We were very poor, but we were happy. In fact, it was in one of those little forest communities when I first saw your father. He was not the mighty, self-assured warrior that you know. He was a young man that was up routing out the remnants of an insurrection. He was so handsome and unsure of himself, I couldn't help loving him."

"Really? That's hard to imagine."

"Well, it was a long time ago. He was there in our area with his father, whom I did not meet until later, which was fortuitous because I might have been scared away from the Dawning family altogether if I had. His father was a harsh and cruel man. Your father was always struggling between appeasing his father and his conscience; the two rarely coincided. I know he wasn't the perfect father, but his father was even worse. Given the upbringing he had, it is a wonder that he turned out as well as he did."

She settled back in her chair: "I remember the time I first saw him—your father, I mean. As I said, he was trying to put down a serf insurrection and capture those involved. The problem was, he well knew the horribly cruel things his father would do to any captured serfs in the name of securing loyalty.

"He came into our town chasing a serf of your grandfather's that had fled the rebellion when the insurrection was crushed. The serfs knew your grandfather and what they were risking, but they had finally revolted because of the miserable living conditions they were forced to endure. Your father, I was later to discover, was personally acquainted with this particular serf. His whole family had died of cholera and starvation. He felt he had nothing left to lose, so he revolted with the rest of them. His name was Lamar, as I recall.

"Braden was questioning my father about dissidents in the area when Lamar, sure that his detection was imminent, jumped up from behind a wood pile by the house and fled into the trees. Your father gave chase. I was a young, impulsive girl and wanted to see what would happen, so I jumped onto the bare back of our old plow horse and rode after them.

"Lamar had such a long head start and your father was wearing so much heavy armor that I figured he would never catch him. But catch him he did. He ran him down over a mile in the heat, and when he caught up to Lamar, he smashed him in the back of the head with his elbow. She made a slight motion with the underside of her elbow to indicate the strike. Lamar sprawled on the ground, dropping the bread and dried meat he had stolen from us. I stayed concealed in the trees where I could see it all. The people in my community were not vassals of your grandfather, and we knew his infamous reputation for brutality. I should have been aware I would not want to see what would become of this unfortunate serf, but I had never seen a real knight before. He was so noble looking in his glittering armor compared to this dirty old serf, I could not help but think he was a hero and the serf was evil. I had to see the denouement.

"Lamar drew the old, rusty sword he had tied to his side and pointed it menacingly at your father. I can still remember the glare from the shiny steel as your father drew his own long sword. He looked like a giant compared to the little peasant. 'Don't do this, Lamar,' he said.

"There were tears running down Lamar's face as he pleaded, 'Master Braden, you have always been good to us, please. We had to. Don't you see? We had to fight. Your father's cruelty is killing us.'

"'Lamar, watch your tongue,' Braden said, enraged by the serf's negative reference to his father.

"'Please, sir, you know what he will do to me if you take me back.'

"'You attacked our home and tried to kill my family; what would you have me do?'

"'Please, sir, I have nothing left,' Lamar pleaded pathetically. The anger seemed to leave Braden, and his sword dropped to his side.

"Suddenly, Lamar charged Braden. Braden swiped the old sword aside. Lamar stood there helplessly and finally dropped to his knees, tears flowing freely. 'Your father has taken *everything from me. My family is dead. I just watched my friends die by his hand, and now I will be returned for him to break me on the rack.'* I cannot imagine a more debased spectacle than that serf at that moment. Lamar dropped his face onto the forest floor.

"I remember so vividly your young father standing over Lamar for a long time. His back was to me, so I could not see his face, but he just stood there holding his sword, looking down at this poor man. I can only imagine what must have been going through his mind. This man had rebelled and had attacked his family, behavior which could not be brooked under any circumstances. However, this serf had indeed been the victim of fortune's cruelest turns. Neither man moved for a long time, and then without a word, Braden raised his sword high over his shoulder and brought it down, severing Lamar's head completely from his body.

"I tried to scream, but my voice caught in my throat. I wanted to turn and run, but I just sat there in the trees, watching. I could not turn away. When your father turned around, his handsome face was tear-streaked. He cleaned his sword and then buried Lamar's body with his own hands. I remember the tender way he laid him in the grave and said a prayer over him.

William was gawking at her. He could not believe what he was hearing.

"You mean he didn't help him? Or at least let him go?" William protested.

Martha smiled sadly her understanding. "I hated your father for that. It seemed so cruel, so horrible, I could not fathom it. In fact, when Braden reappeared around our village again, I would not even speak to him. Eventually, though, I began to realize he was being merciful to Lamar, not cruel. He could not let him go; he had committed treason and would be a danger to his family. But even if he had released him, Lamar had nowhere to go. On the other hand, if he brought him back as a prisoner, he would be tortured and killed in a most horrible way. Braden was doing the only thing he knew he could do to spare Lamar any further suffering."

"I never told your father that I saw that. We never talked about it, but as he got older he got harder and harder, and the tears came less frequently to his eyes. As much as I found the warrior life distasteful, it was what I had agreed to when we were betrothed. What broke my heart was not the ways of the warrior, but watching this good man harden and turn dark. The legendary hero of the Crusades was not the man I married."

William was gaping. He had never heard anything like this.

"The same reason I hated your father at first was the reason I came to love him later. Whatever your father's flaws, he had a mighty heart." His mother seemed to break from her reverie at that point. "I have never told anyone that before," she said, surprised at herself.

"So why bring it up now?" William said, recovering from his shock enough to think it a very odd time for such a story.

"Because I do not want that to happen to you. There is too much good in you. That is too valuable to lose. The world will always have good warriors, even great ones, but it is very short of good men. That is what I mean when I say you are young. Not that you are weak, but that you are a sensitive, good soul, and I can't let anything happen to that. The goodness in you is what will make you a great leader."

"Leader? But I am not going to be a leader. I am the youngest son. John will inherit Dawning Court."

"You do not need to be lord of Dawning Court to be a great leader. Titles do not make a great leader. Braden's father should be proof enough of that. You will always be a leader in everything you do. It is in your nature. It is who you are. So make sure you are a great one, whether as the king of England or the lowliest peasant. Always be true to yourself." She sat for a moment, then abruptly changed the subject. "Leah has been asking to see you, when you feel up to it—"

William almost choked. "Oh, Mother, not now. I am just not up to it. Just give me a day or so."

"She is very insistent."

"Just give me a day or so, please. Then I will go and see her. I promise."

"Okay," she sounded unconvinced, "just see that you do." She rose and started to leave the room.

"Mother," he called after her.

"Yes, dear?"

"What day is it?"

"It's Thursday, dear."

One day! It had been one day since William had been standing in that field a mere hour's ride from his own bed. It was dark when he had stirred last night with John and Martha hovering over him. Therefore, even allowing four hours to clean up the mess caused by the battle and to burn or bury the bodies, his brothers were fighting for hours after he collapsed. They fought at a disadvantage for hours because he was with them.

He leaned back in bed feeling very depressed. Ordinarily a visit from Leah would have been just the thing to lift his spirits, but he couldn't face her with this weighing on him. He felt so ashamed that he doubted he could keep it from her. William sat reflecting on the battle and becoming increasingly melancholy.

He was unaware of how long he sat in that state before a brief knock at the door brought him back to the moment. John walked into the room without waiting for an answer. He was wearing a brown leather tunic that tied down the front and matching breeches now.

"I heard you were awake, thought I would come up and check on you. How are you feeling?" He sat down in the chair next to the bed.

William shrugged, "All right." Then after a pause, "Thank you for saving me out there, John. I am sorry I let you down." He blurted it out lest he choke on the words.

"Saving you? Let me down? What are you talking about?" John seemed genuinely confused.

"You know..." William prodded, hoping John would not make him rehearse the details of his disgrace.

"The skirmish?" John waved it away. "From where I stood it looked like you were doing just fine. He just got in a lucky *shot, but hey, even I had some trouble with that behemoth. That was a big fish to fry on your first fight. You are fearless as a bloody bull, taking on that monster."*

"I let him take my weapon," William could hardly say the words. "I had to be rescued, and as a result, put all my brothers in danger. That is shameful."

"From what I saw even after you lost your weapon, you were still fighting. You are a bloody bull. All we did was move the fight we were engaged in to a slightly different spot on the field. It didn't change anything. Besides, we practically had a fortress behind the pile of bodies you stacked up. Finishing 'em off was easy from there."

William smiled despite himself. John had harbored a deep sense of personal inadequacy for as long as William could remember. He always felt he was never strong enough, good enough, or smart enough. He could see the positive attributes in those around him, but he could not see them in himself. If one listened to John long enough, they could easily come to believe they were something more than mere mortal men. If William allowed himself the luxury, he really could start to believe he had played some great role in the battle.

"Well, anyway, thank you," William finished, wanting to end the matter. "So how did the fight with the giant finally end?"

John looked disgusted. "He ran off, if you can believe that. We were deadlocked, truth be told. Neither of us was really gaining the upper hand, and then all at once, off he ran into the trees. Miserable coward! He must have been some sort of mercenary that was watching the rebellion topple and realized he was not going to get paid that day, eh?" They talked for a while longer about the battle and what had come of it. John finally excused himself, promising to stop by the next day if William was still not up and about.

Henry stopped in later. Henry had little to say and left as quickly as he had come. Thomas was the next visitor that evening. He came bursting through the door still wearing his armor. Thomas' larger than life personality was infectious, and William was cheered somewhat for his visit.

William stayed in his room until the next day. No one else came to see him. He half regretted refusing Leah's visit. He would have very much liked the companionship of his old childhood friend now, but he had no wish to rehash the previous day's events yet again, and more importantly he could never let anyone know of the fear that had taken root in his heart.

William was light-headed when he first climbed out of bed the following morning. He thought to take a walk in the anonymity of the early morning hours. Unfortunately, the castle seemed bustling with life on this particular morning. And as promised, everyone he passed was glowing with praise for his brave deeds and expressed concern over his health. Rather than argue with them, William would force a smile to his lips, thank them for their kind words, assure them he was well, and extricate himself from the situation as quickly as possible.

He was fleeing one such encounter with an elderly servant that had been at Dawning Court since before William was born. The servant called after his retreating back, "The Dawnings have a new prince that will restore them to the glory days of your father!" This sent a shudder through William as it struck at the very heart of the doubts he was harboring.

He made it to the courtyard with some relief. It was still early and the few people who were about were engaged in their daily activities and took little notice of William. It was easy to avoid people out here. He breathed deeply the spring air. He moved over to a small garden adjacent to the main courtyard. It would be empty at this time of day and allow him some peace.

He stood in the privacy of the garden provided by the high hedges and inhaled deeply, extending his arms, closing his eyes and letting the cool breeze wash over him. For the first time since the battle, he started to feel joy at being alive.

"Waiting for the fairies to come and take you away?" a soft alto voice said from behind him.

Despite the start he received from this unexpected interruption, he forced himself to stay standing quietly with his arms extended and eyes closed. He waited as long as he dared without responding. He did not want to seem rude, but he wanted to look like he was at peace, even though he had forgotten all about the beautiful spring morning and was acutely aware of the person behind him. He could hear the rustle of her clothing when she moved and smell her perfume. He was half excited and half annoyed at the interruption. He sighed and dropped his arms, turning on her.

"Does the warrior prince wish to be left alone in his glory?" Leah asked with a wry smile. She looked wonderful. Her slight but curvy form was accentuated nicely under a red dress that tied at the waist. Leah always wore brightly colored materials that stood out dramatically against the drab materials most everyone else chose for their day-to-day wear. Her brown hair hung just past her shoulders and always seemed to have a strand hanging in front of her hazel eyes that she was forever brushing aside.

"I don't remember you being quite so rude. It would seem the time I spent away has not favored you with any more grace than when I left," William returned as if it had been much longer than a few days since he had seen her.

"My character must seem crude and unrefined to a mighty hero such as yourself. Indeed, I can never hope to be worthy of your attention." She curtsied slightly and bowed her head in mock respect.

William nodded approvingly. "Well, just so long as you understand that."

Leah grinned and embraced him fondly. William returned it with his right arm, but kept his wounded left arm at his side. "Are you all right?" she asked, stepping back and inspecting him.

"I'm fine," he said, though not really feeling it.

She looked at him skeptically. "Are you sure?"

He realized that by his tone he was inadvertently inviting her to pry about the very subject that he did not want to talk about. He forced himself to smile. "I'll be all right," he told her.

"Well, I hope so," she said, still looking doubtful; we can't have the Hero of Dawning Court moping around."

"I'm no hero," he said a bit too quickly.

"Well of course you are. Everybody is talking about your glorious battle and they're all saying, "If there is one thing that I know, it's that William Dawning is a hero'. Why I even heard—"

"Stop it!" he said much more forcefully than he had intended. "They carried me away, okay?" he blurted in disgust. "My brothers carried me off the field like a child!"

There was an awkward silence, both of them unsure of what to say. William sat on a nearby bench, and Leah sat next to him, looking intently at his face.

William sighed, realizing there was no way out of telling her now. He told her of arriving in the village and Richard setting the houses on fire and calling out the men. He told her of the battle, and of the fight with the giant, and getting wounded and collapsing. "My brothers surrounded me and fought late into the day to keep me alive and then carried me home and put me in bed." He shook his head in disgust. "All their lives were in danger because I could not hold my own against a bunch of farmers. I was a disgrace."

Leah looked at him for a moment, "Is that it? Is that what's bothering you, that you were carried off a battlefield? Many great warriors have been carried off the field of battle. I understand that your father was even carried off more than once on his many campaigns. That doesn't make you a disgrace. I would say the fact that you stayed and fought bravely until the end against horrible odds lends more credence to the story that you are a hero. I was aware that the stories your brothers were telling of you cutting down legions of enemy soldiers were exaggerated, but maybe they were not exaggerated so much as I believed."

"But all their lives were in danger because of me. They had to protect me," William persisted.

She smiled a disarming smile at him, "So, if it had been one of them, would you have done the same?"

"But it wasn't—"

"No," she cut him off. "Answer the question. Would you have done the same?"

"Of course," he grudgingly conceded. *"But—"*

"No, No," she cut him off again. *"That's it. That is all that is important. You would not even have thought about it. And if you had been wounded or killed in so doing, so be it?"*

William sighed, *"Yes, I suppose so."*

Leah was still grinning, *"Don't you see what this is? It is your pride that's hurt. That is all. Let it go and do better next time,"* she finished, very pleased that she had solved this problem so readily.

"And that's all there is to it? You are very quick to dismiss this."

"And you should be too," she assured him, confident that she had appropriately addressed his concerns.

Just then a dark-haired girl with olive skin who was a few years younger than Leah came into the garden, and William groaned.

"There you are," she said to Leah, *"I have been looking everywhere for you. Mother said you are supposed to be helping her prepare the baskets for the sick, and you are going to be in dutch if you do not make an appearance right now."* She delivered the message with all the gravity of a younger sister trying her best to sound like her mother. *"Edith being ill is no excuse for you to disappear."*

"Hello, Eve," William said without any particular warmth. Eve glared at William. *"Is that all the salutation I get from you, Eve? Where is the love?"* William teased. Her glare turned darker still. Leah tried to suppress a smirk but only half succeeded. William lowered his voice as if speaking in confidence. *"You know, Eve, it is you that I was fighting for out there. When I was out there in the heat of battle, it is the memory of you that kept me going strong."*

"Everyone says you are a hero, but you're just a jerk!" she said with all the feeling she could muster.

"Actually, that is what they were going to put on the banners celebrating my triumphant return," William replied without missing a beat. He moved his hand in front of his face as if envisioning the waving banner in the air. *"All hail the return of

the jerk hero, William. Praise the mighty jerk hero." He dropped his hand down to his side as if deflated, *"But alas, it would not fit on the banner, so they just gave me a stomp on the head instead."*

"Triumphant return? I heard they carried you back home. I wish you had been killed," Eve fumed.

"Eve!" Leah said, shocked. Eve looked down at her feet, embarrassed but still angry. *"Apologize this instant!"*

"Why should I?"

"Now, Eve!" Leah said dangerously.

"I'm sorry," Eve mumbled.

In a calmer voice Leah said, *"Tell Mother that I will be right there."* Eve turned without a word and ran from the garden. Leah stood, preparing to leave. *"I am sorry about that."*

William dismissed it with a wave. Although he had not shown it, secretly her words had stung him, not only because it was true but also because he knew there were many people, not just silly children, that felt the way Eve did. He had hurt a lot of people. But he and Eve had had an antagonistic relationship for as long as he could remember. This was nothing new, and he did not let it get to him for long.

"You really shouldn't tease her like that," Leah chided him for the thousandth time. *"She is growing up and pretty soon will be one of the ladies of the court, and you are going to have her perpetual suitors up here challenging you over her honor."* She smiled as she said it.

"What suitors?"

Leah looked at him oddly. *"You haven't noticed?"*

"It would seem I have not."

"William, Eve is becoming a beautiful young woman. She already has suitors trying to arrange matches with her."

"No, she does not." William refused to believe it. She had always just been Leah's annoying little sister to him, and he could not see her as anything else.

"Oh yes," Leah assured him. *"But father won't hear of it. In fact, he is thinking of shipping her off to France to school, just*

to stave off the inevitable for a few years." She straightened her dress and said, "Well, I better get going."

"Leah," William blurted as she started to go, "there is something else." She turned to face him again. "When I was fighting the giant..."

"Yes," she prodded.

He already regretted even bringing it up, but now that he was this far, he wanted to share with someone the fears that were taking root in his heart. "I was not strong enough. We were locked in a struggle, the giant and I, and I reached down with everything I had, and it was not enough. I was not strong enough to win."

Leah walked back and sat down on the bench next to him and put her arm around his shoulders that were hunched in defeat. "Your strength is what kept you alive."

"But don't you see? There is always going to be someone stronger or better than me, and this man was both. I was powerless against him, and it struck a terror into my heart that I never want to feel again."

She smiled sympathetically. "So what are you saying? You are not going to battle anymore? I am not sure that is up to you."

"When I was out there wounded, I was terrified. My blood mingled with the blood of men I did not even know. I knew then that this is not what I wanted. I do not want to be a knight."

Leah squeezed his shoulder comfortingly. "I am glad you did not want to be there. You are too good a person to ever want to be part of bloodshed and destruction, and I would never want to see that grow on you. But you are a warrior from a warrior family, William. It is part of who you are and it is part of the role you will have to play."

"Thanks a lot," William muttered dejectedly.

She prepared to stand again, knowing her mother was counting the moments until her return. "So you were scared? Feeling fear does not make a coward; giving in to the fear makes a coward, and you did not do that." She faced him. "Thank you for sharing this with me."

He looked up at her for a moment and then looked away, not wanting to meet her eyes. "Thank you for listening."

She put her hand under his chin and raised his eyes to meet hers. "I always believed in you, but now that I know this, you have confirmed my high opinion of you. I believe in you more now than ever."

William forced a smile. "Thank you," he said, knowing that she was genuine.

"Are you going to be alright?"

"Yes, I will be fine. You'd better get going before Eve forms a mob." He resisted the urge to ask her not to betray his confidences to anyone else, but he knew his secrets were safe with Leah.

CHAPTER TWENTY-FOUR

"*Can speed overcome strength?*" *William asked Jurou seriously as he sat puffing heavily on the tatami floor where he had been foiled in a whirlwind attack against his instructor. He was left on the floor gasping for air. This was his first training session since his battle with the giant. Leah's words had been of some comfort to him, but William was determined to go into hard training. For the first time he viewed his training as a matter of life or death. He now saw each lesson as the possible difference between victory and defeat. Every hour he trained prepared him that much more for the next time he faced an opponent who was bigger and stronger. Still, William could not entirely shake the fear that had been planted in his heart that day.*

This particular subject weighed heavily on William's mind, and he valued Jurou's word on it, not only because he respected him as a wise teacher but also because Jurou was about William's height and build, and his prowess as a warrior was legendary. William knew he would never be as strong as Richard or the giant; therefore, if the actual truth was that speed would always be second to strength, than William would always be an inferior warrior. He knew that Jurou would know the truth of this better than anyone.

"Speed can achieve levels of proficiency that a man's natural strength cannot match," Jurou equivocated.

"Why do you hesitate?"

"Speed can overcome, but only as utilized by the most skilled practitioners of the martial arts." The strong will always try to

force a contest of strength. If you oblige them, you will lose. You must keep the contest on your terms, where you are most comfortable."

"Toward that end," William retrieved his bokken from the tatami floor and returned the wooden practice sword to its place on the wall in an act he had decided upon while convalescing.

"Your lesson is not completed. Why do you surrender your weapon so soon?" Jurou demanded.

Walking further down the wall covered in weapons, William pulled the spear from the pegs it rested on. William had trained with all these weapons but had largely focused on the sword as the weapon of choice for a knight. He was re-thinking that now. He stood before Jurou with his new weapon.

Jurou watched him in silence. "By fleeing your fear you are only prolonging the day that you will have to face it," he said wisely. "Pick up your sword and let that day be today," he challenged.

William was looking at the floor, ashamed. He did not like that his mentor saw through him so easily. It was very unusual for William to disobey Jurou, but now he only shook his head and stood his ground. "I am not ready."

Jurou considered for a long moment. "Very well. Defend yourself." Jurou's bokken came up quickly in a flurry of vicious slices that had William instantly on the defensive. It was all he could do to fend off the onslaught of rapid strikes with the slower, more awkward spear. Jurou did not let up, and William found himself stumbling backward under his trainer's aggression.

William was desperate to return a strike but was too off balance to find a break in the combination of blows that had both ends of his spear flailing madly to intercept them. Then William's back was against the wall. Jurou swung a rapid overhead strike with his bokken. William brought the spear up in both hands and caught the wooden blade on the shaft.

Jurou stepped close to William, his left hand locking William's right wrist above his head and the other bringing the blunt tip of his sword to dig into William's belly. He twisted it painfully in the skin to indicate where William would have just been skewered. "You lose."

Jurou backed away a pace. "What is the greatest weakness of the spear?" he demanded, recalling old training drills from William's earliest days under his tutelage.

"In close quarters fighting, there is no room to move," William answered automatically. "Good thing there are very few walls on the battlefield," William muttered sarcastically. He felt that Jurou was simply abusing him to make his point, and he was sulking that he had been so easily bested by his teacher—yet another reminder of how much more skilled Jurou was than he.

"There are many walls in the field," Jurou barked sharply. "A horse, a melee, a barricade. All these things can limit your mobility and limit your options."

"Why are you angry? Do you believe the spear is a viable weapon?" William challenged, looking over the length of it and appreciating the extra reach it gave him over virtually any man, even a giant one. He had not made this decision on a whim; he had been thinking about it ever since he had wished for it in the heat of battle.

"I only have a problem with it if you are using it to hide behind instead of to face your fears."

William looked closely at his mentor. His height, weight, and build were very similar to William's own. Even Jurou's straight black hair and yellow skin resembled William's wavy dark hair and olive skin. Yet for all the similarities, there was something so much more solid about Jurou. Something much more self-assured. Jurou had already proven himself. He already knew what he was capable of, and William was still struggling to discover that in himself.

"I'm not you, Jurou," he said, his eyes again finding safety in the floor. "I may not be good enough. I was not good enough in the field. I failed my first real test. I failed and I had to be rescued."

"Ah, I see you have found a new fear to wear around your neck."

"A new fear?"

"William, when we first started working together all those years ago, what was the biggest fear you struggled to master?"

William shrugged. "I was afraid of everything. I was afraid of having no control of my life and that fear turned into rage."

"That is what we set out to master. We were able to channel that rage into healthy activities that made you a brilliant student. If you fought and lost, it only fueled your desire to improve. Why not channel this experience the same way? Consecrate it for your benefit."

"But I haven't mastered anything," William protested. "My anger still exists. It is just buried deeper now. I still live in fear of it coming out because it is so hard to control." He shook his head and repeated, "So hard. It can take me days or sometimes weeks to suppress it when it gets loose. I am plagued by sleepless nights and horrible designs and schemes I should never want anyone to know about."

"It may never disappear entirely. But you are learning to control it. That is why it is so important not to let another fear worm its way into your heart. You must stay above it. You lived to learn from it. Just be sure you learn the proper lessons."

CHAPTER TWENTY-FIVE

"Will you be requiring my services during your interview with Lady Dawning?" Edith asked Leah the moment they entered the library. Edith had made a habit of delivering her mistress safely to Dawning Castle for her now regular visits and promptly disappearing.

"Of course, Edith. I will send for you when your services are again required." These visits with Lady Dawning had begun not long after William's disappearance. Leah came for news about the family, and Martha had come to enjoy the company. Martha had grown quite fond of this sweet young lady and valued her friendship very much. She had known Leah since she was born and had always known her to be a sweet girl, but now she really found a friend and confidant in this guileless young woman where she had no other.

"I think Edith has found herself romance among your house servants," Leah smiled as the door closed behind Edith's rapidly departing back. "You remember she used to refuse to leave my side. She would sit with us for hours on end as we discussed events and people she did not know. To her it must have been sheer tedium. Now she can't seem to escape fast enough."

"It happens to everyone sooner or later, I'm afraid," Martha replied unconcerned.

Leah seated herself in her usual seat on the sofa. "Now, what news?" she asked anxiously.

"There is still no news," Martha looked at her seriously.

Leah's countenance fell almost imperceptibly, but Martha saw it. "Leah," she said sitting next to the younger woman on the sofa. "Whatever has happened to William, we can't be sure but we have to expect that even if he still lives, he will not return here."

Leah was taken aback. "You must not say such things. Certainly he still lives."

"That may well be, dear, but the reason that William took his leave of us has not materially changed." She sighed. "Leah, I have never known a gentler, more noble heart than yours. Being of Saxon birth, I do not place much stock in hereditary nobility. My very soul shrinks at the idea of aristocracy and that one can be born to nobility. But if ever I knew someone that made me question that, it is you. You are good and noble through and through, and you have been all your life."

Leah blushed and dropped her eyes. "You do flatter me, lady."

Martha dismissed that with a wave. "But you have watched all your friends one by one marry and begin to raise families, and still you are alone. I know you have had many suitors, yet you have refused every suit that is pressed upon you. Why is that?"

"I should be loath to give my heart to one that I could not dedicate myself wholly and completely to."

"Leah," she said seriously, "enough. I know your heart pines for someone, but you are too precious a spirit to waste away in self-imposed solitude." Leah did not speak, so she continued. "I love my son, and there is no one in this world with whom I would rather see him, or any of my sons for that matter. But I would not sacrifice the best years of your womanhood for any of my sons. You are too precious a spirit." A tear found its way to Leah's cheek, but still she did not speak. "I am aware of the visitors to your father's house and the negotiations he is involved in. I believe it to be a choice situation, and I have advised him to accept it. An—"

She stopped suddenly when the library door swung open.

CHAPTER TWENTY-SIX

"Am I interrupting something?" Henry slowed his pace as he entered the library to find his mother and Leah sitting, heads together, conversing quietly. Leah's presence was wholly unexpected, and Henry was dismayed at finding her here on this evening. She was seated in a simple white dress that seemed to complement her beauty in that easy way everything she wore seemed to complement her.

"Actually, son," Martha said, sitting back, "you *are* interrupting," she told him frankly but not in an unfriendly tone.

"Terribly sorry." He performed a mock bow. "I merely thought I would pay my respects since I have only just returned."

"I expected you would be away for at least a few more weeks," she said. "Henry was part of a group of scholars that was asked to review some ancient documents discovered by a group of crusading soldiers in the Holy Land," Martha explained unnecessarily to Leah. "It seems his reputation precedes him." She said the last to Henry himself.

"It turned out to be nothing really." Henry said dismissively. "Some letters of writ concerning the specifics of how an ancient campaign was to be conducted. Important historical documents, perhaps, but certainly nothing that required all the fuss that was made over this. They could have sent them to me and I could have translated them and returned them from the comfort of my own chambers."

Leah wiped her eyes quickly to hide that she had been crying. "I am sure your Lordship is being too modest."

"Not at all. I am happy to help where I can, but I wish they would offer a challenge before wasting my time."

"Henry," his mother reproached him mildly. "Any service to the Church is service to God."

"That is a relief," he said with some bite. "I would hate to think the last three years of my life were wasted. For if I wasn't serving God, who was I serving? Certainly not myself!"

"You forget yourself," Martha Dawning replied sternly. An awkward silence followed.

"Uh," Leah, anxious to break the tension, started. "What will you do now, Sir Henry, with your papal obligations behind you?"

"That is funny you should mention that," he said observing her reaction closely. "I have been disingenuous to claim that my trip was a complete waste, for I have brought back someone with me, a lady."

"Oh?" Martha's eyebrows arched sharply.

"Oh, Henry, that is wonderful," Leah said sweetly. He was disappointed that her happiness seemed genuine.

"And where is this lady?" Martha inquired.

"She was exhausted from the trip, so I had her shown to the guest quarters for the evening."

"And what, may I ask, is the nature of her visit?"

"She is a friend of mine. In fact, Mother, you know her; she is a Mayfield. Mary of Mayfield."

"A Mayfield?" Martha asked, surprised. "I have not heard from them since your father died. They had—" she stopped herself suddenly. "They had some disagreements with your father. Anyway, I should be very pleased to remake the acquaintance of this young lady."

"Tomorrow, Mother," Henry assured her. He had taken a seat in a chair by now and looked to have no intention of departing. "Now, I must know what you two ladies were talking about that so captured your attention."

Martha and Leah looked awkwardly at each other, uncertain of what to tell him. They were spared the difficulty, however, when the door to the library again opened and they all stopped in shock.

CHAPTER TWENTY-SEVEN

"You actually have Richard Dawning?" Her beautiful olive features were solidly chiseled into a demanding countenance. "We must crucify him as an example to all future crusaders that even their mightiest knights offer no challenge for our lowliest farmers." She turned to Amir. "Why did you not tell me who this was you had in the dungeon?"

"Because I knew you would react as you are right now," he grumbled.

"Why should this man evince such emotions from me but nothing from you, from you of all people? How many times must you watch this family destroy the fortunes of those around you before you are willing to act? Allah has dropped this man at your feet and all you do is lock him away? We must exact vengeance for all the wrongs he and his family have done to us and flay the flesh from his body." She insisted.

Amir's eyes flashed dangerously. "Killing this man would bring me pleasure for a moment, but retaining him will bring me victory, and there is no pleasure sweeter than victory. Besides," he smirked despite himself, "I did not say we were going to leave him in peace."

She smiled at the thought of what they may be doing to Richard in the darkness below. "I believe that I would like to see that," she said.

"That will have to wait," Amir said, standing up suddenly. "I have a mission that you are uniquely qualified for. Richard is the strongest of the remaining Dawnings," Amir continued when he could see he had her attention, "and the oldest heir still in good standing with the family."

"And?" She asked impatiently.

"And," he said, "there is much we can use him for. But more importantly, that means there is no one in position to take over the Dawning barony." Anisa was suddenly attentive. "With the only tenable option for Braden Dawning's replacement and the only threat to John Dawning's rightful succession tied to our wrack, it is time for us to act."

"What do you mean?"

"I know John Dawning, and he is of the weakest character. That is why he let his mother push him out of his rightful seat when Braden Dawning died. He has been disinherited and lives in squalor. He is the perfect pawn to gain a foothold in English affairs."

"But you just said he will not contend for the seat."

"On his own he will not, but if we remind him he is the rightful heir and convince him to fight for it, then..." Amir left it hanging.

"I don't understand. If he becomes baron, what makes you think he would be any more sympathetic to our cause than his predecessor?"

Amir looked irritated. "I am disappointed in your limited vision, sister. John will need two things to take the barony. He will need men, which he does not have, and he will need someone there to hold his hand while he walks the road to his destiny, which person he also lacks."

She was nodding now. "And we give him both of those things. At that point we will be indispensable to Baron Dawning. He will have nothing but what we give him, know nothing but what we tell him. He will be the perfect puppet."

Amir grinned at her. "I knew you would catch on."

She stood quickly. "There is much to prepare and we haven't much time."

"Take whatever you need. Stay in constant contact with me, and I will join you when I have... finished with Richard."

CHAPTER TWENTY-EIGHT

"What are the odds of finding my three favorite people awaiting my return?" William asked with a grin from the door of the library. Martha, Leah, and Henry were speechless. "Hmm, perhaps I should come in again and see if we can manage a better reception." He turned and walked out of the room and closed the door behind him. The three occupants all looked at each other in disbelief.

The library door again opened and William marched in. "I have returned!" he announced imperiously.

"How—" Martha began but could not formulate the words. "How did you get in here unannounced?"

"Well, I was hoping you wouldn't ask," William looked embarrassed. "Let's just say Sebastian is going to have a nasty bump on his head when he wakes up."

Martha leapt up. "William, you didn't!" She started for the door.

"Of course not, Mother." He arrested her progression toward the door with his hands on her shoulders. "I lived here all my life. I should be derelict indeed if I could not find my way in past a few house servants, and I do mean few. It is deserted out there since I left."

Martha Dawning's mouth moved, but only tears came instead of words. William embraced her fondly. "I have missed you, too." Leah and Henry were on their feet now.

"What is the meaning of this?" Henry demanded.

William's eyes slid from side to side. "What is the meaning of what?"

"Of this? Barging in here unannounced like this, after all this time?"

"I live here," William replied, moving toward him. "And I intend on sleeping in my chambers tonight, so if you are keeping the chickens there, I suggest you move them at once." He grinned back at his mother. Then without warning he embraced Henry also, who looked very uncomfortable at first, but could not help himself and started to laugh a moment later.

Leah had watched these proceedings without comment, something like silent disbelief playing on her features. William turned and approached her slowly, unsure of what was appropriate after all this time. Did she still have feelings for him? Was she married? If so had they turned to bitterness and resentment? William took her hand searching her deep hazel eyes for some indication of her feelings. He could see the emotion there, but what it heralded he could not be sure. He slowly bowed and kissed her hand, never taking his eyes from hers.

Leah turned her head suddenly, unable to look at him. It stabbed at William. He had never expected that he would return to Dawning Court, so he certainly had not expected that Leah would put her life on hold for him. But neither had his feelings for this girl—woman, he corrected himself—changed. And to see her now—the promise of her childhood had blossomed into a fully magnificent creature at whose feet he would have thrown himself in an instant if he thought it would change anything— made his heart ache.

"You know Baron Braddock is still next door, and I doubt he has softened on the blood oath he swore against you," Henry announced in order to break the moment Leah and William were sharing. "You have put us all in danger by coming here."

"Ah, you are right, of course," William said, tearing his robe off over his head with one hand while he moved over to the sofa. Leah started when she saw what was underneath the robe. The last time any of them had seen him, his armor was gleaming and new. It was now a dull grey. It was stained and scarred on virtually every square inch of it. And while it still retained a certain regal luster, it was clear that it had given its beauty to rescue its owner a thousand times over. Even Henry was startled.

"What have you been doing?" he asked unconsciously.

William glanced down and shrugged. "Oh, it turns out when you try to run a people out of their lands, they don't like it, no matter how many times you insist that God told you to do it. There is just no reasoning with some people. So they protested, usually with sharp objects. Except for this one," he said fingering a recent tear in one of the chest plates. "This one was delivered right here at home."

"What do you mean?" Martha asked.

"Funny you should ask, Mother. That is the reason I'm here now. But wait, it has been so long, we must catch up first."

"William!" His mother chided him. But he did not seem to notice.

"So, everyone well?"

"Sure," Henry answered automatically, falling into his old habit of indulging his constantly flippant younger brother just enough to get what he wanted. He knew from long experience that resisting it only made him that much more perverse.

"Anyone get married?"

"Of course."

"Everyone happy?"

"Why not."

"There, you see, Mother?" he said to her. "Was that so painful? Now we are all caught up and we can get on to business."

Reaching into the folds of his robe he threw a heavy metal object on the table that was standing roughly between them all, and it landed with a clunk. They all turned to look, and Martha gasped. Henry looked quickly back at William. "Is this some sort of joke, little brother?"

"The way my life has worked out," he commented wryly, "I am almost certain that it is. But it is not my joke."

"Where did it come from?" Martha persisted.

"I suspect you know exactly where it came from," William said dryly. "As to how it came, well it was delivered with this letter by two Saracen Men who chose not to tarry long enough to answer questions."

Martha took the offered letter and scanned it quickly. "This is a ransom demand. What is this flaky brown ink its written in?" she said, rubbing the flakes between her fingers.

"That would be blood, Mother," William said casually.

"Presumably Richard's blood." Henry caught the letter as Martha instinctively recoiled in horror. He read over it quickly. Martha backed up and sat down weakly. Leah had not dared herself to interrupt. She was certain this was a dream.

"It's Richard, dear," Martha breathed to Leah by way of explanation. "They have Richard."

"Now we don't know that," Henry objected, still reading the letter. "All we know for sure is that they have Richard's crest that he wore in his breast plate, or perhaps an imitation of it. Richard could be on the other side of the world crusading, and we would have no way of knowing this was a ruse until it was too late. Richard could have lost the insignia in a battle, after which someone found it and hatched this whole farce."

"That's true, but it doesn't really make sense," Martha shook her head. "An outsider would have no way of knowing that we weren't in regular contact with Richard. They would assume that we were sending him regular reinforcements and would be informed of a major development such as Richard being taken prisoner. No, the questions we need to ask are 'Is he dead or alive? Can we pay the ransom? Do we pay the ransom? And either way, how do we go about it'?"

"I don't think so." Henry said. "You are taking too much for granted. All we really know is that someone wants money from us and that they have Richard's insignia." He looked to William for support.

William deflected the question. "Where are John and Thomas? Let us hear their input."

"I will send for Thomas at once," Martha rang for Sebastian. "Send a runner to Thomas and tell him he is needed here this instant. Also make up William's chambers; he will be staying indefinitely."

"Of course, your Grace," the aged servant nodded, not showing the least amount of surprise at William's presence.

"And Sebastian," Martha called to him as he was departing, "not a word about any of this to anyone." He only nodded stoically and closed the library doors behind him.

"Well, someone's obviously gone to great lengths to plan this," Martha said in a depressed tone.

"That someone," Henry pointed out, "may well be Richard himself."

"What do you mean?"

"Mother, consider his history. Suppose now that he needs more money to continue his campaigning. He is low on men and supplies. Where is he going to get it? The Church does not support his unsanctioned campaign. His pride will not allow him to ask us for it, so he figures out another way. He pries the Dawning crest out of his breastplate, sends a note and expects us to send one hundred thousand pounds sterling."

"No, I refuse to believe that," Martha shook her head. Henry looked at William for support, but William only shrugged.

Seeing that he was getting no support for what he believed to be a very likely possibility, Henry changed tacks. "Well," he said, sitting beside the others, "if we accept the note at face value, then I suppose the next question we have to ask ourselves is should we bring him back?"

"Oh, Henry," Martha said reproachfully. "He is your brother."

"Yes, but would we be going to great difficulty and expense to bring something back into our lives we will regret?"

"To be sure, life is quite a bit more vexing when Richard is around," William added sagely. "One never knows what is coming next with him, but one can be sure it is always bad. But on the plus side, everything is quite a bit more entertaining when he's around. We could save a fortune on bards, jesters, and troubadours."

Martha looked down at the floor. "You don't remember Richard as a little boy," she said quietly. "He was so tiny and sweet. He had health problems, you know? We worried about him so much as he began to grow into a timid, sweet boy. I remember any time I looked sad he would come over, climb up on my lap, and hug me because he knew it made me feel better." She smiled at the memory. "It seems so strange that that same boy could have grown up to be so distant. He outgrew his illness, and I suppose he decided he was never going to be weak again. From that time forth he began training incessantly. He kept getting bigger and more aggressive with each passing year until he became the man you both remember. I often wonder how this sickly little boy I used to sit up nights cradling in my arms could have grown to be a stranger to me. He is literally a part of me and yet has become something so unfamiliar. But then all my boys have to a greater or lesser extent grown into someone I hardly recognize. Each one has made choices that have taken them away from me."

Nobody spoke, and Martha's reverie continued. "Children cannot remember all that their parents did for them. That is why a parent always loves a child more than the child loves the parent. But even so, I do sometimes wonder who these men are that call themselves Dawnings. These are surely not the children that played around my feet only a moment ago..." She trailed off with a distant look in her eyes.

The doors opened again and the third Dawning male of the night made his appearance; in walked Thomas. "What is so important that my presence is required at this hour?" he demanded.

"Richard has been taken prisoner," Martha said simply, "and his captors are selling his freedom." Thomas' steps involuntarily slowed to a stop as that washed over him. He looked around at those assembled, trying to collect his thoughts.

"What's she doing here?" he nodded toward the chair Leah had taken after William's arrival. It was next to the arm of the sofa that William was sitting against.

"I will thank you to refer to me as 'he' when you are speaking about me as if I am not present," William responded.

"Perhaps, I should go," Leah said, speaking for the first time since William had come in. She had kept to herself, not feeling it was her place to intrude but neither wanting to withdraw her support from the family at this crucial time.

"I trust Leah implicitly." Martha waved her back down into the chair. "I appreciate your support and welcome your company as long as you feel you are able to stay." Leah nodded demurely and sat back down.

William stood and clasped arms with Thomas warmly. "Little brother," he said. "You do know how to make a return."

"Well, I wanted to give the family a gift that would benefit them, but these two are actually talking about undoing the gift," he said, gesturing to Henry and Martha.

Thomas put his arm around William's shoulders. "They are always like that," he said sympathetically.

"Are you two quite through?" Martha asked.

"Are you?" Thomas looked at William, who shrugged. "Yes, Mother," he announced. "We are quite finished."

They brought Thomas up to speed and left off with the question, "What do we do?"

"Now, I think we can assume the note is genuine," Martha said, cutting to the point. "I received some intelligence a few weeks back that Richard had been involved in a massive battle with the Moors on the Iberian Peninsula, in which he and his mercenaries were soundly defeated. There was no word on what became of him specifically, though, and I have been waiting for some confirmation ever since. I wasn't even sure if it was true until now. But this would seem to fit. Why don't we treat it as if it is?" she suggested.

"Okay, then let's answer some questions right up front." Henry took over again. "Is paying a hundred thousand pounds sterling even an option?" he asked flatly. He remembered all too well the conversation Martha had with the king's messenger.

They all looked at their mother. She slowly shook her head. "No. I don't think we could even pay half that."

"Then, we have to retrieve him by force," Thomas said.

"We could never field an army in time," Henry protested. "They want his ransom delivered on Damascus soil in a month."

"What army?" Thomas said. "It is just a group of brigands." Henry waited for him to elaborate. "Who else takes prisoners and ransoms them? Soldiers do not do that. There is a code of honor that forbids such mercenary behavior among soldiers."

"Wait a minute, how do we know he is even alive?" Henry protested. "It is a fool's charge that trades warm bodies for cold ones. Besides, I have a hard time seeing Richard ever being taken prisoner. He would fight his way out or die trying."

Thomas spread his hands in front of him, "You may well be right, but what choice do we have? We can't take the chance."

"Of course we can! Before we sacrifice men, silver, and time that we do not have to rescue a brother who was nothing more than a burden to us when he was around, let's face the reality. Richard has been dead to us a long time; he just may not have been physically dead until now."

There was silence in the room. "But he's your brother," Martha said quietly.

"Is he?" Henry shot back. "Has he really been a brother, son, or friend to any of us? Now you're advocating putting our lives, as well as others', in danger to retrieve him. And if we die, what becomes of Dawning Court then? Who is going to put things back together without us?"

"What you say is true," Thomas conceded. He actually agreed with Henry completely but saw a chance to win favor with his mother and impress Leah and his recently returned younger brother. "But again, what choice do we have? He is our brother. He is a Dawning. We have all made mistakes, but we cannot leave one of our own in the hands of the enemy. If it were me, I would pray someone would come for me, despite my mistakes. Everything you just said about Richard could be said about me. I am going after him, but I can't do it alone."

There was silence, but no one argued. "Then we proceed as if he is a victim, and we discover his treachery," Henry said reluctantly. "If he is on the other side authoring this mystery, then we discover once and for all how far he has fallen and deal with it at that point."

CHAPTER TWENTY-NINE

"William!" Henry said in a loud voice, startling William from his doze on the sofa.

"What? Who?" he said, looking around confused as if he expected the Moors to come charging through the door.

"You mind looking at Damascus with us?"

"Why? Has it gone missing?"

Henry breathed a heavy sigh of exasperation. "What did you last hear?"

"Uhhm, Richard? Saracens?.." he offered, hoping someone would fill in the rest for him. No one obliged him. "Did you say something about carrier pigeons?" Thomas smirked and reclined in his chair at the table, putting his hands behind his head as he watched the spectacle between the two unfold.

"Unbelievable!" Henry snapped, standing upright from where he had been leaning on the table, holding the rolled map flat. It instantly curled up, forgotten. "Your own brother's life is at stake and maybe yours too. Are you such a buffoon that you cannot pay attention for an hour while we figure out how we are going to get five hundred knights into the region without starting a war?"

"I have the utmost confidence in you, brother. You always were very bright. Now," William said standing. "If we are going into a war with only five hundred knights, I need my rest." And he started to walk for the door.

"It seems the stories we heard of the great warrior and master strategist were exaggerated," Henry fired at him.

"Oh, they almost certainly were," William said without turning back. "All I did was ensure that I got out in one piece." The color drained from Henry's face. Martha quickly stood and rested a placating hand over Henry's trembling one. She stepped over to William.

"William," she said softly, "Henry is very smart, but we need you."

"Oh, this is so boring!" he protested, but seeing she was unmoved tried another tactic. "I'm a foot soldier, what do I know of strategy and battle plans? I just charge in and hope I come out the other end. It does not pay to think too far into the future when you are part of the infantry. The moment you make plans for dinner—" He made a slashing motion with his finger across his throat.

"He should not have to shoulder this burden alone, and what help would Leah and I be in battle plans?"

"Truth be told," William confided in her, "I considered my duty done when I delivered this message. I did not really plan on returning to Damascus anytime soon. I didn't really care for it the first time, you know. Martha dropped her eyes in shame at her son's words. "And this place is so deep in, we could dine with the Caliph of Bagdad. Who is the acting Caliph these days?"

"That'd be An-Nasir," Thomas provided helpfully.

"Right."

"How do you know that?" Henry demanded.

"Thomas just told me." William said, confused. "Thomas, how do you know about the Caliph?"

"Well I-"

"No," Henry barked. "The location. I am not even sure where this place they describe is." He looked down at the letter again. William reached over and snatched the letter from him and turned it over to reveal a hand-drawn map on the reverse side. Henry flushed in embarrassment.

"William," Martha tried again, "surely you will not leave this burden to your brothers alone. This is a responsibility of all worthy Dawning males." The word "worthy" clearly intended to exclude the two remaining brothers that were not present.

William started to protest again when his gaze fell on Leah. Her beautiful hazel eyes met his with a plaintive expression that sent a pang to William's heart.

"William," Martha said in the same soft tone. "Please?"

"Very well, Mother, because your charms are still so irresistible even after all these years. But I doubt my ideas and the current plan are going to mesh very well."

"Why is that?" Martha asked.

"Because you are arming to go against a band of rogues, and that is not who has Richard."

"What?" Martha said, looking at the others. "What do you mean?"

"He has been captured by an army, not by highwaymen."

"How do you know that?" Henry challenged.

"Think about it," William said. "Where was Richard when we last knew for certain of his whereabouts?"

"The Iberian Peninsula," Martha replied, unsure of where he was going with this. "His army was lost to a horde of Moors. We had no word on his individual fortunes until today."

"Now he is certainly being held in Damascus, not far from where they are demanding we meet them in that note. Rogues would not have had the resources or indeed a reason to transport him hundreds of leagues. Besides, the Richard I know would not have been taken captive by a band of rogues. Richard had many shortcomings." He began enumerating them. "A deep thinker?" William chuckled. "Attractive? Certainly not. Kind? Pshaw."

"That's enough, William," Martha said simply.

"I just wanted to be sure we all knew we were talking about the same Richard," William grinned. When no one grinned back, he continued. "Richard was many things, but one to be taken alive by highwaymen? I think his pride alone would have killed them or him on the spot."

"So how many men would you take against this supposed army?" Henry inquired, still unconvinced. "A thousand? Five thousand?"

William shook his head. "Mother, how many men could you spare right now?"

Martha Dawning sucked in her breath slowly. "These are very dangerous times. Peasant uprising, baron wars, King John's misguided exploits, all demand many men at a moment's notice. Quite frankly, I'm nervous about the five hundred we have been considering."

"Exactly," William said as if she had just made his point for him, and started to turn for the door.

"Exactly what?" Henry's irritation was growing by the moment. "You haven't said anything of value at all."

"Oh, did I forget that part?" William said, scratching the back of his head and looking befuddled. "Are you sure I didn't explain my plan between when you asked how many men I wanted and when I asked Mother—"

"Come to the point," Henry barked.

"The point is we leave the five hundred knights at home to defend Dawning Court where they belong. Well, most of them anyway."

Henry started to protest, but Martha interrupted him. "You're talking about subterfuge," she said, looking at William closely.

"I—" he started, but thought better of it. "Yes."

"Tell me what you have in mind."

William laid out for them a crafty but risky plan for Richard's rescue.

"That is very dangerous. You are jeopardizing the lives of every man involved," Thomas pointed out seriously.

"That's true," William said in his same unconcerned way. "But it minimizes the risk to Dawning Court. In this case, the most we lose is fifty men. Besides, how many men does it take to pay some money to some thugs? It's all about making the enemy believe you have a certain number of men regardless of how many you actually have."

"This is madness," Henry said. "We would all certainly be killed."

"I thought you knights loved that sort of thing. What is more glorious than being cut down by an enemy while trying to rescue a fallen brother that nobody really wants rescued? It is the most selfless and noble of deaths."

"Does your own life mean nothing to you?" Henry demanded darkly, glaring at his younger brother.

"Oh, don't worry about me. I am not a knight, so I am allowed to try to keep a cravenly grasp on my worthless little life." He grinned at his brother's scowl and then turned back to his mother. "Anyway, that is what I would do. You may do as you wish. Now if you will excuse me, I really must get some sleep. I'm afraid I am quite the tragic spectacle with no rest. Dishonored, I can accept. But dishonored and unbecoming, well, that will never do."

"And, of course," Henry piped up, "you will not help us if we do not do it your way."

"Oh, on the contrary, brother," William said with a wicked grin. "My mind has been changed by this fair maiden," he said gesturing to Martha. "Where else would I be but in the battle's front? Do it your way if you like and I will ride into doom with you. Or sneak in as I suggested and I will sneak into our destruction right along with you," William puffed up regally. "I have pledged my spear to the cause," he said, snatching it from the corner and raising it high. "And you well know what that is worth!" he declared.

Henry glowered at him. "No, what is that worth?"

William slowly lowered his weapon, looking unsure of himself. "Uh, well, I really did not expect you to put me on the spot like that," he said. "Do I put its value in monetary terms or perhaps in sentimental value?" He raised the weapon again. "It is worth the hearts of twenty fair maidens."

Henry massaged the bridge of his nose with his thumb and forefinger and said nothing. "Good night, William," Martha said, turning back to the map with a tolerant smile.

"Oh and Henry, one more thing," William said as he opened the door to go. Henry looked up. "Remember, I did just pledge my spear, not my sword or dagger, okay? I just wanted to be clear about that."

Henry deliberately ignored him, which made William grin from ear to ear as he left the library.

"Well, it really has gotten late," Leah tried to sound nonchalant moments after the door closed behind William. "I really ought to take my leave," she said, standing and smoothing her dress. "Are you sure there is nothing I can do for you here, lady?"

"No, Leah," Martha said knowingly. "Your companionship through all this has been much needed and much appreciated. I thank you."

"Not at all, lady; I only hope my company was not too much of a burden on you in this difficult time."

"Your company could never be a burden. Let me ring for Sebastian to show you to your room."

"Oh, lady, I would not impose-"

"Nonsense. It is late and you are staying here. Now, I will ring up the servants—"

"Please don't trouble him at this hour, lady. I am sure I can find my own way. I fear I've imposed so often that I know your home as well as my own." Leah was already moving to the door, and Martha smiled indulgently. She looked to Henry, but his gaze was studiously fixed on the map and seemed to be taking no notice of the conversation.

"Leah," Martha said as Leah opened the door.

"Yes, lady?" she turned back respectfully, her tone not betraying a bit of her impatience. "I need not rehearse to you the sensitivity of this matter?"

"No, lady," Leah assured her.

"I must beg that not a word of what you have heard here is ever breathed into an ear that was not present here tonight."

"Of course, lady. I should never—could never—do anything to endanger the Dawnings." Martha nodded, and Leah quietly left the room.

"I am not sure how much I trust that," Henry muttered the moment the door clicked shut. He still did not look up from the table.

"You doubt Leah's loyalty?" Martha asked surprised.

"I think the lady may not be all that she purports to be."

"What a silly thing to say," Martha chided him. "How could anyone, particularly you, think Leah to be anything but the beautiful creature she is?"

"Oh, she is pretty enough," Henry said, his ire rising at his mother's reproach, "but her heart is false." Martha's eyebrows shot up, and he realized he had said too much. "False as all women are... not to be trusted."

"To say nothing of the injustice you have just done to my sex in general," Martha started, "need I remind you that you yourself have brought a young lady home after knowing her but a few weeks; a young lady who at this very moment rests under your largess in our guest chambers? How do you reconcile that to your generous opinion of women?"

"What's this?" Thomas had risen also when Leah departed.

"Oh mother, do not rush to make more out of this than it is. I have become reacquainted with an old friend while in London, and she has accompanied me back to Dawning Court," he explained to Thomas. "It was an idle comment and nothing more, Mother."

"Of course," she said dubiously, her brow still furrowed. "I would remonstrate over the company I was keeping if such idle comments would slip from my tongue without a second thought."

"Why do you persist in your reproof?" Henry demanded. "William uttered nothing but nonsense and stupidity all evening and you reproved him not once!"

"Is that what this is about?" she asked. "William?"

"I am just, umm..." Thomas tried to interrupt and saw they were not listening. "Tomorrow then," he said to no one in particular and slipped out of the room.

"This is not about anything excepting the matter that you seem determined to make it. I am your loyal, faithful son, and yet you see fit to find fault with my every word; meanwhile all your other sons do err grievously, and they are left in peace."

"Whatever are you talking about, Henry?"

"I shall not deign to waste more words on a subject which you have failed entirely to understand the first time through."

"Henry, if this is about William, you are correct. He has a great many faults, and I would never pretend otherwise. But his heart is noble and true. I have always known that about him."

"And what of my heart, Mother?" he said loudly, seeming more enraged by her remarks rather than less.

"Henry, I do not know what you want to hear."

"Is that the best you can manage? I have done everything my entire life exactly according to your expectations. I trained, I studied, I excelled at everything I could. I served in the Crusades to represent the family. And now I am here, leading the recovery efforts of one of my misguided brothers. And the only kind words you can spare for me are 'I don't know what you want me to say'?"

"Henry," Martha said, desperate to calm him down but feeling like everything she said was only enraging him further. "You have no reason to be jealous of William or anyone else." She tried to reach across the table and lay a hand on his cheek but he pulled away. "You are a wonderful boy," she finished flatly.

"Then why is it that I have to demand words of approbation from your mouth? I am certain you would not be saying so had I not insisted. I am your best son. I am the smartest and most loyal. I have done everything you ever wanted of me, but now…"

"Henry, you are a wonderful and loyal son. And if I have ever made you feel one wit less than that, I am deeply and truly sorry. But my son, I fear for you. You have so much cankered up inside you, I fear it is clouding your judgment and skewing your perspective."

"My perspective?" he demanded. "What is askew in your vision, Mother, that you would so willingly sacrifice your most loyal son for your least?" Martha stood helplessly. "Now your sons have once again left it to me to work out the details of this charade. Well, not this time." He dropped his quill and started for the door. If it is not important enough for them to stay focused on it, then neither is it my responsibility.

"Henry, what—" Martha was speechless. Without another word, Henry stalked out and slammed the door behind him.

CHAPTER THIRTY

The library was solid. Najid had searched for some way to overhear what took place in this room. Cracks in the mortar, holes in the ceiling, anything by which he could reliably hear what was taking place inside, but there was none. The only chance he had was of listening at the door. This was very dangerous because the library doors led to a hallway that was a main thoroughfare through Dawning Castle. It was frequently occupied with servants, guests, and Dawnings. And even at that, the regular conversations could not typically be overheard through the thick oak double doors. But if this meeting was what Najid believed it to be, voices might be elevated and discussion heated. He looked up and down the hall for other people, and carefully pressed his ear to the small crack between the double doors that led into the library. It was a muffled rumble at first, but then he was able to make out voices. They were both Dawning men, but he could not tell one Dawning voice from another as their deep baritones were very similar to one another. Nevertheless he could surmise that one was Henry, but he was not sure about the other. So far as Najid knew, Khalid had bought John enough wine to drink himself stupid, and he would be in no condition to consult on serious affairs of state even had he been called upon to do so. Not to mention that John's return to Dawning Castle would have caused enough of a stir among the other house servants that he certainly would have heard about it. No, it was not John. It was someone else, someone new.

Najid could hear that one of them was closer to the door. Close enough that he crouched slightly and readied himself to flee in an instant if the door should unexpectedly open. He could hear more clearly now. They were discussing the ransom. As he listened, his eyes opened wider. He could not believe what an incredible stroke of luck had brought him to this. Allah must indeed be guiding his steps.

"Was there something you needed, Najid?" Sebastian's voice came from behind him, causing him to leap into the air. Najid had been so intent on what was unfolding inside the library that he had not heard him approach.

"Uh—well, I was just—"

"I know very well what you were about," Sebastian chided him in a fatherly tone. "And that will not stand in Dawning Castle!"

Najid knew he was undone, and he dropped both hands to his sides to more easily facilitate the quick draw of the knife concealed at the small of his back. But then Sebastian sighed. "I know servants tend to be a very curious lot, as gossip about their benefactors feeds them day in and day out, but the Dawnings are not like other families. They insist on privacy, and that is a trust that I take very seriously. Do not let me catch you at this business of eavesdropping again." He smiled indulgently, and Najid only nodded mutely.

Najid turned and walked slowly away, wondering if he was making a mistake by letting Sebastian live when he had seen him, a Saracen, obviously listening to the plans being made in response to a Saracen ovation of war. But apparently all the old fool could see was a harmless servant. Najid made a mental note to punish that old man slowly and painfully when the time came, but for now he fairly sprinted to the cave in the woods. He had important news that Anisa must be made aware of. The Dawnings were going to try to appear to have more men than they actually did. That information could be critical to his brethren.

CHAPTER THIRTY-ONE

*S*ince the announcement of Vincent's death on the lists, everything had been a whirlwind. Baron Braddock had men out secretly scouting for William, while Martha Dawning had dispatched Henry to find him before anyone else could. Henry was furious with William. Not only had he stolen Henry's moment of triumph in this competition as the eldest Dawning to ride in it—for it was he that was supposed to ride against Vincent Braddock—but he had disrespected the ancient traditions of the lists, caused a terrible scandal, brought shame on the family, and brought them to the brink of war with the Braddocks. He had already advised his mother to disavow William in an effort to save face and be spared a war they were not prepared for, but she had curtly snubbed him and ordered him to find William and get him to safety while she sorted this out. It infuriated Henry that she was always cleaning up after his brothers. He alone did not make messes, did not bring shame on the family, and he alone was repeatedly overlooked and undervalued for his contributions.

Now that he had realized that William was gone, Henry was forced to admit he had lost another brother, perhaps forever. He sighed with a heavy heart and contemplated the church building before him. It was a stately old church on the grounds within the interior wall of Dawning Court. It had been there from the beginning. And when it was built, Father Garand was there. Henry was not sure at what point the good Father had actually accepted the post, but he had been there as long as Henry could remember and had been a wonderful support to the Dawning family through their many difficult times.

Henry was trying to get his life in order as he would soon be embarking on a crusade of his own and found it helpful to meet with the portly, good-natured Father routinely and pour out his soul to him. It was probably this old habit that took him to the church on this occasion as well. He needed to talk, to unburden his soul and leave them at the feet of someone else; but how could he explain this? Henry's emotions were so bound up inside that he was not even sure what he was feeling. He stopped on a bench that led up the path to the church.

His eyes were downcast, pulled involuntarily down by the heaviness in his heart. He had always hoped that ultimately his family would find prosperity and happiness, but all indications at this time were that they were not headed that way. "What a mess," he said aloud.

He caught a flash of pink on the edge of his vision, looked up, and there she was. His heart stopped and his palms sweated as they always did when she was around. Today of all days he wished she would just pass him by and not say a word, but her friendly nature would never allow that.

"Henry? What a wonderful surprise," she said. "I hope you are not excessively burdened by the events of the last few days."

She always looked so beautiful but made it seem absolutely effortless. Many women spent so much time obviously primping and concerned with their appearance. Leah always seemed to look great without trying. He wondered if it actually was effortless or if that was just part of her charm. He looked up but could not meet her eyes. "I am well, milady. My thanks."

"May I sit with you a moment?" she asked pleasantly. Please just go! He wanted to shout, but he only nodded.

"You will miss him very much." It was not really a question.

Henry shrugged. "He's certainly left a big enough mess to salve any feelings of remorse I may have."

"Henry, you must not be bitter. William did not intend for this to happen."

"Well, what did he intend by making a mockery of every tradition that we place value on?" he demanded, his pent up emotions venting at once. "Honor, valor, courage, he proved well enough that such noble affectations have no place in him."

"Milord!" Leah exclaimed.

Henry sighed again. "I am sorry," he said. "It's just that William never cared about anyone but himself, and now he is reaping the rewards for his many misdeeds."

"Misdeeds?"

Henry looked up, a gleam of hope suddenly appearing on the horizon. "Do you honestly not know?" He searched her face for some sign that she was toying with him.

"Know what?" she asked hesitantly.

"Milady, are you not his friend? Surely his true nature was not lost on you."

Leah looked slightly relieved. "I know that he was subject to fits of extreme passions, but he is a young man; that is not uncommon."

"Extreme passion?" Henry snorted. "Is that how you would characterize it? This was nothing new what William did. The only difference was he did it in the open where he will be held accountable at last."

"Henry, if I did not know better, I might think you inclined toward joy in your brother's misfortunes."

"Joy?" He jumped up from his seat and stepped a few paces away. "Perhaps it is joy that at long last he is being dragged into the light. That his many works in darkness will be seen for what they are. That he will no longer be seen as a hero whose every imperfection is dismissed as roguish charm. Tyler's family fled Dawning Court in fear of William. Callum's family did the same. Even at that age, William was able to so thoroughly terrorize two families of franklins, they had no recourse but to flee. Surely you are not ignorant of these things."

Leah was speechless. Henry knew as soon as he had said it that it was a mistake. Someone as good and kind as Leah could never understand what it was to harbor resentful feelings against members of one's own family.

"Leah," he said, dropping again beside her on the bench. This close to her, her perfume filled his nostrils, and all at once he was afraid he had scared her off, but she did not immediately rise. Every movement was pronounced; he felt each brush of her arm on his shoulder. He could not remember if he had ever been this close to her before, though he had spent so long wishing it might be so. Perhaps with William gone, new opportunities might be opening up. He forced himself to retract some of what he had said. "I only mean that if this is what it takes to rescue my brother from his worst proclivities, then I am happy it happened now, that he may be reclaimed."

"You are lovely today," he said impulsively and immediately felt awkward.

"You are too kind," she said, placing a hand lightly on his arm. She had a curious way of interacting with Henry. He was never sure if she was flirting or completely unaware of how she affected him with the smallest touches.

"Now we are all sad about William, but you must not let it weigh down your spirit. Your own crusade lies just ahead of you, does it not?"

"It is yet a little way off, a few seasons." They sat for a while without saying anything, Leah enjoying the day and Henry trying to think what he could say to Leah to keep her attention now that he had it.

"I had just expected things to be different than they are."

"How so?"

"Well, I expected that through the process of time, my family would all gravitate toward success and happiness. But it seems quite the opposite; they have gravitated toward vice, doubt, and faithlessness."

"Ah," she said knowingly. Leah had always lived at Dawning Court and was therefore privy to many of the machinations of Henry's brothers.

"I mean they all have potential to be such powerful forces for good. All these great warriors to whom I once looked up have hatched a sinister side indeed."

"I suppose being great in one respect does not guarantee happiness," she ventured.

"Thanks, that's very depressing," Henry muttered between his fists that were supporting his head.

"But it doesn't mean they are lost causes either. Part of loving someone means you never give up on them," she said with an intensity that Henry did not understand at the time.

"Well, thus far, everyone seems to be so beset with problems, I am about ready to flee to the Orient," Henry said in a lighter tone that belied his heavy heart. "If you will tell me you have some horrible deed to confess, that is it; I will put my back to this place forever."

"And what trouble could I possibly have gotten into?" she laughed. "Don't you know, it's not appropriate for ladies of the court to get into trouble? It's not 'ladylike.'"

"Good point," Henry said skeptically, being well acquainted with plenty of ladies of the court who were apparently less than ladylike. "Somehow with you, though, I believe it. You've always amazed me. How can someone be so good when it is part of human nature to be so bad?"

"I'm no better than you are," Leah said defensively, as if he had been insulting her.

"How can you, of all people, say that?" Henry objected. "You know better than most the evil that lurks in the hearts of the men in my family, the cruelty we are capable of."

"But that's exactly my point," she said more seriously. "I have always believed in you. Even in your rougher times, I knew there was something special about you, and despite your protestations and your irreverent exterior, you ended up doing what was right. I have always admired that about you."

Henry looked deep into her almond eyes. He felt to take her hand but was too self-conscious about the overly familiar action and instead said, "Do you truly think so?"

She arched her eyebrows. "You are of a different mind on this matter?"

"I only know that I have always thought of myself as the stable one: the one who had to be there, to take responsibility for things because no one else would. But when I call my brothers to repentance, try to get them to own up to their responsibilities, they say, 'who are you to judge us?' and what answer can I make? What can I say that will excuse my own shortcomings? Had I been a better example, I would not be in these predicaments now."

"Please believe me when I say I share in your frustration. If I knew the key to keeping a loved one from making a mistake, I would gladly share it. But we cannot make anyone do anything. All we can do is love them and set an example they will someday want to follow. And you should not excessively flagellate yourself for your shortcomings. We are none of us perfect, but you do bear up under your burdens exceptionally well if I may venture to say so." He looked at her and smiled.

"What?" she asked, suddenly self-conscious.

"You are just too good. You don't understand," he said and then rushed to explain, afraid he had offended her. "You just do not see the evil in people, the wickedness they are capable of. You don't see it in William and you don't see it in me." She did not reply, and Henry rose from the bench uncomfortably. "Milady, I wish to thank you for your kind words and patient ear. I do not find I have too many confidants among my peers these days."

"Well it was my pleasure. I am always privileged to speak to an old friend."

"I- I wonder, Leah, if I might not call upon you at a later time." She looked surprised. "I only feel that I benefit so greatly from your counsel, I should like your permission to seek you out again... should the need arise."

"Of course, Henry. You are always welcome."

Henry was ecstatic. For the first time in his life, he felt he was pursuing more than a mere polite relationship with this girl that he had so long been enamored with. And it seemed that she *was reciprocating, or at least not completely averse to the idea. "Well, I shall look forward to it," he said excitedly and began to walk down the path with a spring in his step. It was only when he had gone some distance that realized he ought to have offered to escort her wherever she was going. That would have been polite, and that would have perhaps garnered him another chance to speak with her. He shook his head in disgust at his own shortsightedness but did not return to the church.*

CHAPTER THIRTY-TWO

When the door closed behind her, Leah rushed down the hall to catch up to William and found him not progressed so far as she might have expected. "William?" she called tentatively. He did not stop, but she observed the slightest hesitation in his step. Leah took a few more steps. "William!" she said louder. "Will you not even spare a moment for an old friend?" she said, catching up to him but stopping several paces away. He turned to face her, and there was a curious look of sadness mingled with pleasure playing across his face. Leah found herself unsure of what to say. There were so many things she was feeling, and so much she wanted to hear. She had envisioned this moment a thousand times, but she suddenly realized that she did not know William's heart any longer, a detail that had been neglected in her sweet day dreams. She knew nothing of his thoughts and feelings and how they might have changed. The boy she was once so close to was a stranger to her now.

"It is wonderful to see you again, milady," William said lightly, though it sounded strained. "The promise of your youth has been fulfilled every wit in the beauty that stands before me now."

"Why do you address me thus?" she said, searching his eyes. "My dear friend whom I have long agonized over at last returns, and this is all you have to say to me. To compliment my beauty or my clothes like I am a silly child." William looked startled.

"You must forgive me my insincerity, milady. Truth be told I do not care for that dress; it makes you appear as an old maid."

"You don't have to be that way with me," Leah persisted. It hurt her that he continued with his flippant act in front of her. "I am your friend, William." She stepped up to him and looked him in the eyes. Hers were brimming with tears despite her best efforts to hold them back. William only looked at her helplessly.

They stood that way for a long moment. There was so much in her heart that she needed to express, but she could see he was not ready. She was so overwrought with William's surprise entrance and the horrible news he bore as well as the grim prospects of what would be necessary to reclaim Richard that she realized she was not prepared for this either. All at once Leah turned and fled down the hall, tears streaming down her cheeks, leaving William standing alone in the deserted hallway.

CHAPTER THIRTY-THREE

Thomas rode toward his home in the moonlight. This all seemed like a dream. William returning a man. He looked exactly the same as he always had except he had filled out now, and the youthful cast to his countenance was gone. He behaved the same, but Thomas thought there was quite a bit more under the surface than there used to be.

And what of this news of Richard? Despite his mother's refusal to hear it, Thomas was not convinced that Richard himself was not behind this. He had sided whole-heartedly with his mother because politically he needed her favor, but secretly he was much more inclined to Henry's perspective. But Henry was not a trustworthy confidant. Thomas could never approach him in confidence and expect that it would remain between them.

Perhaps Richard and William were in cahoots. William returned to deliver the message and ensure they only took enough men that they could easily be defeated... He stopped his horse as the thought struck him. Did he need to return to the castle to warn everyone? He pondered for a moment and shrugged off the thought. That was nonsense. Richard was capable of such a deception, but not William. Of course, how much did he really know about William anymore? He shook his head and clucked his horse into a trot again. What did it matter? He could not prove anything even if he were correct. Groundless paranoia they would call it. For the moment it appeared they were going after Richard.

Thomas did not like Richard. Richard had not been kind to him in his youth, and Thomas had started to entertain the idea of becoming baron of Dawning Court. Richard was the only real threat to that. It was not in Thomas' best interest go after him. Richard would be a hard and ruthless baron if he took over. Thomas was convinced that he would be a peace-loving and wise leader. If they rescued Richard, they might genuinely be doing a disservice not only to themselves but to the people of Dawning Court in general, and indeed to all England. He was not at all sure he wanted Richard back. In fact, he was quite sure no good could come from it.

It was easy for Henry and William to contemplate this fool's errand of going into hostile territory with a tiny force.. Henry and William were unmarried, had no children, had nothing to lose. Thomas had everything to lose. Whether they were successful or not, he would lose the prize he had begun to set his sights on.

He looked down at his paunch bouncing in time with the horse's stride. He was in the worst shape of his life. He could see clearly now that he had lived the soft life of a noble for so long that he was not at all prepared for real battle. His younger brothers, however, were both recently returned from the Crusades and in fighting trim. At his best, Thomas had no doubt that he was more than a match for both of his younger brothers, but now Thomas was having serious misgivings about his own abilities. He stopped in his own training yard, which he had not used in too long a time. He dropped from his saddle and retrieved an old mace from a small outbuilding in which he kept all his training equipment. He walked to a thick post he had buried in the center of his yard. He stared at it for a long moment before reeling back and striking it hard with the round ball of the mace head. He made a solid contact and left a sizable impression in the wood. He felt good about that and opened up a combination of strikes: strike, spin, strike, reverse swing, strike, side-step, underhand strike. Within moments he felt his wrists starting to buckle under the force of the strikes. His breathing was labored, and the force of his swings diminished rapidly. He ordered himself to push through this and find his stride again, and he continued the assault on the post. His speed rapidly slowed, though, and finally in frustration he raised his mace with both hands and brought it down on the post. But his trembling limbs sent his aim askew and he missed completely, bouncing the mace into the ground and losing his grip on it. It bounced up and knocked him on the head soundly before falling forgotten on the turf.

You are going to die fighting for an outcome you do not even desire, he told himself. *You have to stop this thing!*

CHAPTER THIRTY-FOUR

Henry lowered his hand to his side without knocking on the door. He could not disturb her at this hour. As much as he desired company at that moment, there would simply be no excuse for disturbing a young lady at this hour in her own private quarters. What would he say to her? And how was he ever going to tell her after dragging her here all the way from London that he was leaving her here while he went traipsing off into a distant land for reasons he did not fully understand. He sighed to himself and turned to return to his own chambers when the door opened a crack and was presently thrown wide.

"Sir Henry?" Mary's voice sounded surprised, but he noted she was still attired as she had been that day. She apparently was not yet sleeping.

"Forgive me, milady," Henry stammered quickly. "I hope I did not wake you."

Mary laughed. "It is not my custom to retire in my skirts." She looked to either end of the hallway to be sure they were alone and then stood aside, motioning for Henry to keep quiet. "Charlotte is sleeping in the next chamber; I do not wish to disturb her."

"Or explain yourself to her, I would imagine," Henry said in a soft voice but stepped into her chambers. Mary only grimaced in reply.

"I was just finishing up a letter to my mother," Mary explained. "I endeavor to write her as frequently as circumstances permit, at least every day when possible, and I have been neglectful of her on this arduous ride up from London."

"Yes," Henry said, chagrinned. "I do apologize for that. The roads have fallen into surprising disrepair since I last used them."

"Well, never mind that," she said, sitting down on a sofa and indicating he should be seated beside her. She then turned her full attention to him, which Henry found delightful and disconcerting all at once. He loved that when no one else in his life seemed to pay him any attention, she seemed to be fascinated by him, but it equally concerned him that she would soon realize her interest was misplaced and she would tire of him. "What has a great knight strolling the deserted halls of Dawning Castle at this hour?"

"Something has happened, I'm afraid," he said, unsure of what he could or should tell her.

"No," Mary put her hand to her chest. "I fear it is something bad... Sir Henry?" She ventured when he did not immediately respond.

"Forgive me," Henry said, shaking it off. "I was only thinking about what you said just now." He was on his feet, pacing with his hands clasped behind his back. "Something bad has happened, but that is not what has me seeking the comfort of your company at this bewitching hour," he told her. "What is concerning me is that the intended solution to the problem may be even worse than the problem itself."

"Sir Henry," Mary laughed lightly. "You are talking nonsense. Sit here and tell me what is on your mind?"

Henry sat and hesitated for only a moment more. "My brother Richard has fallen into the hands of profligate brigands, and they are holding him unless we meet their demands for silver," he blurted.

Mary was shocked. "Oh, my dear Henry, what a strain this must have put on you." She reached out and stroked his cheek in an eerie similitude of the gesture his mother had made earlier in the study, but Henry did not refuse her. "Whatever will you do?"

Henry was on his feet again. "Well, that is the quandary I am wrestling with. The family has decided to send a small force to rescue Richard, but I am not convinced that is wise. Sacrificing the lives of good men in an ill-judged endeavor seems pointlessly foolhardy to me." Mary said nothing; she only looked thoughtful.

"We don't know anything about what we are up against; we have formulated a daring plan based on pure speculation. There is scarcely one thing about this situation that we know to be true. Such a scheme seems destined to fail."

"Well, I am sure you could not devise a scheme that would be destined to fail." Mary dismissed that concern. "Your intellect is too acute, your mind too keen."

"Therein lies yet another worry," he admitted. Once he began opening up to her, he found he had a hard time stopping. "This is not my plan; in fact, this is the opposite of what I proposed. This was William's idea."

"William?" Mary asked, surprised. "Your disavowed younger brother? But I thought—"

"He is the one who delivered the message…"

"But if he is disavowed, how—"

"He is not truly disavowed. It was just assumed that his actions and the resulting consequences would have warranted that. So when he fled that very night, everyone just assumed he had been disavowed and banished, but no such thing ever happened. Everyone just says it as it conveniently describes the relationship."

"But Sir Henry, if I may, you say a disavowed brother returns in secret with a message that another brother of dubious character is in trouble and needs silver to survive; does that not make both brothers extremely suspect?"

"Yes, it does."

"He then shows up and proposes a course of action different and contrary to your own, a course of action that offers more risk and fewer protections if I am not mistaken?" Henry nodded. "Does that not make this whole situation extremely suspicious?"

Henry nodded again but then spread his hands helplessly. "But what am I to do? I already attempted to express doubts to my mother, and she would not hear it. I do not believe she can tolerate the thought of her son being returned to her corrupt and conspiring after all this time. And even Thomas does not seem to have any reservations whatsoever."

"Surely, you are not bound to participate in a scheme that you know will likely lead to your demise," Mary protested.

Henry sat down again next to her. "Curiously, the very rules of chivalry may demand I lay myself on the altar of sacrifice to my brother's misdeeds."

"That must not be!" Mary protested passionately. "We must—"

"Milady," he smiled at her, "consider the position I am in. Everyone believes my brother to be in mortal danger. As a knight, I cannot refuse to help him. I may suggest that this is a trap and that those who accompany me are riding into certain doom, but as a knight, I would be branded a coward if I refused to do what I could to ameliorate the situation. If I know that they are going into a trap, even if no one else believes me, I am obligated to do what I can to protect the others." There was silence for a long time after he spoke.

"Sir Henry," Mary said with emotion in her voice, "you are the bravest man I have ever known."

"Please, milady," Henry turned to her suddenly. "Please only address me as Henry. Sir Henry is so formal, and it has always weighed on me that... people were always so formal with me when I would wish them to be more intimate friends."

Mary considered him for a moment. "Very well, Henry, I will grant your request if you will in turn call me by my Christian name."

"I would be honored to do so, mila—Mary." He was overcome with a feeling of closeness to this woman. This feeling of affection welled within him as she listened to him and seemed genuinely interested in him, not because she wanted something or was worried about the affect his demise would have on the family, but because she liked him; his well-being was first and foremost on her mind, and it made him feel wonderful.

A wild impulse seized him. As a general rule, Henry tried to resist acting on impulse as it only seemed to bring him humiliation and heartache, but perhaps one more time he would try it—just one last time to gratify his own desires and find that perfect moment that he always believed love was supposed to create.

With no small amount of trepidation, he slowly dropped to one knee before her. "Mary, I know this is a serious breach of etiquette, but I fear there is no time to go through the requisite steps. Only indulge me for a moment. I can face the challenges that lie ahead of me in my life alone. But how much braver and bolder could I be if I had you by my side. Guided by your wisdom and fortified by your love, there is nothing I could not do. Will you give me your hand?"

Mary went white, then blushed, and then laughed and quickly stifled it while he knelt before her.

"Mary?" came a female voice from the next room. "Is everything all right? Are you unwell?"

Mary suddenly looked panicked. "We have awakened Charlotte," she whispered furiously. "She must not find us here like this." Henry was befuddled for a moment before he jumped up. She quietly but quickly ushered him out the door and slipped it shut behind him with only a weak smile for an answer.

He had done it again. He had acted on impulse and revealed his deepest feelings and been rejected. Henry cursed his stupidity aloud as he plodded his way to his own chambers.

CHAPTER THIRTY-FIVE

"We are simply not prepared to ride against the Dawnings at this time," Baron Braddock explained to the rather large Saracen that stood before him not for the first time. "I thought I made that clear during our last interview."

"But they are weak now," the giant persisted. "The serfs are all stirred up, ready to revolt! Will you pass up this prime opportunity to crush your adversaries at long last?"

"As I explained before, the bulk of my armies are committed elsewhere. What remains with me is a skeleton force to protect the realm. Besides, I am not convinced the Dawnings are so weak as you believe them to be. Braden Dawning may indeed be deceased, but Richard yet remains, by all accounts as fierce a warrior as his father, and slightly touched in the head."

"I have spent weeks fomenting this revolt, and all this time I have labored under the belief that if I was able to bring such a condition to pass, I would have your support." The giant flicked a desperate glance at Braddock's personal advisor.

"Don't look to Rafiq for support because he is one of you," Braddock growled at him. "Whatever the color of his skin, be assured that he shares his allegiances with none but me."

"If you will not act now when they are at their weakest," the giant was visibly deflated, "when will you move on them?"

"I am a patient man. I have waited this long; a bit longer could hardly matter."

"But if the Dawnings consolidate power by crushing this rebellion, have you profited from failing to take a stand?"

The baron considered this a moment. "Perhaps you have a point—"

"Right," the giant said excitedly. "We hit them now while they are still in disarray after their father's death. They have had it easy for so long, they don't realize how disorganized they have truly become. We will hit them so fast, they do not realize until it is too late," he almost leapt for joy. "This is the moment I have dreamt of—"

Braddock held up a hand to forestall any more gushing. "You are very quick to assume command of my forces," he said. "What I meant was that if you and your 'rebellion' prove they can make a show against the Dawnings, stand on their own for a time, I will come to your aid."

"What help is that?" Amir demanded. "These are untrained, ill-equipped men. Their numbers may be many but they cannot withstand knights. They need your help!"

"Ah, but now you begin to understand," Braden smiled at Amir. "I am not looking for an excuse to attack Dawning Court. In this day and age, one hardly needs that. I am looking for a clear advantage, and you have nearly admitted your men are not that advantage. But by all means, go," Braddock waived Amir away dismissively, "go lead your little rebellion. It cannot help the Dawnings. And rest assured that if these serfs of yours prove to be equal to the challenge, my men will come over that hill with banners flying."

The Giant turned and stalked out.

CHAPTER THIRTY-SIX

"Race you to the stables," William whispered loudly as they skulked around the courtyard. William's natural strength and dexterity were already starting to favor him in contests of physical prowess against his taller, more slender brother, and he was always anxious to find new feats he could best him at, constantly challenging him over and over until he beat him.

"Are you crazy?" Henry objected. "The guards will see us."

"The guards watch outward not inward, stupid," William told him in a forced nonchalant tone that was deliberately louder than prudence would dictate to show he was not afraid. "Quiet!" Henry hissed at him. They were skipping the day's regime of study and exercise to spend their time fishing and playing. In their naïveté they told themselves that if they left early enough and got back by supper, no one would realize they were gone. Naturally there were a few holes in this plan, but they were easy enough to ignore since they both were fed up with the daily drudgery of tutoring and practice. Who cared about speaking French anyway? They often joked that if they wanted to communicate with a frog, they would send a princess to do it. Their beloved king, King Richard, was mostly French, which was a pill that was hard to swallow, but that was easy enough to dismiss by claiming it was the English blood in him that made him great.

"Who's going to hear us?" William laughed, slapping the stone walls of the castle. "These walls are over ten feet thick."

"The guards will hear us!" Henry hissed.

"Stop worrying about the guards!" he said, annoyed. "They work for us." Then, before Henry could argue, "Last one to the stable is a mangy dog!" And he bounded across the courtyard toward the stables.

Safely away from the castle, they spent the rest of the day swimming and fishing and dozing in the shade of an old elm tree by the pond. They imagined themselves on wild adventures, talked fancifully of running away and living off the land. They were free from lessons, responsibility, and the knowledge that their blissful day was about to be soured by an approaching rider. To their mutual surprise and dismay, the figure solidified into Richard. At once they knew their fun had come to an end.

They watched wordlessly as he rode up and inspected them for a moment. They were still dripping with water. They had braced makeshift fishing rods on some stones on the bank behind them and were each holding a stick like a sword. "We are returning to Dawning Court now!" Young Richard commanded in the unmistakable tone that, though he was still a young man, many were coming to respect and fear.

Though the younger boys were slightly afraid of Richard, they would not have been younger brothers if they simply obeyed. Even so they were too scared to run away, so they did the only thing they could think to do: they stalled. "Mother sent you after us?" William asked, surprised not that she had sent him but that Richard had actually obeyed. He was not known for his cheerful willingness to help with the mundane chores required at court.

"No, actually she sent Edward. But he got no further than the gate where he turned for town and his filthy little strumpet. Now get moving!"

"So you came because you wanted to see us get in trouble?" Henry accused him darkly.

"More precisely to prove a point. John and I have a bet as to how long it will take you two to wash out. He thinks it will take you five or ten years. I believe it will be much sooner than that. Thank you for proving me right."

"I still can't believe Mother sent you," William said as he began collecting his things.

"She was worried about you and needed someone she knew would find you. Sorry we can't all be dogs in heat like Edward."

"Maybe Edward is just a good brother and didn't want to see us get in trouble," Henry grumped.

Richard snorted loudly. "You imbecile! Edward did not fail to find you because he likes you. He is indifferent to you. He doesn't care what happens to you. He cares only about himself."

"And you do care about us?" William asked as they climbed into the saddle.

"Let me put it this way," Richard said as he wheeled his mount toward home, "I care enough to not want you to publicly disgrace our family."

CHAPTER THIRTY-SEVEN

"You know what I almost said to them, to my own brothers?" Richard asked. There was no response, but he knew the voice was not far. He could sense it. "I remember it so well because I wanted desperately to tell them what I was really thinking. I actually wanted to say to them that if they had both drowned in that pond, I would not have cared a bit. I only did not want them doing anything that reflected badly on me. Can you imagine a man feeling that way about his own little brothers? They were young squires behaving as children do. Life for a squire is brutal, demanding, and can be very tedious. I know I ran off more than a few times myself."

"You are learning to empathize. That is good."

Richard snorted in disgust. "Only about thirty years too late."

"These feelings that you are feeling are an important and necessary agent of change. You must understand the mistakes you made and how you should have acted differently. It is also necessary to feel godly sorrow for what you have done and for the length of time you continued on this destructive path. But that sorrow becomes counterproductive after a time. It holds you back from progressing beyond these mistakes just as surely as if you had never realized them at all."

"If I have learned what I am supposed to learn why am I still here?" Richard protested.

"You are not ready to leave yet. If you were released now, you would return to your old ways. I know you think that could not happen," Richard's objections were forestalled. "One does not erase decades of pride, selfishness, and sin by spending a couple of months in here. These are deeply rooted habits that have governed you longer than you realize, each one dragging you down a little further until you are forever bound by them. You were not far from that. What do you suppose would have become of you if you had not lost that last battle?"

"I would have been a great hero," Richard immediately replied, "even greater than my father."

"Perhaps, but what would have happened after? What would have become of you?"

"I would have returned to Dawning Court in triumph."

"And would that great victory have made any difference to your family? All they remember is the way they have been mistreated at your hand. This victory would have done nothing to right those wrongs."

"So what of that? I would have succeeded my father as a great warrior baron. Then my family would have seen that is what I was meant to do."

"And John?"

"What about John?"

"What would you do with him? He is the eldest son and rightful heir of Dawning Court."

"I am confident he would step aside for me."

"And if he didn't? Would you depose him?"

"This is ridiculous. I would be twice the ruler he would be."

"Perhaps, but John has an innate compassion for people that you are only now starting to learn. Wouldn't you agree that was a key to a good ruler?"

"I am twice the man John is and ten times the warrior. How can you say he would be a better ruler than me?"

"You are equating a strong ruler with a good ruler? There is no doubt you would be a stronger ruler than John."

"Exactly. A better ruler."

"I guess that depends on whose perspective you share. To the nobility a strong ruler protects their status and wealth. To the majority of people, the commoners, a good ruler eases their burdens and cares about their general welfare."

"A strong leader can do both," Richard declared.

"So you are convinced you would be a better leader. But it is still John who has the right of succession, not you."

"He would step down," Richard declared.

"And what if he did not?"

"He would!"

"And what if he did not?"

"I doubt it is even an issue. I heard he was on the outs with the family anyway."

"And what if he is not?"

"Then I would remove him!" Richard shouted finally. He then sat in silence for a long time, fuming, with his back against the cold stone and his arms pulling his knees to his chest.

"So there it is. You would have continued to harm your family to further your own selfish ends." There was silence again for a long while.

"Well none of that much matters now because I didn't win. Damned mercenaries!"

CHAPTER THIRTY-EIGHT

"Running away already?"

William started at the direct address and then broke into a grin. "You got my message."

"We weren't quite sure whether to believe it or not. Our long lost hero returned from conquering the holy land," David teased him.

"Conquering the Holy Land?" William was surprised. "Who told you that?"

"Everyone knows about 'the great William of York' and his legendary conquests."

"I'm William of Dawning! You know that, right? I have been down the road, passed out in a brothel for the last several years."

"I thought I remembered you," David laughed.

"That would explain the smell," Neil added.

William looked affronted. "I will thank you not to suggest that the ladies of Chateau Overripe were anything less than impeccably groomed."

"I wasn't," Neil replied. "I was worried for what your lack of grooming might have done to their reputation." They all laughed and embraced fondly after their long absence.

William thought that the intervening years had done very little to change the appearance of his friends, other than having their boyish features hardened into those of men. At 5' 11" and 165 pounds, Neil was a perfectly average figure. Other than his height, there was nothing about his long, bony face and dark hair that parted in the middle to particularly set him apart from a crowd. David was slightly shorter than Neil with curly hair, heavier shoulders and arms; a heavier cast to his face; a smaller, broader nose; and a thicker jaw.

"What are you two hoodlums doing with yourselves?" William asked. "Or is it 'Sir' Hoodlums?"

"Genuflect when you address your betters!" David ordered, still laughing.

"If I see any I will make sure that I do that," William assured him.

"Yes, we are knighted and pledged to Dawning Court, for better or for worse."

"Mostly worse," Neil added without a smile.

"No, wrong attitude, Neil," William chastised him. "It was only by being pledged to Dawning Court that you could be above me as knights and yet still below me as my sworn servants."

"I wonder," David said thoughtfully, "how much of a stir it would make if a young nobleman was run through by his sworn protectors?"

"I think you may have hit upon a grand idea, David," Neil agreed.

"Not much of a stir at all, I'm afraid," William assured them. "If noble knights really want to make a stir in the kingdom, try protecting your charge until he dies of natural causes. That would be something entirely original for a knight." David swung at William, but he dodged aside. "Now, now, you are falling right into the classic profile, I'm afraid." Neil now took up the chase and William was compelled to flee from them. "If you persist in this, you will be no good for the quest I have come to bestow upon your semi-noble persons."

They both stopped suddenly. "What quest?" Neil said seriously.

"Well, that is better," William said, straightening his robe. "The quest to guard my noble person in Damascus."

Neil and David glanced at each other. "Are you in earnest?" David asked.

"I most certainly am, and you can't very well guard my noble person when you are trying to kill me now, can you?"

"Why are you going to Damascus?"

"It seems Richard has gotten himself into a bit of a tight spot, and we thought we would pop over with a few of our boys and lend him a hand."

"When?"

"We depart day after tomorrow."

"That is not much time," David protested.

"It should not take long, only a few of us going, no squires, no more than three pack animals each."

"No squires?" Neil was suspicious.

"What is going on?" David asked.

"I will explain it all later if you choose to accompany me."

"As knights of Dawning Court, you know we are obligated," Neil accused.

"No, not this time. Volunteers only. If you refuse, you will never hear of it again. We are preparing and departing in the greatest secrecy. I am asking you to join me because you are my two oldest friends, both of whom may have families by now, but I did not bother to find out first lest I feel guilty while pressuring you into my service; we may not come back from this one." David and Neil exchanged glances.

"I only point that out in consideration of your heretofore unnamed wives."

"Why do you insist on bringing that up?" Neil demanded heatedly. "Is our duty contingent on whether some floozy awaits our return or not?"

"Neil, he meant nothing by it," David tried to calm him, but it only seemed to make Neil more angry.

"Should we forgo all responsibility and remain at home to ensure that our domestic lives remain intact?"

William glanced back and forth between the two of them. "I'm guessing this is not about Richard," he ventured.

"Never mind! When do we leave?" Neil said abruptly.

"Is he always like this?" William looked to David.

"Most of the time," David responded without missing a beat. "Except when he's asleep; then he is positively angelic."

William turned back to inspect Neil, who was flushing slightly. "I could see that. I bet you are adorable when you're asleep."

"I will not waste any more time here!" Neil declared and walked off quickly in the opposite direction, leaving his two friends behind.

"David?" William said as they watched their friend depart.

"Hmm?"

"What just happened?" In all the years William had known Neil, he had been exceptionally moody, one day pleasant and enjoyable to be around and the next abrasive and intolerable. But this behavior was still unexpected.

"That's what I was trying to warn you about," David sighed. "Neil married a couple of years ago, just after returning from the Holy Land. His wife took their son and slipped away a few weeks ago."

"Slipped away?"

"Took the child and fled the country as best as anyone can figure."

"Fled the country?" William was mildly shocked.

David shrugged. "She didn't exactly leave a letter of explanation. I suppose the simple message was that she would rather leave the life she knew behind and start over in a foreign land than live with Neil any longer. That has to hurt."

"I should think so." William was still looking after Neil.

All at once William was struck with how similar this moment was to a time so many years before. It seemed a lifetime now, but still William reflected on a scene from their past when the three of them had their friendship put to the test, and it nearly broke. The friendship had survived, but it had left a deep rift in the unblemished loyalty of David's friendship toward William. They had never discussed it since that fateful day, and William was not going to bring it up on his first day back with his old friend.

"Privately I think we always ascribed his many foibles to causes incident to youth that would be shed with age and experience," David recalled, mistaking the subject of William's current thoughts. "It seems we were wrong... Can you imagine living with that moody dog day in and day out?"

"I can't even fathom living with him as far as Damascus. But I take it from the way my sworn protector is abandoning me that he will not be accompanying me on that road?"

"Oh, I imagine he will be there. He does not have much choice. None of us do."

"What do you mean?"

David pursed his lips in an unconscious indication that he did not want to continue this conversation.

"What is it?"

"Dawning Court's lands are shrinking, William. We all inherited a certain amount of land when we pledged to your family, but that is where the largess ended. The only income left to us is campaigning or raising crops, and we cannot compete with the serf-grown crop prices."

"But your father's endowment was generous." David's father had served alongside Braden Dawning in the most prosperous days of his campaigning and had been generously rewarded for it.

"My father passed a year or two ago, and with him passed many of our assets to satisfy his great debts. I was essentially forced to start fresh, but..."

"That is nonsense," William protested. "Your father could not have lost everything."

"What? You think this a fabrication?" There was some heat in David's voice. "I have a wife and child to take care of now. I am acutely aware of my circumstances. I do not sleep at night worrying about how I am going to provide for them." The two walked in silence for a few moments until David again spoke. "I'm sorry, I did not mean to snap at you. I know it is not your fault."

"I see this is taking a heavy toll on you. Is everyone feeling this?" William asked.

"Most of the minor nobles are."

They walked in silence for a time until William spoke again, changing the subject. "You did not tell me you were married."

"Oh yes, I am. I have a little girl, too."

"And whom did you press into marrying you?"

David hesitated ever so slightly before responding. "Salena," he said. "I married Salena."

"Is that right?" William asked with a sly smirk on his face. "Salena?"

"Now, I know you two did not always get along, but she has changed a lot."

"Well, congratulations," said William, trying to sound genuine.

"Let us walk toward town. I have to meet a merchant there, but we can pass by my house and you can see the baby. Besides, Salena wants to see you."

They both knew that was a lie, but manners dictated William go along with the charade. "Of course," he agreed as they altered their course onto an adjoining lane. "But I best stay away from town, given that I am a wanted man."

"Is that still not settled?" David stopped walking and looked at William in surprise. "Baron Braddock is an old fool. Accept his challenge, cut his fat belly open, and be done with it."

"Is that all I have to do?" William feigned excitement. "And then will you cut open the bellies of his sons and the armies they will surely bring upon us in retaliation?"

"Well, I uh. . ."

"Yes, I see what that advice is worth. Keep walking, Sir Protector." He pushed David's shoulder to propel him down the road. "For if I follow your advice, I will truly need your services."

"So what about Leah?" David asked as William fell into step beside him again.

"Is that all anyone can ask me about?" William demanded, suddenly heated.

David's brow furrowed. "Have many people been asking you about Leah?"

"No," William admitted frankly. "But it has been on my mind, and I don't care to talk about it."

"That's fine. We all just figured that is what would bring you back here if anything ever could."

"Here we are," David said cheerfully, ignoring William's glare. They were approaching a small cottage set off the side of the road. It was nicely kept, surrounded by trees, but it was surprisingly small. Not much bigger than a serf's cottage.

"What is this?" William asked, stopping in surprise.

"Well, this is where I live, William," David admitted, slightly embarrassed.

"What about Abelin Manor? Your family's house?" William asked, remembering the great stone estate where they had spent so many carefree hours playing as boys.

"I told you, my father had a great many debts when he died. We lost most everything."

"Oh," William said lamely, "I'm sorry. This is nice, though." He wanted to make up for the awkward position he had just put his friend in but did not want to sound overly complimentary, knowing it would sound false.

"Well it's not much, but we are happy here. And all the land back from the road is ours as well."

They walked to the door and David led them inside. "Salena, my dear?" He called as they stepped inside. "I brought someone home to meet Rachel."

They stepped into the main room of the cottage. It was sparsely decorated with a table and chairs. "Oh?" Salena's voice perked up from the next room. She entered with a warm smile which fell to a sickly sneer as she recognized William.

William forced a smile of his own. "Lady Salena, I trust this morning finds you well?"

"Well enough, thank you," came the terse reply.

"William only just returned from overseas. Isn't that wonderful?" David said in an artificially happy tone like a parent trying to convince a child to be excited about something the child hated. "Now he's come to see Rachel."

"She's sleeping," Salena said, her weak smile fading to a frown.

"Oh, sorry," David said quickly. "We'll be quiet." He moved by Salena to the next room. William followed with an apologetic grimace to Salena. He was feeling rather anxious about this situation. He found the inspection and requisite approval of a newborn to be an awkward process under the best of circumstances, but this was an old friend's child, and it was under the scrutiny of a critic in whose eyes he could do no right. If he overdid the praise, she would get offended that he was making sport of their baby, and if he didn't make a big enough fuss, she might complain that he found something wrong with the child.

The next room contained only two beds, a larger one and a small one in the corner on which a little girl lay sprawled in a deep sleep. David crept over to her and looked down with gentle, loving eyes at his little girl. He then waved William over, still looking at his daughter.

William stepped up to the bed in confusion. On the bed lay a chubby girl of about four years old. Her big eyes were closed under her dark locks.

Not knowing what else to do, he reached down and gently stroked her chubby cheek. She stirred slightly but did not wake.

"David, may I speak to you a moment... privately?" Salena said from the doorway.

David sighed, "Of course." He forced a smile for William as he turned and followed her into the next room.

William stood looking over the child as he heard the intense whispered conversation in the other room. He knew it was about him, but what could he do? He wondered what sort of life this child might have. How would she grow up with these parents? She was so innocent now, but she would be saddled with so much from two imperfect people trying to teach and instruct her.

The intensity and the volume of the murmured argument began to grow after a few minutes. William felt very uncomfortable. He did not know if he should stay or quietly slip out. He knew he was the cause of the dispute, but he did not want to abandon David who was, presumably, fighting on his behalf.

After a few minutes, the spat showed no signs of letting up. William called out hesitantly, "David, I'd better get back." The voices broke off and David popped his head into the room. "What? Leaving so soon?"

"I'm afraid I must," said William, pointing his thumb over his shoulder at the door, "I'm just going to go."

"I will at least accompany you to the road."

William would have protested, but he wanted to escape this uncomfortable situation more than he wanted to be polite. "It was good seeing you again. You have a beautiful daughter. You should be very proud." With that, he broke for the door. David caught up to William on the path to the road.

"It seems Salena still has some hard feelings," William observed. "Sorry to cause you all that trouble."

"What?" David objected, acting surprised. "No, that was not about you. We were just in an argument earlier is all."

William stared at him flatly. "I must say I am a little surprised that her feelings are still quite so passionate," he added as if he had not heard David's weak protest.

"Well," David said hesitantly, dropping the charade. "She blames you and your family for a lot of the hardships we are having. I have tried to convince her otherwise, but she's got it in her head that way. And she knew a lot of the things we used to do when we were younger. I have tried to convince her you are a different person, but again, she has not yet seen that."

"She is right not to believe you," William said simply and changed the subject. "You have a very cute daughter, but it raised one interesting question."

"Which was?"

"What have you done with your baby?"

David's face reddened and he looked away. "Salena was pregnant before I left for the Crusades. I did not know until I returned." The scandal that must have created for her to have been pregnant with no husband must have been something. A few of the pieces of this confusing relationship clicked into place.

They reached the road, and William turned to David. "It was great seeing you again. Can I expect to see you in two days?"

"It is not much notice," David said, looking over his shoulder at the house. It was clear he was worrying about informing Salena.

"No, I understand if circumstances will not permit your participation. But would you be good enough to pass the word to any others you know that would be interested? We need about fifty total, and we figure we have about thirty guarantees thus far."

David looked at the ground for a moment. "I will be there, William. And I will bring as many knights as you like," he assured him confidently. "As I said, we all need the work."

"Thank you, David." William smiled. "I look forward to seeing you there."

CHAPTER THIRTY-NINE

The next morning Henry found himself strolling the hallways of Dawning castle. Every hallway, every corner, every room was thick with the shadows of times long past, memories of experiences both joyful and sad. It took but a moment's reflection to resurrect joyous childhood games with his brothers as children. A moment more and painful memories with the same siblings took center stage in his memory.

Henry had been so far removed from these shadows for so long, he was surprised to find them still so poignant. There were many ghosts that he had not had time to come to terms with since his return. He was a different person now and saw things very differently than when he had left. He longed to dissect these phantoms through the glass of his current understanding and experience, but there simply was no time. Nevertheless, there was still something strangely comforting about being back in his old house. Though the large stone hallways of the castle seemed cold and foreboding to some, it was the only home Henry had ever known. Good or bad, the experiences of his childhood had all happened here and this nostalgia was like a warm blanket wrapped around him. Despite all his doubts, fears, and mistakes, as he stood in these halls again, it was easy to believe that all would end well.

But all was not well, he reminded himself. His family was a mess, and he was departing on a dangerous rescue mission from which he might not return for a brother he hardly knew.

"Perhaps I should not celebrate too soon," he said aloud to the empty hallway. Henry had naturally wandered over to the guest wing of Dawning Court to call on the new object of his affection. He knocked on the door of her chamber with no small amount of apprehension given the impulsive proposal of marriage he had issued the previous night that was as yet unanswered. In the clarity of the morning light, Henry regretted having made the impulsive proposal. He wished he could retract it, to excuse it, but what could he do? He wanted to believe that maybe Mary would not mention it, but of course she would have to address it. And what would she say? What did he want her to say?

The door was opened by Charlotte, Mary's dark-haired maid, who curtsied slightly and invited him into the outer room of her chambers. He seated himself but was on his feet again momentarily as Mary entered the room. "Henry, what a pleasant surprise this early in the morning," she said cheerfully. Despite the early hour she was already neatly attired in a comely dress with her hair done up, ready for her day. Henry never could have guessed that he had left her only a few hours before. Mary looked back to Charlotte and waved her away. Charlotte retired to an inner chamber and Mary sat next to Henry and took his hands in hers. "Now, my dear, are you quite sure this is what you do truly desire?" she asked easily but with an intense look in her eye.

"I'm not sure I understand," Henry was assuming she was referring to his extemporaneous proposal the night before but was afraid to assume too much.

"You said something last night that robbed me of sleep. I was up all night thinking about your words just before you stole away and did not allow me a chance to answer properly."

'Stole away?' that was not the way Henry remembered it. He was suddenly very nervous. "Well, it was late," he started to retract his impulsive proposal. "I spoke rash—"

Mary held up a hand to silence him. " I must say, such a proposal intrigues me, but before I can make an answer, there is something else we must speak on before I could even consider mentioning this to my family. "

"Something else?"

"This scheme to rescue your fallen brother," she clarified.

"Oh, that. I do not see what that should have to do with—I do not see that there is any choice. My brother has been captured, and even William has returned to assist in his rescue. What choice could there be for me? Why would there be a choice?" She bit her lip in a coy expression that Henry could not help but find adorable. "Why do you hesitate, my own?" he asked, half laughing.

"I only fear my inability to make myself clearly understood," she said. "You must promise that you will not misunderstand me," she said firmly not in the motherly tone that she tended to take with him but rather as a playful sort of beckoning that invited him to play along. "You will not be cross with me?"

"My dear, as I recall it is you that has occasion to be cross with me rather than the other way around." He was laughing nervously, unsure whether she spoke in earnest or jest. She pouted again, and he hastened to reassure her that he would not be angry with her.

"Now tell me what is troubling you so. Do you fear for my safety?"

"My reticence," she said, "springs not for fear of your safety alone, although of course that is foremost on my mind, but from a number of other factors. Every facet of this mission leads me to believe it is an ill-fated expedition."

Now it was Henry's turn to pout. "Do you think so little of my skills then?"

"Henry, I do not speak to cause you injury but to protect your life. Your past attempts at leadership on the field of battle were disastrous. Even with well-armed and well-trained men, you alone scarcely survived. What chance, then, for this ill-conceived plan?"

"I will not be alone," Henry hastened to reassure her. "William will accompany me." He deliberately did not mention

Thomas, fearing the mention of his name would only give her more cause to doubt him.

"William? But your own tongue has decried him as an arrogant, brash, untrustworthy delinquent. What comfort for the widow-to-be is there in his company? I remember well the story you shared of his infamy and cowardly escape from a tournament of gentlemen."

"From the stories that have reached my ear, he has no equal in battle."

"Exaggerated though those stories most assuredly are, consider this. If things went badly and William had a choice between rescuing his brother or escaping with his life, which would he choose?"

Henry dropped his eyes. "I suppose he would escape."

"Precisely! And then we must consider the quest itself. Why would a good man risk his life and certain prosperity for Richard; for this monster?"

Henry stiffened. "That is my brother."

"Forgive my frankness, Henry, but how would you have me characterize him then?" she asked primly. "How should I refer to a person that has heartlessly heaped scorn, ridicule, and abuse upon the object of my affection since his tenderest days of innocence? Were he not born to the same mother as you, I doubt you would balk at such a designation."

"He is not so bad," Henry said, somewhat embarrassed and unable to meet her gaze.

"He is an animal. He abuses all those under him. He remorselessly slaughters women and children because of their race. Did not your own tongue designate him so when you were first re-acquainting me with your siblings?"

"Even if all that is true, how can I possibly refuse to help my brother in such a time as this? Even my exiled junior, William, is here to assist. It would only reflect badly on me if I refused, whether it was justified or not."

"Reflect badly to whom?" she asked passionately. "To William? What could you possibly care what he thinks?"

"William's opinion is not important to me, but it is important to my mother," Henry said disgustedly. "She treats him like her little prodigal son that can do no wrong. A word from him in the right place might ruin my relationship with her altogether. He could poison her mind against me. Now," he asked at last, "why would you wish me to refuse my responsibility as a knight and a noble of the House of Dawning?"

"Henry, I did not want to bring this up, but have you forgotten so quickly your renouncement of this warrior lifestyle? Is that how little you value your own word, that it is forgotten and the sword taken up again at the first sign of trouble? What is a vow worth that you would so easily drop as soon as the keeping of it occasioned any difficulty? Is that what you think of your vows? Is that all the determination you will put into a marriage vow?"

"I do not understand, Mary. Why do you castigate me for doing what is right?"

"Right for your family, perhaps, but not right for you."

"Speak plainly now, I must know why you are so ardently opposed to this quest."

"Henry," she said frankly, "you should control Dawning Court. You should assume the seat of your departed father. You are the best, the most noble, the most worthy."

"I am the fifth son," he protested weakly.

"Do not insult me that I do not know your heart better than that. You must have considered the possibility."

"Considered, perhaps, but I am the fifth son."

"But you are the first son in standing. Consider, John is a drunk that has been cut off from the family fortune. Edward has disgraced the family and disappeared. He will never be in contention for the seat. Thomas cannot seem to run his own house, let alone a Barony. That leaves you alone to make a serious bid for the seat, save one. Richard. Richard would be a brutal and bloodthirsty leader. And now Richard is imprisoned by the very people he oppressed. Is that not Providence smiling on you? Is this not the same as God's ordination? Would you risk your own latent glory on an endeavor that is destined to fail? Would you save one man when it might cost thousands of others their lives and their happiness? Yet you are intending to rescue him."

There was no response for a moment, and when it came, Henry's voice was very stiff. "I want Dawning Court. I believe I deserve it, and I am happy to watch my inept, pathetic, stupid brothers make decisions that actively or tacitly pass the birthright down to me. But I will not consciously sacrifice one of them just to enrich myself."

"Why do I care more for you than you care for your own life? Why won't you fight for what rightfully belongs to you? Why is your reprehensible family more important to you than I am?"

"T'would that necessity did not demand this of me, Mary, but it does. And until I am master of my own destiny and can choose my own path, I will do what is required of me."

"I am saddened to hear that. I thought I made it clear that ambition and an appreciation for a higher road than the warrior way were essential in a match for me." Henry did not reply. He was so conflicted that an appropriate response utterly failed him. She had told him that she would not marry him if he was willing to be pressed into service by his sense of duty. His misgivings about this ill-fated mission were stronger than ever. And he had once again acted impulsively to follow his heart, and he had again been made the fool for it. He was sick as he stood to formally apologize. "Milady, I am truly sorry that I have brought you here under my hospitality, only to abandon you before you have even had a chance to settle in. I would never have put you in this position had I any inkling such things were afoot. Please feel free to remain at Dawning Court as long as you would like."

It was Mary's turn to be speechless. She had been sure she had him well in hand only a moment before and was dumbstruck when he turned formal and left her. She had arguments prepared for any defense he might make except for this one. How could she argue with this? "I—" she started but stopped.

Henry paused at the door. "I am likely to be very busy preparing for this quest, as we are leaving before dawn in two days; so I fear I will not see you again before then. I am grateful for your friendship in this difficult time and wish you all the best." With that, Henry departed for the courtyard where he knew preparations were being made. He was not happy about leaving Mary this way; he did not blame her. He knew it was his fault for having filled her head with such stories about the shortcomings of his family. If only he had been more reserved. He was just so desperate to win her over to his side before she met the rest of the family and saw their weaknesses reflected in him. But now he was numb as he went about the necessary tasks to prepare for the hard ride they had ahead. Henry had gone from feeling a close kinship with Mary only the night before to feeling completely and utterly alone. What did it matter if he did not survive this journey? Who would really care if he was no more?

CHAPTER FORTY

"They are not here," Martha told Thomas the next morning after William's surprise return. "Henry is visiting with select knights individually to recruit them so as to keep this as quiet as possible."

"So where is William? He should not be out where he can be seen by just anyone."

Martha shrugged. "He said something about meeting someone."

"Leah," Thomas said with some antipathy in his voice. His mother's eyebrows rose. "Would that be a problem if he were?"

Thomas felt a little foolish for letting his jealously show. "You would think he would mind his urgent family business before trotting off with some floozy," he said, using anger to disguise his embarrassment. Thomas had attempted to curry Leah's favor in the absence of his brothers, but to no avail. Leah had spurned his advances. The audacity of that woman! The advantages of a partnership with him should have been obvious, but she pretended not to care about such things. She would care one day.

"I would hardly call Leah a floozy," Martha said dismissively, picking up the parchment in front of her again. "But no, I think he said something about meeting David and Neil."

"Well that's perfect," Thomas said, flopping down in a chair.

"You are in a sour mood this morning," Martha observed.

"Is there some reason I should be otherwise?" Thomas demanded. "I just discovered my brother has been captured and possibly killed; we don't know where he is or who we are going up against; and from the looks of it, my two younger brothers and I are planning on riding in there ourselves and demanding his release. Then to top it off, it is not even important enough to them to be here to finish hammering out our plan."

"Thomas, do not be silly," Martha said. "You know how much there is to be done. They are simply trying to get an early start and will be about later."

"Yes, well, given everything," Thomas broached the subject again hesitantly, "are we making a mistake?"

"I'm surprised to hear you say that."

"I was confident with Henry because he needed to see that everyone else was sure of this quest, but there are a lot of unknowns in this situation."

"Console yourself with the thought that this is all we can do," Martha told him. "We will go forth with faith that we are helping a brother who may one day be returned to us spiritually as well as physically. We must prepare as if it is a trap and leave the rest up to God."

"But it will be risky. Whatever we decide, lives will almost certainly be lost. Is it right to exchange many lives for one, or more to the point, to exchange the lives of valiant warriors who are willing to give themselves in the service of others for the life of a potential tyrant? Is the fact that this is our brother tainting our judgment?"

"Let me ask you," she responded gently. "If this were not your brother but one of your men that were in the same situation, would you go after him?"

"Of course."

"Even though you might lose your life?"

Thomas considered this. He knew there was a time when he would not have hesitated to affirm this, but so much had changed. Was one man worth his own life? The happiness and comfort of his wife and children? "Yes," he reluctantly consented.

"And if you knew you would die in the course of that errand, would you harbor any ill will toward the captive or those who sought his safe return?"

"No, I suppose not."

"Then don't other men deserve the same chance to serve without us assuming it is more than they are willing to give? Do not let the fact that it is your brother taint your judgment."

Thomas was still uneasy about it. Nevertheless, he knew he could not protest much more without his own motives being exposed. "When are William and Thomas returning?" he abruptly changed the subject.

"They should be back this afternoon. I believe Henry wanted to introduce Mary to William," she said. "That should be interesting."

"Ahh, yes. What is she like, this Mary?"

Martha shrugged. "She is a Mayfield, there is little doubt about that."

"Ahh," Thomas said sagely, though he did not understand the significance of that remark at all. Under different circumstances he would have been terribly curious, but not today. He had too much weighing him down.

"Thomas," Martha said suddenly as he rose to depart. "Do be careful. I am risking three of my sons for one son. Bring them all back to me."

"Do not worry yourself, Mother. What could go wrong?" he said with a confidence he did not feel and forced himself to grin at her. "And keep an eye on this place," he said as Sebastian entered the room. "I am convinced that Sebastian is stealing the whole house brick by brick."

"I beg your pardon, Sir Thomas?"

"I am confident that if you check his chambers you will find most of the east wing hidden beneath his mattress."

CHAPTER FORTY-ONE

"Henry? Sir Henry." Henry turned to see Mary hurrying to catch up to him. He froze and his face hardened, the memory of that morning's interview still entirely too fresh in his mind. "I am so glad I found you; I have been looking everywhere."

"Yes, well I have been busy," he said curtly. "I am just on my way now to meet William to check supplies for our journey." He made as if to turn to keep walking, but she put her hand on his arm.

"Sir Henry, in our interview this morning, I fear that I said some things that caused you pain. If that is the case, I deeply regret my words." Henry did not reply, so she continued. "I spoke in a passion roused by the attachment I have come to feel for you in our short time together. If I spoke harshly, it was only because I fear for your safety so. I would have talked you out of this dangerous endeavor for my own selfish motives, but I see that it is something that you must do, and I support you in it and should be honored if I could attend you upon your return."

Henry stared at her, some of his guard relaxing, but he was still suspicious. "Thank you, milady. Your words mean much to me," he said politely but without a great deal of feeling in his voice. "I would have lamented that we had left on anything but the most cordial of terms, and once again, I express my sincere apologies for having brought you to my boyhood home only to abandon you here. I hope you will forgive me my rudeness." He bowed slightly and again started to turn to go.

"Henry," Mary spoke again quickly to keep him from retreating. "I should be very happy here at Dawning Court with you... provided it was my home, too." Henry stared at her and comprehension slowly spread over his face.

"Mary, I—Are you—Who should—" he started and stopped a number of times, then grinned foolishly. "Come now, we must tell everyone!" she smiled back.

"If only you were not leaving so soon," she lamented.

Henry's face hardened at this. "I am sorry, too, but I thought I made it clear that I have no discretion in this matter."

Mary looked away coyly. "I only thought you might have a bit more leverage with your betrothed waiting on you than you did with a childhood friend."

"Unfortunately, a change in my situation has not changed any of the realities that force my hand," Henry said with a hard edge to his voice. "You think I want this? I don't. I was not lying when I said I hate this brutal life. But at the moment there is no help for it. I must ride this last time."

"And you won't think better of your choice of helpmates when you are months on the road?" Her seeming insecurity could not but endear her to Henry that much more.

"Am I so inconstant that you need worry about that? My mind is made up." He took Mary by the shoulders and looked into her eyes. "Mark my words. One month after I return, we shall be wed. And I shall make sure all know it before I depart as a symbol of my commitment."

Mary returned his look with a searching gaze of her own before finally speaking. "I shall wait with baited breath." They both relaxed, and Henry resumed his walk with his betrothed on his arm. "And I shall make all the arrangements."

CHAPTER FORTY-TWO

"There's someone I want you to meet," Henry said, trying to contain his excitement. "This is Mary." He stood aside to draw attention to the short, dark-haired girl beside him.

"Mary, it is a pleasure to meet you," William said bowing, slightly unsure of what the connection between the two was. Mary smiled pleasantly. "William, I presume" she said. "I understand you have only just returned from Egypt. Is that so?"

"I have just returned from…" he stopped himself from repeating the brothel joke he had used with his friends but could not think what to say in its place, so he did not say anything.

"Well, that's wonderful," Mary said cheerfully. "The last time I had the pleasure of seeing you, you were merely a cute little scamp running about the castle getting into mischief."

"That has not changed," Henry chimed in. Mary erupted in a gale of laughter that was far too loud for the jest made, and it took William off guard.

"Last time?" William asked, confused by the reference.

"Oh, I am a Mayfield." "Henry has told me so much about you. I am so pleased we now have the opportunity to meet face to face."

William gave a sly smirk at Henry. "I hope he hasn't told you everything about me," he said, still not sure what Henry's relationship with this young lady was. Was he courting her? Was he hoping William would be interested in her, or did he have different motives altogether? Such information would be very helpful in how charming William thought he should be.

She laughed a light, musical laugh. "No, it was all flattering," she assured him.

"Well, Henry always was a skilled liar," William laughed. "And for that I am grateful." Mary again erupted in loud laughter beyond what would have been expected. William gave Henry a sidelong glance, but Henry was just standing there with an adoring smile on his face, his eyes transfixed on Mary.

"So how has my brother been so blessed as to become reacquainted with you?" William asked, seeing that Henry's interest in this young woman was far more than cursory.

"Sir Henry was part of a group of scholars that was reviewing some ancient papal documents found by some of our crusading soldiers in the Holy Land. I saw him and was instantly taken with his knowledge of ancient languages and scripture." She smiled up at Henry and closed the gap between them, hugging his arm. "And he was so adorable, I was instantly smitten."

Henry flushed. He had never been particularly suave where women were concerned, so it seemed incredible to see this outgoing, charming lady shamelessly flattering him. It was either a match made in Heaven or something else entirely, but it was clear Henry was accepting it at face value. "Is that right?" William turned the conversation to Henry to take the pressure of carrying it off of himself. That Henry was a gifted scholar was true, but William was trying to remember if he had ever met a woman that was charmed by that. William found himself wondering if this girl could possibly be what she seemed. Henry shrugged mildly. "That is fairly accurate."

"Well, how is it that the Mayfields have such a lovely daughter that we were not aware of?" William asked.

Mary swatted the air toward William. "I believe your brother might be trying to charm me away," she said to Henry.

"T'would that I had the power, lady" William said without enthusiasm. He was quite sure he was out of things to discuss with this young lady. At this last remark Mary smiled up at Henry, who stood close and put his arm around her shoulders.

"Well that's wonderful. I do hope we will be seeing more of you, then," William said, not meaning a word of it.

"Actually that's why I wanted you two to meet. I hope that we will be seeing a lot of Mary. She and I… are betrothed." Henry announced a little shyly.

William almost choked, then caught himself and forced a smile. "Is that right? Oh, how wonderful," William feigned excitement.

"I am afraid that I must divest myself of the company of you two charming gentlemen lest I keep my lady in waiting, waiting," Mary glanced at William to see if he had caught the jest.

He gave a hollow chuckle, "Oh my, we wouldn't want that, lest she become a lady in mourning, this morning."

"So soon?" Henry protested. They both ignored William. "I was hoping you could spend the morning with us." William cringed inwardly at the thought.

"Now I mustn't keep Charlotte," she said sternly. Then more gently, "I will see you later." She smiled at him and then turned to William. "William, it was very nice to re-make your acquaintance."

William bowed a bit awkwardly. "The pleasure was all mine, milady."

***

They both watched her shapely figure retreating, each thinking his own thoughts that were very different from the other, until she was out of earshot. "A lot has happened since we last saw each other," William said conversationally. As a result of William's flight after the tournament, they had not seen each other in over four years.

"Remember when we were talking all those years ago?" Henry said thoughtfully. "I predicted that the next five years were going to be dramatic for our family." They automatically fell into stride beside each other. "I feel like that prediction has been borne out. In some ways I feel as if I never left, and in others everything seems so different. We should probably begin by inspecting the stables to be sure we have the mounts that will be required."

"Via the Battlements?"

"William, we must make haste—" Henry began.

"Forgive me, Sir Henry. I have been granted a reprieve of a single day to visit my childhood home. Part of me wants to visit one or two of our childhood haunts."

Henry grumbled but did not protest further as they walked toward the battlements of Dawning Court where they used to play as children. "So you mean the last five years were all your fault?" William teased him. "Then you have some serious explaining to do."

"It sounds silly, but I mean it," Henry explained. "It pertains to anyone you care to look at. John is still married, but his relationship is worse than ever, and things may have changed irrevocably for the worse. Richard is still lost to distant lands searching for glory, or at least that is what I assumed before your arrival. Thomas now has two children that are laying bare the weakness in his marriage that we all knew was there. And I don't know about you, but I have been forever changed by my time over… there…" he trailed off, his eyes distant.

"That is very true," William agreed emphatically. "I used to have this bone tooth necklace that I loved. Well, I dropped it somewhere over there, and I think I shan't see the likes of it again." Henry shook his head and ignored the comment. "And now I've met Mary," he said suddenly, snapping out of it. "You see, everything is the same and yet quite different. It can never be like it was again."

They mounted the staircase of a tower. "I noticed Edward was conspicuously absent from your list."

Henry shrugged. "Edward is still persisting in his libidinous fantasy world. I can't imagine that too much has changed for him. Besides, you know we don't mention his name around here," Henry added with a sardonic smirk.

"That is right," William agreed quickly. "What was it we used to call him as children? Whipping Boy? Let us refer to him as Whipping Boy," William declared. "Then we shall never be in danger of violating the unspoken command to never utter our brother's name."

"You know, it was so long ago, all that happened with Edward, I'm not sure if I remember it accurately." Henry broached the subject. He remembered perfectly what took place with his brother but wanted to query William's memories and feelings in general on the subject as he was the youngest Dawning.

They emerged on the top of the battlements to stroll the length of them. They were mostly unoccupied these days except for a soldier at each end, keeping watch. As such, it was generally a peaceful place.

"What's to remember?" William said carelessly. "The family outfitted him with enough equipment and money to sustain a small army. He rode out of Dawning Court with our expectation that he would join up with the soldiers crusading in the Holy Land. Next thing we heard, he had not gone to Jerusalem at all but had taken the money and supplies intended for the cause and had set himself up in Europe, where he began his search for the pure carnal man."

"I remember him sitting on his horse in his armor with all his pack animals around him. Even at that age, I remember thinking he did not look ready for what he was getting into." Henry filled in the sympathetic details that William had omitted. Henry sat on the inside edge of the battlements. William shrugged and threw himself onto his back across the opposite parapet. Henry cringed as William came to rest with one arm and one leg hanging carelessly over the fifty foot drop. "What are you doing?" Henry demanded of his younger brother. "Have you no concern for your own life at all?"

William looked up at him in surprise. "What are you talking about, Mother?"

"Why would you deliberately move to the very precipice of disaster?"

"This is where I'm comfortable."

"Well, it makes me quite uncomfortable."

William groaned. "Do not trouble yourself; I assure you I am quite well."

"Yes, well, the onus will fall on me to explain to Mother where the red stains on the rocks below came from. So for my sake, please..."

"Oh Henry, you will never change. How's this?" William rolled up on his right side so no body parts were dangling off the edge and propped his head on his hand.

"What are you talking about? I have changed," Henry said, slightly affronted.

"No you haven't," William said simply. "You have not changed because people do not change. You are as you have always been. Your brothers are the same as they have always been. Only their circumstances have changed. The difficulties you observe they are having now are merely the fulfilling of the promise of the weakness of their characters that was always present."

Henry reddened at being contradicted so directly. "Well you have changed," he asserted in anger. "Before you left, you weren't such a buffoon that it is impossible to carry on a conversation with you."

The corners of William's mouth tilted up, but he did his best to suppress them. "Actually, my brother, I have changed least of all. You might say I died the day I left and have not changed a bit since then."

"You know, I have had communications with Edward over the years," Henry blurted out suddenly, looking down at the stone beneath his feet and deliberately not responding to William's last comment.

"Whipping Boy," William corrected him.

Henry forced himself not to be baited by his brother. "I looked up to him more than any of my brothers. When he did what he did, it broke my heart. I had to know why, so I began corresponding with him." He looked up again at William for a reaction to this revelation, but William was only on his back again staring up at the sky, so he plunged on. "He said that he had never been prepared to go to battle and that the family had pushed him into it. You remember he was always much more fond of books and romancing the girls of the court? Even his sword skills were with the rapier, a weapon far more suited to gentlemen dueling than real combat. Anyway, he said everything just got out of hand until he knew it was too late, and he knew he couldn't go back home and face everyone in disgrace. He would be—was branded a coward for what he did, so he used what funds had been sent with him to start a new life."

"Well, if he had only told us so," William said with mock sympathy. "We would have gladly rewarded his cowardice with the money meant to support our knights, God's knights. He did not have to take it and reserve himself a special seat in Hell for his treason."

Henry diverted his gaze from William. "He was excommunicated for what he did. But that is what made it impossible for him to ever return and put things right. Edward's not a bad person, he just did some dumb things."

"What makes a person bad if not his actions?" William laughed, still gazing up at the sky and swinging his legs carelessly over the edge of the parapet. "Make no mistake about it; Edward is a bad person."

"How can you, of all people, say such a thing?" Henry demanded indignantly.

William raised his head to observe Henry's agitation. "And you just assume that I do not consider myself of dubious character? Oh, I have no illusions about my own standing in the hereafter. And by the way, The Whipping Boy did not just defy the family or the Church; he rebelled against everyone! His decisions were tantamount to betrayal of his church and his God. He stole from us, and he brought shame on the family."

"Betrayal?" Henry objected.

"He cut off the supplies to our own soldiers!" William interrupted his protest. "That is something the enemy does," William reminded him, as if Henry were a slow child.

"He was pushed into something he wasn't ready for," Henry said, starting to get very agitated himself. "His own mother was not even sensitive to his plight. She of all people should have understood that he was not like his brothers. She never asked what he wanted or if he was ready for that. She just expected he would do exactly as John and Richard had done."

"You're actually ascribing the blame for his actions to our mother?" William seemed genuinely amused. "She was alone, doing the best she could, with sons who were only interested in exploiting her for personal gain. It was a miracle that she even managed to fund his crusade, let alone outfit him as well as she did. And then she had to contrive to replace the money the Church was counting on that he had deprived them of. And apparently you do not recall that we did not have it. Whatever happened to personal responsibility? Wouldn't the time for Edward to step up have been before she spent all the remaining silver believing she could trust in her son? Before the family sacrificed so much?"

"Who are you to judge him?" The anger was showing clearly in Henry's voice now. "He was doing the best he could with a family who did not understand him and Church leaders he believes are nothing but a bunch of greedy old men who use guilt to keep everyone in line. Therefore, in his mind he was not betraying the Lord but doing the best he could despite knowing the family would never understand."

"Ah yes, I am sure the Whipping Boy's actions were predicated on the corruption of the Church and not the lusts of his own heart. It is exceedingly fortuitous for him that everyone is responsible for the Whipping Boy's actions except the Whipping Boy."

"Stop calling him that!"

"But Henry, have you forgotten that you were the one who assigned him his flattering nomenclature?"

"I'm not saying he doesn't have responsibility for this!" Henry's voice was still raised. "I'm just saying there are mitigating circumstances that no one ever considers, and I think he came off looking far worse in this than he had to."

"That is probably true," William conceded sarcastically. "I suppose we overlooked it amid all his attempts to return the money, attain forgiveness, and make amends for what he had done. Silly us." His tone changed abruptly. "Edward knew exactly what he was doing when he rode out of here."

"See," Henry was stabbing a finger at William, "that's the kind of attitude that makes it impossible for him to ever set things right, and everyone around here has it. It is no surprise he fled!" Henry turned away angrily and looked out over the yellow fields of Dawning Court, fuming.

"Are you saying Edward has intimated some desire to make amends?" William's voice was softer now, as he sat up on the stone. Henry did not respond. "Of course he hasn't," William answered for him. "So why are you trying so diligently to offer a defense for him that he has not even bothered to offer for himself?"

Henry did not respond for a long time. He just stood staring into the distance, the fall breeze washing over him. "I think I understand him," he breathed at last.

"There is a big difference between understanding him and agreeing with him."

"I didn't say I agreed with him," Henry spat angrily and did not speak more.

Henry had more contact with Edward than he had let on, and he no longer shared in the repugnance for Edward's actions that everyone else seemed to. He had hoped the outcast William of all people would see his side, but he either did not care to see another side or was simply having too much fun antagonizing Henry to have a serious discussion on the subject. William was only playing him, Henry knew that. He was saying whatever he had to to get a rise out of his older brother. And just as when they were kids, Henry could not help reacting to it, which only set William off that much more. He stood in silence for a long time. Finally he turned to find William walking one foot in front of the other on the very edge of the parapet, arms extended for balance.

Henry shook his head. "Have you completely taken leave of your senses?"

William shook his head, not taking his eyes off what he was doing. "No, but for a moment I thought you might have lost your wits and we might be here for a while, so I thought I'd better entertain myself." Henry knew it was pointless to argue with him, so he began walking for the far staircase to descend the wall.

"How did you meet Mary?" William asked without preamble, jumping down beside him.

"Just like she said," Henry said tersely.

"Well that's exciting. I am sorry to see you fall, though. William tried to return to normal conversation. "I suppose I will be the only one left."

"Well you won't be standing much longer, either," Henry said without thinking.

"Me?" William asked surprised. "What did I do?"

Henry forced his voice to sound normal and even careless, but he could not hide the catch in it when he said, "Leah? Where is that going?"

It startled William to hear that spoken aloud. "How did we go from being friends to getting married, just like that? Besides, I have barely had a chance to speak to Leah since getting home. Do you know something I don't?"

"Oh, come on," Henry pushed, "you know everyone has been thinking this way since you were fourteen! Are you trying to tell me you have never thought about it?"

"And what, pray tell, makes you believe a maid as eminently good and respectable would even consider the suit of an outcast?" William protested.

"Hmmm, you're right," Henry folded his arms and tapped his chin in mock concentration. "How would one tell such a thing? A beautiful, charming girl that could have had just about any man in the kingdom is still not married when all of her peers are already having children. I would say she is waiting for something, wouldn't you?" Henry gave William a sidelong glance and was surprised to see his brow furrowed and a scowl on his face. He pretended not to notice. "What do you suppose that something could be?"

"I don't know," William grumped. "I have only just returned. Must I be pressed with this before I have even had a chance to collect myself? Wait a moment. Leah is not married?"

"What do you think we have been talking about?"

"I don't know, weren't you listening either?"

"You really didn't know?" Henry asked seriously.

"I—I just assumed..." he stuttered.

Henry sighed. "No, William, Leah is not married, and I can assure you it is not for a lack of suitors."

"I... didn't know," William said in an unusually thick voice.

"Well, I wouldn't wait too long to move if I were you," Henry warned. "A woman like that, I might snatch her up myself." It was painful and even slightly embarrassing for Henry to speak of Leah in this way to the very man that prevented him from having her. It hurt him deeply that all his accomplishments and accolades were not enough to outshine the memory of his wayward brother. They ought to have been. She should have seen! But alas, she did not, and he was doing the only logical thing: he was moving on.

"My thanks for that," William replied sarcastically. "I really needed that."

CHAPTER FORTY-THREE

William entered the library through the dark oak double doors to find his mother in front of a map laid out on a large table. "Planning a trip?" he asked lightly. He came over to see the map of mainland Europe. William turned to Sebastian, who had dutifully followed him into the library. "Go find Henry immediately and get him over here. It is urgent."

"Yes, sir, and where might I find Sir Henry?" He asked.

"I don't kno—He mentioned meeting up with Mary this afternoon; they are probably on the grounds, perhaps out by the gate."

"Very good, sir," and Sebastian withdrew.

"He is wasting time with Mary when we have so much to do?" Martha asked, surprised.

"Now now, Mother," William chided her lightly with his eyes on the map. "Young love must not be suppressed. It is such a delicate thing."

"Is it?" she asked, looking at him meaningfully. William pretended not to catch the meaning.

"I have no reason to think otherwise. All the bards say so, and if I cannot trust the tale of a beggar with a lute then who can I trust?"

Martha watched her youngest son measuring distances and considering routes for a time before speaking again. "You know, I am so proud of you," she said with emotion in her voice. "I know why you did what you did. I know that you have spent the last four years serving God, and now you are here to help a fallen brother." William looked up, surprised at the comment. "I worried so much about you when you were younger. You had so much anger in you, I prayed continually that you would not go down some dark road and be lost to us forever."

William was uncomfortable with her openness and at again being reminded of his many mistakes. He tried to subtly but quickly put an end to this discussion. "Well, thank you for not giving up on me. It looks like your prayers worked, because I am okay." He then added, "What is more powerful than the prayer of a mother?"

"Apparently the vices of my other sons are more powerful than that," she said, the disgust returning to her voice. "I am so grateful I have you. At least one of my sons is striving toward becoming a true man."

"Well, I fear you do me too much credit, Mother. Besides, what of Henry? He fulfilled an honorable campaign. It looks as though he is about to be married to a good... political match," he added the word 'political' to qualify the statement so full of misgivings for him. "And he is on his way here to help us finalize a course of action."

"That's true," she agreed hesitantly.

"However?"

"I have worried about Henry for a long time. He seems to be staying on the very edge of the straight and narrow path of righteousness, but only barely. He does what is right, but I wonder if he is doing it for the wrong reasons. It is as if he is so filled with doubts and misgivings every step of the way that in an instant, he could be another Edward."

William shrugged. He could not help but think of the undue amount of sympathy for Edward that Henry had expressed during their earlier conversation. It would seem there was more to his feelings after all. "You may be right, but what's to be done? For the moment, he is holding true. Let us worry about those who are falling all around us rather than borrow worry from some future events that may never come to pass."

"I know you're right, but it is a Mother's job to worry. And I am worried about him."

They stopped as the door opened and in glided Henry. He was dressed in a fine silk doublet with the short cloak that had been made for his trip to London and his soft, upturned shoes instead of his utilitarian boots. "What are you wearing?" William grinned wickedly.

"I was with Mary," Henry said primly, tossing his hat on a table. "I prefer not to look like I just wandered in off the front lines when I see her."

"You didn't mind looking like a worker this morning," William commented dryly.

"Don't be silly," Henry said, disgusted. "I would not wear finely tailored clothes to make preparations to go to battle."

"No," William agreed. "You wouldn't want to get dirt on them and hide how ugly they are."

"I should be remiss indeed if I took fashion tips from someone who has been living in the squalor of a military camp for years."

Just then, Thomas walked in. "What's with the jester outfit?" he asked casually.

Henry colored. "I will have you know, this is what all the nobles in London are wearing now."

"Hmm, well let's hope it stays in London. All right, do we still think this is a good idea?" he queried.

"As good an idea as it ever was," William replied.

"You do not sound too optimistic, little brother. Should it concern me that the author of this plan does not even have confidence in it?"

William held up his hands defensively. "I only said it was a better plan than the one that was under consideration—less risk. I never said it was a good plan."

"Well, it is a little late to be hearing this," Thomas said, surprisingly upset by William's comment.

"Forgive me, I should have notified you last month that in a few weeks we are going to be made aware of a situation about which we would need to make a rapid series of determinations with insufficient information, and that I will not be confident in the recommendations I make under those circumstances."

"Enough," Henry interrupted. "Thomas, you are correct. It is not a good plan. It is too elaborate and there is too much that can go wrong. Nevertheless, William is also correct that it minimizes the risk to Dawning Court and gives us a counterattack in the event of a trap, which this almost certainly is. Now let us get down to it. William how many men were you able to recruit?"

"So that is it?" Thomas was incredulous. "Everyone acknowledges this is a plan fraught with problems and yet we are simply going to go through with it because we won't lose that many men? What about us? We are Dawning Court! The three of us are the last worthy Dawning males, and we are going to sacrifice our lives for a very dangerous, very unworthy brother?"

"I thought we had been through all this," Henry sighed. "Thomas, we simply do not have time to rehash it. Besides, you were certain enough last night about this."

"I only said we should go after him; I never agreed to this plan."

"Follow your conscience, Thomas," Martha told him. "If you are willing to be here, then we need you to be here; if you are not, there is no time to convince you."

"We have a few hours of daylight left," Henry added, now over by the table with the map laid out on it. "We will likely be up most of the night preparing and have no more time to discuss this."

Thomas dropped into his seat. "I thought we might at least determine we are making a wise decision before we worked out the logistics of it."

"We are doing the best we can, Thomas," Martha assured him. "That is all we can do." Thomas did not respond.

"I received word from David that he had commitments from ten knights including himself," William interjected.

"Very well. I have attained commitments from almost thirty others. Thomas, if you were able to get ten, then we should have the fifty we need... Thomas?"

Thomas was still staring thoughtfully into space. "Thomas?" Martha repeated.

"Hmm? Oh, yes I did find ten knights willing to do it, although it was not easy. There is much concern about leaving so late in the season."

"Excellent," Henry said, showing some excitement for the first time. "With the three of us, then we have the fifty we were hoping for. Now let us consider the route we might take." He turned to the map laid out before them with Richard's blood red crest acting as one of the paperweights. "Though it will cost us some time, I think we are better off staying on land as far as it were possible—"

"Time is the one thing we do not have," Thomas interrupted. "We are leaving far too late in the year. We are going to get caught in the winter snows."

"I don't think so," Henry said, still looking at the map. "We will need to set a blistering pace just to reach the designated meeting spot. If we retrieve Richard quickly and return at the same pace, we should just beat the snows, if not some chilly nights."

"And if the snows come early this year?"

"What do you want me to say, Thomas?" Henry asked. "Do you want a promise that all will go according to plan? Because I cannot give you that."

"This idea is looking worse and worse all the time," Thomas grumbled, folding his arms and sitting back in his chair.

Henry ignored him. "Now, let's consider the specific route we will take..."

CHAPTER FORTY-FOUR

Thomas returned home in the early evening with more reservations than ever about the journey they were to embark on the very next day. He retrieved his mace from where it lay forgotten in the training yard. He was half surprised his children had not found it and suspended it from the tallest branches of a tree somewhere as part of a game, as they did with everything else of his. He swung it and was unpleasantly surprised to feel how sore he had become just from the previous evening's exertion. His hands were bruised and his back, arms, and chest were aching. He opened up another series of strikes on the training pole and found himself winded even more quickly than the previous night.

"I'm going to die," he declared aloud. How had he let himself slip so far? "I need a drink." He again dropped the mace, and instead of going inside to spend the remainder of the evening with his family as he had anticipated, he climbed back in the saddle and made his way to the tavern he had come to know so well in recent times.

He was hoping to find John there. John would be someone he could commiserate with. He was not disappointed. "What are you doing here?" he said to his half-inebriated brother.

"I jussht shtopped in for a pint," he said with a slur in his speech. "Have a drrink. H- He ish b-buying." He indicated the tall Saracen merchant that had financed so many of their drinking binges before. He always seemed happy to do it, claiming that it was his privilege to attempt to win the favor of the family of benefactors." For the first time, there seemed something sinister about this merchant's motives to Thomas. Perhaps it was all this talk about the Saracen capturing and ransoming of his brother, but he did not wholly trust this merchant.

"Where have you been?" Thomas asked urgently, sitting across the table from John. "We have been looking everywhere for you."

"Who hash?" John tried to focus his blurry eyes on Thomas.

"There is much afoot that we would have had your council on," Thomas said cryptically as there were many people about.

"Whatever it wash, mine wash more import-ant," John grinned and leaned forward unsteadily in his chair. "I've had her! The most beaut- beautiful woman in the wor-ld."

Thomas sighed as he realized his brother's company was going to be of little value to him tonight. He contemplated the drink of brown liquid that was placed in front of him. He really did want it. He wanted it to calm his nerves and comfort him that all would be well, when he was not at all sure that it would be. Thomas watched John guzzle down another mug and grin at him. He was carefree, and that is what Thomas needed at the moment. He drank down his own cup. The warming effects were slow to come, however, so despite his resolve to only have a drink or two, he had another, and another, and before long, his fears did dissipate. He spent the remainder of the night with his closest brother singing drinking songs and not bothered at all about the morning to come.

CHAPTER FORTY-FIVE

David rode over to the old cottage road that his widowed mother occupied since his father's death and the loss of the family estate. Her little place was set back deep on his own land well away from the road. He found that he did not frequently visit his mother these days as her life was a reminder of all that had gone wrong in his own. There was a substantial gap between the life he had envisioned for himself and the life he was actually leading. Salena took Rachel and checked in on her each day, and he contented himself with that. It was sobering for him, but before each campaign he forced himself to visit her on the chance that he might not return.

"How are you, Mother?" Bronia Abelin started almost imperceptibly at being suddenly interrupted. She was sitting by the fire, staring at a large book in her lap.

She glared up at her son with a hand over her racing heart. "Have you no manners whatsoever?"

David kissed her as he entered, "I am afraid I never did; is it only now that you are noticing that? Forgive me for startling you."

"I did not hear you come in," she admitted.

"I shouldn't wonder, you seem to be so deeply engrossed in that book it is a surprise I have even now been noticed. Good book?"

"Hmm? Oh, I don't know," she said, holding it up so he could see the title.

"*Historia Regum Britanniae,* by Geoffrey Monmouth," he read aloud. "Well that should keep you occupied for a while. It is a pity that Bishop Monmouth's flair for the fantastic was not matched by his attention to accuracy; that could have been a truly valuable work."

"I have been on the first page for two hours," Bronia admitted.

"I admire your diligence, but you would best leave off conversation with me if you maintain hope of finishing it before it decays," he smiled.

She grimaced. "I have had a lot on my mind of late, David. Very nice of you to pay your respects," she added as an afterthought with only thinly veiled reproof in her voice.

"Yes, well, I have been busy," he said, sitting down on the edge of a chair as if he might flee at any moment. David never knew what mood he might find her in, and he was not yet certain if he would find it prudent to beat a hasty retreat. "Now tell me, what has occupied you so completely that even the fanciful tales of Geoffrey Monmouth cannot capture your attention?"

She closed the book on her lap and looked at her son. "In earnest, David, it is you that has been occupying my thoughts of late."

"Is that so?" He said without enthusiasm. He knew whenever she was having thoughts of him, it likely meant an ugly reproach was to follow.

"The shade of Lyn has been to visit me," she announced.

"That's strange, Mother, he never visits me." David replied flippantly.

"Don't be impertinent," she hissed. "He sits with me even now. He was a good boy. The boy that was going to restore this family to prominence."

"I am aware of that," David sighed, tired of the same old litany of his long lost older brother. He had barely known him as Lyn had been some ten years his senior and had died as a young man early in his career. Their father had put all his time and attention into Lyn's education and training and always overlooked David himself. After Lyn's death, his father filled the void left behind with outside interests such as drinking and gambling. It did not seem to occur to him that he had another son that may also benefit from his attention.

"I cannot seem to make sense of fate's capricious hand. Of the group Lyn was with, Richard and John Dawning and some of their friends, he had a better heart and more to lose than any of them. If any of the rest of them had been struck down, it would have been less of a loss for mankind than losing Lyn. The others did not have wives or children. There would have been fewer people hurt as a result of their loss than his." Lyn had taken a wife very young, and she had been pregnant when he died. "Lyn was a good boy."

David flushed with anger. He had of course heard the theoretical comparisons many times before, but it was he that had been taking care of her all these years. Yet all she ever said was how he didn't measure up to the imagined man that his deceased older brother would have become. Though she had deliberately not used his name in the comparison, he understood that the implication was there. When David opened his mouth to respond, it all came out in a gush. "In a strict comparison of the worth of a soul, it seems you are overlooking a few things. I loved Lyn, too. He was a good boy and a good brother who was on his way to becoming a good man; however, he died before things got really bad. Before father died and the debt collectors came. It is I who have taken care of your person since that time. Doubtless, you believe Lyn would have fulfilled that calling more ably, and perhaps so, but he is not here to do so. Yes, Lyn did leave more behind than the others, but it does not necessarily follow that he would have more in the end."

"It is in poor taste to speak ill of Lyn under the circumstances," she protested. "Lyn was going to restore our family back to prominence."

"But he did not, did he?" David said, frustrated with her unwillingness to concede even the smallest point.

"Why did he have to die at all? It just seems so senseless. "

"It is senseless, Mother! Death is completely arbitrary. Where one stands on the battle lines, an argument with the wrong person, choosing one horse rather than another, death turns on the smallest things. So rather than lamenting the premature demise of your good son, perhaps your prayers would be better spent on the son you were left with."

"What can we do except be prepared for death?" she said as if he had not spoken. "We must live in such a manner that we needn't fear the great beyond. Are *you* prepared for death, David?" she asked suddenly, and David averted his eyes. "This is why you have been the subject of so much anxiety on my part. The reason you have not lived up to your brother's potential is because you have not lived up to *your* potential. The reason you have not restored this family to prominence is because you have not restored this family to prominence." David furrowed his brow, his confusion overriding his defensive instinct for the moment. "David, you have contented yourself with 'good enough' in life. At some point you stopped striving for perfection. You no longer sought for greatness in this life and settled for merely good enough." She held up a hand to stave off the inevitable objections from her son. "Oh, it was in keeping with your amiable nature, but it prevented you from truly excelling, from truly shining. You will not leave the mark that Lyn would have, that you could have, because you gave up on yourself. You settled. You settled for your wife, your service as a knight, your religion. Your devotion to anything has only been skin deep because you would not do what was necessary to earn the deeper convictions and corresponding strength of character that came with those trials."

David did not reply. He only kept his eyes downcast and said nothing.

"David, what is the meaning of life; or rather, what is the meaning of your life?"

"I know the gospel," he grumbled into his chest.

"It is not a question I am looking for you to answer for me, but answer within your own heart, David. What is the meaning of *your* life? What is the focus of your life that makes all the hardships worth enduring? When that is clear to you, your life will take on a meaning of its own."

David considered for a time and finally sighed. "I feel quite rudderless," he confessed.

"You cannot steer your life by your emotions alone. Emotions are far too fickle to steer you true. Rather, when you are strong, use your heart to guide your intellect. When you are weak, intellectually stay the course until your strength returns." She stood up to indicate their interview was at an end. "I know you have come here because you are departing soon with the others."

David looked up, surprised. "But—How—"

"Hold strong to what you have always known to be right," she interrupted him, "and I have no doubt you will come through this with courage and nobility."

He forced a smile and gratefully stood to leave. "My thanks, Mother."

"My son, you must decide once and for all what you believe. Only then will you be free of the self-imposed shackles that bind you."

CHAPTER FORTY-SIX

"So, if you did have the chance to go back and make amends, what would you do differently?"

"Everything," Richard answered.

"But those things that were so horrible before would still be there. Your family that was so intolerable would still be intolerable. Your mother that did not give you the respect you deserve would not have changed."

Richard remembered how it enraged him that his family did not hold him in awe. Everywhere he went he was treated with deference, if not reverence. Everyone either feared or respected him, but his brothers would still tease and argue with him, as if unaware that they were nothing compared to him. His mother would still make demands on him as if her agenda was more important than his. He could still feel the warm ire rising in him as he remembered the treatment he received at the hands of his family.

"Here you are, lower and more debased than you ever imagined possible, and still your pride controls your emotions?"

Richard started to lash out at the voice but stopped. He did not want it to go away again. He felt lower than ever and did not want to be alone right now. He also sensed that on this point the voice was right.

Thinking further, he could remember fond times, training with John, or teaching his younger brothers tricks for the battlefield or giving them advice on their training routine to make them stronger or faster. Though that was often an inconvenience to him, he yearned to be back on the training grounds of Dawning Court, fencing with blunted swords or wrestling with William and Henry when they were little.

He smiled to himself to remember the times he pitted Edward and Thomas against each other. He would have them face off, usually against their will, for his own amusement. He told himself at the time that it was for their own good. He was teaching them how to fight even when their heart was not in it, but he knew they held resentment toward him for that. Thomas seemed to have understood as he matured that it was just the kind of thing older brothers did to their younger siblings, but he remembered well the look that Edward gave him over his bloody nose and tear-filled eyes. Now it seemed there was a connection between that experience and the increasing distance Edward put between them as he matured. For the first time Richard began to feel guilty for those youthful indiscretions.

"Perhaps you were not perfect, either," the voice suggested calmly, continuing the thought he was having.

"Perhaps not, but really now," Richard protested, "we were kids, all of us. Anyway, Thomas seems to be okay with it."

"But Thomas is a pleaser by nature; it would not have served him to hold a grudge. Edward was more sensitive, like a soft piece of wood he bears the marks of every such encounter until his scarred surface barely resembles the original."

"You are blaming me for all Edward's problems? That's ridiculous. The disaster that Edward became was not because of some childhood games. And even if I *was* in the wrong, isn't Edward responsible for his own actions? We all experience hardships, but we get past it. We move on."

"You are missing the point. Your brothers lost their father when they were very young. So it fell to you and John to fill that role. What did you do to help them, to nurture them?"

"Don't put that on me. I am not their father, never claimed to be, never wanted to be. It's not my fault our father died. Anyway, I was young, too."

"Of course you were, but was your sensitive younger brother better or worse off because of your influence?"

Richard was surprised by the question. "I tried to make him stronger by pushing him," Richard protested, his words sounding empty even to himself. "I tried to teach him how to stand up for himself. All he ever did was sit and read. He was never going to become great that way."

"Was he better or worse for your influence?" the voice repeated.

"Worse," Richard grudgingly admitted. "I never really liked him. It used to bother me how awkward he was and how long it took him to learn anything that required coordination. He seemed content to just spend his whole life wrapped up in books about other people doing great things while never doing anything himself."

"And how did that hurt you?"

"Well… it didn't. I was just embarrassed by it," Richard admitted. "But certainly you cannot be implying that what he was doing was healthy, either."

"And whose choice was that to make?"

Richard shrugged, feeling an overwhelming sense of remorse to remember the awkward, withdrawn little boy that was afraid of the world and cowered from the sport they made of him. "I should have protected him. I should have encouraged him and then maybe he would have wanted to get outside of himself." Tears were in his eyes as Richard began to cry for the many wounds he had inflicted on those he should have been watching over. "I was stronger, and they should have been able to look to me for protection as their elder brother rather than as their biggest antagonist." He sobbed harder still as if saying the words were tearing the emotions from his body. "But I never did. All of my family is worse off because I have lived." Richard sat in his dark, cold cell and sobbed the first tears he had shed since he was a little boy.

CHAPTER FORTY-SEVEN

"Edith, please see to the horses," Leah said. "I fear we have ridden them beyond their strength in this heat." Edith nodded and led the lathered animals away toward the stable.

Leah turned the corner and there he was, loading a wagon hitched to a pack animal with heavy burlap bags of grain for transport into the yard. He had filled out since he had left; he was much broader and thicker now, his arms larger and his face more defined, stronger. He had become a man. Leah approached slowly, not wanting to interrupt but wanting his attention before Edith returned and they could no longer speak openly.

William placed a sack on the back of the wagon and stopped to wipe the sweat from his brow. He pushed his bangs out of the way and noticed her standing there. A pained expression flashed across his countenance before being replaced by a forced smile. "Leah," he said softly but made no move toward her. "I hope this day finds you well."

"Not so well as I could have wished," she replied. "My oldest friend returns from a four-year absence and neglects to call on me." She was trying to affect a playful tone, not wanting a repetition of their previous encounter, but it was strained even in her own ears.

He stroked the side of the horse absently as he gazed at her plaintively in her riding clothes with her face flushed nicely from the exertion of the ride. "Ah, yes, well I must beg your forgiveness on that score, milady. But would you believe it? It is rumored that there are those hereabout that would do me harm? Me! I know," he said, raising a hand to forestall her imaginary objection, "it is unthinkable. It is no doubt a rumor started by someone jealous of the many glorious honors that have been showered upon me by the locals."

"How have you been, William?" she asked, locking his gaze with her own.

"I uh. . ." he stumbled over his words. Leah was so guileless, it made it difficult for him to maintain his flippant attitude around her without feeling vulgar. "My dear, I have seen the world and much that is in it. My mind has been expanded by God's creation and withered by the meanness of man," he said expansively as though he had been a pilgrim on a journey of spiritual enlightenment.

Leah took another step toward him, vexed by his refusal to speak to her as a confidant. "You know that I remain ever your faithful friend?" she assured him. "I am as interested in your well-being now as ever I was." He only looked away. "Do you believe me?"

He smiled at her sadly. "I know your heart is and has always been true." They were silent for a long time as they gazed into each other's eyes, hers so hopeful and his so sad. "And what of you? I expected you would be married with many children about your feet."

It was Leah's turn to avert her eyes. "No," was all she said.

"Leah—" William blurted but brought himself up short. She looked up hopefully. "Leah," he sighed. "Pray tell me that one such as yourself, so beautiful, so good is not pining for something that can never be."

"I am not sure what you mean," she dropped her gaze again.

"My soul is dark and depraved. I have been cast out and hunted. I am despised such that even Lucifer himself will not reclaim my soul. I live in limbo until the final state of my soul is determined and consigned to my eternity."

"Why would you say such horrible things?" she asked, now taking a slow step toward him. She was disturbed by what she was hearing but encouraged that he had dropped his flippant manner and was speaking to her from his heart.

"I have seen so much of the darkness of mankind, I have seen—I have done so much that convinces me man is not worth saving, that all this despicable race should be wiped from the face of the earth."

"So you made mistakes," she protested passionately. "We all have. You should not have to carry those with you the rest of your life."

"Do I have the right to forgive myself when those I hurt clearly have not forgiven me?" he queried. "The mistakes I have made, the evil I have committed can never be undone. The lives I have taken, the scars I have left on the lives of all those around me will never vanish. Is it right that I should not carry the burden of these things when others must carry it forever more?"

"No, you do not have the right. You have the duty to put these things away. You have done what you could to make amends, you have spent years serving God. It is not your right to take the power of forgiveness that the Lord has reserved for himself and put it in the hands of lesser men and women. Repenting means to turn away from your sins. What more can a penitent man do to show he has turned away from his sins than what you have done?"

"I am grateful for your confidence in me, but it is quite unwarranted. You cannot and I hope never do know even half of the evils I have done, or you would turn from me and never again look back." William smiled wanly. "You know, even in the service of God I was lengthening out my time in purgatory." Leah did not reply, so he continued. "The horrors of war make people do things they would not otherwise do. They blur the line between right and wrong; they turn the clear cut black and white boundary of everyday life on its head. And if you are the victor, it is left only to your conscience to determine whether you were acting for the cause of good or of evil, and I stopped asking that question a long time ago."

"I know you had to do horrible things, things that I cannot even imagine; but my confidence in you evinces many certainties regarding your behavior. You were forced to make decisions that no one should have to make, but I know your character, and I know you made the best decisions possible. I know that your men were better off because you were their leader than had it been someone else. It is only because you are good that you are weighed down by these things. You must forgive yourself your mistakes. Living under a constant barrage of our own failings is too much for anyone to withstand for long."

"In all that, the only thing that has kept me from surrendering to utter despair—one thought, one memory has made me question whether there might not be something deeper, more beautiful, more gentle in this world than what I see, better than what I have become. I cannot bear the thought of that perfection, all the potential for happiness and good that it entails, going unrealized in the shadow of a sweetly loyal but misplaced affection."

"You assume too much."

"Leah, tell me it is so, and I will believe you," he said, suddenly intent on her. "Tell me you would not pass on a single moment of happiness because of some pour soul that will never be worthy of you. Tell me, and I will be satisfied."

"You have my word that I shall not deprive myself of a happy situation," she assured him. "But I will also firmly promise that I shall not be matched with one who does not have my heart... and has no probability of earning it." She again met his eyes and held his gaze. All the years they had been apart passed in that moment. He was so guarded, there were so many demons he had yet to confront, but he was still the good-hearted young man with whom she had spent her youth.

"Leah," he sighed. "I am not my own agent. There is much I would have done differently if I knew then what I know now. There is so much good I could have done. How easily could I have made changes that would have put my life to good use instead of wasting it?"

"But don't you see, don't you see?" Leah seized on the opportunity. "You cannot go back, but you will one day find yourself thinking the same thoughts about today. Your willingness to throw away today because of mistakes made yesterday will rob you of a joyful tomorrow, just as surely as the mistakes of yesterday have robbed you of the joy you might have had today."

"Why do you do this to me?" He suddenly seized her by the shoulders. "My life is forfeit. God has not forgiven me!"

"William," she said, fearful of his passion. "I don't know what you mean. Please, you're hurting me."

"Why can't you see this? You will be the instrument of my downfall."

"William, please," she pleaded, not scared of him but discomfited by this insensibility that she did not recognize in him.

"The moment I care about something, the moment I have something to lose, he will take it from me."

"Who who will take it from you?"

"Aren't you listening to me?" He released her suddenly and turned away.

"I am listening, but you are not making sense."

"God will take it from me! I should have been struck down a thousand times on the field of battle, and yet here I stand because I was expecting death, because I looked for it. I would have embraced death. And here I am staring at goodness and beauty in the face that tantalizes me with a life of contented happiness. It can never be! I live because there is no reason for me to live. I live because my death would be no punishment. The moment I have hope, the instant I have an expectation of a life beyond this hollow existence, I am a dead man!"

Leah's brow furrowed. At first she thought him to be joking but shortly came to be disturbed by his words. "William, God is not punishing you."

"Then who else?" he demanded, taking several steps away to separate himself. "The devil, given leave to dispose of me as he would, would snatch my soul and seal me his as my soul is primed. It is only God's power then that would preserve me. Yet my actions do not warrant such protection." William turned back to her and looked deep into her eyes, and his voice softened. "You do not understand..." he sighed and sat heavily on the sacks of grain he had been loading onto the wagon. "I have scarcely taken a step in this life that I have not left a wake of devastation in my path. Even in my attempts to atone for it, I was only lengthening out my time in purgatory. Returning hom—here—is the best reminder I might have had of that."

"But you are not that person anymore," Leah protested, "that person who did those things."

"That's where you are wrong," he cut across her. "I am exactly the same person that I ever was. If you believe you see improvement in my character, I assure you it is only your affection that colors me in better shades than I deserve."

"So you made mistakes. We all have. You should not have to carry those with you the rest of your life," Leah protested. He smiled at her. "What?" she asked, suddenly self-conscious.

"You are just too good; you do not understand."

"My confidence in you evinces many certainties regarding your behavior," she repeated.

"I should very much like to know on what foundation such confidence is placed." William folded his arms, looking slightly amused at her.

Leah was unsure of herself. She felt it was important to say just the right thing here, but she did not know what that was. She had always believed in William's nature, that he ultimately always did the right thing, but she did not know how to make him believe that of himself. "The mistakes you made in your early years, you never intended the harm that came as a result."

"Not at all. I always intended the harm I caused. Granted, there may have been unintended consequences, but I always intended to hurt those that crossed me, and any who stood on their behalf were counted as enemies along with them."

She made a face at his argument, and William started to turn away. So she changed tacks, feeling that time was growing short. "Your life is a gift!" she said passionately. "What are you doing with that gift?" William stopped short, half turned from her. Leah became conscious of her own labored breathing. She had not been aware of how impassioned she had become. She heard Edith approaching. "Please do not waste it," she implored him softly, turned, and was gone, leaving William alone with his haunted thoughts.

CHAPTER FORTY-EIGHT

David leaned over to kiss his little daughter's angelic sleeping face. "Are you leaving now, Daddy?"

"You are supposed to be asleep," he tried to sound stern but could not hide his smile.

"I wanted to be awake when you left."

"Well, I am glad you are, but we must be very quiet so as not to disturb your mother."

"Daddy, are you going to die?" she asked suddenly.

"Whatever are you talking about, Rachel? Why would you ask such a thing?"

"Mommy said you were going away on a dangerous journey and you could get hurt or even die."

"She did, did she? Well, your mother worries about me a lot."

"Is that true?"

"Impossible," he said flatly. "You remember that story I told you about the knight that vanquished the dragon? Well I am traveling with my friend William, and he is a magical warrior."

"Like the knight in the story?" she asked in awe.

"No," he said mysteriously. "He is like the dragon."

"The dragon? But the knight slayed the dragon," she protested.

"No, he only vanquished him. You cannot kill a dragon. All you can do is send him away for a while."

Her eyes opened wide. "Your friend is magic like the dragon?"

"I think he might be. I don't believe he can be killed, and the way he moves on the battlefield is nothing short of magical."

"And he will keep you safe?"

"Actually, your daddy is going to keep him safe." Rachel's eyes opened even wider. "You must be magic, too."

David laughed and hugged her. "You know, I think I may be." He stood to leave after kissing her one more time and committing her to return to sleep.

"Daddy?" she said as he neared the door.

"Yes, dear?" he turned back indulgently.

"Is your friend really that strong?"

"He is the greatest warrior I have ever known... now go to sleep."

CHAPTER FORTY-NINE

The sun would not be up for an hour or more when Henry walked into the courtyard that was already bustling with activity. They were leaving under the cover of darkness to attract as little attention as possible.

Henry scanned the crowd for familiar faces. David and Neil were there; Henry was not surprised. They were William's oldest friends. Who else would William have been able to go to? He saw several other familiar faces, some who had come willingly, others who had grudgingly agreed after trying to negotiate a price for their services. While technically obligated as sworn knights of Dawning Court, it was not uncommon for unscrupulous knights to cite some important but non-essential, official duty as an excuse to not fight when they were called upon. It was a tried and true political method of soliciting more money from their liege to pay the "fees" for someone else to maintain the critical "duties" that would be neglected in the knight's absence, and with a volunteer request such as this, it was a prime opportunity. Henry, of course, would have none of that, but he wondered if either of William's old friends had employed such a scheme. He had known them both over the years, and Neil in particular seemed somewhat more mercenary than David. If either of them were going to employ such a device, it would definitely be Neil, he thought.

Beyond those two Henry spotted Roland. Thomas and William were nowhere to be seen yet. He chastised himself for not ensuring that William had not fled during the night again. Then he realized how cynical he was being and reminded himself to be on guard for that.

Into the torchlit courtyard an old familiar face came into view leading a fully-loaded mount and several pack animals behind him. Henry was shocked. "Anthony?" He took a few quick strides to his cousin.

Anthony grinned a warm smile under his brown locks. "Well met, Henry."

"Well met, Anthony. What wind have you blown in on?"

"My family was in the area transacting some... business, and I heard of the trouble. What could I do but offer my sword?"

Henry frowned. "I might have known we could not have kept this a secret," he grumbled. "Are you quite committed to this cause? It will be very dangerous."

"I am certain. This is your brother, and I am here to help." They clasped each other's arms in the only form of an embrace their heavy armor would allow. "I am very much cheered to see you. It eases my burden somewhat," Henry told him.

"Is this all who are riding with us?" Anthony asked skeptically, looking around at the relatively scant number of knights, a number that seemed even smaller with no squires, servants, or drummer boys.

Henry nodded. "I will explain more when the time comes, but we thought stealth would serve us better than force on this occasion." Anthony nodded his understanding, surveying the other knights in various stages of preparations.

These men were a mere fraction of the armies that Braden Dawning had commanded, but in the decade-and-a-half since his death, funds had dwindled and so had the knights and soldiers that remained faithful to the Dawnings. These fifty men represented approximately a fifth of the entire ready complement of knights of Dawning Court with perhaps a thousand more available from surrounding friendly areas that could be called upon in a pinch—provided the pinch was not the neighboring friendly areas no longer being friendly.

Martha had entrusted this piece of information to her boys on the previous night that they might understand the gravity of the situation as well as the tremendous trust that was being placed on them and this mission. It was by virtue of this secret as well as a general ignorance of the deep divisions in the house of Dawning that kept would-be enemies at bay.

"Sir Anthony, I trust you will excuse me while I check on the men." Anthony nodded his ascent, and Henry made his way over to Roland via David and Neil, greeting various friends and acquaintances as he went.

The two were sitting casually, trying to outdo the other with past accounts of battles in which they had allegedly participated. "Have you had adequate time to prepare?" They had each prepared their respective supplies at their individual homes and arrived ready to go, as opposed to the routine militia that relied on Dawning Court to provide everything from their weapons to their food.

"No, frankly," David said, "but I did not think the enemy would wait on me."

"I have been ready for an hour," Neil said shortly, making no effort to hide the annoyance he was feeling at being made to wait.

"Have you made doubly sure you have all you need?" asked Henry, ignoring his tone. "We intend to travel very quickly, and there will be very little chance to forage, hunt, or acquire needed supplies." If you need more supplies, now is the time. Everyone else is stocking up," Henry added, noticing David's single sparsely-loaded pack animal. Virtually every other knight traveled with at least three other animals to carry additional food, clothing, armor, and weapons and would have more had they allowed it. But David had only the one. Henry felt certain that this was a result of circumstance rather than choice.

"I am prepared," Neil said shortly.

"As am I," David added.

Just then one of the stable boys walked over with a bag of supplies over his shoulder. "Pardon me, sir— sirs," he said, addressing David but looking up at each of them. "Sir William requests that you would take this," he said to David.

"William is not a knight," Henry said primly. "Do not refer to him as sir."

"Yes, sir," the servant replied quickly. "Forgive me, sir, but to a lowly stable lad, everyone with a sword looks to be a knight."

"What is it you want?" Henry said angrily.

"Sir Will—What I mean to say is, Lord William—saw you were not carrying overly much and thought you might take some of his excess," he said to David, who looked at his own sparsely-loaded animal and crimsoned.

"He said no such thing!" Henry said to the servant, unwilling to believe that William would be so insensitive.

"He most certainly did," the servant replied defensively.

"Where is 'Sir' William?" Henry demanded. "I would have words with him."

"It's quite all right," David said quickly to avoid any additional embarrassment he might suffer by this turning into an argument. "I do have the space, and I am happy to take it."

Henry watched David and the lad secure the additional weight with a scowl. "Well that is my brother—selfish to the very last."

"You," he said to the stable lad when he finished securing the load. "You know my brother Thomas?" The servant nodded. "Good, go to his house, rouse him if necessary, but have him here within the hour. We will not wait longer if he tarries. Be sure you make that clear to him."

The lad raced from the yard, and Henry excused himself to speak to his old friend. "Sir Roland, I trust this morning finds you well."

Roland grinned at him. "How could it not? We are riding out just like a storybook-fabled knight."

"Hmm, well from where I sit the differences are quite striking."

"How so?" Roland asked, continuing to lash gear to his sumpter horse.

Henry leaned against the post of the stable he was standing near. "As a child I loved the stories of brave knights that would slay an evil dragon and save a beautiful princess. There was never any doubt about the outcome. It was exciting but comfortable to go along for the ride. The knights in the stories were shallow creatures that exuded nothing but nobility and bravery; indeed, that was the very purpose for which they were created. They never doubted, regretted, or second-guessed themselves. They knew what they had to do and they did it, knowing that everything would work out in the end."

Roland grinned at him. "Maybe this is the purpose for which you were created."

Henry chuckled. How could he ever have known that the dragons he was destined to contend with were, in reality, the evil machinations of men. Now he was fighting foes he could not see or touch as they all too frequently inhabited the persons of his own friends and family and even himself. How did one fight such insidious monsters that were constantly rooting into the hearts of men: dragons of vice, dragons of pride, jealousies, selfishness, anger, hatred? "My purpose indeed."

Henry eventually found his way into the saddle of the large brown stallion that had been prepared for him. A large muscular beast, this was a warhorse bred to be the noble steed of a gallant knight on a glorious quest. William's identically clad mare stood by ready to go, but his brother had not yet made an appearance this morning.

The large double doors of the castle opened and out strode Mary like a beam of light in the shadowy courtyard. She was dressed in a white gown and looked radiant despite the early hour. She walked straight to Henry, who came out of his saddle to meet her. "Lady, what brings—"

"Sir Henry, there are some details of our impending nuptials that I should like to discuss before your departure this morning." Henry took her by the hand and led her to the edge of the light where they began talking very animatedly.

***

William walked into the bustling courtyard with a smile on his face. This was a life he understood. He would soon be leaving all the confusion and difficulty of life at Dawning Court behind him and trading it for the mercurial life of the warrior. That was where he was comfortable. He already felt comfortably anonymous in the bustle of the knights. He had even stowed the bulky traveling robe for the time being, allowing that in this company of all companies, riding under the Dawning banner, he would not worry about being someone else. If this was to be his last ride, as it very possibly was, he had no need of such ploys. There was something liberating about that idea.

He spotted Neil and David talking on one side of the courtyard and Henry standing off to the side with Mary talking. Henry spotted him and detached himself from Mary.

"William!" Henry barked in irritation. "How can you be such an insensitive cad to David?"

"Henry, I am doing my best to stay awake at this early hour, and listening to you is not conducive to remaining conscious. Be brief and tell me what you are babbling about?" Then, as if to illustrate his point, he emitted a ponderous yawn.

Leah's voice from nearby caused them both to jump. They turned to find her much as Mary was, completely made up and radiant despite the early hour. Edith was a pace behind, observing the commotion with an indifferent frown. Leah had awakened her very early with the announcement that they were going to see the knights off. Edith had complained and attempted to dissuade her, but to no avail.

Leah still had not told Edith of her interview with William the previous day and therefore could not explain that it had been weighing heavily on her, not only because of William's disturbing ideas about the dark destiny he seemed to have envisioned for himself but also because of her reaction to him.

He had returned for only a moment, and instead of showing him how overjoyed she was to see him again and how much she had longed for this occasion, she had greeted him only with tears and reproof. They had always shared a connection in their humor and playful attitude, and she was determined to prove to William that that connection was still there. The old friend he had left behind all those years before was not gone, and there was a reason for him to return to this place. She forced a smile and said cheerfully, "Well, it seems I am in luck."

William grinned, and Henry immediately stepped toward her. "Milady, what are you doing out here at this hour?"

"Where else would I be when my heroes were riding out on their noble quest?" she replied with no trace of the early hour showing in either her voice or manner.

"It seems the only people that don't know about our secret departure are my brothers," William said, still smiling. He turned to Henry. "You did tell them, right?"

Henry frowned. "Yes, of course I told them."

"Well that's good," he said. "Because it may be that they are insensitive cads like me, and then where would we be?"

Henry stiffened. "Well what would you call it when a man with so much excess that he cannot carry it all asks the one man without enough to carry it for him?"

"I call it practical. What?" William protested the frown Henry gave him. "He had room, and I have so much that I could not use it all on two of these journeys," he said meaningfully. It took Henry a moment to understand. Feeling slightly embarrassed, he dropped it; they turned back to Leah, who wore a slight smirk on her smooth features.

"Milady," Henry said with a bow, "may we have your blessing on this quest?"

"You know that you have it, Sir Henry."

"Milady," William said with a bow, mocking Henry, "there is a small token I would request of you in the event that I do not return from this excursion into the very pit of Hell," he said dramatically.

"Anything," Leah laughed.

"Should I not return, will you be so good as to take a moment each day to say a curse over two of my brothers? Henry for making me go on this quest to rescue Richard, and Richard for needing to be rescued."

Leah bit her bottom lip in mock consternation. "Well, I said I will, so I am bound. Forgive me, Sir Henry." She placed a hand on his as she laughed lightly. Henry could not help laughing with her.

"I don't believe I have had the pleasure," Mary interrupted.

Henry jumped again and immediately withdrew a step from Leah. "Milady, of course, what has become of my manners?" He introduced Leah to Mary.

Leah curtsied politely. "It is a pleasure, Lady. Your reputation precedes you."

"Yes, well one can hardly be betrothed to Henry Dawning for a moment without your name being known." She smiled at Henry.

William choked and started to cough, which earned him another glare from Henry, but Leah stepped in quickly, "That is wonderful," she said to them both. "I'm sure you will both be very happy. Oh, but to have to be separated from your betrothed in the very spring of your engagement can hardly sit well with you."

"It is the life of the companion of a warrior prince," Mary said primly to Leah.

"Indeed it would seem so," she said, giving William a sidelong glance.

"Only tell me there is still time, milady, to steal you away for myself," William said flippantly after recovering himself.

Mary turned to him and smiled warmly. "I'm sorry, my heart belongs to this Dawning," she said, interlacing her arm with Henry's.

"Nonsense, one Dawning is pretty much like the rest. We all share a similar voice, facial structure, and a belief that we alone are unique in this world."

"If you will excuse my brother's crass behavior, chivalry was the main lesson neglected by Jurou," Henry said, interposing himself between them as he turned Mary away.

"I think he is actually going to do it," William said confidentially to Leah as they watched their retreating backs. "I think he is actually going to marry Mary... in a marriage ceremony... where much merriment will be made of mary... iage."

"Is that a problem?" Leah asked back in the same quiet tone.

"I don't know, I have only met her once. But given my policy of always saying the first thing that comes into my head, I am going to say... yes."

Leah looked thoughtful. "I wonder if she will remain at Dawning Court while you are away. I should like to get to know her better."

"I should think she almost has to," William affirmed, giving Leah a suspicious glance at the change in her demeanor since the previous day. "I doubt her family wants her back."

Leah swatted his arm, "William Dawning!"

"What? I may not be a knight, but I am not blind, or more importantly deaf. Speaking of which," he said, looking over her shoulder and around.

"What are you looking for?"

"Where is Eve?" he asked curiously. "Not that I expected her to come out and greet me, but wherever you were, your four-foot shadow was never far behind."

"My sister is away at boarding school in France, attempting to fend off an army of young men bent on stealing her virtue," Leah smiled.

"What?" William said, surprised. "Little Eve?"

"I tried for years to tell you that this was coming, but you could never see past the obnoxious child you knew."

"There was more to see?"

Leah smiled despite herself. "She was obnoxious."

"She really was, wasn't she?" William laughed.

"Only to you," Leah laughed with him. "To everyone else she was charming—just as sweet as can be."

"Yes, why was that?"

"You really don't know?" Leah asked, surprised.

William shrugged. "I always assumed it was because I was stealing her older sister and closest friend away from her."

"No," Leah said, even more surprise registering on her face. "No, just the opposite. She was infatuated with you."

"You gest!"

"She was not jealous of my attention, she was jealous of yours."

William shook his head. "How did I miss that?"

"Well, because you always looked at her as the little sister. To you she was just a child who did not have those sorts of thoughts and feelings."

"Perhaps you're right. No wonder she was always angry with me. Whoops. Sorry, Eve," he said to the air.

"You may have the chance to tell her in person," Leah said. "She will be back here in a few weeks. She has finished school. I guess the question is will she come back betrothed or not?"

"I can't even imagine little Eve as someone's wife. The mind recoils at the thought… She'll probably inform his parents every time he does something she does not approve of."

Leah smiled. "And what of you?" she changed the subject abruptly. "Will you exact promises from a lady without offering something in return?"

"Promises? Oh the cursing, that's right." He bowed graciously. "Of course, milady, whatever a lowly servant of uh—himself can do."

"When you do return from this adventure, I will require a pledge of something very dear to you," she said slyly. There was a mischievous smile playing on her lips. William bowed again.

"All that is mine is yours, dear lady, only—" he hesitated.

"Only?"

"Only I do not expect to return this way again soon. If and when we rescue my errant sibling and he is assured of safe passage home, I have pressing business that requires my attention elsewhere. Which thing breaks my heart to tell," he continued once again in his light-hearted manner, failing to notice her smile disappear, "as I am always delighted to live among those who would as happily stretch my neck from a tree as speak to me. No, no," he said in mock modesty, "they are not wrong to hold me in such high esteem. My natural charm and way with people has earned me all the respect and admiration that is lavished upon me."

"William," she said seriously, stepping up to him. "Will you not return this way?" She was trying to keep her tone neutral, but her resolve to remain light hearted crumbled in something near panic. A plea was evident in her voice.

"Milady," Edith chimed in for the first time. "We are not alone here." She was looking at the others in the yard that might be observing this, but no one seemed to be paying attention.

William looked at Leah, confused. "I am afraid I cannot. I did not mean to come back here like this; it was only this unexpected ransom note that brought me here as it is."

"William, these are dangerous times for Dawning Court. You do not know the intrigues that are afoot."

"Yes, milady. But the precarious state of my family's affairs could only be rendered more so by my presence."

"William," her voice caught in her throat, "the fortunes of those that are dear to you may shortly be at stake." She looked at him meaningfully, but he did not understand her and assumed she was still referring to his family.

"All will be well, Leah," he reassured her. "Sufficient is the strength of the family yet to wrestle with whatever might come this way. They will hold their own."

"And if they cannot?"

"They will." He forced a smile to his lips. His heart ached to have her so close at long last only to once again be leaving her. Why couldn't he just take her away with him? Why not just that? *And then what, you fool? Leave her poverty-stricken and alone when you die, as you surely will? How would she be better for that?* William shook his head and dropped his eyes, and Henry stepped up beside him.

"We have a problem."

"Only one?" William was relieved by the distraction. "Then we are doing better than usual." Leah retreated quietly into the settling commotion of the courtyard.

"Thomas is gone."

"Gone?"

"I mean he is not here, so I sent a runner to his house, and he has not been home all night. I sent him to the tavern, and it is locked up tight. He is missing."

William shrugged. "How many men do we have?"

"Fifty, with Anthony's fortuitous arrival."

"So what's the problem?"

"Our brother is missing," Henry reiterated.

"Do you believe him to actually be in any danger?"

Henry hesitated. "Well no, I suppose not."

"Then we ride without him. Either he will catch up to us or he will not. We cannot lose a whole day because he is passed out somewhere." Henry looked indecisive, so William changed the subject. "You should say something to the men before we go," William said quietly.

"Why?"

"You know, to inspire them. To remind them of their noble quest and let them know who's in charge, that sort of thing."

"I don't think so. If you are feeling to make a speech this morning, you go right ahead," Henry said tersely.

William shrugged and climbed into the saddle, looking for Leah. He spotted her some distance off, speaking to Anthony. Mary again joined Henry. "Milady," William said to her. "It is regrettable that your nuptials will be delayed on such unpleasant business as this."

"Concern not yourself with such trifles," Mary said cheerfully. "And I will do the same. Your errand is far more important than our nuptials, which may be celebrated at any time." She smiled warmly at her betrothed. "And how much happier will that day be when the whole family is reunited?" William choked on his reply and started coughing again.

"Any time?" Henry announced grandly. "Nonsense. I make it known to all within the sound of my voice to stand as witness here and now that our wedding will not be a day later than three weeks after our return to Dawning Court."

Mary beamed up at him and turned to William. "You just make sure you bring him back in one piece."

"Certainly you jest," William tried to recover himself. "I am relying on my elder brother to get us all home in one piece."

Mary laughed a soft, musical sound in the early morning solemnity. "Now, Sir Henry, if I may have a word." She pulled Henry aside to confer with him privately once again.

Just then the double doors of the castle were thrown open wide and all eyes turned to see four fully-armored knights carrying a large silver chest into the courtyard. Two of the knights carried it between them in one hand each by a heavy handle on each side. The other two walked, hands on hilts, scanning the yard for potential threats. These four knights had been specifically charged to see this chest safely to its destination regardless of what else may happen.

The four knights secured the chest to the back of a sumpter horse and mounted one at a time. They then took positions on every side of it, openly armed to the teeth as a message to any would-be thieves to think twice.

"I still say it would have made more sense to hide the money," Henry grumbled to Mary. "Why make it a target like this?"

"Did you tell them that?"

Henry nodded. "We discussed it. Thomas and William felt that since nobody locally knows what we're about and they are certainly not going to attack an armed cavalcade of knights on a moment's notice, the only real fear we have is treachery from the Moors who are expecting it. If that is their intention, they will attack us regardless of whether they see it or not. In that event, how much better to have it properly defended than to have it stowed in our saddle bags? I still don't like it."

Mary looked at him seriously.

"Henry, who is in command of these men?"

Henry furrowed his brow in confusion. "I am not clear—"

"Who is leading these men?" Mary said more firmly.

"I—that is to say, we don't—we haven't—"

"Who, Henry? Your drunken brother? Your disavowed brother? One of your men?" she demanded. "Henry, you are in command! You must take charge where you have heretofore failed."

"Failed? I—" She nodded in the direction of William, who was pulling his horse around to the front of the men who were just now starting to settle down and look for direction.

William stood in his stirrups and shouted, "Thank you all for being here today. Your loyalty is much appreciate—"

"Are we going to let the Moors do this to us?" Henry called from where he had just leapt into his own saddle. Every head immediately turned from William to Henry. "Are we going to let them take a son of England and extort payment for his safe return? Payment which they will then use to kill more of our people and arm against our knights?" Henry was speaking very loudly. As the eastern horizon began to glow behind him, he looked every inch the holy warrior. "I cannot speak for you, but as for me, this will not stand. And with Heaven's armies by my side, I will right this wrong that has been perpetrated on our people and on our family. And we will show the next would-be extortionist the fire of the wrath of God! Now who is with me?"

A great cheer rose from the courtyard, and the men fell into line behind Henry as he galloped out of the courtyard. Their destination was weeks away, rendering any gallop ultimately pointless as a time-saving device, but he knew it was important to go with the excitement of the moment. He let the men charge for a league before slowing to a trot.

William caught up to Henry when they had slowed down. "Thanks for warning me back there," he said, obviously irritated.

"About what?" Henry asked without looking at him.

"About your speech. You could have just told me rather than making me look like a fool."

"I took your advice," he said simply. "About getting the men charged up and showing them who is in charge." He looked directly at William. "And I am in charge."

"You want to be in charge?" William grinned wickedly. "You are welcome. I want to command about as much as I want to be drawn and quartered. Besides, it always entertains me to watch the heights a man's vanity can take him to before dropping him off the edge. And who is better at vanity than the chivalry?"

"Your jealousy again reveals you," Henry said. "I would have you remember that it was your actions alone that exempted you from the honors of knighthood."

"Is that what it is, jealousy?" William was still grinning. "I had not realized it, being masked so well in disdain as it is." Henry's jaw tightened, but he said nothing, and William dropped back.

CHAPTER FIFTY

"Your father would like to speak with you," Martha said to John when she walked into the room where he was sitting.

John was instantly on his feet. "Me?" he asked nervously. "I—"

"John," Martha smiled her understanding at her son through her fatigue. The long weeks at the bedside of her husband were for naught. His condition was not improving despite her best efforts, and the strain was beginning to show on her. "I know you are worried, John." She approached him as he stood agitatedly, wiping his palms nervously.

"What does he want?"

"I am not sure what he wants, John, but I have an idea." Seeing that John was not satisfied with that, she explained further. "You will be leaving for the Holy Land soon, and he may be afraid that he will not get to see you again. I would expect that he wants to resolve some things with you. John," she said, taking her son's shoulders firmly and looking into his eyes. "You are a noble warrior. It does not suit you to always be doubting yourself. You will soon travel to a foreign land and fight for the Church as is expected of you. You have been knighted for your willingness to serve, and you deserve it. I know your character, John, and I promise you that when it really matters, when you are called upon, you will perform admirably."

John dropped his eyes as his mother spoke, not wanting her to see that he was doubting her words even as she told him not to. He only nodded in response. "Now go, go to your father."

John walked nervously from the room. His father had taken ill a few months ago, and John had not seen him since he became bedridden. He felt guilty about not making more of an effort but feared his own awkwardness in that situation. He had an abiding need to address the wrongs Braden had done him over the years but was terrified to do so. He was spared this, however, by the physician's forbidding any presence in Braden's room that was not required to be there.

John's tension grew as he walked the halls and mounted the stairs to his father's bedchamber. Why would Braden request his presence now? Was his mother correct? Would his father apologize? He had never heard his father apologize to anyone for anything. But now, as his health declined, did he recognize the damage he had done to his little son? John could remember every epithet, every insult his father had flung at him; but more than that, John could remember the beatings, the pain, the fear, trying vainly to fight off his much larger father when it seemed a sort of madness was upon him. John would try to get away, to cry, to fight, but nothing placated Braden in this state until exhaustion took his rage from him.

And now, as he prepared to depart as part of a campaign to Damascus that would take him away from his home, his family, and Lindsay for several years, John wanted his father to approve of him more than anything in the world. All his life he had dreamed of faithfully serving under his father. He imagined how much Braden would come to rely on him and how much he would value him. That was all John had ever wanted. And maybe now, if his mother was right, all would be well. Maybe Braden believed in him after all. Perhaps, at long last, Braden would tell his son how much he loved him and how proud he was of him.

John gently knocked on the thick oak door of his father's bedchamber. He heard nothing from inside. He took a deep breath to steel himself and pushed the door open. The room was *dimly lit, the only light peeking in from around the shuttered window. There was a large four-poster bed along one wall that was made of a dark cherry wood. The bedclothes were drawn back from the side facing the door of the room. Braden's tall form stretched across the full length of the mattress, but he had lost a great deal of weight, and he was very thin now. His breathing was labored and audible as soon as John entered the room.*

John slowly approached the bed, his heart thundering in his chest. He was shocked to see the drawn and withered countenance of his only very recently vigorous and strong father. "You wanted to see me, father?" His voice trembled as he spoke.

Braden Dawning's voice croaked from his throat. He had to stop for breath after every couple of words. This made his speech halting and slow. "You are... departing... Crusades."

"Yes, shortly, Father."

"You... will be general? Lead... own crusade?"

"I am not certain, Father. I do not know how I may fare over there."

There was a long silence before Braden spoke again.

"You lost... tournament... to Collin Braddock?"

John dropped his head. "Yes, Father. I lost this year by one point. I was wearing this new armor, and it—"

"You... courting a peasant?"

"Courting? Lindsay? No, of course not. We are just friends."

"You... marry her." There was an accusation in his weak voice, and it trembled with emotion.

"No, Father, no," John hastened to reassure him.

"You are..."

"What is it, Father?" John knelt beside his bed.

"John, you are... a disgrace... to Dawning name." John was stunned. "Never be baron."

The tears stood in John's eyes as he struggled for a response. When the words finally came to John, they poured out very rapidly.

"Father, I will make you proud. I will show you that I can do it. I will serve the Church honorably. I am a knight now. Father, all these things I do, I do for you. I am not as good as you, but I will make you proud. Please, Father, please, tell me you approve of me."

"Richard is... my first... best son... He will... make me proud... he will be baron."

"Oh, Father," John hung his head as Braden waved him away. "Father, I do not care about being baron, but surely this cannot be your only message to me." Braden fumbled for the bell on his end table and rang it as violently as he could manage with his feeble strength. The servants shortly appeared and stood hesitatingly as they saw what was happening.

"Please, Father," John was pleading desperately. "I beg you to spare some kind word for me. I am your son, I have always done the best I could. I am sorry if it was not good enough; but I tried, and I will try harder."

Braden gesticulated violently with one weak arm until the servants dragged John from Braden's bedside and out of the room.

CHAPTER FIFTY-ONE

John fled. The hot tears were streaming down his face, and he was humiliated. He ran from the castle and into the fields surrounding Dawning Court. He ran blindly for a while before finding his way inevitably to Lindsay. "John, what is the matter?" He hugged her closely to him, wanting to hide his tears from her but unable to do so as they poured anew at her compassion.

When he was able to calm down, he told her as candidly as he could about his interview with his father. "Well, that is nonsense," Lindsay replied. "You have not even had a chance to prove yourself."

"Maybe he is right," John said from where he sat, shoulders slumped, utterly defeated. "For the last few years, it is all I can do to keep up with Richard in the training yard. He seems to grow stronger by the day, and I have to train harder and longer to try to keep up. Maybe Richard would be the better leader."

"What does that have to do with it?" Lindsay protested. "You are the eldest Dawning; the birthright belongs to you."

"Don't you understand, Lindsay? The Dawnings are first and foremost warriors. Everything else—the barony, the wealth, all came as a result of being powerful warriors. If Richard is better than me, then he is a more deserving heir than I am..." John trailed off, a thoughtful expression in his eyes.

"But he is not a nicer person than you," she said, failing to comprehend the problem.

John could not help chortling. "And why does that matter?"

Lindsay pouted. "It matters to me."

"You know, maybe it is not all bad," John said, reaching out and touching her smooth skin. "If I am not baron, we could be together."

Lindsay lit up as she always did at the mention of this. She was younger than John, and in moments like this when she got the girlish glee in her eyes at the thought of being married, John was reminded that she was not, in fact, very far removed from girlhood. "Oh, John, wouldn't that be wonderful?" she said. "We would have a house together and little sons and daughters." Lindsay twirled in place as she thought of it.

John smiled indulgently. There was something about her simple innocence that he found irresistible. He had spent so much time with the people at court that were constantly scheming and plotting that it was truly refreshing to be with a woman that was so guileless. "Lady Lindsay Dawning, the wife of Sir John Dawning, the great knight." Lindsay tried the title out, and John sank back into his melancholy.

"Things are not working out the way I had imagined them."

Lindsay stopped twirling, and sat next to him. "What do you want with your life, John?"

"I want to be a great warrior baron like my father," John said to the ground. "But I am not him. Richard is more like my father than I am. He is strong and hard. I am soft and weak compared to him."

"Well, I think you are the mightiest warrior in the kingdom," Lindsay said, leaning against his large arm. It was ludicrous to say that an untried eighteen-year-old was the mightiest warrior, John knew, but he appreciated the sentiment and wrapped his arm around her.

"That's it!" John snapped his fingers. "I can settle this once and for all."

Lindsay sat up. "What do you mean?"

"All I have to do is prove that I am a superior warrior to Richard, and all this will be behind me. I will have proven to Richard and to my father that I deserve to be the heir of Dawning Court."

"But—" Lindsay started to protest. There was something about this idea that seemed wrong, but she could not seem to articulate it. "But what if—" she stopped again, frustrated that she could not think. But John did not seem to notice as he became more and more excited.

"This is the answer! I will prove that I am the best Dawning and am rightfully the first son and therefore the first choice."

"But what if your father does not change his mind?"

"He will have to. Don't you see?" John was on his feet in his excitement. "If I best his favorite son, I will be proving that I deserve to be the first heir of Dawning Court."

"But what if you lose to Richard?" At last Lindsay was able to lay hold on the thought that had been just out of reach, but John did not hear her. He was already sprinting for the castle to put his plan into action.

CHAPTER FIFTY-TWO

Thomas awoke in a haze with John nudging him roughly with his foot. "Come on, I want you to meet someone." Thomas looked around to try to gain his bearings. They seemed to be in the guest house of his estate, but he could not remember how they had come to be there. He vaguely recalled arguing with Henry and William about something and getting drunk with John, but little else. Judging by the numerous empty wine bottles littering the wrecked room, they must have brought the binge here to the relative privacy of Thomas' guest house. It was probable that no one, including Thomas' wife, Annie, knew they were there.

"Get up," John said again.

"What are you talking about?" Thomas asked annoyed. "Who do you want me to meet?"

"You'll see. Get up. We have to go."

"What? No, we'll do it tomorrow. I need sleep."

"No, it has to be now. Let's go." John walked toward the door.

"I will never forgive you for this," Thomas said and dragged himself painfully to his feet. His head swam, and he felt nauseous. Thomas stood unsteadily in place for a moment. "I think I know why our father banned alcohol at Dawning Court," he said, trying to get his eyes to focus clearly. "Anything that makes a man feel like this has to come straight from the devil himself."

"That's true," John said, throwing his cloak over his shoulders. "But you will forget this discomfort, and you will do it again," he added mildly as he fastened the clasp. He had been drinking longer than Thomas and was more familiar with the after-effects of alcohol.

"What are you saying?" Thomas protested. "I will never put myself—ahh, you're right," he conceded. He took a few shaky steps forward, and by the time they reached the door he was walking fairly steadily.

"What is this? Where are you taking me?" Thomas complained as they stumbled through the woods in the darkness. At John's insistence they had abandoned their horses a half-mile back, and he would only answer Thomas' protests with a terse "You'll see."

They entered a small clearing in the trees where Thomas bent over, bracing his hands on his knees to rest. He was still trying to shake off the after-effects of the night's heavy drinking. "You know I am truly starting to believe you are taking me somewhere you can hide my body and no one will ever find it."

"Oh, quit your belly aching, we are almost there." John dismissed his complaints.

"Well, if whatever unholy tryst you have planned does not lead to my demise," Thomas panted, doubled over, "this grim death march you have brought me on certainly will."

"We'll rest here," John allowed in recognition of Thomas' abysmal condition. He seated himself on the soft turf and leaned back against a rock. He interlaced his fingers on top of his head. "Thomas, did you ever think there was more to life than this?"

"What? What are you talking about?" Thomas asked, sprawling on the soft terrain. "I have really let myself go," he exclaimed.

"I mean," John said, ignoring the comment, "did you ever feel like you were meant for greater things but you just did not have the tools to achieve your destiny? I often feel as though I were the hero from some epic tale, but somehow I have wandered into the wrong story. Have you ever felt as if you were lost in a pathetic farce of some sort?"

"What? You mean, did I think my life would amount to more than a mediocre house, two children, and a nagging wife, only to die in a clearing in a forest that leads to the seventh circle of hell?" Thomas was now lying flat on his back on the ground, his rotund belly heaving up and down as he continued to struggle for breath. "I suppose that has occurred to me. Why?"

"Well, what if there was still a chance to live your dream. Would you seize it?"

Thomas lifted his head off the ground and stared at John. "What are you talking about?"

"Let me start again," John said, leaning forward intently. "What is it that you always wanted to be? Even as a child, how did you truly want your life to turn out?"

"As a child?" Thomas exclaimed. "Children are stupid. Believe me, I know. I have two of my own." Catching John's expression that was not one of amusement, he dropped his head back on the ground. "When I didn't want to be a fairy princess, I wanted to be the cook because he could do all those great tricks with the knives and make delicious veal." Thomas lifted his head again suddenly and looked at John. In a quite serious tone, he said, "Are you going to give me the chance to be a fairy princess, John?"

"I'm serious. How did you imagine your life would turn out?" John persisted.

"All right, all right," Thomas sat up. "I don't know what I wanted," he said reluctantly. His relationship with John was based more on a general disgust with life in general rather than on any actual deep bond. Thomas had thought it an unspoken understanding between them that everything was fair game for humor and mockery and did not like the turn this conversation had taken. "I suppose I just always assumed I would end up great, you know, like our father." Thomas immediately regretted saying it and tried to qualify his statement. "I mean great like everyone thought he was, as great as his legend. I know he wasn't much of a father."

"Not much of a father?" John repeated incredulously. "He was nothing but a bully, a pathetic thug that beat up on those weaker than him. Even his own children, whom he was supposed to protect, were fair game!" John spat angrily.

"Yes, well, as the oldest you got that much worse than the rest of us," Thomas uttered placatingly.

"But I understand what you're saying," John continued in a calmer tone. "We were born to a powerful family, a family of legend; we were meant to be great. So why aren't we?"

Thomas shrugged. "Why don't you ask William and Henry? Apparently they have it figured out. They both returned from the Holy Land as heroes, although William is cocky and Henry is self-righteous. But as you say, it is the reputation that matters, not the person underneath."

"So why are they celebrated heroes and we are forgotten drunks? Didn't we do everything they did exactly, plus more?" John pressed.

"Drunks? Speak for yourself," Thomas protested briefly, but then moved on. "Well, I know William's campaign was marvelously successful. I mean capturing Damietta. How many times have they tried to take that city? And Henry is a tragic hero that fought desperately to save his men and barely made it out alive..." Thomas dropped his head. "I guess I was just along for the ride when I was over there. I did nothing to distinguish myself. I just put in the time and tried to get out alive."

"No, don't do that!" John interrupted. "You are blaming yourself. I spent years blaming myself, but it is not my fault any more than it is yours. Consider what Henry and William had that we did not." Seeing Thomas' blank stare, he answered his own question. "They were given every advantage. As the youngest children, they were spoiled rotten. No expense was spared for them. They were given everything." John moved closer to Thomas and leaned in anxiously. "Ask yourself, would Damietta have been taken if William wasn't there?" Thomas shrugged, so John answered for him. "Of course it would have. You cannot in all earnestness tell me you think William was integral to that victory."

"Ok, so it would have been taken anyway," Thomas conceded. "What's your point?"

"My point is that he is a hero because he was there, because of the tools he was given, not because there is anything special about him. And what of Henry? What would you do if you got into a situation where you were vastly outnumbered and your men were being routed? Exactly, you would fight like a wild dog just to stay alive. And that is exactly what Henry did. He fought out of fear and desperation just to stay alive. Survival made him a hero. He did no differently than you or I would have done in the same situation, yet he is a hero because of his circumstances. And he knows it. That is why he has never been the same since returning."

"All right," Thomas said thoughtfully, "if that's true, then what about Richard? He has a mighty reputation. He is more feared than both Henry and William put together. But Mother does not care for him any better than she does either of us."

"That is precisely my point," John said excitedly as if Thomas had just walked right into his trap. "What makes Richard different from William or Henry?" He answered again without waiting for Thomas' response. "The fact that he was willing to take what he needed to be great. He did not wait for it to be handed to him; he took what he needed and became greater than all of us."

"Yes, but he's a complete ass that nobody wants around. Everyone is scared of him," Thomas countered.

John shook his head. "You are missing the point. "It is the reputation that matters, not the person behind it, remember? It is taking the glory for yourself."

"What are you getting at, John? This doesn't sound like you," Thomas said dubiously.

"That is why I brought you here. I have been talking to some people lately who have been expanding my thinking. They are who I wanted you to meet." He turned to the trees, "You there?" he called into the darkness.

A dark-robed figured stepped from the shadows into the clearing. Thomas immediately climbed into a crouching, guarded position, unsure of what to expect. He watched in amazement as John got to his feet, hurried over to the figure, and kissed it. The two approached Thomas side by side. John extended his arm around the slender form under the light, clinging robe. The thin figure drew back her hood to reveal the finely chiseled features and dark skin of the prettiest Moor woman Thomas had ever seen. "Thomas, this is Anisa," John said proudly from her side.

Thomas realized he was still crouching and stood self-consciously. "Uhhm, well met, milady?" Thomas said with a slight bow, his customary nervousness around beautiful women returning immediately. Anisa nodded slightly in acknowledgment.

"Anisa and her friends are the ones I was telling you about," John clarified unnecessarily.

"Friends?" Thomas glanced about the dark tree line nervously.

"Oh, they're not here," John explained. "I meet Anisa here, and she takes me to them." Anisa gave an almost imperceptible shake of her head toward John.

"What is it?" John turned to her, drawing Thomas' attention to the action.

"My darling, you did not tell me you were bringing anyone with you," Anisa said in a smooth alto voice with just the trace of an accent that made her seem even more exotic. "We are not prepared for visitors," she said in a tone that belied her displeasure.

"What of that? This is my brother; we can trust him," John said, giving an embarrassed sidelong glance at Thomas. Anisa gave a noncommittal grunt and sat down on a stump facing Thomas. Thomas could not help but see this exchange as a displeased mother chastising a child that did not understand what he had done wrong.

"Now, Sir Thomas, would you be good enough to enlighten me as to what your brother has told you of me?" Anisa continued in her mother hen tone.

"I regret to say, my dear brother has seen fit to impart very little of such a lovely subject," Thomas switched into very formal language as he always tended to do when attractive women were present. Not because it impressed them, for he had yet to meet one that was openly impressed by it, but because he thought they should be impressed by it. "Only just now he mentioned that he had been privileged to partake of an expanded understanding regarding what station in life a person is relegated to." She arched an eyebrow slightly at this.

"Is that so? And what has he told you?"

Thomas shrugged. "Very little, I fear. He alluded to a certain possibility that you possessed means whereby one could seize the helm of one's abysmal life and redirect it." He became uncomfortable with her silence and added, "Have I erred in my understanding?"

"That depends," she said slowly.

"On what might that depend, milady?"

"On the reason you have found yourself in this 'abysmal course of life'."

Thomas considered this for a moment. He had never said anything of himself, and for Anisa to direct such an implication toward him was the height of rudeness. On the other hand, if she did have a way to help him and he denied needing any help, well that, too, was rather foolish. Thomas decided to walk a middle ground and neither confirm nor deny what she had said. "Are you inquiring about my humble life, milady? Are you asking for the reason I believe it to be humble or the reason it actually is?" Thomas asked lightly. "Because the two are not always the same thing."

"You are mistaken!" Anisa sat forward with startling vehemence. "There is no difference! Our reality is what we perceive. That is all that matters. That is all that is important. Anything else is merely second-guessing ourselves, and great men do not doubt themselves."

Thomas looked at John for guidance, as he was taken aback by what he felt was a resounding rebuff by this foreign woman. John merely raised his eyebrows, pleased that his brother was confounded by Anisa. Having been the recipient of many such tongue lashings himself, it now instilled a certain sense of pride to see how ruthlessly efficient his woman could be. She was so different from other women. She did not get hung up on ceremony. She was strong and intelligent and refused to be treated otherwise simply because she was a Saracen or a woman.

"What is it you are looking for, and what difference could it make to you who or what I have become?" Thomas was angry and embarrassed at having this strange woman blatantly humiliate him in front of his brother when he was merely trying to hold a pleasant conversation. The fact that she was beautiful and a foreigner only made the insult that much worse.

"It does not make any difference to me," Anisa said primly. "But it ought to be a matter of some importance to you. Now, who made you this way?"

"What way?" Thomas demanded in confused irritation.

"Who made you into this?" She gestured at him in disgust.

"What ar—"

"Who made you a drain on your family?" Anisa cut him off, her demanding tone growing with each question.

"I'm no—"

"Who made you a useless leech on your own people?" she demanded still more loudly.

Thomas was shocked. How dare she speak to him in such a tone! He had a mind to strike the belligerence from her mouth. "I make my own—" Thomas' voice was rising in anger now.

"You were born of a great family. Why are you the least among them?"

"I am—"

"Who made you so soft, so spoiled? You are nothing compared to any of your family. Why?"

"I am better than—" he shouted, but Anisa was already talking over him.

"You are the worst of the Dawnings. You could not even stand up for yourself. You are weak. How is it that you have no strength when all your brothers are powerful warriors?" Thomas was furious and tried a number of times to interrupt, but Anisa plunged on, enraging him further. "You are a rotund, lazy dog! How can you bear to be the one Dawning that is looked at like that?" This cut Thomas very deeply as he had always been acutely aware of his size. Though he made light of it in public, he always felt that was how people actually viewed him: as the adopted Dawning. All his brothers were handsome, strong, and charismatic, and he was ugly and fat.

"Close your mouth, woman!" Thomas' face was red, and he was trembling with rage. "Lest I close it for you."

"You are the reason your life is worthless! You are nothing to the rest of your family."

Thomas lunged forward and crossed Anisa's chin with the back of his hand. She gasped and fell backward. "I could be the greatest Dawning!" he shouted at her. "I am only here because my mother turned me into a simpering servant beholden to her. I should be the greatest Dawning!"

John immediately leapt to Anisa's aid, interposing himself between her and Thomas. "What is wrong with you, Thomas?" he shouted. "Are you all right, Anisa?" he asked, gently helping her to her feet. "I am so sorry about that. I am so sorry," he sounded almost pathetic.

He did not notice the faintest of smiles cross her lips as she raised her hand to feel the trickle of blood that was coming from her broken lip.

CHAPTER FIFTY-THREE

"I think we are done here," Anisa said shortly and disappeared into the trees. Thomas was already descending the hill to the horses again.

John started to go after Thomas and then realized Anisa was leaving and turned to follow her, but she was already out of sight. "Anisa?" he called but was answered only with darkness. Frustrated, he turned to pursue Thomas. "What was that about?" he demanded of Thomas when he had caught up to him. "How dare you strike a woman, and especially Anisa?"

Thomas rounded on John. "She had better learn her place or she will get worse than that!"

John retreated a step, surprised by the venom in Thomas' voice. He raised his hand in submission. "Anisa forgot her place, I will grant you that. But striking her? I did not expect such behavior from you, Thomas. Particularly toward someone who has done so much for me."

"And what exactly has she done for you, John?" Thomas was walking again with John a pace behind. "You are still married; do you remember that?"

"Anisa has reminded me that there is more to life than the miserable existence I am living...more than the life you are living," he added after a brief pause.

"What are you talking about?" Thomas demanded. "You are living in exactly the same manner you have been for years. Simply because some little trollop has shot a little ray of dirty excitement into your life does not mean your situation has improved—"

"Anisa is not a trollop!" John insisted. "And I will not permit you to speak of her that way."

"Then what is she, John?" Thomas stopped his rapid descent long enough to wait for an answer. John became uncomfortable and did not reply. "Uh huh," Thomas said and continued his descent. "Are you telling me you are not intimate with that woman?"

"I would never—" John feigned shock. Then, under Thomas' level gaze, "How did you know?" He gasped.

"I am not blind. I saw that woman, and I know you," Thomas said simply. "Adultery is a big one," Thomas said off-handedly, "even for you."

"You have the audacity to judge me?" John demanded. "Who is the first to pick up the strumpets hanging around the tavern?"

"That is not adultery," John said. "That is only… letting off steam. Those women mean nothing to me, but this," he said, pointing back up the hill, "is clearly something more dangerous."

"It's not adultery," John instinctively protested, but then rethought his approach. "At least, I don't want it to be. I am trying to find a gentle way to let Lindsay down and release her."

"It's not that easy," Thomas replied. He was still walking rapidly and responding in an indifferent tone of someone who had no more than an academic interest in the subject at hand. "You have to get permission from the Church, which you will not get, and even then Lindsay will be a marked woman. Nobody will touch her. You will ruin her life."

"You don't really believe all that, do you? About the Church and their power?"

"Were you married in a church?" Thomas asked simply.

"You know I was," John responded sullenly.

"Then you will have to get the Church's consent for a divorce."

"So you do believe the clergy have power?" John again plied Thomas.

"Of course they have power," Thomas replied. "The people give them the power, and as long as that remains unchanged, the Church has power."

"So you don't believe they get their power from God?"

Thomas' pace unconsciously slowed as he considered this. "I think they are men. Some good and some not."

"So why be bound by their authority? It's your choice."

"Because they have the power. There is no choice."

"But what if there was an alternative that would distribute the power differently, and you would have the ability to overthrow all these silly, antiquated traditions?"

"What are you talking about?"

"I am talking about us being in control. You and me. We could rule Dawning Court and maybe England. We could change all these old, unjust laws. We would be just rulers because we know what it is to be poor and be subject to unjust laws."

"How could we rule England?" Thomas asked, his interest piqued despite himself.

"One step at a time." John saw Thomas' growing excitement and his passion grew. "We start with Dawning Court. Then we expand from there."

"I am not fighting my own family," Thomas said simply, losing interest and continuing to the horses.

"Don't you see, Thomas?" John snatched Thomas' arm and turned him around. "We won't have to fight our own family. I am the rightful heir of Dawning Court. Legally, our mother cannot keep it from me."

"What about the other brothers? If she wants them to stop you, they will."

"I don't think so, but should such events come to pass, you are correct, they may be able to stop me. But they could not possibly stop both of us. Richard is the only cause for worry and if we act quickly, we will be in power before he ever returns from the mainland."

Thomas suddenly smacked his head dramatically. "Richard!"

"Spare no thought for Richard. He is hundreds of leagues away."

Thomas' heart sank as he realized that he had missed the other knights' departure. He briefly considered racing home, throwing together some quick preparations, and pursuing them but shortly discarded the idea. They were setting a brutal pace that he would have had a difficult time keeping up with in his present condition even had he departed with them. Catching them now was unlikely. Plus, he did not know what he would be doing it for. He truly did not want to be with them.

"Thomas?"

"Richard..." he started to explain but realized he would have to admit his negligence if he did, "will not be a concern. What about the others?"

John looked as though he would inquire further but did not. "Edward is not a problem... Even if he were here, he would not be an obstacle to us."

"William and Henry will not step aside for you."

"They are just pups! They could not stop us should we pursue this. Do you see it? We would go from miserable nothings, begging for a handout, to the most powerful land barons in all of England. Think then what possibilities would lie at our feet!"

John watched as the excitement grew in Thomas' eyes. "You see? You see?" he giggled delightedly. "This is what I have been talking about. This is how close we are to greatness, if we are only willing to seize it."

"We would need men," Thomas said, "at least for a show of force if we are to be taken seriously."

"That is where Anisa and her friends come in," John said delicately.

Thomas was instantly suspicious. When it was he and John leading such a movement, he liked the idea. He knew they could control it. But the outsiders made him nervous. "She is a Moor, isn't she?"

"And?"

"And? We are fighting the Moors, John. They are the enemy."

"Only because the Church has made them so. What have the Saracens actually done to us? What reason do we really have to hate them?" John said quickly, asking well-rehearsed questions. "You are not simple-minded enough to be bound by such foolish, manufactured racism are you?"

"What I think about them is not important. What they think about us is. They see us as the enemy."

"That is an unfair generalization. All Saracens do not hate us, just as all English do not hate Saracens."

"John, what possible interest could they have in helping you do this, except to gain a stronghold in England?"

"Help *us*," John corrected him. "They are interested in garnering goodwill among the English. They are trying to find advocates who will help them appeal to the kings of Europe and the Pope. They are just people trying to live, and they are trying to stop the genocide in their home countries."

Thomas stared at him. "You do not honestly believe that?"

"Thomas," John implored him. "This could work. We have everything we need right here. A new and brighter day is about to dawn for us."

Thomas turned and continued walking. "I thought for a moment that you had a real plan. Handing the barony over to the Moors is not my idea of a real plan."

John did not follow him this time. "You are being too cynical, Thomas," he called after him. "Think about it. Don't you want something better for Hannah and Harry? A powerful father they can respect? This is your only chance."

Thomas continued down the hill in silence.

CHAPTER FIFTY-FOUR

"I tell you a house cat is lazier!" A familiar voice rang out not far behind William.

"You've been touched! A sloth is renowned for being the slowest, laziest animal in the world. They have even coined a word to mean exactly that because of the sloth. Maybe you have heard it: 'sloth'," Neil retorted.

"No, no," David was shaking his head. "Slow I will give you, but a sloth will take steps for self-preservation when necessary. You can drop a mouse in front of my wife's cat, and it might swipe a paw at it before it goes back to sleep. And that only if it is feeling playful."

"Self-preservation? A sloth's method of self-preservation is to sit there and hope predators will think it's already dead and leave it alone."

"That's a possum."

"Uh, sloths do it, too," Neil said lamely. "Anyway, I'll wager you drop a dog in front of your wife's cat, and you will witness self-preservation."

"I am not so sure. That cat is so fat and lazy that I fully expect it would simply go back to sleep and assume someone would take care of the dog for it."

"Sir Knights, I beg you, accept my gauntlet and issue a formal challenge in a proper manner," William interjected helpfully. "A knights' duel would settle this matter once and for all."

"William, you decide," David turned to William. "I say cats are the stupidest, laziest animal, and Neil says sloths. Which is it?"

"Well, seeing as how I am an authority on animal husbandry, I am glad you two have chosen to appeal to my wisdom on this all important subject," William said loftily, ignoring their derisive snorts. "The answer to the question you pose as to which is the stupidest, laziest animal is simple," he said slowly and took a deep breath before expounding on it. "The answer is you are both wrong." They stared at him in anticipation of the wisdom he was about to impart to them. "I had this French teacher once that was so—"

David and Neil both groaned loudly, cutting off the rest of his explanation. "I ought to run you through for that," David said, reaching for the well-worn hilt of his sword.

"With that old sword of yours?" Neil laughed. "You better have him get the cut started for you."

"What's wrong with my sword?" David pulled it from its scabbard and inspected the short, thick blade that he had carried since before he was knighted.

"Nothing is wrong with that old, leaf-shaped blade. Particularly if you are fond of antiques."

"This was my father's sword. It is very strong."

"It's so strong because it's an inch thick," Neil laughed.

"It has not failed me yet. Look, it even has this burnished hilt with my family crest on it," he offered, showing the distinct hilt of the weapon that made it easily identifiable from other weapons of that variety. "William, you can appreciate that," he appealed to his friend.

"It is an old weapon, David. They have better techniques for forging stronger blades these days."

"Oh right, I forgot who I'm talking to. Sir 'I-carry-nothing-but-Damascus-steel'."

"What, this?" William brandished the point of his spear.

"That is not wootz steel," Neil offered. "Wootz steel has clearly visible striations from where the metal is folded; this is something else altogether." He moved his horse in to get a closer look at the head of the weapon.

"Damascus steel," David corrected him.

"It was wootz steel before coming to Damascus," Neil dismissed him. "Wootz is made by combining glass with iron ore and charcoal into ingots that are used to forge the blades. These ingots are melted and folded together over and over to make an amazingly strong and sharp metal the likes of which the world has never known. But this, I have never seen this. The blade is perfectly smooth, and the bands in the metal are much closer together than the wootz variety. Almost as if they were cosmetic. This metal has been folded many, many more times than a wootz blade."

William withdrew the head of his spear from their immediate inspection, feeling self-conscious.

"How do you know so much about it?" David asked in irritation.

"My uncle is a blacksmith," Neil shrugged. "I often worked in his shop until I became a full squire. Where did you get that blade?" he asked of William.

"From Jurou," William replied self-consciously.

"And your sword is made of the same metal?" William nodded. "I hope you thanked Jurou," Neil said in amazement. "What you are carrying are not valuable weapons but priceless artifacts that may have taken a smith a lifetime to forge."

William said nothing. He knew they were valuable and had tried to refuse Jurou when he had offered them, but Jurou had insisted. It was on the eve of his first real battle that he had given him the sword. Suddenly, William was not sure he had shown the appropriate gratitude for these weapons that were like an extension of himself now. He could not imagine going into battle with a cheaply made weapon that may break or that was unbalanced . The weapons really were a marvelous advantage and had undoubtedly saved his life more times than he could count.

"You carry Damascus steel then?" David asked Neil, stubbornly refusing to be corrected.

Neil shook his head. "I would carry wootz blades if I could afford them; but alas, I cannot."

"Yes, that Damascus steel does make quality weapons."

"Wootz steel is the best steel man has ever known. But not just anyone can make it."

"I have been all over the Holy Land, and I know where I can buy Damascus steel, but nobody ever mentions wootz."

"Wootz is the English version of the Indian word for steel, where people think it originated from, although it actually probably came from China."

"Well then, aren't we insulting the Chinese by referring to it by an Indian word? We better just call it Damascus steel to avoid that all together."

"Wootz!"

"Damascus!"

"Wootz!"

CHAPTER FIFTY-FIVE

"So it was the fault of the mercenaries?" the voice probed in that calm manner that was beginning to infuriate Richard.

"Well it certainly was not mine."

"Doesn't a good leader recognize the limitations of his men?"

"I was well aware of their limitations, I just did not count on the size of the horde we were up against," Richard said defensively.

"When you saw the Saracens amassing on the opposite hill, why did you not change tactics while there was still time?"

"There was no time. Even if we had retreated at that point, they would have pursued, and things would have been even worse."

"Worse? What could be worse to you than utter, humiliating defeat and degrading captivity?"

"I could be dead," Richard suggested.

"So you would rather be here than be dead?"

Richard thought about it for a moment. "I suppose I would," he grudgingly admitted.

CHAPTER FIFTY-SIX

*T*he training yard was, as yet, empty. The sun had just barely risen, but John had been up for some time. He was very nervous about this challenge. He had watched Richard progress and increase in strength to the point that he now feared that Richard was not only stronger than he was but also a better warrior. He was warmed up and well-practiced by the time Richard came stumbling into the yard, still trying to buckle on his armor. His hair was a mess, and his eyes were still blurry with sleep.

"Ack!" Richard exclaimed, shielding his eyes from the first strong rays of morning light shining over the wall. "This challenge is ridiculous," he grumbled to John. "And it is even more ridiculous that you would choose this unholy hour in which to do it."

"I would have thought you would welcome this opportunity," John said seriously. "You are always insinuating you are superior in strength and skill; now is your chance to prove it once and for all."

"This is laughable," Richard said, forcing a chuckle in one final attempt at levity.

"Good, then it should be quite fun. Choose a weapon."

Richard passed the blunted metal swords and picked up a wooden practice sword. "I trust blood will not be necessary!" he grumbled.

"I'm willing if you are," John said seriously, determined not to back down from any challenge that Richard might issue. Richard only shook his head as he slid his helmet into place and walked to the middle of the yard.

"Shall we say three clean strikes to the head or body?" Richard asked. John nodded and took his place, facing his brother several yards away. *"We don't have to do this,"* Richard said one last time, and John smiled under his visor. He knew that for all his blustering and bravado, his younger brother was scared of him.

"Call it!" John commanded.

Richard sighed and said *"Begin!"* sharply.

John took three quick strides and began raining a series of furious blows down on Richard. Richard blocked and parried as he fell back under the onslaught. He saw at once that this was not a game to John but a serious test of his machismo, as he feared it would be. John feigned to his left and Richard went to block the imaginary strike, only to receive a stunning blow to his other side. *"That's one!"* John shouted before Richard had even realized what had happened.

They walked back to their starting marks and noticed that the yard was no longer empty. The trainees had begun to fall out for their morning exercises, and the spectacle of the two eldest Dawning boys fencing was a sight indeed. Both boys were large and strong and skilled at their craft. They were widely respected and admired by the younger men for this.

John could almost feel the tension rise as people began to gather round. Richard led this round with a sharp thrust which John did not expect. John slashed violently downward to block the strike, but he missed, and his wooden weapon struck the ground. Before he could retract it, Richard stomped down on it with his boot, wrenching it from John's hand. Richard immediately delivered a wringing blow to John's helmet, which sent him staggering back holding the sides of his visor in pain. The frustration John felt at losing this round in such an obvious way was only compounded when Richard gallantly returned his practice sword to him.

They again took their marks. John was determined he would not be made to look the fool again by his younger, more inexperienced brother. John again launched into a series of blows at the outset of the third round, but rather than falling back under them, Richard matched him blow for blow. Richard swung at his legs, which John desperately blocked. Though the shot would not have counted in their contest, it had escalated beyond that now. When his guard was lowered to protect his legs, Richard slipped one gauntleted hand off his weapon and smashed it into John's visor.

John was furious and drew his sword back in both hands to return the blow. Richard quickly stabbed the wooden blade into John's armored torso. "Hit," he said, but John did not stop. He brought his weapon down on Richard's shoulder so hard the wood shattered over his armor.

Richard swore, dropped the wooden sword, and dove at John. John pivoted and shoved him past, but he did not get completely clear, and they both went down in a clash of metal. The struggle continued as they rolled on the ground. At last Richard came up sitting on John's chest. He tore John's helmet from his head and struck him across the face with it.

A deep gash opened up on John's chin, and blood poured from it, drenching his hair and covering his neck. John bounced Richard off of himself. Richard was inflexible because of his armor and unseated relatively easily. They both regained their feet and squared off again. Richard removed his own helmet.

John smashed Richard across the face with a heavy blow. Richard instantly answered with two punches of his own that stunned John. John swung a wild left cross at Richard, which hit him and glanced off with minimal effect.

Richard saw John was teetering and delivered two quick jabs followed by three rapid alternating hooks that left John lying in the dirt, bleeding from his chin, lip, and nose. The effusion of blood made his wounds look far more gruesome than they actually were. Richard stood over the brother he had bested and kicked his leg. "Now you know," he said seriously. "I am better than you, I am stronger than you, Dawning Court is mine for the taking. Don't ever forget that." With that he turned and strode away, leaving his brother bleeding in the dirt of the exercise yard.

CHAPTER FIFTY-SEVEN

*T*hey were riding into an unknown little town together, three young men that had decided on an extemporaneous trip south as was common to them in those giddy, carefree days of youth. The three friends had saddled up on a whim and decided to see where the road would take them. With limited supplies, they jumped from town to town, reveling in the new experiences each new place brought with it.

Riding up beside a dark, middle-aged man with a craggy face and thick, unkempt beard, William leaned over slightly in the saddle, resting his forearm on his thigh. "Pardon me, my good man, but where might three newcomers find rest and refreshment in this town?" he asked jovially.

The stranger looked up at William with no trace of civility; instead something more akin to anger showed clearly on his craggy features. "Next town over," he said.

His tone instantly irritated William. "Well, I can see that thinking is not your forte," William rejoined in the same jovial tone he had been using. "You may not have understood when I said 'this' town that I meant the town that you yourself are standing in."

"I would hate to dirty up your pretty little outfit," the villager threatened. "So why don't you and your friends run along before I have to hurt you." He said the last in a very menacing tone.

"Neil," William looked up at Neil, who was watching quietly, "do you remember Lady Flaverly? The nasty old woman that used to tutor us in French? Doesn't he look just like Lady Flaverly?"

Neil squinted at him, "Mmm...." he stared thoughtfully.

"I mean Lady Flaverly if she had less facial hair," William clarified.

"You know, I can see a resemblance. See if he will put on a bonnet."

William turned back to the red-faced villager and smiled, somewhat embarrassed, "Would you mind terribly? You do so resemble an old friend of ours, and we just want to make sure you are not her."

Neil leaned closer from his saddle and whispered to him, "Lady Flaverly, is that you? Est-ce que c'est vous?" he repeated in French.

The villager was shaking with indignation. "Nobles," he spat, "I wouldn't pay a pound to save the whole lot a ya!" and walked away.

Neil and William erupted into fits of laughter at his retreating back. David, too, forced a weak laugh but obviously had reservations.

"What is the matter with you?" William asked as he struggled for breath between fresh fits of laughter.

"Why was he so angry?" David asked, looking after him.

"Who knows?" William dismissed it while wiping tears from his eyes. "He is probably just upset with the hand life has dealt him. You know, looking like an old French crone as he does. Who wouldn't be upset about that?"

"But didn't you notice how angry he seemed to be when we arrived?" David said thoughtfully. "And every comment he made was about nobles."

"So what's your point?" Neil asked, bringing his laughter under control again.

"I think there might be things transpiring in this town that we are not—and perhaps do not want to be—aware of."

Just then William glanced up and noticed the sign for the tavern hanging above the door. "Well this is a lucky coincidence," he said, dismounting.

"I don't think we should stop here," David said, looking around at the empty street nervously.

"What are you talking about, David?" William asked, exhausted from the long day of riding.

"There is a lot of civil unrest in some parts of our country, and I think we should move on to the next town."

"Why? Because of one angry villager and his bad attitude? Look, I'm hungry and I'm tired and I'm going in here to get some food. If you want to wait with the horses, you are welcome to." Neil also dismounted.

"But didn't you notice? It was like that villager was standing guard. He might be fetching his friends as we speak. It's not worth the risk. Let's move on." David was still in the saddle.

"We are nobles from Dawning Court and will not be discriminated against in some nothing town." William began to lead his horse around the side. "Where is the stable boy? What kind of place is this?"

"It's fine," Neil assured David and followed William around the side. Reluctantly David followed suit.

They tied their horses up and walked into the tavern that was darkening as the sun descended behind the hills. There was already a roaring fire in the large hearth, and the tavern was surprisingly full. There were fifteen men gathered around, focused on a central orator who stood in front of the fire. They were all drinking and making a healthy racket. They did not seem to notice the three enter and approach the bar.

The tavern keeper was dropping off a round of drinks to the assembled crowd. "What'll it be?" he asked, returning to the bar while wiping his hands on his apron. He glanced at the three and then did a double take, his jaw dropping slightly.

This was not a completely uncommon reaction for the three, however, as they had a habit of showing up in the smallest backwater dives in the region, places where no nobleman had *previously set foot.* "What is on the menu?" William asked, taking no notice of the tavern keeper's reaction.

The tavern keeper leaned in. "Are the young lords quite sure they want to eat here?" The three looked at each other confused, while David's apprehension grew.

"Food's not very good, huh?" William asked knowingly, in the same confidential tone the tavern keeper was using.

"No, milord, the food is fine," he fidgeted a moment and then said, "what'll it be?"

William raised an eyebrow but ordered whatever they had available. The bartender produced a game hen, fully prepared, astonishingly quickly. The three tore into it and turned to observe the entertainment that had attracted the attention of the crowd.

They were casually leaning against the bar, eating, when David nudged William in the ribs meaningfully to draw his attention to the speaker at the hearth. "... they take enough of our crops that we can't feed our families," he was saying animatedly, sloshing ale over the side of his cup as he spoke. "And what do they offer in return? Protection from invaders that do not exist!" The group roared their support. "They are bleeding us for taxes to support their lavish, soft lives while we slave day and night. Our women and children get sick and die from not having enough food and warmth." Another angry cheer rose from the assembly. "The nobles of this country are bleeding it to death, one peasant at a time!" William almost spit out his drink. "They take and take and give nothing back. We must do something about this!" There was another cheer.

David leaned over to the other two and whispered, "We need to leave now!"

"I will not!" William said. "I will defend the nobility against this unfounded slander even if no one else will!" He set his drink down purposefully and stood up.

David grabbed his sleeve, "William, no!" he whispered urgently. "They have been drinking, and they are working up to something."

"This is nonsense," William muttered angrily, shrugging off David's restraining hand, "claiming we are just a waste."

"The nobles don't do anything with the tax money?" William raised his voice over the speaker. All attention immediately turned to him. "What about that wall you all live behind? Taxes paid for that," William said, referring to a wall they had a passed a ways back. He hoped he was correct in assuming that it was similar to Dawning Court's walls of defense that protected most of the locals of the area.

"You mean the wall you took our money for and then forced us to build, noble?" The orator by the hearth answered, uttering "noble" as an epithet. William's clothes and speech immediately identified him as a member of the ruling class to all present.

"And the houses many of you live in, those were built with your tax money."

"You call those shanties houses? They don't keep the rain off or the wind out, so what good are they?" The crowd murmured their agreement.

"Then why live in them if they are no better than sleeping outside?" William challenged.

"You come here from your palace and tell us to be grateful for our shacks?" the orator demanded.

"I come here to tell you there are more things afoot than you can imagine in your simple, safe lives. The nobles answer to the king, they keep the country safe, they keep the region safe from neighboring expansionists, and they train to fight to defend your security with their very lives."

"To defend your easy life and your property, you mean. We are not property!" he roared back, and several of the crowd stood up.

"The nobles do God's work." This came from Neil, who was standing beside William to face the crowd. "This man," he said, indicating William, has trained his whole life and will shortly depart to fight in the Holy Land in order to return it to God's chosen people. This edict comes from the Papacy and is God's word. Who among you has made such a pledge or risked so much?"

"God's war? What do we care about God's war when we can't feed our families? Wait a moment. You are not from around here, are you?" the orator said, squinting blurry eyes at the crest that affixed William's cloak about his shoulders. "Who are you?" The crowd was on its feet now and turned to face the young nobles.

"We are servants of Dawning Court," Neil said proudly, puffing out his chest and turning his nose up a bit.

"You insolent prigs are from the north and come here to try to tell us our business?" the orator roared, and as a group they began to advance on the young men. William glanced at Neil for direction, but Neil held his ground insolently as he stared down the rabble.

William turned to consult with David only to find an empty stool where he had been sitting. He quickly scanned the tavern. David was standing in the shadows by the door, silently watching.

The young men were shortly surrounded by the angry tavern clientele, who began jeering and shoving at them.

This was inconceivable that peasants would be laying hands on noblemen with impunity, but it was happening. William tried to call for David, but David quietly slipped out the door. William and Neil had no weapons on them and were afraid to act for fear of escalating the situation.

One of the group shoved William hard from behind. He stumbled forward and roughly fell into the arms of more drunken ruffians.

Neil stepped up to the brute that had shoved William and struck him across the chin. "You have no right to touch a noble, especially a Dawning!" he declared.

The crowd fell all over both of them, holding fast their arms and legs. The orator stepped up and looked closely at William. "Well, I did not realize we had a Dawning on our hands." He made a mock bow. "I am honored."

William was furious. He wanted to fight, he was ready to fight, but he could not understand how the situation had turned so bad so quickly. It seemed like a dream to him that they could be at the mercy of these men that twenty minutes before were not even a part of their lives. Should he fight? He asked himself for the tenth time. Or would that only make things worse? How could they be worse? He glanced at Neil, whom William knew was waiting for his cue from William. But still William hesitated. Confusion and fear clouded his judgment. Were they going to die here? How bad would this really get? "What is this about?" he demanded.

"This is about spoiled, rich children putting their noses where they do not belong," the orator patted both William and Neil down and relieved them of their purses. "We do appreciate you stopping by," he said. "Thank you for donating to the cause. He was hefting the small leather pouches in his hand. "I bet this is more money than the group of us make in a year. Show these fine noblemen the door," he said.

Neil and William were roughly propelled to the door and tossed out into the street with more than a few punches and kicks leveled at their persons.

They landed roughly in the street. They regained their feet, humiliated and angry. Neil was sputtering with fury, "How dare they lay—Who do they think..." William silently dusted his clothes off and assessed the damage done to insure there were no serious physical injuries. He was embarrassed and ashamed that he had not acted when not only his life but that of his friend might have depended on it. And he felt betrayed by David, who had abandoned them altogether. There were so many emotions running through his head that the whole experience felt like a dream.

William silently led Neil, still sputtering angrily, around the side of the tavern to retrieve their horses. David was waiting on his horse when they came around the corner. "Where were you?" Neil demanded. "We needed you!"

"I told you not to go in there! I practically begged you not to," David shot back.

"What difference does that make?" Neil yelled at him. "We are your friends, and we needed you."

"I told you to leave that alone, but you were determined to pick a fight with that drunken rabble. If you want to put your neck on the line for nothing, that's fine, but count me out. You have gotten me into enough scrapes in our time." He directed this last at William, who said nothing. The fog of confusion in his mind was growing all the more thick as he tried to process the events of the last few minutes.

"You despicable coward!" Neil hurled the insult venomously at David. "We could have been killed!"

"Correct, because you repeatedly ignored me. If you had listened to me at any point, you would not have gotten into that situation. If that mob had decided they wanted your blood, what good would it have done for me to die, too?"

"It might have saved your soul," Neil uttered in a deathly quiet voice, and then turned to William as William climbed on his horse. "We are marching straight to the local baron and demanding he burn this town to the ground. Then we are going to find each of them, especially that thief that robbed us, and we are going to have him drawn and quartered."

"Why? Because you started a fight with them?" David chided.

"You shut your mouth!" Neil screamed, stabbing a finger at David. "You have no right to speak about this! Just shut your mouth! Now which way to the castle?" He was scanning the countryside in the fading light.

William settled into his saddle. "Let's forget about it," he said distractedly. "I just want to go home."

"You're right, let's bring back our own knights and do it ourselves," Neil agreed, misinterpreting William's intent. "That will be much more satisfying."

William shook his head and pointed his horse's face down the road. "I just want to forget this whole thing ever happened," he said.

"You cannot let this stand!" Neil insisted vehemently. "This sort of behavior leads to anarchy and revolution. We must respond."

"I said I just want to forget it ever happened," William repeated.

"Well, I will not forget this," Neil rode out ahead of them in fury. "I will not forget. This cannot stand." William followed him but did not catch up to him for a long while. He thought they both needed some time to think. He did, however, stay ahead of David as he could not face him right then. He was angry at David's betrayal. He had always felt David was his closer friend, but here, when it mattered the most, Neil had proved himself more valiant than David. William would have never imagined this turn of events, but here it was. It seemed so incongruous with the people he thought he knew. But he felt a new appreciation and respect for Neil that he had not previously known.

Eventually William caught up to Neil and awkwardly thanked him for coming to his defense. William was ashamed of himself for his failure to act and tried to explain away his hesitation as shock. He hoped it did not look as much like cowardice as he feared.

Neither of them spoke to David for the remainder of the trip. When they did resume interaction with him weeks later, this incident was never discussed. It was too sore a subject for the suddenly fragile friendship to weather.

CHAPTER FIFTY-EIGHT

"Henry, help me!" Leah screamed at him through the clash of metal and the screams of men. How had she gotten here? Henry started to push through the crowded battlefield toward her when from the other direction he heard another scream. He turned to see Mary there, screaming for him to help her. He hesitated. Before him Richard lay prostrate. He knew he needed to get to him quickly or all would be lost, but how could he sacrifice the best person he had ever known? And what of Mary? Could he give up the only woman who had ever accepted him for one who had openly rejected him on two occasions?

The man in white returned. He saw now that it was white armor that shone in the sun like an aura of light. He swooped in and grabbed Leah around the waist and spirited her away. He still did not show his face, but Henry felt he knew better than ever who this man was.

The battle raged on, and Henry had to make his decision. He turned to chase after Leah as she reached her arms back toward him over the shoulders of her captor, who was still running. All at once a grey cast came over her form, cracks appeared on her vivid countenance, and she collapsed into dust.

Henry stopped and spun back to Mary to rescue her, but as he neared her young, voluptuous form, it turned dark and rotten. Her skin pulled tight like dried out leather, and her arms that were open in desperation seemed to now be determined to hold him and squeeze the life from him.

Henry remembered his duty now that these two were out of the way. Richard's form was still lying helmetless in his blood-red armor, clutching a sword at his chest as if he were on his funeral bier. He may no longer be alive, but this is what Henry was here for.

He fought his way through the melee to his brother's body, but when he got there he looked down on the form only to see Patrick, his young lieutenant's body lying there, his eyes wide open and staring at Henry.

Henry sat bolt upright in cold sweat, his breathing very rapid. He looked around in the dark, and it took him several moments to realize where he was. He slowly lay back on his bed roll as his breathing slowed. He rubbed the back of one trembling hand over his eyes. The dreams were getting more vivid as they approached Damascus. Was he going mad, or did these dreams mean something? Leah turning to dust was easy: he had lost her. The man in white had to be William, but he could never see his face. What could that mean? Perhaps that reflected his understanding that he did not know William, or at least did not know what would make Leah willing to forgo every other opportunity at a good match for his sake.

What about Mary? Did her rotting visage represent some corruption deep down? Or did his turning toward Leah first make him too late to save her, and he lost both of them? And what of Richard's body? That could be only a representation of what he expected they would find on this quest, the dead body of his brother. Patrick's face, of course, could simply be his guilt over that boy's death. Patrick's mother, he realized, was still unaware of his demise. She could have guessed by now, but he had sworn to protect the boy. The spot Henry lay on at that moment was not half a day's ride from the small village where he had taken Patrick into his army. He could... Henry cringed at the thought. He shied away from having to dredge up that memory again–from having to face the grief-stricken mother. But perhaps this would put the shade of Patrick away, that it would no longer haunt his dreams.

Henry lay until just before dawn, turning these thoughts over in his mind, when at last he jumped up and went and shook William. William was half on his feet, reaching for his spear before his eyes were even fully open. "What is it? What's the problem?"

"Nothing, everything is fine," Henry whispered quickly, trying to calm him down. "Only I need you to come with me. There is something I have to do."

William looked around in confusion. "I know what you have to do: rescue Richard. We are already doing that."

"No, something else. Look, I can't explain now, but it is not far from here. We will catch up to the others before nightfall if we hurry. Will you ride with me? I have already saddled your horse."

William looked at his brother suspiciously for a moment, but deciding he looked more confused than sinister, he shrugged and began packing his bedroll in the dark.

CHAPTER FIFTY-NINE

"This is something I have to do," Henry said impatiently to William as he reined his horse in by the small cottage that was set by itself in the middle of a large track on overgrown fields.

"Well, that is fine," William said, squinting up at the late afternoon sun. "But this was a bit more out of the way then you indicated. If we are going to rejoin the others tonight, you had best hurry."

"Then we will catch them tomorrow," Henry snapped.

"Since both Dawning men have abandoned this fool's errand of a rescue, I would not advise being gone long. It will not take long for the men to get nervous."

"Just keep an eye out."

"An eye out for whom?"

"Anyone bad!" Henry's patience was getting shorter by the moment as he contemplated the task at hand.

"Does that count you, too? Cause in this mood, I would say that you are bad."

Henry ignored him and stepped off the road to knock on the door of the cottage. It was some moments before the door was opened by a very elderly woman. She looked Henry up and down. As she recognized him and understood the errand he was must be on, she almost fainted.

Henry stepped forward quickly to support her. "You have come to tell me you did not protect my boy as you promised you would," she said to him as he eased her down on one of the few chairs in the shabby one-room cottage. "You took Patrick from me." There was no accusation in her voice; it was merely a statement. She did not look at Henry as she said this.

Henry hung his head. "I did all I could," he said feebly. "I tried to protect him, but we were overrun. Everyone was killed that day. No one survived."

"And yet here you stand," she said simply, still not looking at him.

Her words stung Henry very badly as this same thought had sprung into his mind a thousand times before.

"He fought bravely–Patrick, I mean. He never despaired, never shied away from onerous duties. He was a remarkable soldier."

"So remarkable that you pledged to protect him. You are a knight, are you not?" Henry nodded. "Is not your oath your bond?" Again Henry nodded. "Then how can it be that you stand here while my Patrick is moldering in the ground?" She still spoke calmly and without anger, but that made her words all the more piercing. "Should not my last son have been safe from all danger until you yourself were dead and unable to protect him any longer?"

There was a long silence before Henry drew out a small pouch of coins. "I did all I could for your son, but that battle was... beyond my control. I recognize his loss is going to be a hardship to you both emotionally and temporally. There is nothing I can do for the first, but I can help with the second." He held out the pouch to her. "I wish to do what I can to ameliorate some of the difficulty Patrick's absence will cause." She did not look at him, nor did she take the offered coins. "I am sorry," Henry said as he turned to leave the cottage. If there was any way I could trade places with your son, I would do so, but I cannot, so I do what I am able to do." He dropped the bag of coins on the table as he exited the cottage, more determined than ever to free himself from this miserable life. The fear, the pain, the death, and then the aftermath—the eternal aftermath that would never leave him be.

Henry left the cottage. William was still sitting astride his horse but wore a knowing expression on his face. "You all right?" He asked as Henry mounted in silence.

"I hate this," Henry muttered darkly.

"Hate what?"

This life of chivalry and war. This is not what I want out of my life. Not at all."

CHAPTER SIXTY

"You shouldn't have been there in the first place!" David said angrily. "I told you that going in. Do you remember that?" William said nothing. The truth was William did not remember that. "Not only did you not listen to me but you went in and antagonized a bunch of drunken ruffians. Should I then have had to die with you?"

William had brought up the incident to David on this long ride in an effort to resolve it within himself, and things had quickly declined. It was one big blemish that William could not understand in a long history of unwavering friendship, but David had never apologized, nor had they ever spoken of it after the fact. It was a source of tension that William did not particularly want to dredge up, but he had dredged it up and here they were.

"I was just being who I was, I suppose. You, on the other hand, were being someone I do not recognize. Perhaps if you warn me of such transformations in the future, I can make my decisions based on that."

"Just being yourself?" David demanded. "Do you know how much trouble came down on my head simply because of my association with you while you were 'being yourself'? There was a very real possibility those men could have strung you up. I was not going to go swing beside you for no good reason. If you chose to throw your life away, did that mean I had to follow?" The last was not a question, but William chose to answer it anyway.

"Yes, actually, that was part of your pledg—"

"If the roles were reversed and I was inciting a row for no good reason with people that were going to kill me, you cannot, in earnest, tell me you would not have done the same."

"In earnest?" William was incredulous. "Can there truly be any question that I would have remained by your side until the bitter end? For me, there would have been no option. You were my friend, and that was enough." William was surprised by David's insinuation, as one of William's youthful characteristics had been a fierce loyalty to his friends. He would often make enemies of those he felt had wronged his friends, even when those that were wronged did not feel strongly enough to do the same. He was quick to anger and slow to forgive. Once an enemy, always an enemy. "But I understand that hero charade is not for everyone." William no longer became so impassioned over every slight, but he recognized that that had been part of his character while he was growing up and was very surprised that David did not seem to remember that detail. Perhaps it was a memory of convenience. "Neil did not hesitate. Neil, whose bond of friendship has been up and down since we were very young, did not hesitate. And yet you, my oldest friend, not only had to think but judged that my life was not worth defending."

"You're questioning my loyalty? After all we have been through?"

"That is what so disturbs me about this," William was saying in a slightly antagonistic tone. Though he was speaking his real feelings, he could not seem to let them out in a vulnerable, sympathetic way. "I cannot reconcile this behavior in our history. I broached the subject in the hope of making peace with it. Instead I find myself doubting your loyalty on every occasion in which we rode into danger. I had always assumed I had a trusted companion by my side. It seems that I actually had no one watching my back at all. Now I understand that your highest priority was protecting your own skin."

"How dare you accuse me of cowardice?" David yelled. "You of all people, who have so frequently put others in the path of danger on a whim and then fled when you were finally directly challenged because of your actions. You left us all behind. Now you accuse me of not being loyal to you. I was the only one who stuck by you through it all; nobody else was willing to take that place. In fact, I was often told that you were going to get us both killed, and I thought on that day you were about to prove that prophetic."

"It causes me serious misgivings about our current situation," William said as if he had not heard David's protestations. "I believe that I will have you reassigned to a different detail, something that will keep you out of harm's way, where you will not find it necessary to make those sorts of decisions regarding whose skin to save first."

"You're what? Because of something that happened when we were children? That was a lifetime ago."

"That's right, we were children, making decisions that would shape the men we would become. You have never once expressed any regret over what happened. To the contrary, you have defended your position with much passion. This quest is too dangerous and too important to take any chances."

"I come out here to help rescue your brother, and you treat me like this?"

"For all I know you deem this to be an unworthy suicide mission also and are not to be depended on." William turned his mount.

"William," David called in a pleading tone. William turned his head to the side to indicate that he was listening. "What about Neil?"

"Neil stays with me," William declared firmly. "I need people I can count on, and whatever Neil's faults, he has proven his loyalty."

"But removing me from your detail? It's a disgrace, and he will know it as such."

"That's where your thoughts lie? Your reputation? Not our friendship or your personal worthiness but your reputation?"

"You made the decision about our friendship. I am trying to salvage the only thing I can."

"Pity you were not as concerned with such things all those years ago. It is said that one sees the essence of a person when times are at their worst. Not in the fat times but in the lean times does a man reveal himself for what he truly is. I am very sorry for what you are revealing." William rode away. The truth was he was not overly concerned that David would have failed in his responsibility as part of his personal detachment; but in his anger he knew it was an affront to David that would wound him deeply and would be a small recompense for the wound that David had forced him to bear all these years. And objectively, no one could fault this move given the facts. Nevertheless, William felt in his heart that David would not abandon him here.

What David had said about leading them into trouble was basically true. Though often more of a consequence of his outspoken youthful disdain for virtually everyone and everything than any conscious desire to seek out trouble, William was the impetus for far more sticky situations than mild-mannered David would have, of his own accord, found his way into.

Even now, as William's anger cooled, he suspected David's behavior on that fateful occasion may have been an attempt to teach William a lesson about his own brash behavior. It may have been an action more attributable to his youthful frustration over his friend's repeated poor choices than out of any real maliciousness on David's part. The burden of William's friendship was a responsibility that not too many people could or would carry for long. William steeled himself against such thoughts.

CHAPTER SIXTY-ONE

"Anthony, please come with me," William said as he walked by his distant cousin who was casually conversing with a group of soldiers. Surprised by the request, Anthony hastened to follow. Anthony was William's grandfather's sister's husband's niece's son, and though it was a serious breach of etiquette from a young nobleman who was supposed to have the genealogy of every duke and earl in the country memorized, William never knew what exactly that made him in relation to Anthony, so he always just called him his cousin, and Anthony did not seem to mind. To William this was one more sign he was never meant for court life.

He did not know Anthony very well as his father was Sicilian and Anthony had grown up in the kingdom of Sicily. But William knew him to be dependable, if not the most skilled cavalier, and he knew Anthony had come running when he heard Richard was in trouble. That was worth a lot to William at the moment when loyalty was at a premium. And for reasons that William did not understand, Anthony had always looked up to the Dawning boys despite his own siblings being more financially successful and therefore more secure and socially refined. But there was something about the Dawnings that intrigued Anthony.

When they were out of earshot of the others, William turned to Anthony and inspected him to be sure he was making the right decision. His armor was burnished to a high shine. He was an average build, slightly taller than William himself if not so heavily muscled, with brown eyes and brown hair that had a slight curl to it but laid flat atop his head and was cut straight at the bangs. His round face gave him a gentle boyish appearance. William instinctively wanted to ask him what he was doing here, but instead said, "Anthony, I would like for you to be part of my personal detail for the remainder of our voyage."

"Uh, yes, Sir William," Anthony said, still unsure of what was happening. "But I thought your detail was already complete."

"Bah, is anything ever complete?" William said dismissively. "Henry was worried about the command structure of the guards, so I divided them into two separate groups and put David over one of those..."

"Sir Henry was worried about the command?" Anthony asked, surprised. "Wasn't it he who created it?"

"Or maybe not," William waved a hand in the air. "I cannot keep up with everything I say. Anyway, I have an opening to fill, and I need someone I can trust to fill it. I would like to offer that place to you."

"It would be my honor," Anthony saluted with a fist over his heart and a slight, stiff bow. William suppressed his smile, knowing this to be a sincere gesture of respect from Anthony. Anthony was older and a knight but had insisted since their outset on treating William as a member of his own class with all due formalities.

"Thank you, Sir Anthony." William put a hand on his shoulder warmly. "I cannot express how comforted I feel to have you by my side. There is one thing you should be aware of before accepting my offer, however. This is one of the most dangerous positions on this quest. Perhaps you have family considerations..."

"Family considerations?"

"A wife, children, a family?"

"Oh, no sir. I do not have a wife."

"Really? No wife?" William could not hide his surprise at this. Besides being slightly older than the typical marrying age,

Anthony seemed content in life. William assumed he must be settled domestically.

"No, but I hope to correct that shortly," he said and flushed at the admission.

"Anthony," William said in a mock serious tone. "Are you betrothed?" Anthony flushed more still.

"Not exactly," he shrugged. "My father is trying to arrange a situation as we speak. Thus I was in the area when I heard of the trouble with Richard. But Sir William," he confided, "she is the most beautiful woman I have ever seen. I cannot believe she is not yet wed."

"Well, there's more to a lady than a beautiful face," William cautioned. Then feeling he was sounding too silly, he added, "There is the size of her dowry as well."

"Oh I know, but she is sweet and clever, too. I mean I have only met with her on three occasions, but she is all I can think about. I feel like I am floating on a cloud all the time." Anthony sighed, clearly enamored with thoughts of his new love.

William laughed. "Why, Sir Anthony, I do believe you are in love," he teased. Anthony did not seem to notice; he just stood there with a silly grin on his face, staring off into space.

"Sir Anthony, why don't I get someone else for this post? You clearly have much to live for."

This snapped Anthony out of his dreamy state. "What? No! I will not dishonor you."

William put his hands on Anthony's shoulders and looked him in the eye. "I know, but you are clearly very distracted, as well you should be. It sounds as though you have met a wonderful girl. But we simply cannot afford any mistakes."

William started to walk away, but Anthony held his arm. "My duty comes first. Give me a chance. I will not let you down." There was great earnestness in his eyes. He seemed to William so childlike, so humble.

"Okay Anthony, okay." William patted his arm "I believe you, and I offer my thanks."

William walked away, hoping he had made the right decision. He trusted Anthony, but he was having visions of telling a sobbing young lady and her parents that this young man had been killed in combat. Still, there was nothing to be done about it now without insulting Anthony's honor. How curious, William thought, was this honor business. If he were to move Anthony to a safer post, his honor would be offended, and he may never forgive William even though William would have been protecting his life. Yet, it was perceived that he was doing Anthony some great favor by putting him out front where the danger would be greatest. Sometimes things ended up quite backwards in this world, William thought, quite backwards indeed.

CHAPTER SIXTY-TWO

"Let me cut his throat!" Khalid growled, pulling a long, curved dagger from the folds of his robe.

Anisa gingerly touched the wound on her lip that Thomas had given her in his rage. "No," she snapped.

"He is unarmed! He is a fool! I could destroy him before he even knows what happened."

"And what of John, you fool? Will you kill him as well?" She glared at Khalid, expecting him to be more astute rather than emotional. "You would have to, and then what? Or will you just explain to him that his brother dared to lay hands on your lover and you could not take it?" Khalid gritted his teeth but replaced his weapon. "So much better, then, to drive a wedge between John and the last of his brothers that might turn him from this path."

"Wedge? What wedge?"

"Don't you see? Thomas Dawning has just struck the woman John is in love with. He will necessarily protect me and tacitly our plans from further assault from his brother. That means he will continue to cleave to us while withdrawing from the last brother still at Dawning Court."

Khalid gave a noncommittal grunt.

"Besides, a Dawning even more proud, passionate, and easily manipulated than John could be very useful to us."

"Useful?" Khalid snorted. "How so?"

"Thomas will be the last living Dawning male when Amir is through with the others. If John becomes a problem, then we will have a backup." Anisa was still fingering the split in her lip thoughtfully as she looked into the trees after them.

"What do you have in mind?"

"Perhaps I need to pay Thomas a visit and be sure his 'heart' is in the right place should we need him."

CHAPTER SIXTY-THREE

"Do you believe in God, Richard?" the voice asked. "No," he said at last. "At least, not the God that was taught to me since infancy. I don't believe all that."

"Yet had you adhered to those teachings, you would not sit where you sit today."

"Ignorance is bliss, is that it? I could be happy and deceived or discerning and suffer the consequences?" Richard challenged. "There is no God... unless... unless you're God." There was no response. "But I believe you are part of me," Richard continued. "So either you are part of me and there is no God as I have suggested, or you are God *and* a part of me. Maybe that is what God is; maybe God is simply the good inside all of us, and we as humans call that collective good 'God'."

"You lean too much to your own reason, Richard. There is nothing so flawed or prone to fallacy as the reasoning of man."

"But if there is a God, surely the reasoning I have applied, the reasoning you say is so fallible, is his creation. What else, if not the ability to reason, separates man from the beasts?"

"Every man is given his agency and, necessarily, his reason. If a man could not reason, what good would his agency be? How could he reason through problems and make correct decisions? But just as that reason can point him toward the light, it can be manipulated to justify whatever he wants to believe. Your philosophy can be bent, twisted, and manipulated to justify any idea that may appeal to you, just as you have done here. Where is it written that God's commands must match what people want to believe in their hearts? Is not that completely backward?"

"But if I don't feel it in my heart, how can I trust anything save my reason?" Richard protested.

"Because you *can* feel it in your heart, but that does not mean that you cannot feel incorrect things as well. Consider this: How do you know there is no God?" Richard did not immediately respond. "With all you have been taught concerning the danger of rejecting God as he has been shown to you, you must be certain. You must feel it somewhere deeper than reason that you are correct?"

"I do."

"Then what is it?"

Richard was silent for a long time before he finally responded. "When I was little and my father was routinely pummeling John, I came to know fear. I remember seeing the insane look in my father's eyes. All reason and love was absent; he was totally out of control. These fisticuffs were a near nightly occurrence at their worst, and the family lived in fear. We were overjoyed when Father would leave on a crusade or diplomatic mission because for a time we would have peace." Richard trailed off in reflection. "I was so scared for my brother. I could see the toll it was taking on him, and I was afraid Father would kill him. But I was mostly afraid for myself. I was afraid that I would be next. Countless nights I fled the scene of the brutal beatings for the safety of my chamber, and with all the earnestness of a child's soul, I would pray that the violence would end. I asked God to take away the beatings, the violence, and the fear; and God did not answer my prayers. The prayers of an innocent little boy pleading for help went unheard. That's when I knew I was on my own. That's when I knew my only defense was to be stronger, faster, braver than my father. I would never be a victim, and all who came after me would regret it dearly, be it family or foe."

"Fear and faith cannot mutually exist, Richard. One will always drive out the other. You see how that fear grew in your heart until it replaced your faith?"

"It was not the fear that replaced my faith. It is the fact that my faithful prayers were not answered even in my time of greatest need."

"But wasn't your prayer answered?"

"No, it wasn't."

"What became of your father?"

"A few years later he took ill from the fever and was bedridden for a time before finally accommodating us all by dying. It was the first good thing he ever did for his family," Richard said flatly in a voice devoid of emotion.

"Didn't that solve your problem?"

"His death? Are you saying that is how a little boy's prayers are answered? By killing a family member years later? I wish I had known that before; I could have saved myself a lot of trouble with the campaigns," he finished sarcastically.

"God would not take away your father's agency, so he could not make him stop what he was doing; but he would not allow him to continue hurting an innocent, faithful child. What options were left?"

"So he killed him?" Richard asked incredulously.

"No, the fever killed your father. But perhaps he was not granted the protection that might have been granted to a more faithful man."

"Perhaps I was not, either," Richard said softly to himself. He laid his head back against the wall. He suddenly did not feel like talking anymore.

"While horrible, Richard, those experiences by your own admission shaped the man who sits here today. They are inseparable. The one thing you seem to value about yourself is your prowess as a warrior. You would not be that if not for your father. It was his physical characteristics that grant you the strength you have. It was his passion that made him a devastating force of war, which you inherited in your discipline and relentless pursuit of grandeur; and it was that passion that drove him to the abuses you have detailed and that motivated you to surpass all others in strength. You cannot have one without the other."

Richard made no reply.

CHAPTER SIXTY-FOUR

"Are you sure you understand?" Henry asked David and Spencer again. They repeated the instructions yet again. "Then go with God, gentleman." They both saluted him and wheeled their horses to the north. "There is not much time," Henry repeated. "We will buy you all the time we can, but you must ride swiftly."

David and Spencer led thirty-four of the knights to the east, leaving only Henry, William, the knights of the chest, and their small personal detachments. As they prepared to make camp several hours earlier than usual, it was a lonely feeling. Henry had not realized the security that came in being in the company of so many trained warriors dedicated to the cause. They were only fourteen strong now, and there were not many ways to divide up the duties. They were all kept busy setting up tents, tending to the mounts, cooking, or taking watch.

Though he kept his reservations to himself, Henry could not ignore the many potential flaws in this daring plan of William's. It was not a good plan. There was too much that could go wrong, too many things unaccounted for; and he knew he was completely at the mercy of David and Spencer. If they made a mistake, got lost, or even were waylaid, he would not know until it was too late. And at that point it would be too late for them all.

CHAPTER SIXTY-FIVE

"*There is no easy way to say this, John, so I am just going to come right out and say it.*" Martha was sitting with her recently returned son in the library. He would not meet her eyes as she spoke. "I have grave concerns about the peasant girl, Lindsay. Here you are on the very eve of your assumption to the baron's seat, and you are neglecting all of your duties at Dawning Court in order to fraternize with this girl."

"Why should it matter who I choose to associate with?" John grumbled. "You were a peasant girl when father found you."

"Sit down, John." Martha motioned him into a seat opposite her own. "I know my words now must seem the height of hypocrisy, but you must understand that we live in a very different England now than your father and I did. The responsibilities that weigh on your shoulders as baron are very great. Your father made his greatness. Therefore, there was no expectation on him in the beginning. He took a small, relatively unknown–albeit strong–barony and turned it into one of the strongest in England. But had he chosen to remain in obscurity, no one would have really thought much of it. But now he has raised a standard that you regrettably must carry."

"Regrettably? Why regrettably? Because I am not as good as my father?" John was suddenly heated. "Mother, do you think I do not know that? Do you think I do not feel my *unworthiness—the disappointment I bring on my family? Is there anyone that feels that more acutely than I do?"*

Martha raised her hand to calm him. "You misunderstand me. Regrettable because it is not fair to you. Regrettable because the obligations of the position do not allow you freedom. There are things that you are required to do for the office that would not matter so much if you were in the place of one of your younger brothers." John looked at her but said nothing. "John," she said firmly. "The baron of Dawning Court may not marry a villein. Our barony is in trouble. The wolves are at the gate. A wise political marriage may be the only thing that saves us at this point."

"Mother I—" John started and stopped, again looking at the floor.

"What is it, John?" Martha asked, a slight edge in her voice. But John did not answer. "Is this more about that peasant girl? Because I will not hear any more of that. Once you have been in the Baron's seat for a short while, you will understand the shadows that are looming over us."

"Lindsay! Her name is Lindsay," John barked. An awkward silence followed.

"John, do you know the reason I did not call you home from the Crusades when your father passed but rather chose to act as regent while you served out your time in the Holy Land? Do you suppose that I enjoy this duty?"

"No, I suppose not," John answered reluctantly.

"Then why not call you home immediately to assume your position?"

John shrugged. "I suppose you thought I was too young."

"That's partially correct. I wanted you to learn to be a warrior—a leader while over there—and return to me a man ready to assume power. Of course many rulers have assumed power younger than you, but these are turbulent times, and a power void, or even the perception of a void due to a weak leader, in the middle of this nationwide struggle of barons would be too much temptation. It would virtually guarantee we went to war. But now you have been returned for over a year and have never once made any mention of becoming baron."

"I uh, well," John stumbled over his words as he had not expected his Mother to be so direct.

"This role is not for me," Martha told him. "I was never meant to sit in this place and do not relish remaining here one moment longer than I must. You have returned, and you are ready to take your rightful place as baron."

"I—but—" John stammered.

"I will help you, of course," she reassured him. "I will not leave you without support."

"But I am not ready."

"Not ready?"

"I just don't yet feel ready to take over the affairs of Dawning Court."

"Do you still doubt yourself? Didn't you command men in the Holy Land?"

John hesitated. "I lead some men, but I never achieved any position of real power... I am not my father."

"Not your father?" Martha asked, confused.

"He was a general of his own army, leading his own crusades by the time he was my age."

"John, no one expects you to be your father—"

"I—" he interrupted her but stopped. "I am just not ready to take over," he said softly, shaking his head.

Martha gave him a long, searching look, which he did not raise his eyes to meet. "Perhaps you are not ready," she said at last. "Take what time you need to be comfortable with this great responsibility. But remember, John, no one ever knows for sure how they will bear up under the mantle of leadership until they wear it."

"I am sorry, Mother. I know I continue to disappoint you and fathe—you."

"That I am ready to be done with this, it is true. But you would disappoint me far more if you took your inheritance before you were ready and squandered it. Nevertheless, I would urge you in the strongest possible terms to begin preparing to *become Baron Dawning. That means you must behave accordingly. It does you no good to fraternize with peasant women. Please conduct yourself in a manner befitting the heir of one of the most powerful baronies in all of England."*

John only nodded, still unable to meet her gaze.

CHAPTER SIXTY-SIX

"We best ask someone," William said.
"Yes, good idea," Henry agreed sarcastically. "Pardon me, can you tell me where the Moors who have kidnapped our brother are requiring we meet them in order to pay the ransom to get him back?"

William stared at him. "Perhaps I had better do the talking." They were riding through a small Moor Village within a couple of days' journey from their meeting spot.

"I must concur with your brother, Sir Henry," Anthony put in. "It is a local map. Why don't we ask the locals?"

"I don't even know what dialect they speak in such a place. It may be completely incomprehensible to me."

"Why would you not be able to speak it? You speak Arabic," Roland pointed out.

"I speak classical Arabic, the language spoken in the Qur'an, and I have studied a few other dialects. But dialectal Arabic is the result of the language merging with other languages over time. This practice will sometimes make one dialect virtually incomprehensible to someone just a few leagues down the road."

"Perhaps you should just try," Anthony suggested "We do not want to make a mistake with something of this import."

"Fine." Henry drew his horse up beside an elderly Saracen woman who, unlike everyone else, did not flee at the sight of the armed knights. In fact, she did not seem to notice them at all. "Pardon me. Would you tell us where these crossroads are that are indicated on this map?" Henry addressed her in perfect erudite Arabic. She chattered at him but did not divert from her destination. Henry said a few more lines to her and she responded, but not in a conversational manner.

"You see?" he said to his companions. "I told you I could not understand this crazy dialect. I cannot even get her to look at that map."

"Give me that," William said in disgust and hopped off his horse. He walked alongside the elderly lady and began to speak to her. Henry translated for those who did not understand.

"He is speaking about the weather. She commented that it is still hot. He offered to help her with her bundle, which of course she refused. He is saying something about his brother, meeting or finding his brother." William was holding the map in front of her. Henry furrowed his brow as the woman began gesturing and pointing.

"Well?" Roland prodded. "What are they saying?"

"I don't know," Henry admitted, his brow still furrowed.

A few minutes later William returned to his mount and handed the map back to Henry. "Well, what did she say?" they asked.

"She said we are on the wrong road. There is a parallel road over those hills that will take us to this place. She also invoked Allah's blessing on us if we are here only to find our brother. I won't tell you what she said if we are crusaders," William grinned.

"How did you learn that?" Henry asked in a tone that was almost a challenge. "This dialect, I mean? I have made a study of this language. I have read every book I could find in Arabic, and I cannot understand it all. How could it be that you know this dialect and I don't?"

"We must have ridden through these parts at some point in the past, and I picked it up," William shrugged.

"You don't just pick up Arabic," Henry insisted.

"It seems I did," William grinned and rode ahead to converse with Neil.

"That is unbelievable!" Henry fumed.

"What is the problem?" Roland asked.

"Yes," Anthony added. "It seems quite fortuitous that he was able to get the information we needed."

"You do not understand!" Henry was still angry. "William is a bungler. He has never applied himself to anything. He has run rampant through his life and destroyed everything he touches. Yet somehow everything comes easily to him. I have to work for everything I have, my knowledge, my family, my skills, and it is all just dropped into his lap!"

"Don't you think you're being a bit severe?" Roland suggested hesitantly.

"No, I do not! I have lived with this my whole life. He appreciates nothing he has. I have worked for everything. I took responsibility for my campaign through the Holy Land. When my leaders fell, I shouldered the burden and led my troops to accomplish what had to be done. Now my name is forever associated with a humiliating, disgraceful defeat. William floats through in the infantry of all places and is considered a hero! I do everything I can to protect my family; he abandons us for years, and still it is him that my family loves best. I have to struggle to find and keep a worthwhile woman; he has women throwing their lives away in the hope that they might catch a glimpse of him again one day." Henry was gritting his teeth.

Roland and Anthony exchanged uncomfortable glances. "What is it that you want, Henry? Would you prefer your brother did not have good fortune?"

"No, it would be wrong for me to wish ill upon my brother. I only want him to feel the weight of the responsibility that is on his shoulders. I carry it with me every day of my life, and he seems oblivious to the pressures that are on him."

Neither Anthony nor Roland spoke, unsure of what to say to this.

"Brother, may I have a word with you?" William called suddenly, dropping back to join them.

"Of course," Henry said neutrally and followed William's horse a little way off the road, out of earshot of the others.

"I did not want to say anything that might alarm the others, but the old woman back there said something else," William told him, squinting at the horizon. "She said this place is right near the foot of Mount Alamut, that mountain in the distance," he said pointing.

"Alamut? Alamut?" Henry repeated, while William waited for him to remember something he was sure his brother would know. "The Nizari!" Henry snapped. "Mount Alamut is the fortress location of the mythical group of the Nizari."

"She said something about these Nizari," William replied. "I offered her a handkerchief, but it turns out she was not sneezing."

"Very funny, brother. Our problems just got a lot bigger than I thought."

"Should we tell the others?" William asked dubiously.

"I think we need to bring the others in on this at once." Henry declared. "But only Roland, Niel, and Anthony," he said. "We don't need any panicky idiots doing something unpredictable right now."

They called the others to them, and Henry took over. "We have reason to believe that this meeting place is at the foot of that mountain," he pointed, "Mount Alamut. The mountain fortress of the Nizari," he explained. He was rewarded with blank stares. "Surely you know the Nizari?"

"You mean those Moors that use all those crazy herbs before battle to dull pain and give them mythical strength?" Neil shrugged. "What's different now that we know the enemy's name?"

"It is not just an ordinary army," Henry explained. "The Nizari are a radical Muslim group. The stories about them are no doubt exaggerated, but it is impossible to separate fact from fiction anymore. The Hashasheen, as they were designated by their enemies because of the herbs they were said to imbibe, were a splinter group from the Isma'ili Fatimid, the Shia Muslims. They disagreed over the leadership, as is usually the case in these situations, much like Pope Innocent III and King John disagreed over the new archbishop of Canterbury.

Anyway, the Nizari, or al-Da'wa al-Jadīda as they refer to themselves, split off. Their name means New Mission to distinguish themselves from the Old Mission, the Fatmid. The Nizari did not have the manpower to fight traditional armies, so they became a secret society of intrigue and assassination. They train men and women known as Fedayeen to infiltrate governments, societies, armies, everywhere. That is what they do best."

Neil shrugged. "It sounds like good news for our purposes. We were expecting an army, and they will not have one. We deliver the ransom, get our man, and go home."

"The danger is the farther reaching effects of this group. They could have men anywhere. They very well might have men at Dawning Court. No Saracen is above suspicion. They might be perfectly harmless, but we would never know until it was too late."

They rode for a time in silence, each pondering this new information.

"So I guess she was not sneezing, then," William repeated to lighten the mood. "You know, brother, I could hear your little tirade about me from where I was riding." An awkward silence followed William's declaration as they waited for his reaction. "A bungler, eh? You know this is the same as when we were children. If we did not let you be King Richard in our games, you acted like this." Still no one spoke. "You remember, when we used to pretend to be at the siege of Chalus-Chabrol."

"Oh please, no," Henry dropped his face into his hand.

"No no, this is exactly the same thing. You're just mad that I am not Pierre Basile anymore and you don't get to be king."

"Oh? This I have to hear," Anthony prodded.

"Henry, because he was older, always insisted on being King Richard and pouted for hours if we did not let him. He would play King Richard, and I always had to be Pierre Basile, the boy who shot King Richard with his crossbow." William grinned to recount the dramatic scene that they had reenacted a thousand times as boys. "He would lay dying from the gangrenous shoulder wound my errant bolt had caused and look down at me and say magnanimously, 'Free this child, for he has stood boldly in the face of insurmountable odds and defended himself with only a frying pan. What's more, take one hundred shillings from my purse and bestow it upon the lad. No harm will come upon you today.'" William was dramatically reenacting the larger-than-life portrayals of their boyhood game.

Neil, Anthony, and Roland were all roaring with laughter. "I cannot restrain the tears, your majesty," Neil interjected. "Your soul is too noble for words!"

"Don't waste too many tears on him," William said. "No sooner had his King Richard breathed his last breath then he was on his feet again as the cruel Captain Mercadier. 'This boy has killed our beloved king. Seize him and have the flesh flayed from his body!'"

"At which point, as I recall," Henry shot back, "you would then act out a violent, horrible torture victim, writhing and screaming at your punishment. Which was a just punishment, by the way."

"Well I could not be upstaged by my older brother, now, could I?"

"That shouldn't surprise you," Neil added. "William is still determined not to be upstaged by anyone."

William grinned at him. "The jealousy of the lesser players is always directed at those actors with important parts. I ignore you."

William and Neil rode up ahead, still laughing at the old story, but Henry was obviously agitated. So they rode in silence to find the new road to Mount Alamut.

CHAPTER SIXTY-SEVEN

"Mother, that servant you sent me is so lazy, you may as well have sent no one at all!" The anger was apparent in Thomas' voice.

Martha looked up in her customary posture, hunched over the small writing table. "Walter? That's strange. I never had any complaints about him in the two years he was in my house."

"Well of course not, but you have enough help to cover for him. But in my home where the help is so sparse, his failure to perform is far more apparent."

"Well then, you must send him away at once," Martha insisted.

"I was going to do just that," Thomas assured her. "But then I started talking to him, and he has a family with a sick child, and I could not bear to release him despite his lackluster performance..." Thomas hesitated slightly. "But because he is not pulling his weight, I really need someone to step in for him."

"Strange, I don't remember hearing anything about a sick child, and I make it my business to know about such matters where they concern those who serve in my house."

"Well, it sounds like it is a pretty recent occurrence. He has taken ill suddenly," Thomas said quickly. "You probably would not have heard about it." He looked forlornly at her. "It was a big disappointment because Annie was so looking forward to his help to really put the affairs of the house in order. And he is just not much help at all. Annie is really struggling, I'm afraid."

"Well perhaps if you were not too busy drinking yourself to death, you would have more time to help her," Martha said sharply.

"What are you talking about?" Thomas demanded. Never one to be called out for his faults, Thomas' ire rose instantly.

"Your brothers are off attempting to rescue Richard without you because you were so drunk as to be incoherent when they needed you."

"I already told you of the difficulty I had. They tasked me to find John and see about enlisting his help. I found him in the most wretched condition, I feared for his life. Truthfully, I did. I dared not leave him, but I never imagined they would depart without me. They did not even let me know." Thomas shook his head regretfully.

"Of course, and the last time you were seen before that, you and John were getting liquored up in some seedy little tavern."

"Who told you that? Did Henry tell you that? I knew he would take it like that. I was not drinking! I do not drink! I was there trying to talk some sense into John. And, yes, John was drinking, he has a problem. But unlike Henry, I thought his safety more important than reporting his indiscretion back to you. I was not willing to abandon him in some dirty little tavern in that condition. He would have been at the mercy of any common rogue that might perpetrate any form of evil upon him. I cannot believe Henry ran back and told you that 'we' were drunk." The disgust was apparent as he spat the last part out.

"And why must it have been reported to me? Do I not have eyes to see and a mind of my own to understand?"

Thomas sat down looking burdened. "John was in a pretty dark place. He made me follow him into the woods, and I was very afraid he would do something drastic. So I stayed with him. He opened up to me, and I sat with him all night while he cried and lamented his life. He was talking about trying to take Dawning Court back by force. I talked him out of it, but he's not in a good state. I just cannot believe Henry claimed I was drunk. Anything to turn you against me, I suppose."

"And why would he want to do that?"

"To curry favor with you, of course. Richard is out, Edward's out, John is out. If he makes me look bad, then there is no one left between him and the baron's seat.

"Ah, I was not aware his sights were set on Dawning Court."

"Well what else? Mark my words, he has designs of his own. More so than perhaps any of the other sons."

"Well it is good to know you are completely innocent of such aspirations yourself," Martha said absently, but she wore a thoughtful expression.

"I never said that," Thomas said, looking at the ground. "It may be that I have spent too much time with John. I am so worried about losing my brother, I'm sure I have seen too much of the other side. I know I do not help Annie enough. And now that's she's pregn—" he stopped abruptly when Martha looked up sharply.

"She's what?"

"Oh well, you might as well know. We have not officially announced it yet, but Annie is pregnant." Martha could only stare at her son. "That is why that lackadaisical servant has been such a disappointment. We truly need the extra help."

"She's pregnant again? What terrible luck." As it usually was, Martha's honest reaction was the first to show.

"Well it wasn't exactly luck," Thomas said bashfully.

Martha's eyes narrowed. "You mean you planned this?"

"What difference does it make? I want five or six children; I figured I might as well get to it."

"That's wonderful. You are living in a family-owned house, constantly begging for handouts, the children you do have spend most of their time naked in the mud, you and your wife can hardly speak a civil word to each other, and it seemed a logical time to you to have another child? Because more children will make any bad relationship better, right?"

"Now you're trying to tell me how to live my life?" Thomas fired back defensively.

"Why should I bother? You never listen. You never seem to learn anything from others' mistakes but seemed determined to make every single one yourself." Thomas' lips pursed into an angry line. "Annie does not have easy pregnancies! She cannot manage the house as it is. How will she fare while pregnant and caring for two young children?"

"That's why I need more help," Thomas pleaded desperately.

"You put me in a difficult place here. On the one hand I think you need to feel the sting of your own bad decisions; but on the other I cannot sit by and watch a family collapse in upon itself if there is something I can do to prevent it. What shall I do?"

Thomas' face broke into an involuntary half smirk because he knew she was about to give in. But to conceal his smugness he quipped, "You could send another servant like the last one. Then you are not really helping me, and your conscience is placated."

Martha could not help laughing. "I'll see what I can do," she sighed.

"Thank you," Thomas said, standing up to leave. "Thank you for everything, Mother. What would I do without you?"

"Probably learn to stand on your own two feet and be a man," she said, but smiled tolerantly as he kissed her and left the room, excited that he had once again gotten his way.

But as Thomas left the castle, his mother's final words kept echoing in his head: "Stand on your own two feet and become a man." So Anisa was right. Even his own mother did not think of him as a man.

Perhaps he was not a man after all. He began to feel that a display of his prowess was necessary. He could no longer be the lovable jester that everyone laughed at and dismissed. His fist tightened on the reins. Those that did not take him seriously now would tremble at the very mention of his name.

He bypassed his house and the chance to tell Annie the good news and went straight to the training yard.

CHAPTER SIXTY-EIGHT

"It is time," Henry said to the few knights that remained with him. We cannot all go to the meeting."

"Sir Henry," said Timothy. "Would it not be better, safer, I mean, if we all went?"

Henry shook his head. "It is too much leverage that we cannot afford them right now. If their intentions are to dispatch us, they will be heavily armed, and they will have us all. We would have already sprung the trap while trying to set it." He looked around at the eight knights and William assembled around him. "Only one of us must go. His safety will be in his fleet-footedness. There would be little value in disposing of a single knight, and the Moors will know that. If they are truly after money, they would not dare harm him. And if they are after all of our heads, disposing of the one would only warn us of their treachery."

"And what if in their rage over not being obeyed, they murder Richard *and* the unsuspecting knight?" Timothy asked boldly. "Who would you send on such a fool's errand?" Henry inspected each of the faces of the young knights in turn.

William was standing at the back of the group, leaning on his spear, munching casually on a hunk of dried meat, entertained by the proceedings as he often seemed to be. As Henry inspected each face as a potential candidate for this errand, William was nodding fervently or shaking his head to vote for who he thought should be chosen. His votes tended to be indications of how much he liked or disliked each particular knight more than any actual considerations of the skills required. Henry deliberately ignored William until finally his gaze came to rest on his younger brother. It stopped there. "Ahhh, not me," William whined loudly.

"Who else?" Henry challenged.

"Anyone, I don't care. Send the little guy," he said, gesturing at Timothy with his jerky. "Or send Anthony. It is his job to protect my person." He said the last with conviction as if the matter were settled.

"Would your conscience allow you to send men into a dangerous situation into which you would not willingly go yourself?" Henry asked primly.

William did not answer for a moment while he chewed and swallowed. Then, "Definitely," he said, taking another bite of his jerky. "It seems to me that that is the point of being the leader."

Henry stepped up to him and spoke quietly, hoping the other men could not overhear. Timothy gave Anthony a sidelong glance. "William, you know as well as anyone how dangerous this mission is, but it must be done. The whole thing turns on this meeting. We need someone who can think on the spot. This was your plan; you must make it work."

"I never said anything about riding out of my way that far in this heat," William protested. "You go, and I will wait here under that shade tree and be very anxious until you return."

Henry pulled him aside a few steps. "You know there is no one here that is your equal in one-to-many combat. If things go badly, you stand the best chance of anyone of getting out alive. That is a fact! All foolishness aside, there is no one else to do this."

"Ohh," he protested again. "Are you really making me do this?"

"You have to do it, William. Now," he said, looking at the sun, "you haven't much time; you had best be off."

Henry gritted his teeth and forced himself to listen to William's complaints all the way to his horse as he gave William a leg up into the saddle. William looked down at him from his perch. "This is because I made fun of your short cloak, isn't it?"

Henry smiled despite himself. "Yes, it is. Now go!" He slapped the rump of William's mount and sent it galloping off with William still calling complaints over his shoulder until he was out of earshot.

Timothy stepped up beside Anthony, who had watched the whole exchange with interest. "Sir, meaning no disrespect to the noble family, but would it not have been better to send a knight for such an important task?"

"Sir Henry knows what he is doing," Anthony assured him, still looking after the brothers. "There is no better choice for this than William."

"But Sir, what assurance have we that he will carry out this critical task? Or that he is even able?"

"Don't worry about that, Sir Timothy. I give you my word of honor that William will fulfill this mission."

"Is that your word to give, sir?"

Anthony stiffened slightly at being second-guessed by this younger knight. "William will accomplish this task," Anthony said firmly. "Nothing can dissuade him from it now. Should all the forces of Damascus be lying in wait for him, he will ride into their midst and deliver his message."

Timothy bit his lip for a moment to repress his insolence but finally could not restrain himself. "How can you hold such confidence in a disavowed son of a nobleman?"

Anthony ruminated for a moment. "William Dawning cares nothing for his own life, and nothing is impossible to the man who has nothing to lose."

"Sir Anthony, I would never contradict you; however, the only thing he was concerned about was his own life. He does not share your valor or courage or that of the Dawning family."

Anthony smiled at Timothy and patted him on the shoulder. "It appears so to you, because you are seeing exactly what he wants you to see." With that, he returned to his preparations.

CHAPTER SIXTY-NINE

"It was high noon when Abdul and Imar rode out into the crossroads. They had been hiding in the hills since before dawn to ensure the Dawnings did not attempt some bit of treachery. There had been no sign of the knights, but they had fifty men hiding in the rocks on either side of the road in case the treachery was yet to come. They were sure the Dawnings would try something; they just were not sure what that might be. They had to come for their brother. The ransom note had indicated they were to meet here at high noon on this very day. The plan from there was simple: The Dawnings would deliver the money. Abdul was to lead them back near mount Alamut, where Richard would be delivered to them. They would then be allowed to return the way they had come, where the fifty men in hiding would fall on them and destroy the Dawnings at the moment they thought they had attained their freedom. The plan was brilliantly simple, as most good plans were. It eliminated the Dawnings and had them paying for the privilege of dying at the hand of the Nizari. It was wonderful.

But noon came and went and still no Dawnings appeared. In fact, no one at all appeared on the desolate road. Abdul began to grow uneasy. "They are not coming?" Imar asked, putting a voice to Abdul's own fears.

"Nonsense," Abdul quickly reassured him. "They must come if they have any hope of retrieving their brother. They do not know who we are, and they have no other means of contacting us other than this prearranged time and place. They will be here."

Two more hours passed, and they began to get even more nervous about it. Abdul was particularly terrified of returning to Amir and informing him that the Dawnings had not come. Amir did not handle disappointment well.

"They are not coming," Imar said again. It was no longer a question. It was hot, and he was tired of standing on this dusty road; and he was starting to feel more than a little foolish.

"They will be here!" Abdul insisted, unwilling to consider the alternative.

"But what if they do not come?" Imar suggested.

"They are here! Our spies saw them entering our land not two days ago. They are here. Why bother coming all this way if they did not intend to meet us and get their brother back?"

"Our forward posts could have been mistaken. One group of European dogs in armor looks much like another." Imar was again articulating Abdul's fears, and it was making him angry.

"They had a chest and the Dawnings' insignia! They are here!"

"What if they were waylaid on the road, and the group that was seen was merely the victors carrying the spoils."

"Flying the Dawnings' banner?" Abdul was almost yelling now in his agitation.

"Of course. As a celebration of their victory, or even as a deliberate gesture to throw us off, ."

"That's enough! They will be here. Hold your tongue until then." Abdul's authority over Imar was only consensual and both men knew that, but Abdul frequently got his way by virtue of being bad-tempered. Nevertheless, as the day wore on, neither Abdul's tacit authority nor his surly nature were enough to keep Imar from voicing his concerns.

"Abdul?" he asked somewhat hesitantly.

"Yes?" Abdul sighed.

"What do we do if they do not come? I mean, what is the alternate plan?" Abdul did not answer. He did not tell him there was no alternate plan. It was never even considered that the

Dawnings would not appear. For the fiftieth time Abdul wished Amir were there personally. He would know what to do. He could handle every situation. And what's more, he would know that this was not Abdul's fault. He would see that Abdul was right where he was supposed to be, on time and ready to go.

"I wonder if the Dawnings are standing on some other deserted road this very moment, wondering why we have not kept to the agreement, wondering why we would not come for our money," Imar grinned. "Maybe they are just lost. Wouldn't that be interesting?"

"You think this is funny, fool?" Abdul growled angrily. "Do you know what Amir will do to us if we return empty-handed? Do you understand the penalty for failure?"

"Do not call me fool!" Imar groused. "Amir cannot possibly blame us if they do not show up."

"Is that a chance you wish to take? Are you willing to stake your life on our leader's understanding nature?"

"Amir is not my leader. Hassan Ibn Sabbah is my leader. He is the Imam, not Amir."

"That's fine, but Hassan is not going to kill us because the Dawnings got lost in a foreign land!"

Imar was forced to face the reality of what Abdul was saying. "What do we do? Should we go look for them?"

"Where would we start looking?"

"Perhaps we should send men up and down the road to be sure they are not waiting nearby."

"They are not nearby, you fool!"

"Then what do you want to do? You tell me to be serious because we might die over this, and then you do not want to do anything to fix it. And I am not a fool!"

Abdul inhaled in preparation to deliver a blistering tongue lashing. Imar braced himself, but the expected attack never came. Abdul's attention was suddenly captured by a lone figure that appeared on the road approaching them.

The figure was strangely garbed in white and gold armor. He did not look like an English knight but was clearly not a local character. He had to be with the Dawnings' party, Abdul concluded silently.

"You do not appear to have our money," Abdul said menacingly as the figure came into earshot.

"Nor do you appear to have Richard Dawning," the loan figure was trying to sound casual.

"We have him. Once payment has been made, he will be produced."

"Hmm, that is a good plan; but it strikes me that it has a few trapdoors in it. All for me."

"Do you want him killed now?" Abdul demanded.

William just shrugged. "There is some debate among our party as to whether you actually have him at all, and in the unlikely event that you do in fact have him, whether he is alive or not. Your appearance here empty-handed does not help those trying to make a case for you."

"You would leave us sitting here for hours and then show up here empty-handed and test my patience? Perhaps the prisoner's severed hand would convey a sense of urgency for you?"

"I appreciate the offer, but I doubt I would recognize his hand; and once again, that does not bolster your claim that he is alive. I know my brother, and I doubt very much you could take a hand from his live body. No, I'm afraid we will have to see him in person."

"So you are a Dawning?" The Saracen said, suddenly perking up. William cursed himself for letting that slip. He had wanted to conceal it. If they believed him to be a simple messenger, they had no leverage over him. But as a Dawning...

"We have your ransom, but we will not hand it over without our brother present," he said, ignoring the question.

"You do not trust us?"

William stared at him for a moment, trying to think of an appropriate response. What did one say to the men that were holding a loved one for ransom when asked about their integrity? He could not think of anything appropriate. "So here is how we will do this, and this is the only way we will do business with your il—" He stopped short of overtly insulting them. "—with you. There is a meadow off the road from here about a league west. Do you know the place of which I speak?"

"There will be no changing the deal!" Abdul roared, fearful that he was losing control.

"Now don't be silly. I'm sure this is not a personal vendetta. You are a man of business. It is the money that interests you. Surely, you can see that this location, surrounded by your men, is not a neutral location. If it is a legitimate exchange that you desire, then you will have no objection to my terms. Now, do you know the meadow of which I speak?"

"We know it, but—"

"No!" William cut him off, going on the offensive. He had to keep him off balance. "These are the only terms under which we will agree to the demands of cowardly scavengers! We will meet there. Our brother will accompany you. We will wait until sunset, then we will return to England whether you have shown yourself or not. If Richard is not with you, there will be no deal. If you do not appear by sunset, there will be no deal. If you bring more than eight men with you, there will be no deal. If we see you approaching with any more than that, there will be no deal. That is all." William started to turn away.

"We will not do it!" The Saracen screamed.

"Then you will remain in poverty."

"We will kill your brother!" The desperation was plain in Abdul's voice.

William shrugged. "That is unlikely. If he is in fact alive, it would cost you a hundred thousand pounds to kill him. Therein lies the difficulty for one in your position. There is but one card to play, and once it is played the game is over." William turned and began to walk back down the road.

"What's to keep us from killing you right now?"

William did not look back as he spoke. "What would that profit you? That will not get you what you want. You are a man of business. This is not personal." If William had known how wrong he was, he would not have been so brazen.

Abdul was in a veritable panic as he watched William walk away and imagined having to relate this to Amir. "Seize him!"

he yelled to the men lying in wait along the roadside. The first notes of the battle cries from the men concealed in the rocks were just heard after William was already a good distance down the road. When he reached a certain point, he cut sharply off the road, leapt over some boulders, and was gone as suddenly as he had appeared. The Nizari pursued him, but by the time they reached the top of the boulders that veiled his escape, he was only a fading speck of a galloping rider on the plane beyond.

"Well that worked," Imar chortled. Abdul glared at him. "He obviously knew what we were planning."

Abdul wheeled his horse toward Alamut. "Reassemble the men. I will report what has happened." Imar nodded mutely, knowing Abdul was riding into danger when Amir's anger was at its peak.

CHAPTER SEVENTY

"I weary of hearing the virtues of my mother espoused incessantly!" John snapped, this being a particularly sore subject for him.

"She's a strong woman, Sir John," Anisa persisted.

"When my father was alive, all I ever heard is what a great warrior he was and what a powerful man. Will you now take up my mother's banner? The woman who despised me so as to throw me out and deny me my inheritance?"

"That's what I was referring to. It takes a strong woman to do that to the son of Braden Dawning, particularly when she has no specific right to do so. But people still respect her decision. Even you honor it."

"What honor? I do not honor it. But what choice did I have?"

"Ah, poor John," she said in a tone she would use to address a child. "You were merely a hapless victim of circumstances."

"Do not do that," John warned dangerously. "Do not mock me."

"Then act like a man," Anisa said acidly. "You are a victim only because you allow it of yourself. Take charge of the situation! Take back what is rightfully yours! Take back your life!"

John was silent until something struck him. "What concern is this to you?"

"How can you ask me that?" Anisa demanded angrily. "You are my business, and I want what's best for you, even if you do not spare a thought for it."

Ordinarily when she got angry, John immediately backed down; but he was tired this evening, and he felt particularly weary of her constant prodding and probing into affairs he felt were not her concern. "My mistake. I naturally assumed you loved me for who I am, not my station in life. I did not realize I had inadvertently picked up a social climbing whore." He knew he had gone too far, but as was so often the case, his better judgment kicked in a moment too late.

Anisa's dark eyes blazed. She drew herself up in preparation for her retaliation. "Actually I fell in love with the person I thought you could become. That is the person that was attractive to me." Then in a calmer voice, "Quite frankly, I could never love such a pathetic spectacle."

John shrunk under her derision. He wanted to yell and lash out against Anisa for saying such things, but her assessment was fair. He had made a disaster of his life. He had nothing to show for his first almost four decades of life: no wealth, no power, no accomplishments. He was in a loveless marriage, with no children. All that he had was standing in front of him denouncing his many shortcomings. Small wonder she could not love him. He could not even love himself. He suddenly felt weak in the knees and half sat, half collapsed onto a rock. He dropped his face into his hands as he could not bear to look at the woman who was staring so carelessly into his naked soul. She knew him too well. She knew his faults and his weaknesses as if she had made a careful study of his life and personality. For all the talk, the flippancy, and the bravado, at the end of the day John had no deep-seated strength to draw on. He had never sown the seeds that would sustain him in his need; and now that it was required, his soul was naked and bleeding, and he was alone.

Anisa stared at him with contempt in her eyes. Then slowly she softened and felt pity for this tortured soul that was wracked with silent sobs. For the briefest of moments, she felt guilt for using him this way. But she knew it was for the greater good and quickly dismissed those feelings.

She sighed, walked over and sat beside him, put a tender arm around him, and hugged him to her breast. He sobbed into her for a time, a weak, pathetic man. When his tears started to abate, she opened her robe near his face enough to tantalize him. John did not immediately respond. She gently lifted his chin to face her and kissed him, softly at first. When he began to return it, she added passion to her kiss, almost violence. She would restore his confidence by making him feel he was a great lover and seal him to her that much more assuredly. As she surrendered to his embrace, she knew that he was hers to do with as she pleased. Men were so easily manipulated. She smiled slightly to herself at the overwhelming sense of power she felt even while pretending to succumb to him.

CHAPTER SEVENTY-ONE

"Are you prepared, Sir David?" Spencer asked as he slipped into the clearing in which David was making his final preparations.

David looked up and grinned. "Lightning courses through my veins, and there is thunder in my sword arm. I am indestructible today."

"Do you understand the aim clearly?" Spencer asked with a nervous expression.

"I understand," David assured him. "Why do you fret so?"

Spencer grunted. "Am I so obvious, then?"

"Sir Spencer," David grinned, "you are without guile. Now, what concerns you?"

"This plan... there is far too much that can go wrong. If we are seen, if we are late, if we are early, if the Moors do something unexpected, if—"

David held up a hand to forestall him. "I believe I understand the gist of your concerns. Please stop before I lose my nerve all together."

"You do jest, but what is to become of us? Are we to throw our lives upon the altar of chivalry for the small chance that we can rescue a fellow countryman?"

David looked around to be sure no one else was within earshot, took Spencer by the arm, and led him deeper into the forest to be sure they were not overheard. "What are you saying? Where is your honor?"

Spencer looked very uncomfortable. "Of course, I only venture to share these thoughts with you as I know you must harbor similar sentiments after William Dawning humiliated you."

David sighed and sat back on a fallen tree. "Sir Spencer, I understand there is great danger in this endeavor; but we are men of honor. We do not pick our battles based on the probability of success; we choose our battles based upon right and wrong."

"You are correct, of course. It is only—" He stopped and looked away.

"It is only what, Sir Knight?" David prodded. "Speak plainly now. Fear no reproach from me."

Spencer looked at him for a long moment, gauging whether he could trust him. And as people so often did with David, he continued, "As we have ridden through these unfamiliar territories, I have been impressed by how much life I have yet to live. I have not yet found a wife, there is much of the world that I have yet to explore, and for the first time, I feel—" He stopped again.

"Fear?" David asked simply. Spencer recoiled at the word.

"Regret. Regret for having willingly offered my life with so little consideration."

"Ah, your spirit was willing, but your flesh grows weak, eh?" David chuckled. Spencer stiffened at the remark.

"Sir Spencer, there is nothing to be ashamed of. I have a little girl at home that I love above all else in this world; but I do not regret being here. Your willingness to volunteer only betokens a noble heart and brave spirit. Anything we may feel later is our brain telling us our noble heart and brave spirit are going to get us killed." David grinned at him again.

"Are you ready to make such a sacrifice for the Dawnings then? Do you not carry enough animosity for them to make the exchange of your life for a Dawning seem an obscenity? You have a family to raise. These Dawnings have none of that."

David was quiet for a long time. The words of his final conversation with his mother echoed in his head. What if this was the end? Was he ready to die? A great ball of ice formed in the pit of his stomach. There was more to his mother's words than he had been willing to admit even to himself. He pushed those thoughts away and stood to face Spencer. "We are here because it is right, not because it is safe. We are sworn to the Dawnings, and we give what is needed without counting the cost. It is not our place to weigh our lives in the balance against anyone else. If we all did that, there would be no such thing as valor, only base, cravenly self-preservation." He put his hand on Spencer's shoulder. "It is fine to be scared, as long as we still do what is required of us when the time comes. I will be there when I am needed, and I know I will see you there too. That same heart that made you stand up to be counted with the other men out here today would never allow you to flee before the job was done."

"Well, of course, I would never even consider flight!" Spencer declared, but a look of relief passed over his face to know he was not the only one who thought of such things. He made a slight bow and turned to leave.

"Sir Spencer," David brought him up short. "I would not worry too much. The Dawnings have a way of getting out of these scrapes. Believe me when I say that none of them should be alive today for some of the scrapes they have ridden into."

Spencer smirked slightly. "Lightning coursing through your veins?"

David smiled back. "And thunder in my sword arm." David patted him on the shoulder and returned to his horse.

CHAPTER SEVENTY-TWO

Abdul jumped off the heavily-lathered horse back at Mount Alamut. He had ridden full tilt to deliver this news to Amir. If they were going to get back to the designated meeting spot by sunset, they had no time to lose. The English had very cleverly left them no time to plan any sort of intrigue. Abdul was in a panic to deliver the news, but he hoped the frenzied feeling he was experiencing would be infectious and Amir would be too preoccupied to take his displeasure out on the messenger.

He raced into the cave at the foot of the mountain that was frequently used for coordinating such operations. It was much less remote than the near impregnable fortress on top of Alamut. Amir was inside, waiting expectantly. "What took you so long?" he growled.

"The Dawnings, they did not come."

"What?" Amir roared, leaping to his feet.

"They only just now sent a messenger." Abdul deliberately did not mention the fact that the messenger was a Dawning. "He said they would only exchange the money for their brother if we met them in a place of their choosing, a meadow about a league west of the crossroads. He said we had till sunset or they would return to England with the money." Abdul gasped the explanation out, still winded from his hard ride.

"Those Dawnings think they can dictate the rules to us?" Amir roared and hurled his terracotta cup into the wall, where it shattered. "I will show them not to play games with me." Amir snatched a knife from the table and turned toward the cells where the Dawning prisoner was being held.

"Amir," Bashir stepped forward. "If you kill him, we get nothing." Amir stopped, looking at him with a slightly crazed look.

"Then I will just take a foot for their impudence."

"He would not survive it!" Bashir implored him. "He is too weak. He would not survive."

Amir fixed his crazed eyes on him once more before turning and hurling the knife in frustration against the same wall that had spelled the end for his cup just moments before.

"Let us take all our men," Bashir suggested. "We will arrive at this meadow, overwhelm the Dawnings, and claim our money."

"Actually," Abdul piped up hesitantly. "They said if they see more than eight men approaching, they will not be there when we arrive and we will never see them again."

"The arrogance!" Amir swore.

"We haven't much time," Abdul offered and then withdrew into the shadows, fearing he had overstepped his bounds.

Amir pounded his fist on the table. "I will slaughter every last one of these Dawnings with my own hands!" he roared. The cave stood silent while Amir regained control of himself. "Here is what we will do. Bashir, you collect thirteen other men, and we will ride out with the prisoner to meet them."

"But they said—" Bashir objected.

"I know what they said!" Amir's words were punctuated by his pounding of the table again. "The Dawnings are not making the rules here!"

"But what if—"

"They will not. We are not a big enough force to panic the arrogant Christians. They will not be sure if their message was communicated clearly or not; and when they see we have their brother, they will risk it. Our scouts reported that they are fourteen strong. We will be fifteen. The meadow of which they speak is about an hour's ride from here. Abdul," he said, jabbing a finger at him, "in a quarter of an hour, you will take everyone with you and ride to that meadow. That will give us time to complete our business and if necessary to stall them until you arrive."

"But won't they see us coming?" Abdul asked hesitantly.

"Not in time to react to it. If we went together they would see it. But if you are a quarter hour behind us, no warning can be sent in time to be of any value. They will not be warned of their impending doom until it is too late to react." Abdul was unconvinced, but his doubt was quickly replaced by his fear of Amir. He nodded mutely and hurried out of the cave to prepare the men.

CHAPTER SEVENTY-THREE

"Nothing to say, Richard?" The voice asked after Richard had trailed off mid-sentence and not spoken again for hours.

"I get it now," Richard whispered hoarsely. "I finally understand."

"What is it you have come to understand?"

"That day on the battlefield, the day they put me in here..."

"Yes?"

"I did not survive."

"What do you mean?"

"I have died, and this is Hell. It all makes sense now. That is why I have not seen any person except vague shadows since that day. It answers why I am always too cold or too hot. It is why I never have enough to eat, and why it is always dark." He broke off in a coughing fit.

"But you are not alone. I am here with you."

Richard smiled in the darkness. "And I even understand you at last," he said. "You are the cruelest part of Hell. You are the endless misery, the fire and brimstone. You rest with me eternally to repeatedly dredge up the evil I have done and the wrongs I have perpetrated. And there is plenty to dredge up because I have lived a sinful life, and now I am reaping the reward for it. This is the eternity I have earned." He broke into another fit of coughing.

There was only silence. But this silence was different from those that preceded his revelation. There was no expectation that anything would break the silence. It held a depth that was unfathomable and which made his once mighty heart begin to shrink in his bosom. How small and forgotten he was. How ironic that someone who had fed off of the adoration of others would now forever wither and crumble in anonymity, forgotten by both the living and the dead. Ironic indeed. Truly each man's hell is of his own fashioning, devised by the very acts and deeds that earned him his place in the forgotten depths of the netherworld.

Richard was sitting with his back against the cold, damp wall. He felt to cry for his plight, but the tears did not come. He tried to force them, hoping for the cleansing it might bring. But there was to be no release. Instead he sat numbly and stared with unfocused eyes at the oblivion that stretched before him. He felt his body slide down the wall to his left and his head hit the floor. He was powerless to move his arms or legs. He did not even have strength enough to maintain his sitting position. It was as if a giant weight had settled on him that he could not bear up under. This was his eternity.

He began to imagine that he heard sounds off in the blackness: Metal scraping on stone, some faint voices exchanging words. Richard smiled faintly. It was amazing what the mind would invent to try and comprehend the incomprehensible.

More sounds now, a footfall, a bolt being drawn back. The filthy moist air of his cell seemed to swirl and before him stood the silhouettes of figures: ghostly images that no doubt had come to usher him to an even darker circle of Hell now that he had discovered the secret of this one.

Harsh commands were barked in a guttural language that Richard did not understand: the language of the damned. The silhouettes seemed to float in front of him. Then he felt himself being propelled by unseen hands. Up and into the darkness he was dragged.

CHAPTER SEVENTY-FOUR

The fourteen men rode slowly across the field in the setting sun. The meadow was approximately two hundred yards long and about the same distance wide. It was enclosed on three sides by a thick tree line that light scarcely penetrated. And what did manage to pierce the canopy was only enough to illuminate the first few rows of trunks. It was blackness beyond that. The fourth side opened up to the main highway, which ran beside it out of the mountains and back into the desert. William and Henry rode in front with Neil and Anthony and their six companions fanned out behind them. Behind these rode the four knights of the chest, their burden still sitting atop the unfortunate sumpter horse that was led between the first two knights with the last two bringing up the rear, ever vigilant for treachery.

They approached the small party of Moors, all mounted, horses shoulder to shoulder, some fifteen strong. The two center-most Moors sat with the gaunt figure of a man between them. William leaned over to Henry. "That's not Richard," he said of the shriveled form that could scarcely keep himself upright in the saddle. There was a rope tied around his neck, the other end wrapped firmly around the hand of one of his guards. His hands were bound behind his back, and he was blindfolded. The reins of his horse were held by a giant of a man with long dark hair and a scar running down his left cheek. A memory stirred, and William leaned over to Henry again. "That's the giant!" he whispered urgently to Henry.

"What?" Henry did not understand.

"That's the giant who fought with John until he fled...when we were kids. This is a trap."

"Of course it's a trap," Henry muttered out of the corner of his mouth. He was not particularly interested in William's ramblings at the moment. "But what choice do we have but to play it out?" They continued their slow, plodding advance in the fading sunlight and stopped fifteen feet shy of the mounted Moor line that was spread out flank to flank beside the remains of their prisoner.

"I am glad you were able to make it," Henry said conversationally.

"You should consider yourself fortunate that we did not dispatch him for your treachery," the one with the rope in hand said in heavily accented English.

"Now what good would that have done?" Henry asked casually. "We both have an objective here. Let us keep that in mind, and we may both get what we want. Now, where is our brother?"

"Who do you think this is?" the one with the rope asked, shaking the rope of his prisoner.

"That skeleton is not our brother. It appears that perhaps you have the wrong man or the wrong family."

"This murderous dog *is* your brother! He elbowed the gaunt, filthy figure in the rib sharply. "Speak. Let them hear your voice," he ordered. The figure flinched but gave no other sign of life.

"Speak!" he repeated, raising his voice sharply. When no sound was forthcoming, he jerked the rope in his hand so sharply that the tall figure tumbled off of his horse, gasping for air.

William seized this opportunity to jump from his horse and race over to the prisoner in the guise of helping him. He would settle the question once and for all. The man with the rope started to protest, but the giant silenced him with a wave of his hand. There was little doubt about who was in charge.

William reached the figure and helped him into a sitting position. He removed the blindfold and could scarcely recognize the sickly figure before him as his once great brother. Richard's eyes were dreamy and he did not seem to see William. "Richard? Richard? Can you hear me?" William tried to get his attention, but Richard did not respond. William quickly checked him over for wounds, but other than bruises and slight lacerations he could find nothing in the filth that covered him from head to toe. "It is Richard," he called back to the group. "Neil, come and help me," he said as he attempted to help his brother to his feet.

"Not so fast. Where's our money?" the man with the rope demanded.

William glared at him for a moment before turning back to the group and beckoning. "Bring the chest over," he called. "Neil, now!" he repeated more forcefully. Neil hesitated only a moment before jumping down from his horse and hurrying over to them as fast as his heavy armor would permit.

The four knights of the chest slowly rode forward, their burden between them. After a long journey, they were relieved to deliver up this heavy charge safe and sound.

William put his head under Richard's left shoulder and lifted him off the ground. He stumbled slightly under the weight as he found that Richard could not or would not support himself. He stumbled sideways a few steps and found himself in front of the giant's horse. William looked up into the face of the man from so many years of nightmares. The long, stringy hair seemed unchanged, but his face looked harder and older than William remembered it. Nevertheless, he still seemed as intimidating as William remembered him. His larger than life presence had not simply been enlarged in William's imagination over the years. This man was immense.

The giant smiled his recognition and leaned down close to William. "You were very foolish to bring so many of your family along. But I thank you for it as you have made my job so much the easier. And this time there is no one to protect you."

William's heart grew cold with fear. He was aghast that the giant was as much as admitting to him his intention for treachery. He was unsure how to react. He briefly considered yelling a warning, "It's a trap!" But that would only panic his men, who were already expecting a trap; and he and Richard were extremely vulnerable at that moment, particularly with his spear stowed safely on his horse. Whatever the Moors had in mind, he had already walked into it, and there was nothing to do but let it be sprung. Then Neil was there, sliding in under Richard's other arm, and together they began carrying him across the intervening distance to the extra mount they had brought. The Moor holding Richard's leash reluctantly relinquished his grip on it as the chest was brought forward.

William could see the Moors slowly begin to fan out in a half circle with the giant in their center. He hastened his step without being too obvious about it. He feared that abrupt movements would startle the others and trigger the springing of the trap that much sooner.

The knights, too, moved slowly. They were setting the chest in front of the Moors as William and Neil were pushing Richard onto the back of a riderless horse, the reins of which were held by Anthony.

"Open it!" the Moor spokesman barked. Timothy removed a key from within his armor and threw it in front of the Moor as he had been instructed. The Moor glared at him and slowly climbed off his horse to retrieve the heavy key. He picked it up and looked around to make sure everything was as it should be. No tricks. Then dropping to one knee before the massive iron chest, he greedily fitted the key into the lock. He twisted it until the lock released with a snap. Grasping the heavy lid with both hands, he excitedly but almost reverentially raised the lid and peered inside. "What the—"

***

The leader of the band leaned forward in his saddle to try to get a better view of the clearing through the trees. The anxiety was plain on his face. He realized this was a good enough ruse at first glance, but their deception would be quickly discovered. Nevertheless, all they needed were a few moments; that would be enough. It had to be enough. Still, he hated that he was this far away. The tree line was too far away from the knights in the middle, but the distance did alleviate any suspicion of a trap.

He gripped his sword nervously as he watched two English knights usher a third person back to their party. He hated waiting, and he wished he could ride out now. He drew his sword when he saw the Nizari spreading out to encircle the knights. This was it, they were about to strike. He raised his sword as a sign for the men to prepare themselves. He just needed the signal.

A moment later it came! His arm plunged and he jabbed his heels into his horse's flanks. His men exploded from the tree line. The group in the middle of the clearing froze as they grasped the scene before them. Just then another group of similarly clad men broke from the opposite tree line, and the two groups converged on the men in the middle.

***

Henry recognized the Moor armor on the charging men and shouted out a warning. "Treachery! Fall back, men! Fall back!"

The Moor giant stood in his stirrups and shouted, "Kill the Dawnings!"

Anthony, still holding the reins of Richard's horse, pushed the wavering figure down over the neck of his horse to stabilize him and drove his spurs into the side of his own animal. It bounded forward with such force that he was scarcely able to retain his grip on the reins of Richard's horse and stay in his own saddle.

William and Neil immediately moved to cover his escape and deter any would-be pursuers. A group of the encircling Moors charged, and William bounded forward to meet them, spear in hand, swinging it in wide vertical arcs on either side of him. He caught the first Moor on his unprotected head, unseating him; a second on the opposite side saw it coming just at the last moment and, jerking violently backwards, lost his balance and fell out of his saddle. The other three passed by out of reach. William reined in his horse to turn for another pass. Then Neil was there. He rammed his heavy broad sword under the breastplate of the first. Instead of turning to pursue William, the remaining two turned on Neil.

Fencing from horseback was always awkward. The advantage the horse offered was that of height and leverage. It offered the rider the freedom to rain down blows with impunity on the infantry; however, when facing other mounted opponents at a standstill, the horse could quickly become a hindrance. Nevertheless, none of the combatants were willing to give the other the advantage by dismounting; therefore, they continued their awkward ballet as the horses clumsily sidestepped one another. The first Moor struck a heavy overhand blow, which Neil caught with the flat of his blade. But the nose of the rider's horse bumped into the flank of Neil's animal, causing it to canter away slightly. This moved him out of range of the second Moor's strike. Neil then righted himself and struck back at his opponents, but both strikes were parried.

William wheeled his horse and rammed his spear into the throat of the first recently unhorsed Moor, then brought a heavy blow down on the top of the second retreating figure, cracking his skull and dropping him where he stood. He whirled his mount and thrust his spear into the exposed back of one of those fencing with Neil. Wrenching his weapon back violently, William stabbed at the second man; but his spear point was knocked aside. Nevertheless, this movement left the man exposed to Neil, who took full advantage of it and cut him out of his saddle.

William pulled his horse around to survey the battle field. All was chaos. Henry and the remaining knights were outnumbered at least three to one. William scanned the meadow for the giant. He located him on the opposite side of the field, calmly watching what transpired. William spurred his horse forward to work his way to him.

***

The bandits from the trees were upon them, riding through their ranks and crossing swords with the knights. The first side made a pass, leaving several saddles empty. As they charged among the men, Henry easily deflected the clumsy stroke of one bandit and then blocked a second stroke from a rider closely following the first. Suddenly the second wave of bandits was upon them, wiping out yet another group of men. The first made a wide circle and again rode back into the fight.

Henry drove his sword at the closest Moor who had been one of Richard's captors. His blow was deflected and countered. Henry caught this counterstrike on his small buckler strapped to his forearm and struck back quickly, but to no avail—the Moor's shield took the blow with ease. The two were locked in this struggle until the Moor's mount, reacting to a nearby pass of a bandit, turned. The Moor wheeled completely around to take a swing at the bandit. Henry took this opportunity and, rising in his stirrups, brought his blade down on the helmet of the Moor with both hands, cleaving into it and finishing him.

A small group of bandits surrounded the chest and jumped down to collect it. The Moor that had been looking into the chest stood suddenly and rammed his sword into one of the closest rogues, only to have the next one cut him down where he stood. His face did not even register the surprise at the fatal blow, so swiftly was he dispatched.

***

The giant was not overlooked in this all-encompassing melee. It was the wild running bandits that took notice of him first. A small group of them broke away and rode to meet him. The giant held aloft a large mace on a chain with spikes jutting from it. He began swinging it above his head. The first bandit to reach him caught the full force of the blow on his shield. The spikes did not penetrate the heavy shield, but the sheer weight of the blow shattered his arm. He screamed in pain and hunched protectively over his arm in the saddle. Another bandit was there, and the giant redirected the strike intended to finish the first man at the second. He dodged to the side, feeling the wind as the deadly mace rushed over his face. The giant kept the weight of the mighty weapon spinning in circles and immediately came around with another blow, but the bandit was also stabbing at him and he was forced to intercept the bandit's blade with this swing. He struck it with enough force that the bandit's sword was swept from his hand and went spinning to the earth.

As the giant's mace came around again, his opponent leapt from his stirrups, hitting the giant in the chest with his shoulder and sending them both tumbling to the ground. The giant lost his grip on his own weapon, and the momentum of the swinging mace carried it some distance across the meadow before it came to rest in the dirt.

From across the field, William saw his chance and began carving his way toward the giant, his spear spinning and twirling, both ends finding targets in the fray. He was not careful to dispose of the Moors that he encountered. His only focus was on getting by them.

The bandits had succeeded in loading the chest on horseback and were leading the heavily-laden animal back into the trees. With the disappearance of the chest, the motivation for all three groups enmeshed in the melee seemed to vanish. Henry recalled the remaining knights to him. Two of the saddles were empty from the skirmish. The Moors, their numbers now cut in half, broke and fled in confusion. The bandits retreated as suddenly as they had appeared, leaving behind several of their wounded.

The giant, however, was otherwise occupied and could not beat a retreat with his men. He and the bandit wrestled to get to the fallen sword, which lay close to where they had landed. The bandit smashed the giant in the face with his elbow and jumped to his feet to run for the sword; but the giant, recovering quickly, brought a massive fist into the side of his knee, knocking it out from under him. The giant then lunged from all fours at the fallen weapon. The bandit desperately grabbed and hugged the giant's legs, bringing him down mid-lunge into the dirt; but the giant's reach was just long enough that, even being brought up short, he was still able to wrap his hand around the weapon while he kept his opponent busy with a flurry of kicks. The bandit rolled once to get away and looked up just in time to see his own leaf-shaped blade slicing the air toward him. It was stopped only a moment shy on the shaft of William's spear. William made no attempt to hide from the giant the smug smile that he wore on his lips as their eyes met. The giant was now lying on his stomach, prostrate in the dirt, as William stood over him, weapon ready, every advantage his. Their eyes met, and for just an instant William saw fear in the giant's eyes, replaced rapidly by rage. He roared and began hacking furiously at William's feet and legs.

William easily stepped out of reach and reversed his swing, bringing the blunt end of the spear sharply against the giant's hand. The bandit's sword landed in the dirt several feet away, and again everything froze as William and the giant stared each other down.

"I know not what perceived wrong you have received that you should harbor such malice against my family, but it matters not now. You die as you have lived, like a dog in the dirt."

The corners of the giant's mouth flicking up in the traces of a smile that he could not repress were the only warning William had of the attack. He jammed his spear straight back and caught the belly of the first of a group of Nizari charging to the aid of their leader. Maintaining his grip on his weapon, William executed a quick forward roll to keep him clear of the others and came up facing this new group of enemies. He was aware of the giant crawling quickly out of reach, but there was nothing to be done about it for the present.

Before him stood three Saracen soldiers, the fourth down on his knees, looking in shock at the blood covering the hands that were pressed over his belly wound.

By now the bandit had recovered his weapon just as he was attacked by a fifth man who made a clumsy lunge with his long sword. The bandit quickly sidestepped it, knocked the blade down with his own heavy weapon, and swung up along the length of the Moor's extended arm to find his unprotected neck.

The whole exchange had taken only a moment, but the giant had regained his weapon and was charging back toward William. The bandit, heedless of the direction the giant was headed, interposed himself in his path. Their fight was not complete.

"Not now!" the giant roared, unleashing a furious assault on him. "You are not important. Stand aside!" It is difficult to block a mace on a chain with a sword as the chain tends to wrap over the blade and cause unexpected results, such as broken blades, or even the swordsman losing his grip all together. As such, the bandit did not try to block the fierce strikes from the stronger man. Instead, he rather skillfully deflected them. But the giant did not lose his momentum—each time a stroke was deflected, he continued his strike, bringing his heavy weapon around again and again until he found a weakness in the bandit's defense. A hesitation, a misjudged parry, or a misstep and it would all be over.

Meanwhile, William faced his new attackers across only a few yards of ground. They knew who he was and were in no hurry to rush him now that his back was not to them. It was too dangerous, and none of them wanted to be the first into the devil's teeth. William's focus was only on his targets. His anger at this injustice was focused on them and only them. He was cognizant, however, of the fencing match taking place between the giant and the bandit not far from him, and he knew he needed to end this quickly. He studied the men closely. One Moor in the rear was protecting a wounded knee. Another had his guard low from trying to use a weapon that was clearly too heavy for him, and the third looked ready to retreat at any moment. William was studying them so closely that he failed to notice still another Saracen approaching from the rear.

Without warning William leapt, feinted a quick stab of his weapon at the antsy opponent, who promptly jumped backward. He dropped and spun, kicking his heel out, taking out the man with the bad knee who had instinctively shifted his weight back to it when William advanced. As a result, when William connected with it, it popped and he screamed as his leg folded under him. William did not stop spinning but came up with his spear coming around at head level, catching the claymore-wielding Saracen in the face as he attempted a stab at William. William had the reach on him, however, and he lost his right eye to the point of William's spear before he could make contact with his thrusting attack.

William withdrew a step to assess just in time for the Saracen quietly approaching from behind to get there. William was still unaware of him when the Saracen made a savage stab at his unprotected back.

* * *

The bandit saw what was happening. He saw the man sneaking up behind the English knight and knew that if this assassin succeeded, he would be outnumbered quite suddenly. He tried to call out but it was useless. The knight was too engaged to hear him. The giant at last started to tire in his barrage of assaults, and the bandit caught the handle of the mace from a clumsier stroke on the base of his blade. It slid down to his hilt, and he and the giant were eye to eye. There was something strangely familiar about this face now that he was up close, but he was sure that he did not know him. The bandit slammed his right elbow into the giant's face while maintaining his hold on his blade. The giant stumbled back, jerking his mace free with his right hand as his left hand came up to his face.

The bandit saw his chance to finish this, but just then the other Saracen was rearing back to strike the unsuspecting knight's back. Without hesitation, he turned. "William!" he roared and hurled his sword end over end. The Saracen heard him shout and paused just long enough for William to dive aside and avoid the thrust. The Saracen lurched back out of the way, and the bandit's spinning blade made a deep gash in his right arm that was yet extended from attack.

The giant did not hesitate, and the bandit turned to face him just in time to see the mace come down toward him with crushing force. The bandit lurched at the last moment so that, instead of hitting him in the head as was intended, the mace smashed down on his clavicle with the spikes cutting deep into his body. The force of the blow made the bandit's left side go instantly slack, and he started to collapse. The giant brought the mace up and around in a heavy underhand swing into the bandit's chest as he pitched forward. The force of the blow spun the bandit's entire body around so that he landed on his face in the opposite direction he had been falling.

"No!" William screamed, desperate to end this struggle quickly. He was aware that even as he traded blows with this wounded man, the Saracen with the broken knee had struggled to his feet. William extended his spear straight on and charged the Moor that had been at his back. It was a foolish move that left William open to an easy parry and counterstrike, but so surprised was the Saracen after fending off strike after strike of oblique attacks that his parry was too little too late, and his blade was dashed aside by the force of William's drive, which plunged into his stomach. William took a hopping step forward and kicked the body off his weapon with a foot to the dying man's chest. Whirling his spear, he spun round and hurled it with all the force of his panic at the crippled man who was even then hobbling toward him. The Saracen's dark eyes grew wide in the instant he recognized his fate but knew there was no way he would avoid it. The spear entered his chest, and the finely crafted head of the weapon exploded out the back of his leather armor, carrying his body back as his feet came up, propelled rearward by the force of the strike. He landed on the earth several feet back from where he had last stood, the spearhead driven into the earth by the weight of his body.

Seeing that the field was rapidly emptying of all but the English knights, the giant crossed the short distance to his horse, slowed just long enough to retrieve something from the grass, and leapt into his saddle to gallop to the safety of the trees.

William raced over to the bandit, who was lying in a heap on the ground. Panic seized him, and William slid in the dirt on his knees in his haste. A glance was all it took for the shock to jolt through his body. The giant was instantly forgotten. He turned the bandit onto his back. William could hear a wet sucking noise as the bandit tried to inhale. "David, you're going to be all right," William said desperately. "Henry! Henry, its David!" he screamed. His friend was still alive but could not speak because of his wound.

David's light blue eyes were wide, and panic was plain in them. He opened his mouth to speak, but no sound came. "Relax," William said too forcefully. He was trying to hide his own panic as he cradled his friend's torso on his lap. He tore a strip of cloth from his clothing and held it over the gaping wound that was all that remained of his crushed clavicle and shoulder. The cloth was instantly soaked in blood. William was consumed with too many emotions to articulate. He had seen too many wounded men to fool himself; he knew David's wound was mortal, and he had no idea what to say that might comfort him. So instead he yelled, "Hurry!" as Henry and Neil raced across the field toward them. The remaining knights were dressing the wounds of the injured.

"David, I'm sorry," William said. "I'm sorry that I was not with you. I'm sorry that I did not get to you. I'm sorry I was not a better friend to you." The words were spilling out as he watched the light dim in the eyes of his oldest friend.

The terror in David's faced increased as he felt the darkness closing in on him. He gripped at William's arm frantically in pain and desperation, his back arching in pain. The end was near. William tried to imagine what would be on his mind at this moment if their roles were reversed. He offered a silent desperate prayer for his friend. "David," he said in a calm voice, hoping that David could not see the tears that were streaming down his face or hear them choking his voice, "be comforted. Salena and Rachel will be watched over." David's body began to spasm. William gripped his hand tightly through it. "Do not fear the reaper," he said gently. "He takes you to the arms of our loving Savior, as you lived in honor and glory."

David's arm slackened and his eyes went dark as the light of his spirit slipped from him. "Goodbye, my friend," William said through tears that flowed freely down his face.

Then Henry and Neil were beside him. Henry squatted and gently checked David's breathing and heartbeat. It took only a moment to confirm what he already knew. Neil stood in shock and said nothing.

Henry put his hand on William's shoulder. William, still kneeling by the body of his friend, was unable to stem the flow of tears. "He was a good friend to you, and he died with honor on a noble quest in the field of battle," Henry said awkwardly. "No knight can ask for more than that. He will be buried with honor."

"No," William choked through his tears. "We will take him with us!"

"Toward what end?"

"He deserves a proper burial in his own soil." William was climbing to his feet again.

"His body will never survive the trip home. It is too far," Henry protested. "Let him be buried with dignity here rather than as a bloated, stinking corpse in England."

"We will bury him in The Holy Roman Empire then. I will not leave him here in this unholy place."

"But this is the land where our Lord walked, the land of Abraham," Henry argued. "This is the Holy Land."

"It is not dirt that makes a place holy; it is the actions of the people who occupy the land." William turned back to look at his friend's body. "The Lord lived among these people because they were the most wicked in the world, and now it is occupied by filthy heathens that are no better. I will not have him left here in this place. We take him with us."

Henry wanted to argue, but he saw the futility of fighting it. "Wrap him up," he ordered two knights working nearby. "He's coming with us. Now let's be off immediately. It is not safe here."

As if to punctuate his statement, he stopped.

"I want—" William started.

"Shh!" Henry ordered sharply. "Listen!"

The meadow seemed eerily quiet now. A strange contrast to a bloody field that moments before had been steeped in commotion and death. Then they felt it. It was a sensation more felt than heard, a dull rumble like thunder in the distance. "They're coming," Henry said, and all at once everyone was moving. Henry broke for his horse and shouted to the other knights. "They are coming! Ride, ride!"

"Neil, help me!" William ordered as he was shouldering the body of his friend.

Neil looked around nervously and then helped William throw David's body over the back of his horse. There was no time to secure him. William jumped into the saddle and spurred his horse forward as Neil raced to his own mount.

They broke into the tree line as a small army of Nizari made a wide sweep from the road into the meadow, only to find an empty pasture that could have lain undisturbed for years.

***

440 The Knights Dawning

The Nizari reined in sharply and surveyed the meadow. Abdul had expected to find Amir, Bashir, and a group of knights. Instead all he found was an empty meadow in which scarcely a twig was moving. For the briefest of moments, Abdul knew panic as he thought they had the wrong location. But upon closer inspection, he could see dead among the grasses. This must be the place.

He quickly counted the dead—only seven and none of them Amir. So, where were the knights? Where were the English dead? What had happened here? "The trees!" he answered his own question. "They must be fleeing into the trees, and Amir is pursuing them." They might be getting away, he thought again with some panic due to the displeasure he knew another failure would most certainly arouse in Amir. Abdul could not afford another failure. He needed to act quickly. "This way," he ordered and charged forward. "Three lines," he commanded without pause. The group divided into three separate arms and thundered into the trees. Abdul's line charged directly into the trees at the far end of the meadows, while the other two groups split into a "Y" shape around the center group and entered the tree line at opposite angles. Abdul was counting on the fact that if the knights were fleeing, they would be in a dead run and would not be taking the time for subterfuge, making them easy to track.

William had ridden fifty yards into the trees and could not hold the body of his friend on his mount any longer. It was a dead weight now and rolled and flopped with each bounce, threatening to fall off the back or either side of his horse. "I have to secure David... David's body," he called to Neil. Neil flashed a sour expression at him but did not say a word. They heard the Moors crashing into the trees behind them. It sounded like they were approaching from every quarter. William's horse leapt over a protruding root, and he lost his hold of his friend's body as it bounced off the back of his horse. William started to rein in his mount to retrieve it as Neil came soaring by. He saw what was happening and grabbed onto the bridal of William's slowing mount. "Keep going, you fool!" he ordered, jerking the bridal and the horse back into a run.

They crossed a clearing in the trees, and a rope snapped up behind them at thigh level. It was wound around two trees and held by a mounted knight on either side. A moment later the fleet-footed Arabians came crashing through the trees after them, the three separate lines converging on their target. With a horrible sound the first and second line of horses hit the rope and collapsed in a terrible mass of bodies rolling and crushing each other. The horses' cries mixed with those of their riders in an unholy noise that signaled to the knights the success of their trap. They tied off the ends of the rope and disappeared into the trees.

The Nizari lines continued the pursuit as best they could only to find arrows whizzing around them. They plinked off their armor and pierced the flanks of their generally unprotected mounts. They turned to identify a specific archer only to be assaulted from every other direction with a barrage of arrows, making it impossible to focus an attack on any one target. They were equipped only for hand to hand combat and had nothing prepared with which to return fire. It did not take the Nizari long to realize they were in a losing situation. It was only a moment later that Abdul sounded the retreat. The Nizari turned and fled from the forest graveyard as fast as they had come, several of the riders pausing only long enough to pick up now horse-less comrades.

With the Nizari routed for the moment, the last of the English knights fled the forest after the main contingent of men.

CHAPTER SEVENTY-FIVE

"One of you must have tipped them off," Bashir shouted at Ibrahim. "How else could they have known where we were? How else could they have known about the money?"

"I don't know how they knew those things. I do not even know who they were!" Ibrahim persisted. "Those were not our men. Were they Jews, renegades, outsiders, who? That is the important question."

"You imbecile!" Bashir shot back. "They could be nothing more than mercenaries. What matters is who in our house has turned on his brothers for the love of lucre." Bashir snatched a long dagger that had been stuck into the wooden table top and slowly paced the room looking closely into each face of the survivors. To a man they nervously looked at the floor and then back at Bashir for fear of looking guilty; then, afraid meeting his eyes would be construed as a challenge, they again lowered their gaze.

Bashir suddenly seized Mustafa by the hair and yanked his head back. "Why have you done this thing? You will die for your infidelity!" Bashir drew the dagger back. "Now I send you to Hell with all liars, and you will never see a pound of that money!"

"Stop, you fool!" Amir yelled from the doorway. He stepped into the dark room and slammed the heavy door so hard it reverberated through the chamber. Amir's massive bulk filled the landing by the door. He could not even stand upright until he had descended the three stairs to the main level. "You look for enemies where there are none while the real enemy casually strolls out of our land with our money and our erstwhile prisoner, laughing at us." Amir brought the heavy English broad sword with the antique leaf blade crashing down on the table.

Everyone stared in silence at their leader. "They were English! The bandits were English!" The room immediately broke into a clamor of questions and murmured conversations.

Bashir stepped forward. "Why, because one of them had an English sword? The Europeans have made so many unholy crusades into our land, English weapons are easier to acquire than our own."

"A-an-and" Ibrahim added hesitantly, hoping to ingratiate himself with Bashir without angering Amir, "I did see the knights fighting with the bandits."

Amir rested both palms on the table, trying to control his anger. "Did any of you," he asked in a deadly quiet voice while casting his eyes about the room, "did even one of you see a bandit kill a knight or a knight kill a bandit?"

Each of the men in the room looked at those around him to see if anyone was volunteering. "No, but—"

"Did you?" Amir roared. The room fell silent. "Well, I killed a bandit. The same one who donated this sword." He began pacing the room, looking into each of the exhausted faces individually. "And I looked into his eyes. He had blue eyes! We were duped, and we stood by and did nothing! Instead of three dead Dawnings, we have lost men of our own and given them back the one brother who can and may make a serious claim for the throne." Amir snatched the sword and cleaved several large chunks out of the table with the heavy blade. "This could destroy everything."

"So what do we do, Amir?" Bashir asked his brother. "Do we go after them?"

"It's too late for that. We have to change the plan. And we have to ensure there are no more mistakes! I will go to England personally and stick this sword into the hearts of those English dogs, one by one."

CHAPTER SEVENTY-SIX

The next evening Henry's small band met up with Anthony, Richard, and their knight escort, as well as the large group of bandits with the chest. When Henry arrived in camp, the others were already celebrating their victory with copious amounts of liquor. William and Neil had caught up with Henry and the others earlier that day.

Anthony came forward to meet them, grinning broadly. "I cannot believe that worked," he said slapping William on the shoulder as he climbed out of the saddle. "That could not have gone better," Anthony continued to the weary and solemn knights.

"David did not make it," William said simply as he handed the reins of his horse over for care. "Now, where's my brother?"

Anthony's countenance fell instantly. "My deepest regrets, William... Richard is in my tent. He is under constant supervision. He... is not well," he warned.

William put a hand heavy with fatigue on Anthony's shoulder. "You performed nobly, my friend. My sincere thanks for everything."

Anthony looked embarrassed. "It was no more than my duty," he said modestly. William made his way immediately to Anthony's tent while Henry began barking orders at the celebrating men. "We are not safe yet! We are still on enemy soil, and they could still be in pursuit. I want the guard at each post doubled. All other non-essential men are to bed down immediately. We leave before first light."

"But Sir Henry," came the protest, "we are only taking a bit of wine for a job well done."

"The job is done when we are back in England. Then I will celebrate with you, but not before!" The men grudgingly obeyed.

"Uh, Sir Henry?" Timothy hesitated from behind Henry. Henry turned to face him. "Sir Henry, what shall we do with the chest?" Timothy was one of the knights that had been charged with the safe delivery of the chest. Two of his comrades had been in the foremost ranks on foot when everything broke loose and had been wounded in the resulting skirmish. Henry stared at him blankly. "The chest, sir," Timothy repeated, unsure of what more needed to be said. "We were charged with its delivery, which charge we have honorably fulfilled, but now we have it back. What is our obligation?" he asked delicately.

"Bury it," Henry ordered simply.

"Sir Henry?" Timothy asked in confusion.

"Bury it," Henry repeated.

"But sir, all that money—"

"Is worthless," Henry cut him off. "The chest is full of scrap iron. You are welcome to it, if you are so inclined, but it is up to you to convey it back."

"I do not understand. We risked our lives for scrap iron?"

"No, you have risked your life on the Baroness of Dawning Court's behalf, as a knight sworn to her is obliged to do." Henry stepped up close to Timothy, a full head taller than he, and stared sternly down at the younger man.

Timothy took half a step back unconsciously. "But the Baroness lied to us," he said without thinking.

"I would guard my tongue carefully if I were you," Henry warned dangerously.

"She told us the ransom money was in there."

"Not at all. What she said was exactly the truth. She told you Richard Dawning had been ransomed for a hundred thousand pounds sterling. All the payment that would be offered was in that chest. The Dawnings do not submit to extortion. And we do not pay the enemies of the Church from the family's coffers."

"But she could have told us," Timothy protested, unconsciously taking another step back as Henry's ire rose.

"Would you truly have been willing to die for a chest full of lead? Of course not!" Henry answered his own question. "We needed men who would defend that chest with their lives, and that would only happen if it was believed to be valuable. You have done a marvelous job in protecting it, for which you may be justly proud of your feats. And I assure you, your service will not be forgotten."

"I understand," Timothy replied, dropping his eyes to the earth. "We will leave it here."

"Apparently your understanding is yet lacking. You will bury it."

"But why?"

Henry pinched the bridge of his nose with one gauntleted hand and tried to quell his impatience at being questioned. "Sir Timothy, what were our objectives on this quest? What was the entire reason of this elaborate charade?"

"One was to get your brother back safely," Timothy said hesitantly as Henry ticked off each item on the fingers of one hand. "Two was to retain control of the chest." Henry flipped up a second finger, still rubbing his nose with the other hand. "And three was to keep the Moors from ever knowing we had duped them."

"Correct. Therefore, if we drop the chest here and they find it, even if they had never realized the Moor bandits were actually English knights, they will know we never had any intention of paying them. Do you wish to make our family and lands the focus of a Nizari grudge?"

"No, sir. But if I may say so, sir, it looks as though it may be too late to prevent that." With that, Timothy walked away to find help to dig a large hole.

Henry found himself alone and for the first time pondering upon what the long-term ramifications of their actions might be. All the hours in the war room, all the long days in the saddle, all the idle discussions that passed between them, they never considered the probability of retaliation, largely because they did not think they were up against a group that was capable of moving outside of their present sphere. He now realized they were at odds with a group large enough to project their influence all the way to England. Simply returning home was no guarantee of safety. It would not be an invading army that would follow; this group didn't work like that. It would be something much more insidious they would have to watch for... something he now feared the Nizari may be unveiling already. Perhaps Richard's kidnapping was never the goal at all but merely a distraction to remove the Dawnings and their knights from Dawning Court.

CHAPTER SEVENTY-SEVEN

William walked into the dimly lit tent. The only light was provided by what little sunlight filtered in through the cracks in the tent. There was a mound enveloped in shadow in the center of the floor that he took to be Richard's body. Another shadow sitting nearby quickly rose when William entered. "How is he?" William asked quietly so as not to disturb his brother.

"Not well, I'm afraid, William," the figure in the shadows replied. William could not make out who it was in this light, but it really did not matter. "He is disoriented and confused. He does not say much, but what he does say is incomprehensible. And to make matters worse, he is running a fever. It is not too extreme yet, but given his weakened condition and the urgency to keep moving, I greatly fear complications."

William nodded his understanding. All knights had some training in the healing arts. It was a necessary part of their training that enabled any knight to look after a fallen comrade. "Has he eaten anything?"

"Very little, and then only with much coaxing. He does not seem to feel he needs to eat."

"You have my thanks. I will stay with him for a while," William said, stepping up closer to the mound in shadows on the floor. "You should rest."

The shadowy form nodded and withdrew.

William checked carefully around him in the darkness to make sure the ground was clear and sat next to Richard, leaning back against a pile of gear. He surveyed the tent as his eyes adjusted to the low light. It was not much to look at: just an old, fading tent, the white canvas walls yellowing with age. There was a pile of equipment in the corner, some of which was currently serving as William's back rest. He inspected Richard's long form lying prone before him. Even with a blanket blurring the lines of his actual shape, William could scarcely believe this gaunt, frail figure that lay before him was his mighty brother. Richard had always been larger than life. Though William did not necessarily care for many things about Richard, he had never known him any other way. It was difficult to conceive how this situation came to pass.

Two dark circles glimmering in the darkness near Richard's head gave William a violent start. Richard's eyes were open and staring directly at him. "Richard?" William said quietly, sitting upright. "Are you awake? It's me, William."

"William?" cracked a dry, weak voice that did not resemble the Dawning men's deep, booming baritone at all.

Richard sighed weakly and pulled the blanket up to his chin. "You are not really William, of course. You are just another reminder of where I failed as a brother and as a person, no doubt. Well, I am very sorry I was not there for you."

"Do not worry yourself over such things," William said dismissively. "How are you feeling?"

Richard stared at him for a long time. "You really do not harbor any malice toward me?" he asked incredulously.

"Of course not," William assured him. "Stop talking nonsense."

"Then what are you still doing here?" he asked. "Perhaps you cannot go until I have forgiven myself." Richard stopped suddenly, the dark, glowing orbs of his eyes growing large. "Unless you, too, are here. You, too, are in Hell." He began to shake his head, and his voice cracked with emotion. "Oh no, not you, William. Not here. What did you do? How did it happen?"

An eerie chill crept up William's spine as he listened to Richard's ramblings. "I do not understand, Richard. Nothing happened to me. We rescued you from the Moors. We are taking you home to Dawning Court."

"Then you don't know? I suppose it took me a while to figure it out too," he said to himself. "Were you involved in a big battle recently? A battle that you narrowly escaped?"

William shrugged. "We fought today and it became... chaotic at one point."

Richard slowly moved a clammy hand onto William's. "William, if you are here with me," he said slowly, "you did not survive the battle today."

The chill washed over William again. "Richard, where do you think you are?"

"Why, William..." he said, a tear on his cheek glistening in the lamp light, "We are in Hell." Richard drifted into unconsciousness again, leaving William alone with the eerie images he had conjured.

CHAPTER SEVENTY-EIGHT

The rain kept coming. The world was soaked and cold. Everyone had retreated to the safety of their tents to wait out the weather. Only those on guard duty and the occasional unfortunate occupant of a tent that had given way to a small flood were exposed. All sound was muffled by the sizzling rain drops blanketing the land.

Loneliness had settled on William, who was not ordinarily subject to the pangs of solitude. He valued peace and quiet very much and under normal circumstances he might have been grateful for the respite, but not today. Today the absence of David was palpable. He had tried his best not to think about David since that dark day, but now his mind was filled with nothing else. He felt very alone.

Even Neil had kept his distance since that day, and William was grateful for that. Neil had a curious knack for saying the wrong things at the wrong time, and William was not emotionally prepared for that. Though Neil had proved a valiant friend, David had always acted as a buffer in their personal relationship. William could not help but wonder if Neil blamed him for what happened. Of course he blamed himself, so why would Neil feel otherwise? If he had just left David in his personal detail, where he was originally stationed, he would still be here. But then someone else would likely be in his place. Did that make it less regrettable?

William sighed over the sea of questions that had no answers. Nevertheless, that did not keep him from being mired down in them for the rest of the solitary day.

In the silence of his tent, the chill pressed in. He half expected to step outside and find himself back in time. The air was the same. The rain, the smells were similar except for the sea air. There was no smell of the sea here now. Just for an instant William wondered if he could step out of his tent and find David there all those years before on that fateful trip to the seaside...

"I can't believe this rain won't let up," David said walking in, carrying some semi-dry twigs he had wrapped in his cloak. "I'm worried about that berm above us; it is saturated and could give way, sending us right over the cliff." He shook his head. "I still can't believe I let you talk me into this; the ocean in October. Well, anyway, we should move the tent just in case."

"What?" William protested. "The few remaining items that are not wet or muddy would surely be drenched in such an endeavor. The berm is fine."

"Perhaps we should head for home," David suggested. "I cannot even see the ocean for the fog."

"What are you saying?" William pulled the flap of the tent back to reveal a spectacular view of a grey ocean that blurred into the horizon of dark ominous clouds forming a single grey mass. They were very exposed on the rocky cliff where they had pitched their tent the day before. "Tell me that sight does not stir your soul," William challenged, half in jest.

"That sight terrifies me. Look at the weather that is headed this way."

William snorted. "You mean headed away from us."

David walked to the door of the tent. "Watch the clouds, William. Those are headed right this way."

"No, they are not," William countered, taking a second look at the sky. "They are clearly... well, heading toward us. What's your point?"

"My point is that this is going to get worse before it gets better! We are soaked already, and that berm behind us is about to give out." The berm David was referring to was a high mound of grass and dirt that had overrun the rocky outcropping where they were camped. It sat about fifteen feet behind and stood some ten feet high, and was even now breaking loose enough to run a small stream of water down around their tent. William looked at the clouds rolling in off the sea. They seemed to be getting darker by the moment. He watched the steady stream of water running out from underneath the tent and looked at David.

"I say we weather the storm like men, not run away like mice." William could not completely suppress his grin as David became even more agitated.

"That berm is coming down, and I will not be here when it does," David said, stomping over to his bedroll and beginning to collect his things.

"That berm would not dare come down on noblemen. We are the princes of our country, and we own that berm," William declared authoritatively. "It has not the audacity to sweep us away like some poor peasants."

"Did you hit your head recently?" David asked, rolling up his bedroll. Just then a bolt of lightning flashed so close, the entire tent was set aglow. A mighty peel of thunder shook the ground they were resting on and, as if to punctuate the moment, a hole opened in the saturated rear wall of the tent and the small lake that was collecting there began flowing through the center of the tent.

William looked down at the water running over his boot. Looking up, he held up one finger and declared, "I have made a decision. We shall move on."

"You've gone quite mad, Caligula," David said, picking up his saddle. William knew they needed to move quickly, but he was having too much fun to stop there.

"David," he commanded, "fetch me my cloak," and he gave two small claps as a sign that his command should be obeyed immediately. David ignored him and pushed past with his *saddle and gear, heading out to the horses.* "You would abandon your master?" William called, throwing on his damp cloak, snatching up his saddle, and hurrying out after David. "What sort of servant are you to run away at the first sign of trouble? You must have some French in your lineage which, I should point out, you have never divulged," William said gleefully as they saddled their animals. Just then with a mighty rush the berm gave way and swept the tent in a great wave of mud and water over the edge of the cliff and down into the violently rolling sea a hundred feet below, taking with it all of William's gear except for his saddle, which was now on his horse.

Wordlessly the pair stared at the edge the tent had gone over. When the dramatic scene had ended and only the sound of rain and running water remained, they both raced over to the cliff edge to inspect the aftermath. A hundred feet below they could see a small white spot floating on the violent swells. "Well," William said after watching it for a moment, "go get it."

"I'm not going to get it. You go get it." David shot back.

"I would, but when we were hunting yesterday I really hurt my shoulder," William said, grabbing his right shoulder and working it around painfully. "And one can't scale a hundred-foot rock wall in a storm if one's shoulder is compromised."

"How come you are just mentioning this now?" David asked, obviously not believing a word of it.

"I do not like to burden my friends with my injuries," William said with suitably understated heroics.

"Really?" David asked dubiously. "How very gallant of you. You know it's interesting that you would say that because I remember a creag match last year in which you twisted your ankle."

"So?"

"So you spoke of little else for three days. In fact, you still bring it up occasionally."

"Look, are you going to go get that or not?" William persisted.

"No, I'm not," David rejoined without the slightest hesitation.

William sat back away from the edge. "Well if you're not going to get it, and I can't because of my ankle—"

"Shoulder."

"Right. Then what do we do?"

David thought about it for a moment and then said, "We have enough to get home because my gear is all intact. It might be a little bit rough, but we'll be fine."

They returned to their horses. David did not voice the chills that ran down his spine as he considered how close to disaster they had come. But William, noticing he had no bedroll or dry clothes to change into, managed to voice what was on his mind. "Ahh, David?"

"Yes?"

"Would you like to trade gear? I should think you will find mine ever so much easier to carry." David shook his head in disbelief, climbed into his saddle, and started for home...

William smiled to remember now as he sat in silence in his tent, Richard's occasional incoherent murmurs his only company. He wished David were here to reminisce about that day with him. But the unrequited desire only made the loneliness bore into his soul that much deeper, and a great sadness began to settle on him. It was difficult for an individual to find a friend that could tolerate him, but finding someone who understood or appreciated him was rare indeed.

CHAPTER SEVENTY-NINE

It was day three of the downpour. There was nothing in the camp that was not soaked and muddy. The men were soaked, and dry firewood was not to be found. That left them cold, with only dry rations to nibble on that were tough on the teeth, did little to fill the belly, and left the knights miserable and depressed. William sat with Richard in his own tent, which had sprung a leak. He was using a cooking pot to catch the water, but having moisture penetrate his only shelter seemed to make it all the more dark and depressing. William hated being soggy. He had spent so much time in that condition over the course of his campaigns that he had come to detest the feeling.

Henry came in, stripping off his soaked cloak. "I am so tired of this rain!" he was almost shouting in frustration.

"I know," William agreed. He was reclined on his saddle with his fingers interlaced behind his head, watching Richard thoughtfully.

Henry walked over to a small steel kettle and poured some thin soup into a small cup. "That's cold," William said casually without looking at him.

"So is everything else," Henry grumbled before swallowing the bitter drink down. "This weather is going to make traveling interesting. There is nothing like calf-high mud to slow down progress."

"We cannot move now anyway. Richard's fever is up, and look at him." Richard was under three blankets and shivering violently.

"We have to get back," Henry said. "And the sooner we get him into a warm bed with regular warm meals, the better."

"I agree, but if we move him now, in this weather, all he will get out of it is a cold grave. He cannot be moved until this fever breaks"

"I do not think that's a good idea—" Henry began.

"Henry, he is at death's door; these next few hours are critical. I'm not moving him!" William insisted.

"If we wait any longer, you are guaranteeing we get caught in the snow! What then? Hunker down and wait for spring while we watch our men die from starvation and exposure? And what if the Nizari have figured out our little trick and are riding us down as we speak? Then we all die for the sake of one sick man who may die anyway?"

"You may continue on if you like, but I am not going anywhere until this fever breaks."

"It is the epitome of irony that we went to all this trouble and lost a good man only to lose Richard to a fever after the fact," Henry said bitterly. "What a waste."

"Do not speak such tripe in here!" William barked. "We are staying to ensure our effort was not wasted and that David's life was not spent for naught. Now why don't you do something useful, like find some dry wood so we can make a fire."

Henry looked at him for a moment and then slammed down the empty cup and pulled on his wet cloak. "You know, I think I liked flippant William better," he grumbled.

"Isn't this exactly what you wished for, brother? That I would feel the weight of the burdens I carry? Well, I am feeling them now." William's voice cracked, and he turned his head away.

Henry stopped for a moment. "William, I know you are sick over David. I know you feel responsible. Believe me, I understand better than I can convey. I wish there was something I could say that would accelerate the grieving process, but there isn't. What is absolutely imperative, however, is that you maintain objectivity through this. Maintaining your reason is more important than ever, or you may find the weight of many deaths added to the weight of your friend's."

"All those I have heretofore lost in battle were associations that I only knew because of the battle; they were not a part of who I was. But now my life is forever changed because of this. A part of me that infuses my past will not extend into my future."

Henry squeezed William's shoulder. "You want to know what I have always most admired about you? The thing I wish that I had, that you have?" William did not respond, so he continued. "Your indomitable spirit. No matter what came, it never seemed to faze you."

William laughed through the tears. "I thought that drove you to distraction."

Henry smiled and stood. "I did not say it did not tax me to no end. I only said I wished I shared that spirit." And he stepped back out into the rain.

"William?" Richard asked through chattering teeth.

"Yes, Richard?" William said, leaning forward, looking after Henry. Richard lay there shivering under his blankets. His eyes were so narrow that William was unsure if he was still awake. William settled back after a moment, assuming Richard had drifted off again.

"It is so dark. So dark," Richard muttered suddenly.

"What do you mean?" Much of what Richard said appeared on the surface to be nothing but nonsense, but William would listen closely for insights or clues into his dementia.

It was several moments before Richard spoke again, "S- so dark."

William shook his head. "The tent? Would you like more light?"

"Their souls are so dark." Richard lapsed back into silence. William was unsure if there was some profound message to be garnered here or if Richard's comments were merely the bleating of a demented mind.

"William," Richard whispered so softly it took William a moment to realize he had spoken at all. William leaned in close to him and put his ear near his mouth.

"I'm here, Richard," he assured him.

"William, I have seen it."

"Seen what, Richard?"

"I have seen it," he was still speaking in a soft whisper as if he were afraid of being overheard. "I have seen the Hell of Hells where Lucifer lives. I have seen it." A chill ran down William's spine. "It is darkness—cold, lonely darkness. There is no light, no peace, only angry, bitter darkness and nothing else." William waited. "I'm so scared, William. I don't want to go there. I don't want to go there!" Tears began to flow from Richard's eyes.

"You won't," William reassured him weakly, surprised that his own voice cracked with emotion. "You are safe now."

"I feel the black enveloping the darkest parts of me and pulling me down. It wants me back. The blackness wants me." Richard's breathing became very rapid as panic set in.

William seized the once mighty shoulders in his grip and spoke in a firm, commanding voice. "Listen to me, Richard. The devil shall not have you today."

"He is coming for me! I have done so much evil—too much to ever be forgiven." His eyes opened wide at William, and he whispered, "So many things I did not realize—so many things that were sealing my soul to him. I did not know, William. I did not understand."

"In God's name, we have snatched you from the jaws of Hell, and he will not have you today!" A moment later the panic passed, and Richard's rapid breathing slowed. He settled into a fitful sleep once again.

William sat back, surprisingly shaken by the experience. Whatever Richard was seeing and feeling, he clearly believed he was looking into the seventh circle of hell and it was looking back at him, reaching out to claim him as its own. William felt it all around him and suddenly had an overwhelming desire to go out into the air and walk around, but he did not dare leave

Richard for fear that somehow the gate to Hell would open up and claim his brother if he were not there.

William could not help but reflect on his own past misdeeds. If Hell were reclaiming all those that were fit to be taken, why not take him as well as Richard? All at once William was standing back in Dawning Castle as a young man.

CHAPTER EIGHTY

"*You* will report every evening and weekend until the property is repaired and restitution has been made!" Martha ordered William.
 William glared at her defiantly. "Who said it was me?" He asked, revealing what was foremost on his mind.
 "I am sufficiently satisfied that it was you, and you will make amends with the tailor."
 It had been him, of course, William and his friends, that smashed the window and vandalized the contents of the tailor's shop after the tailor chased them off that day from loitering about the square. But William had not been alone, and only one that was among his friends could have betrayed him.
 "I want to know who told you!" William said darkly. He did not bother arguing the punishment as he knew no headway would be made on that account, nor would he betray the friends that were with him as he had so clearly been betrayed.
 "We are finished here," Martha said with a note of finality in her voice.
 "Tell me who betrayed me!" William shouted at her.
 Her countenance darkened even more. "Get control of yourself, William. Now leave me!"
 William stood defiantly rooted in place for another moment, reluctant to give up his object. But seeing it was pointless, he fled the castle to find Neil and David waiting for him

inconspicuously in the courtyard. They were anxious to know of his fate, but even more anxious to know of their own.

"What happened?" they asked, quickening their stride to keep up with William's agitated pace. "Are we in for it, too?"

"Your names were not mentioned," William indicated disconsolately. "I need to know who is behind this. Who betrayed me?"

Relief being so freshly on them, they were anxious to accommodate their doomed friend. "It had to be Callum and Tyler!" Neil suddenly exclaimed. They have been working extra hours in the fields for the last few days. I could not understand why, except now it all makes sense. They are being punished for their complicity in the act and must have given your name as the perpetrator."

"My mother sounded as if she believed I alone was responsible for this. They must have incriminated me alone in this!" William suddenly diverted onto a side road. The blood was pounding in his head like a drum beat.

"Where are you going now?" David asked nervously.

"I am going to pay my friends a visit." He put extra emphasis on the word *friends.* David and Neil exchanged nervous glances but hurried to keep up.

There was a small, one-room cottage on the edge of Callum's family estate that was generally unused. This is where the boys tended to congregate in their leisure hours in the evenings. As it was near dusk, William guessed that they might be found here. When they reached the small place, set some distance from the main stone house, he was not disappointed to see a light glowing inside. He heard Callum and Tyler laughing inside, and the warm passion he had been nursing swelled into a great rage. How dare they laugh and make merry while their cowardly hearts had been contemplating his destruction!

Exercising a good deal of self-restraint, William knocked gently on the door. The laughter inside immediately ceased, and there was silence for a few moments inside. Then hesitantly the door opened, and Callum's thick frame stood before William, *with Tyler peeking over his shoulder. "William," he said with surprise and nervousness. "I am surprised to find you here."*

William's head was low and he was looking right through Callum, struggling to restrain his fury. "How are you, Callum?" he asked darkly. Just then a small blonde face peaked out from under Callum's right arm. The boys were not alone. For the briefest of moments, William's resolve faltered, but he reassured himself that whatever consequences Callum and Tyler were about to suffer was a result of their actions, not his own.

"I am well," Callum said nervously. "My cousin Maria is up from London visiting with us."

"That's very fortunate," William said, still staring through him with the same grim expression. The pounding in his head was a virtual torrent now.

"Fortunate? Why? What do you mean?"

"That way there will be someone to collect your bodies." Callum's surprised expression immediately fell to one of anger. "I know it was you two cravenly swine that had the audacity to implicate me in this when you yourselves stood right next to me through every step of it."

"You don't know what you are talking about. Now why don't you just get out of here!"

"I know a miserable cur when I see one." William was still speaking in the same darkly calm voice, though he could hardly hear for the roar in his head. "Now how shall we do this? I will take you each alone or both together." Through all this, Neil and David, with a presentiment of what was coming, had remained but had stood several paces back so as not to be associated with what they knew their friend was likely to do. But they knew equally well that trying to dissuade him from anything in his wrath only threatened to turn his anger on them.

"How dare you come into Callum's house and call him out?" Tyler's voice cracked as he became impassioned also.

"You two now have a wrong to right. Let us settle this, you worthless dogs!"

"Leave my family's land!" Callum ordered and started to shut the door. William struck suddenly and without warning. He smashed the door inward with his foot with such force that it crashed open and hit Callum. He fell backward, his nose splattering blood on the door and running down his face. Maria screamed and retreated to a corner.

"You think this is over? You think I am finished with you?" William roared as he rushed into the cottage. Tyler swore and leapt to Callum's defense. With a hop, William crossed the short distance to meet him and shot his foot out sideways, planting it into Tyler's stomach. He used his momentum to lift Tyler off the floor and send him careening back into the wall. Maria's repeated screams gave William a sense of satisfaction.

Callum was on his knees, holding his nose. "You maniac," he said. A crack of William's elbow temporarily silenced him. William turned back to Tyler, who was just leveling a weak punch at him, still out of breath from the blow he had received. With a scoff William caught the blow across both his upraised forearms. He seized Tyler's wrist with his left hand and struck him a quick, stunning blow in the face. In such a state, Tyler was unable to resist William twisting his wrist upward into his own shoulder in a very unnatural state that made Tyler rise on his toes to try to relieve the pain that was shooting through his wrist and arm.

"Did you think I was not going to know it was you?" William demanded to Tyler's squirming face as he writhed in the grasp that William had on him, a hold easy enough to maintain with a single hand. "Did you think I would not find out you had betrayed me?"

"I'm sorry," Tyler said desperately. "But they knew already. They already knew who it was." He was vainly trying to pry William's fingers loose from his wrist.

"It was all of us!" William roared. Suddenly he released Tyler as his hair was seized from behind and his head jerked back. He put his own hand over the one threatening to pull his hair out and pivoted, using his elbow to break the grip, albeit painfully. There was the petite blond-haired, green-eyed girl.

William's rage was now upon this attractive, young, terrified girl. Knowing she was defenseless, he threw his whole shoulder into a devastating punch that instantly crumpled her tiny frame to the floor. William would remember vividly, even years later, the white dress with elaborate needlework across the bodice, and how the rough material felt on his knuckles.

"William, that's enough!" Neil yelled from where he had hesitated by the doorway. He had an idea of what William was about, but all had happened so quickly, he did not know what to do; but this was too much. David had not come into the cottage at all. William slammed his foot straight back at Tyler, whom he sensed more than heard about to attack from behind. His foot struck Tyler in the same spot as before, and Tyler crumpled to the floor.

The blood pounding in William's ears subsided now. All he heard was Tyler's gasping for breath and Maria sobbing on the floor of the cottage. "It seems you have chosen sides poorly," William lorded over them.

"William, let's go," Neil ordered.

But William was not without a sense that there would be repercussions from this. "If I ever hear of this, I will be back. There is no place you can hide from me. Mark my words!" He did not know if his threat would do any good to two such cowardly souls, nor did he know where this would end if they continued to push him. Perhaps there was only one inevitable conclusion.

CHAPTER EIGHTY-ONE

"Ah ha! You're a laborer in a tailor's shop!" Eve called at William, just out of arm's reach as he was painting the front of the shop. He had finally acknowledged that he had wronged the tailor and apologized as best one could apologize without a trace of humility. Now he was only anxious to be free again.

Eve and her little friends had happened upon him as he performed his duty and were now teasing him incessantly. "William Dawning is going to be a laborer all his life. End up with an ugly wife." They sang and danced around just out of reach.

"Eve! Go away!" he ordered, knowing his irritation was only fueling their game.

"Don't be cross with me because you're bad. It's your own fault you're here." This infuriated William all the more.

"How can such a tubby girl have such a small brain?" he demanded of her. Her face fell at the insult, and he knew he had scored. Eve was no heavier than any other little girl her age, but that didn't matter because she irritated William to no end, and she was always around when he least had the patience to deal with her.

"I may not be smart, but I'm smart enough not to have to repair a shop like a tradesman!" she shot back.

"That is true, you little toad. Because someone is always cleaning up your messes for you. If not for Leah, your family would have turned you out ages ago."

Her face fell again. "They would not!"

"Oh, but they would," William said in a confidential voice. Leah told me that they had not wanted you. And when you were another girl instead of a boy, which is what they really wanted, they had tried to deliver you to a monastery."

Her upper lip quivered. "You are a liar! A laborer and a liar!"

William shrugged nonchalantly. "Think that if you like, but I have seen the monastery where they left you on the steps. It was only Leah that brought you back."

Eve looked nervous now. "I am going to ask them if that's true, and they are going to say you are a liar."

"Oh, they have all made a pact that they would never tell you they tried. You see, they might want to try again, and they can't let you be suspicious or you might mark your way home somehow."

Tears stood in Eve's eyes now that she attempted to hide behind her long, dark curls. "You are a liar, and I hate you."

"Go ahead and run home as fast as those chubby little legs will carry you and ask them. They will pretend to be surprised and say that it is all nonsense, and then you will know that what I have said is the whole truth." She turned to hide her tears from him and began walking away. "Eve," William called after her. She pretended to ignore him, but he knew by the way she cocked her head slightly that she was listening. "They did not want to give you up only because you are so simple-minded, but also because you are so homely. That should be of some comfort to you."

Eve suddenly ran back to him with tears running down her face and kicked him in the shin. William grabbed his shin in one hand and with the other hand still holding the paintbrush flicked it so a heavy spray of paint splattered all over her face, hair, and clothes. She ran away sobbing, and William rubbed his painful shin in mild satisfaction that he had won the day.

He finished up for the evening and was just leaving the square when a slender figure appeared on the road in step with him. "Are you going home?" she asked casually.

"It seems like the thing to do," William observed dryly. "Every moment I am out and about, I seem to find myself in more trouble. What brings you out today? Come to mock me in my humble labors, too?"

"Too?" Leah asked.

"Your sister was here earlier."

"Was she, now?" Understanding dawned on Leah's face. "That explains the multicolored child that came home in a fit of hysterics with tales of being assaulted by the worst brute imaginable. She curiously left out the part you just mentioned."

"Well she would, now, wouldn't she?"

"I expect. It makes her less sympathetic if she includes that part."

"I quite frankly do not know how you tolerate that little monster." Leah started to reply, but William continued. "There is no possibility that you two can actually be related. She is scheming, conniving, obnoxious, and a homely creature to boot. She must take after your father." Leah did not immediately respond, and William, sensing the awkwardness, attempted to lighten the mood by continuing. "Never have two people plotted so hard for my undoing as Eve and your father. I should be quite happy if they both just disappeared tomorrow and were never heard from again." He had meant this to sound light, but Leah stopped and was staring at him. She was not laughing.

"William, I understand that you have your differences with my family," Leah said softly, still holding his gaze. "But they are my family, to whom I am indebted for everything. I love them dearly despite their not always seeing things as I might wish, and I cannot tolerate such awful things being directed against them, particularly from one who professes to be my friend." William was embarrassed by her words and felt slightly jealous at what he perceived to be her favoring them over himself.

"Leah, I don't understand," he said, flushing. "Families only bring exasperation and trials. What does it profit you to be so loyal to them?"

"I understand how you may feel that way," she said; she still had not moved as if she had not yet determined whether she would continue in his company or not. "But you must understand and give equal consideration to the fact that I do not feel that way about my own family. I love them for all their quirks and foibles."

"I am sorry... if I offended you," William said, qualifying his apology as he did not regret his words against her family in the least degree.

"Do we have an understanding?" she asked seriously. William nodded mutely. He was silently angered by her reproach but did not dare push her on this subject. "So are you about finished? At the tailor's shop, I mean?" Leah asked, returning to their former conversation.

"Another day or two, I suppose." He tried to sound casual again as well.

"This seems like a lot of work for one night's rabble rousing with your friends," she chided him mildly.

"That had not occurred to me. Although if it had not been for my friends, I never would have been caught," he offered with some amount of pride.

"You never did explain to me how that happened. It wasn't Neil and David, I trust."

"No, it was not Neil and David."

"Who, then? Have you had a falling out with them?"

"We had a falling out," William said, deliberately avoiding her question. "But it has all been settled now." While he did not regret what he had done to Callum and Tyler, he knew that Leah, as good and sweet as she was, would never understand it. He felt it necessary to conceal certain things from her. That night was one of those things. They were the enemy and had made themselves so by their actions, and all that had happened to them happened in consequence of those actions. But Leah was too sweet and naïve to see this. All she would hear is that he had attacked his friends in their own house. She could never understand, so it was imperative that she never know.

"I'm glad of that," she said.

William was very uncomfortable now. He did not like the way this conversation was going and was feeling very out of sorts since her reproach. After a moment's hesitation, he decided to end it. "Leah, I have just remembered, there is something I am very late for. Will you excuse me?"

Leah looked surprised. "Well of course, but what could—" William did not wait for her to finish but broke into a sprint. He was not the least bit subtle, he knew, but all he cared for at that moment was to extricate himself from this uncomfortable situation.

"I will see you soon," he called over his shoulder and abandoned her there on the road alone.

CHAPTER EIGHTY-TWO

"Gentlemen," Anisa said cheerfully as she walked into the cave, tracking in the light blanket of snow that was covering the ground. "It would seem our brother has succeeded. Winter is upon us and there is no sign of the Dawnings or their party. The Barony is as good as ours." There was a general murmur of approval among those assembled. Anisa could not hide her excitement that such a big piece of this elaborate plan had fallen into place.

"I fear your celebratory overtures are premature, milady," Khalid said, walking into the cave after her. "I have only just received word that the Dawnings betrayed our people and have once again left many dead in their wake. They are returning to Dawning Court even now."

"What?! But that cannot be true!" Anisa's heart sank. "Surely we would have heard..."

Khalid spread his hands before him. "I cannot explain why they have not yet returned. I cannot even tell you how they eluded our brother, but it would seem they have and that they are expected back any day now."

"No, no, this cannot be," Najid, the Dawnings' house servant, protested. "I warned you they were only bringing a small force. I told you what to expect. What more could we have done?" There was a general sense of dread in the dank cave as the chill set in on them more deeply. "All that we have worked for is slipping away."

"Nonsense," Khalid said dismissively. "We still proceed with the plan."

"How can we proceed with the plan? How do we stop the Dawnings in their homeland with a weakened force when we could not stop them with our whole army on our own land?" Rafiq demanded.

"I told you not to underestimate them! I warned you!" Anisa breathed.

"Amir is bringing men with him," Khalid explained.

"Excellent," Anisa perked up again. "Provided he has arrived by Henry's wedding day, then John will make his declaration, they will resist, and as John's loyal subjects we will have no choice but to cut them down."

"Won't that cause a problem with John?" Rafiq asked dubiously.

"I have no intention of seeking John's approval. He certainly won't like it, but once it is done, I will help him to see the necessity of such a step. We are so close, we cannot let this opportunity slip through our fingers."

"The timing will be critical," Khalid pointed out. "We will have to take them completely unawares, and we have to get all the Dawnings together. If even one escapes, he could and would incite a revolt. We do not have the manpower to contend with a large force."

Anisa nodded her understanding. "I think it may be time that John sets a date to become a man."

CHAPTER EIGHTY-THREE

Leah dropped her needlework for the tenth time. She rose and walked to a window and opened the shutters to peer out at the snow-covered landscape. Where were they? They should have been back by now. Why weren't they here? Why had they not sent word? All these questions and a thousand others had occupied her mind with increasing frequency since the weather turned. She sighed and closed the shutters again, sat back down near the fire, and picked up her needlework once again. She was determined to get her mind off of this. She stared into the fire for a long time before dropping it again.

Suddenly from the lookouts came a trumpeted call. They had returned! The advanced lookout would have spotted them first and trumpeted the warning back to the sentries posted at Dawning Court's inner walls, who in turn trumpeted the news to all those around Dawning Court; the brothers had returned. Leah was one of those who heard the call. She dropped her needle and thread and jumped up to check over her dress. She was not at all happy with what she was wearing, considered changing, and then decided there was no time. She rushed for the door but was brought up short by a vision of a potentially awkward scene that unfolded in her mind's eye. But she had to know if they were successful or not. She had to know if everyone was well. "Of course he—they—are well. We would have received word if it were otherwise," she assured herself. "Maybe it is better not to go?" She wrung her hands anxiously and paced nervously. She would have to decide shortly in order to allow time to meet them at the gate. Now that this moment had arrived, she had no idea how to handle it. How could she have let herself get into this situation? And how could she bear to tell William? Tears sprang into her eyes, but she quickly composed herself. Now was not the time. "He—they—will be expecting me. I'm going", she determined.

Before she could think better of it, she threw a cloak over her shoulders and raced out the door to the small stable attached to her house. She had a servant bring the carriage around while she waited, pacing anxiously.

In a few moments she was on the road heading for the main gate. She could not imagine a more bittersweet moment. "This is not a situation of your own making," she reminded herself. "You did not want it this way, either." But that did little to cure the sick feeling in her stomach.

Leah came upon a familiar figure: a woman walking on the road carrying a young child. "Salena?" she said, ordering her driver to slow. "You've heard the news?"

"Oh, hello, Leah," Salena looked up in surprise. "Yes, we were just on our way to greet them."

"Well, you certainly are not going to walk there; hand Rachel to me," Leah said and took the little girl up, setting her on the seat next to her. Rachel smiled at Leah and swung her legs off the seat of the carriage. Salena climbed aboard. "Thank you," she said as she seated herself self-consciously on the wooden seat. She did not try to make an excuse as to why she was walking. Leah was the one person Salena felt was not judging her. "And thank you again for the basket of treats the other day. You are too thoughtful."

"Not at all," Leah replied modestly. "If you ever need anything, please let me know." The carriage resumed its brisk pace.

"You are alone?" Salena asked, surprised at the notable absence of Edith.

Leah looked embarrassed. "Edith was not available when the call came, and I did not think I could afford to wait. But she is such a dear, she will forgive me." She looked worried for a moment, but the look quickly fled. "But I now have you with me, so there is nothing improper in this."

"I wish I had your independent spirit, Leah," Salena confessed. "I feel so dependent on David. I do not know what I would do if anything should ever happen to him. I thought I would go quite mad awaiting his return, and Rachel, of course, misses him terribly."

"I am sure of it," Leah agreed, looking at the dark-haired little girl humming to herself on the seat between them. "I can't believe how big you are getting," she said to the little girl, who only smiled and continued to kick her legs and hum.

"You think so?" Salena asked in surprise. "I don't feel like she is growing at all."

"Well, she is still quite petite, but each time I see her she looks more the little lady than ever before." Salena could not help smiling at the compliment.

"I have been so worried. Since they left, I mean." Salena said suddenly as if confessing some great sin. "In earnest, when David told me William was making him go on this silly adventure, it was all I could do not to march up to the castle and spit in William's face."

There were so many things about that statement that infuriated Leah that she bit down on her tongue to keep from showing her anger in a decidedly un-ladylike way. Instead she responded to the last item of contention. "I would hardly call a quest to rescue a family member held hostage a 'silly adventure'," she said somewhat stiffly.

Salena sighed. "I know. I just do not trust William. Anything he is involved in is dubious."

Leah reminded herself of how young Salena actually was and that she and William's relationship had gotten off to a bad start. "Salena, William really has changed from the surly teenager you remember. You must forgive the past and let him be a different person."

"Certainly you don't trust him!" Salena said, shocked. "You know him better than anyone."

"That's right, and I would trust him with my life. In fact, even as a teenager there would have been no one I trusted with my life more."

Salena nodded reluctantly. "David said he's a great fighter."

"It has nothing to do with that," Leah assured her. "I know he had a rough exterior and sometimes still does, but if you had taken the time to get to know William like I did, you would find one of the most courageous and noble hearts ever to reside in the bosom of a man."

Salena listened patiently, then said, "But the things he said, the danger he brought down upon my David's head because of his stupid pride. If you ask me, you could take the entire Dawning family and—"

"That's enough!" Leah cut her off, shocked that Salena could be so insensitive to speak that way about one of her best friends, much less the local family of benefactors.

"Oh, I am sorry, Leah, I forget he is your friend." Salena dropped her head so her long, dark hair would hide her coloring face.

"That's right, he is my friend, and there are things I will not hear."

"But surely you do not deny that you have seen him do some questionable things," Salena persisted with a peculiar blindness to the propriety of the situation.

"Perhaps," Leah shot back hotly, "but I have also seen him do some of the sweetest, most noble things I have ever witnessed. Now mind your tongue."

They rode on in silence for a time, Leah fuming and Salena too embarrassed to speak further. Finally Leah said, "You know, Salena, it is not good for you to carry this bitterness around with you. It only hurts you, and it cankers your lovely soul in a way that spills out onto all those around you. You must get rid of it." More silence followed. At last Salena spoke. "You are right, Leah. Every time I think of the Dawnings, and especially William, I become incensed; but if you see something more, then it must be as you say. For you are a woman of impeccable judgment."

Leah smiled at Salena. "Just give him a chance. I promise you will be glad you did."

"Oh, I've missed David so much," Salena abruptly changed the subject. "I am so relieved he's back, I cannot even express it. I will throw my arms around him and drag him home and lock him up to ensure he never has any thoughts of leaving again."

Leah smiled, suppressing the wicked thoughts she herself was having. She, too, had missed her friend very much.

They reached the gate just in time to see the multicolored flags of the knights appear on the horizon. They were home. Leah and Salena jumped down from the carriage, barely able to contain their excitement. Over the hill they rode, armor glittering in the sun, plumes bright and beautiful. William was the only one that could be easily distinguished from the others because of his unique white armor. All the other knights were only distinguishable from small variations in similar suits of iron and their individual crests. It was necessary to get up close to find an individual within the group.

There was quite a welcoming party assembled at the gates now, and Salena realized she would not be seen among the others. Forgetting her decorum, a veneer that was always rather thin on Salena anyway, she scooped up Rachel and hurried out towards the knights when they were still fifty yards away. She spotted William and set a course for him, expecting to find David somewhere close by. Leah sighed and then hurried after Salena, giggling in excitement in spite of herself.

As they got closer, William spurred his horse ahead of the others, leading a riderless horse with him. Leah's heart leapt with excitement as he rode toward her, then she knew something was wrong. She saw it before Salena, who was looking past William to find her husband. Leah's legs suddenly felt weak, and she stopped in place ten yards behind Salena. She did not want to see the scene that was about to unfold, but she could not look away.

William dismounted and dropped to one knee before Salena, still holding the reins of the riderless horse in one hand. There were tears in his eyes, and though Leah could not hear the words being said, she knew what news he was conveying. A horrible, heart-wrenching wail broke from Salena that merely confirmed Leah's fears.

"You did this!" she shrieked at William. "You took my David from me!" William kept his head bowed before her, saying nothing. The strength went from Salena's limbs, and her knees buckled slightly. She looked as though she might drop Rachel. Only her fury at William kept her on her feet. "He was a hundred times the man you will ever be! And you took him from me. You took my baby's father from her!" she screamed at William between great, wracking sobs.

Leah raced up to them and pulled Rachel from Salena's arms, tears streaming down her own face. She cradled Rachel in one arm and put her free arm around Salena and pulled her tightly to her, turning Salena's bereaved face from William. She held Salena as her body shook and tears poured from her.

It broke Leah's heart to see William kneeling alone, struggling to control his own emotions. She longed to run to him as she saw the water dripping from his downcast face and his body rigid with the strain of maintaining his composure. But she knew Salena needed her more at the moment and William would not have it any other way. Salena turned back as Leah led her back to the gates. "You killed my David. I will never forgive you. Never!"

Everyone had frozen at this dramatic scene. The knights accompanying William had stopped some distance behind, and their eager families had also waited, somehow sensing what was happening. No one wished to be involved in the scene before them: the dramatic portrayal of the moment in which each of their greatest fears was realized. Everyone waited with a solemn respect for Salena to be escorted away from the gate before resuming the joyous reunions of their own.

Leah glanced one last time over her shoulder as she departed from the field. The iconic scene of the lonely knight brought to his knees by his burdens would be forever impressed in her memory. These men sacrificed more than she had recognized, and she longed to be with William now.

Henry appeared at his side. He stood silently erect beside his brother while the scene passed away; neither moved, neither spoke. They shared in that moment the deep personal losses they both had suffered.

CHAPTER EIGHTY-FOUR

"They have returned!" Anisa's eyes flashed in fury. "How could you have let this happen?" They were meeting deep in the trees as usual.

"Me?" John protested. "I was not even there."

"You should have been there. You could have ensured this did not happen."

"What do you mean by that?"

"You allowed the most viable threat to your assumption of power to be returned as a hero on the eve of your triumphant declaration. You should have been there to guarantee this did not happen."

"Are you suggesting that I kill my own brother at his weakest?"

"You would not have had to kill him; you would only have needed to ensure the appropriate arrangements could be made for him."

"Perhaps we have different ideas of what I am willing to do for this." John's reticence suddenly resurfaced.

"Do not be such a simpleton!" Anisa's dark eyes were blazing. "Do you honestly believe that you will have to make no sacrifice for this? That attitude has made you the pathetic shell of a man that you are today."

John was stung by her words. "I did not even know they were going after him. I did not even know Richard had been captured."

"It is your responsibility to know. You should be involved with everything that happens at Dawning Court right now. One ugly surprise like this could ruin everything. Is that what you want? Do you want to spend the rest of your life tending dead crops and living in a ditch in a drunken stupor?" Anisa began a full frontal assault as she usually did during disagreements, and, as was usually the case, John was quelled by her fury.

"I'm sorry," he said desperately. "It will not happen again."

"I know it won't," Anisa said, regaining some of her composure. "Amir is coming in person to ensure that it will not."

"Amir is coming here?" John was shocked. They had always spoken of Amir as a mystical figure: a sage, warrior, and mystic all rolled into one; but he had never really expected to meet him.

"He believes that we have handled this too incompetently, and he must oversee it personally to guarantee success."

"I'm touched that he would be so concerned with the plight of one foreign knight in a small barony so far away," John said, somewhat confused as to why he would be so. Anisa did not explain. Since arguing with Thomas that day in the forest, the peculiarity of this situation had been more pronounced than ever before. Now this 'Amir' was coming to take over the planning of John's ascension to power. What would he expect in return? Would those helping him be more loyal to Amir than to John? "Is there going to be a conflict of leadership?" John asked tentatively, afraid to set Anisa off again.

"Why would there be?" was all she said.

"Good." John's eyebrows knitted together in perplexity. Perhaps he and she were not so closely aligned after all. He wanted to push the matter further, but Anisa interrupted him.

"We will need to act quickly before Richard has a chance to regain his strength and mount any serious resistance."

"When?"

"We need to ensure the entire family is together in order to control the situation." She interlaced her fingers behind her back and pursed her lips thoughtfully. "When would you expect them to all be together next?"

"Hmm," John said thoughtfully. He did not want to admit to Anisa that he was so estranged from the rest of the family that he was completely unaware of all travel and upcoming events. All except one. He snapped his fingers excitedly. "Henry's wedding. There is no question that they will be married in the church, and even if Richard is convalescing, he will be in attendance. The entire family is guaranteed to be there."

"Perfect," Anisa said, feeling his excitement. Her beautiful face brightened noticeably. John was happy to see that. She treated him much better when she was happy, and he was the one that had made her happy. "When is that?"

"A few weeks."

She stroked her chin thoughtfully. "It will be close, but I think we can do it. We will have to begin preparations immediately." She turned to retreat into the trees.

"Anisa," John called, seeing her depart unexpectedly. She stopped. "Aren't you and I going to have any time?"

She half smiled over her shoulder at him. "Of course. I will meet you tonight. In the meantime, keep a close eye on your family and apprise me immediately of anything out of the ordinary."

"Of course," he said quickly, anxious to reassure her. He was already thinking about their time together that evening. No business, just closeness and pleasure. He needed her and was feeling the distance that had kept them apart for too long. He turned to descend the mountain with thoughts of the evening to come filling his head.

CHAPTER EIGHTY-FIVE

When everyone had passed on to be with their families, Henry started for Dawning castle. It hurt him that there was no one waiting for him. He really had hoped Mary would be there and that everyone would see his betrothed coming out to support her man; and for the first time in his life, his reality might match his dreams, with the damsel breathlessly awaiting the return of her hero from abroad.

But of course he knew that was foolishness. She no doubt had returned to Mayfield long ago. Why would she have remained here in a barony full of strangers when her own people were just a few days away? Henry sighed. He was finally having the triumphal return he had always dreamt of and there was no one who even cared. He had led a handful of men into the jaws of death, and they had snatched Richard out while only losing one man. While he was not at all happy about David's loss, the loss of only one man on the expedition was a far better result than even he himself had dared hope for.

He dropped his horse at the stable to be cared for and walked the length of the courtyard back to the castle. Still, the lonely hero returning from a thankless quest to rescue a fallen brother, only to find himself all alone once again, also somehow fit the idea he always had of his role in the family. He was glad in a way there was no celebration held, no reward for what he had done. It helped solidify that he had done this thing for selfless reasons rather than some deep down selfish desire.

That was important to him after the conversation he and Mary had had the night before his departure. He was still smarting from the disparaging comments she had made to him. After stewing on these things for so many weeks, he had begun to think that perhaps she was not a good match for him after all.

Henry was ripped from his reverie by the apparition that appeared in the path before him. Mary was radiant in a white dress that could not but remind him of a wedding gown. Henry was unsure of how he would be received after all this, after completing a mission that she was so adamantly opposed to. And he was not really sure how he felt anymore.

He stared at her from fifteen paces away. Neither moved; neither spoke, till suddenly she broke and ran as well as her cumbersome clothing would allow her and embraced him. Henry stumbled backward from the forceful embrace, but all at once all was forgiven. Here was someone that did care about him. He was not about to give that up.

CHAPTER EIGHTY-SIX

"Mother, I'm afraid I must be off," William announced without preamble, walking into the library.

She looked up in mild surprise and then rose to meet him. "I will not insult you by trying to talk you out of it. You are old enough to know your own mind." She put her hands on his shoulders. "You have done the family a great service. I know the price you paid by coming back here, but I am not sorry for it because it has proved to everyone the greatness of your heart. A greatness that I always knew was there. But I am sorry that your burdens are a little heavier for your experience here. I know why you do what you do, William. I only wish you would not do it."

William smiled a sad smile at her. "You wish I didn't do most of the things I have done in my life. Why should this be any different?"

She smiled back. "If you would start listening to me, then you might find you had an easier time in this life. You will miss your brother's wedding?"

William spread his hands helplessly. "I would not choose to, as it is hard to find food as plentiful as it is in a wedding, but Braddock will certainly be watching the wedding party for me. It may be that he has heard of my return by now, and he may arrive here at any moment."

"You are leaving soon, then, I take it."

"Tonight, under cover of darkness. It is too dangerous for me to travel these parts by day." William shook his head with a wry smile, tinged with sadness. "I never would have thought I would be an outlaw in my own home."

"William, I would caution you—what is it?"

William held his hand up to silence her. He had his head cocked, listening intently. After a moment he made a motion for her to keep talking as he crept for the door. "Uh yes, well I was only saying that you had best be warned that this time, if you leave, it is going to cost you something that I believe is most dear to your heart—"

William flung the door open suddenly, without warning, and leapt into the empty hall. All was quiet. He stood listening for a moment before reentering the library. Martha's eyebrows were raised expectantly. "Nothing." He shook his head. "Only I was sure I heard someone."

"You are too paranoid. It comes from too many years at war. It would take your father months to settle down after he returned from a campaign."

"Yes, that is probably it," he said skeptically. "You trust your house servants?"

"Yes, I trust them."

"Well, anyway," he embraced his mother, "I have so missed the reassurance of my mother's presence. I love you, Mother." She could not suppress the tears.

"Please return to us as soon as you can."

He stepped back and looked for something to say to reassure her. "I will see what I can do about Henry's wedding. The wedding party would not be complete without the disavowed son of the Dawnings."

"I would never disavow you," Martha said, wiping her eyes.

William looked at her seriously. "I know, but you should have."

She shook her head. "I could not do it then, and I could never do it now."

"Should Braddock ever ask you directly, you may be bringing a war on Dawning Court that we are not strong enough to fight."

"That old fool and I have an unspoken understanding. He never asks me about that directly, and I never give him any reason to suspect that I have done otherwise."

"I mean it, Mother. If it comes to that, you do not for one second hesitate to disavow me. It doesn't matter anyway."

"It matters to me!" Martha said passionately. "You are my son! I will not disavow you for no good reason, and I will not pretend I have done so if I have not!"

William smiled another sad smile. "Very well, Mother. Thank you for believing in me."

"I know you try to hide a heart that grieves for your friend, William. It is okay to grieve. It is okay that something penetrated the façade. It is not a weakness to care."

"I am quite sure I do not know to what you are referring. Any sadness you detect is only for my extremely chaffed hind quarters—riding in the rain, you know—that will be put in the saddle yet again." He tried to sound light, but it sounded forced.

"It is okay to grieve. I loved David, too. He was like one of my own children, he was around so often when you were boys."

"And Salena and Rachel?" he asked.

"Are to be well taken care of. I have put all that you asked in place for them. They will live better now than they did when he was alive."

"That is well." He embraced her one more time and left her alone in the large, empty library, which suddenly seemed colder and emptier than it had moments before.

CHAPTER EIGHTY-SEVEN

"You will never go all the way to the top!" William taunted David.

"I will so," David said and wrapped the rope over his shoulder to climb one branch higher.

"That's not the top," Neil pointed out.

David looked up at the remaining flimsy branches and gulped. "Those branches won't even hold my weight," he protested.

"Of course they will!" William persisted, only slightly nervous for his friend's safety. "Look at that bird sitting above you. It's barely bending that branch, and you aren't even going that high. You'll be fine."

David reached one trembling hand up to the next branch and stopped short of hoisting himself up. "If I do this, you have to do it too," he bargained.

"I'm not doing it," Neil muttered to William out of the side of his mouth.

"Of course we'll do it," William called up as if Neil had not said anything.

David looked back down at the ground many feet below and back up at the last few branches he thought he could reasonably scale. Then, one by one, he slowly pulled himself up, hugging the tapering trunk as closely as possible while trying to hide his trepidation from his sniggering friends below.

"It's going to be the best swing ever," William encouraged him from the ground. The opposite end of the rope David was carrying was tied off to a branch of another larger tree right beside them, and David was now higher than the tied knot on the other tree. None of them had ever swung from that high before, but now that they had turned ten, they felt it was time to really test their mettle. They had spent the day venturing into the forests around Dawning Court to find wild beasts to slay and prove themselves; but finding the forest dragons to be largely hunted to extinction, they decided to bring their test of manhood to the old rope swing. "How are you ever going to fight in the Crusades if you're afraid of a tree?" William taunted to spur David through his hesitation.

"There's an old adage that says if you're afraid of a tree, you're afraid of a Moor," Neil supplied helpfully.

"Shut Up!" David barked, their comments starting to grate on his fraying nerves.

"There's an old adage that if you can't shut your friends up, you can't even beat a Frenchman," William instantly retorted.

"Can you beat a Frenchman, David?" Neil yelled. "There is no way I'm doing that," he again muttered to William. David had reached the last branch. He had his hand on it, but when he tried to hoist himself up, his strength failed him.

"You know, I can see over the battlements from here," David called down trying to sound casual and to disguise the terror he was feeling.

"You see?" William yelled back. "You've been on the battlements hundreds of times, so what are you worried about?"

"Of course, the battlements don't shake like this," Neil called and started to push on the trunk of the tree. He was small enough that he could only elicit the smallest movement from the branches above, but it was enough to send the frazzled boy into a panic.

"Stop it!" David shrieked at him.

"Stop it, Neil," William said nervously but could not help grinning at David's reaction.

David pulled himself carefully onto the uppermost branch of the old oak tree. He moved very slowly, trying to maintain a grip with both hands as he turned himself around. Though he was only about ten feet higher than where they had been swinging from previously, he could not empty his mind of the premonitions of pain and death. "This is crazy," he called down weakly.

"Just do it!" came the unsympathetic response from his friends.

David held his breath, took a hold of one of the knots on the rope and carefully slid the attached wooden plank between his legs, feeling as though he would lose his footing at any moment. He was set, and since he could see no way out of it, he tried to jump off the branch. His fear once again robbed his legs of their strength, however, and his "jump" devolved into a mere buckling of the knees. But that was enough, and away he went in a virtual free fall. The wind rushed past him, his heart stopped, and he was unaware of the high falsetto scream that filled the air as he descended. But then the old rope went taught and swung him over past the next tree and high into the air, where the rope slackened again; and once again David's piercing scream rang out as he now made a similar journey backward. Again the rope caught and swung him back up near his original perch, though not quite so high as before.

After a few more swings, David came to a halt, laughing. Neil and William quickly ran up to him with a newfound respect in their eyes. "I can't believe you did it," William said.

"I thought you were dead," Neil added.

"It was actually pretty easy," David said nonchalantly. "I would even do it again… sometime," he added quickly so as not to find himself back up in the tree. "Here you go," he said, holding out the swing to the other two.

"I'm not doing that," Neil again reiterated and took a step back.

"Well?" David extended it to William. "We had a deal." William hesitantly took the rope from his hand, thereby tacitly accepting the challenge, and immediately wished he hadn't. "It is so much fun," David assured him. William wrapped the rope around himself and started his ascent. "Just don't die."

"You know they say if you can do it backward," Neil immediately started taunting him when he was in the lower bows, "you will be able to beat a whole army of Vikings."

"That's true," David added immediately, glad to be the one on the ground now. "I have heard a lot of people say that."

William determined he was not going to let his fear get to him. He put it out of his mind and began climbing. David had done it and been fine, so what did he have to worry about? He climbed up past their usual launching branch and ignored his friends' teasing from below. But he, too, found his limbs inadvertently slowing as he approached the upper branches. Nevertheless, he slid and scraped his way to the top and turned to face outward from the trunk for the first time. He immediately felt light-headed. The distance from this height looked twice as high as it had from the ground. William stood for a moment, desperately trying to think of an excuse to get out of this.

"If you die, can I have your saddle?" David was yelling at him.

"If I die, I have decreed that you two are to be stuffed and put on my grave," William called back. Seizing the rope, he slid the swing between his legs before his fear got the best of him. In a few moments he would be down, and all would be well.

He stepped off the branch before he had a chance to think about it and was vaguely aware that he, too, was now screaming like a little girl. He fell fast; the wind was deafening. He completely lost sight of his friends and the world around him. All he could see was that ground rushing up toward him. Then, as it always had, the old rope creaked, the branch gave slightly, and William swung up to the opposite side of the pendulum.

William then made the descent from the other side, using his weight to spin himself around to face the ground. Again the rope caught him and started to swing him up, but this time the old rope had frayed too much from years of weathering, and the strain was too much for it. The rope snapped off where it was knotted around the limb just as William was beginning his ascent for the second time. The rope let go, and he was hurled through the air another ten feet before he crashed into the ground, tailbone first. Stars exploded before his eyes, and everything went black.

After a brief moment of shock, Neil and David were there. "What do we do?" Neil shrieked in panic.

"Go get someone!" David yelled, his voice cracking from the fear. Neil dashed off for the castle, and David knelt down next to his friend, unsure of what to do. "William, can you hear me?" There was no response. "William!" David sat there helplessly, with no idea what to do. In desperation, David said a fervent prayer for William's safety. With all the feeling of his young heart, he implored the Heavens that everything would be well with his friend.

Neil sprinted around the outer wall of the castle and into the training yard. John was there, running through practice drills with his long sword. "I need help!" he shouted. "William, William has fallen!"

John immediately dropped his sword and raced out after Neil, who was already on his way back. He overtook him as he came around the wall and saw William lying on the ground with David sitting over him. "Oh please, no," John said aloud, fearing the worst and redoubling his speed. David stood as he raced up, relief at their arrival clearly showing on his face.

"He's still not awake, and his lips are turning blue," David supplied.

"What happened?" John demanded. William was very pale, and his lips did appear to be turning blue. He quickly checked William's neck for a heartbeat and was relieved when he felt it. Then, not waiting for the stammered explanation from David and Neil, he scooped William's limp form up and ran for the castle.

He ran inside, crashed through the doors of an adjacent sitting room, laid William on a sofa, and began calling for servants and barking orders for medicines. "I prayed for him," David admitted quietly as he looked over John's shoulder."

"I have been praying nonstop," Neil added, unsure if he should be ashamed or proud of this fact.

"That may be the only thing we can do," John said. "He was searching for a heartbeat again when William's eyes opened. Everyone froze in anticipation. "William," John said quietly with Neil and David looking anxiously over his shoulder. "William, are you all right?" William rolled his eyes around the room to try to assess the situation. "William?" John repeated.

"John," William replied quietly.

"Yes?"

"Stay off the rope swing. I think the rope's ready to break." The room breathed a collective sigh of relief.

"Do you have any idea how scared I was?"

"You should have seen it from my side," William offered somewhat weakly.

John smiled his relief. "One of these days, I will not be here when you need me."

"Yes, you will."

CHAPTER EIGHTY-EIGHT

"So where is he?" Mary asked impatiently.
"I don't know," Henry shrugged. For as long as I can remember, he has never been on time to anything."
"Well that is the very sole of impropriety," Mary said. "No gentleman would keep a lady waiting."
"No gentleman would do half the things he has done." Henry said, scanning the distance for some sign of him. Henry was seated in the carriage where he sat next to Mary, holding the reins of the twin white horses bridled to it.
"He's probably drunk and won't show up at all. Or better yet, he will stagger over to us inebriated."
"I doubt it," Henry contradicted her lightly. "John likes to make big appearances, and he is not going to want to look foolish in front of my betrothed when he meets her for the first time. He used to make brazen overtures to Leah with William right there. It was very embarrassing. And though she was good-natured enough about it, he was humiliating himself, and everyone could see it except for him. Do not be surprised if he conducts himself similarly with you."
"Well I assure you, I will not be dallying with any of your brothers," Mary said indignantly as she smoothed her skirts.
"Well that's good," Henry said without emotion, still scanning the horizon.
"So what do you mean, 'make a big entrance'?" Mary asked. "I thought he didn't have any money."

"He doesn't," Henry explained. "But that is how John differs from my other brothers. Instead of leeching off the family, he struck out on his own to prove himself. Each time he resurfaces after a long absence, he tries desperately to appear as if he has come into his own. He will borrow, beg, or steal to get what he needs to look the part... and it seems today is no exception," he finished as John came riding over the crest of the hill in a finely tailored black tunic with gold embroidery on the chest and a matching black cloak flapping behind him. He rode atop a fine Arabian horse with slender legs and a thin mane, the traits that distinguished these animals from the massive war horses that were bred locally.

John rode up to the carriage, a slight hesitation before jumping down from the saddle was the only sign that belied his nervousness under his confident and casual air. "Henry, so good to see you," he said, opening his arms expansively as he approached the carriage. Henry jumped down and embraced him.

"How have you been, John?"

"Can't complain," he said, patting the tapered nose of his fine animal.

"Yes, I noticed that," Henry said despite himself. He hated feeding into John's delusions, hated even more the idea that John thought he was fooling him, but he could not help himself. "That's a beautiful animal. It must have cost a king's ransom."

John shrugged, "I know some people, so maybe it only cost King John's ransom but certainly not King Richard's." He laughed loudly, and Henry laughed at the irreverent snipe at the unpopular monarch.

"And how is your wife?" John's countenance darkened for just a moment before brightening again.

"Fine, fine. She wants to have a baby," he told him. "And you are well?"

Just then Henry remembered Mary still seated behind him in the carriage. "Can't complain," he said, gesturing to her.

"Yes, I noticed that," John said, echoing Henry's words from a moment before. He leaned in confidentially and said, "She's a beautiful animal." Henry laughed despite himself, and Mary blushed furiously. Though she was out of earshot, she knew they were talking about her.

"John, I would like you to meet my betrothed, Mary." Henry offered his hand to Mary as she stepped down from the carriage.

"Milady, you are even more beautiful then was described to me," John said, taking her free hand and bowing deeply.

"And you are exactly as was described to me." Mary's pleasant tone masked the acid in her words.

John paused at the comment. He knew full well that the descriptions of him that were floating around were far from flattering. He was well aware that he was being insulted. "Milady, you do me an injustice," he said, hiding the blow she had dealt him with humor. "I am a modern crusader for the underdog. The powers that be have vilified me for their own ends, but I am a champion of the poor and outcast." He bowed humbly again.

"I am certain you are, sir," Mary said without missing a beat. "Shall we be off, then?" she asked no one in particular.

"Of course," John said, looking to Henry for some reaction to gauge the exchange that had just taken place. But Henry was busying himself at the carriage as if he had not noticed anything out of the ordinary.

John climbed into the saddle, resisted the urge to gallop away from what promised to be an unpleasant afternoon, and pulled his horse in beside the carriage.

"You know, it's interesting that the Arabs breed such fine animals," Henry said conversationally as they rode. "In my time over there, our cavalry typically outnumbered theirs five to one. You would think that everyone would be mounted with such fine animals available to them."

"Well, you must remember," John pontificated in a light air, "the average Arab is a merchant first and a warrior second. His country could be going up in flames, and he would still be selling the torches to the enemy." Henry snorted, and Mary laughed a melodious laugh.

John looked at her in surprise. He again glanced at Henry for some indication of her seemingly incongruous actions, and again Henry was looking elsewhere as if he was not aware of anything unusual in her behavior.

"I understand that the selective breeding of the animals makes them quite rare, even in their own country," Mary offered, "whereas in England we sell anything that looks the part. It can have brittle hip joints, soft hooves, and be dumb as a post from years of inbreeding; but if it looks big and strong, we don't care."

John again glanced at Henry, but this time he was rewarded with an explanation. "Mary is very interested in animal husbandry," he explained.

"I love animals," she added. "And that one you are riding is a beautiful specimen indeed. Tell me, where did you acquire such a rare find?"

John patted the animal's neck appreciatively. "This was a gift from a friend," he again dismissed the question. "And you are correct. It seems a shame to put a saddle on an animal this fine, but I tell you, I have never ridden a horse that seems so at home with a saddle. This animal seems to know what I am thinking before I do."

"Is it fast?" Mary asked, unable to keep her keen interest in the animal from showing.

"Oh, milady, it is like riding the wind," he assured her. "You positively must ride her as soon as it can be arranged."

"Oh no, I couldn't," Mary said, suddenly embarrassed.

"I insist. It is an experience you will not soon forget. The next time you visit Dawning Square, have your saddle brought. We will saddle her for you, and you can see what all the fuss is really about."

"Well that's very kind of you, John. I should like that very much." She smiled to herself.

The rest of the afternoon passed in easy frivolity. John was every bit the gentleman, and Mary laughed at every jest and gesture. John took his leave in the early evening.

"John, you really must come and see us again soon," Mary said to him as he prepared to depart. "I do not remember when I have enjoyed myself quite so much."

John bowed from the saddle and promised he would do his best. With a florid touch, his horse reared and darted away. Henry and Mary stood side by side and watched him depart.

"What a despicable person," Mary started the moment he was out of earshot. "Can you believe the way he was so brazen, as if I was some floozy that was going to be taken in by that?"

"I don't know, you seemed to be enjoying yourself," Henry said as he started packing up.

"Why, because I was polite? It was exactly as you said. He was desperately attempting to prove he was a nobleman."

"He is a nobleman."

"That is what made it all the more pathetic."

"He does need desperately to prove himself. That is why he was so weak. He wants me to be impressed with him and you to like him."

Mary breathed a sigh of relief. "Well, I am just glad that is over. What an ordeal. Each new family member I meet is more trying than the last," Mary said, settling back on the carriage as Henry put the last few things from the picnic in it.

"You think that was rough? I was raised with them."

CHAPTER EIGHTY-NINE

"You can't leave!" Leah was standing in the middle of the road in the moonlight, just outside of Dawning Castle. Her cloak was blowing about in the wind, revealing the hem of her nightgown below.

"Where did you ever get such a preposterous ide—" William started to deny the accusation but was interrupted.

"Don't bother trying to deny it. I know. Edith told me."

"Edith? How did sh—"

"Haven't you learned that running away fixes nothing?"

William reluctantly climbed out of his saddle. He approached her with a forced grin. "You know, this is the first time in my life I have ever seen you not perfectly made up."

"You left for four years before, and what is resolved because of it?"

"You're still lovely."

She punched him hard in the chest. "Leaving now will not fix anything."

William stumbled back slightly, more in shock than pain. "On the contrary, my leaving took care of all these problems; it was my returning that has stirred them all up again."

"You are needed here! This experience should have taught you that if nothing else. The family is rudderless."

"My family does alright."

"It is not just about them! Everyone suffers when the Dawnings suffer. Without solid leadership, rival barons are emboldened, uprisings increase, and lives are destroyed."

"Leah!" William interjected firmly. "Don't you see? All those things are happening since my return. I have returned Richard. If he survives, he will make a strong enough leader to make the barons think twice before attacking Dawning Court. And my leaving is the best guarantee that we will not soon face an attack of the barons. If I stay, I am guaranteeing a confrontation with Baron Braddock."

"Then fix it! Answer his challenge!"

"Answer his challenge?"

"Yes! You are not a scared, untried youth anymore. I know what you are. That foolish old baron challenged William Dawning the boy. He does not stand a chance against William Dawning the man!" She took a step toward him. "Answer his challenge, and put this foolishness behind you forever. Build a life here where you are needed more than you can ever know."

"What has aroused such passion in you?" William half laughed. "I have made it clear from the moment I set foot in Dawning Castle that this was how it must be."

"Are you so stupid you cannot see what lies before you?" Leah choked on the emotion in her voice. William opened his mouth to speak, but no words came. He had never seen Leah in such a state, and he certainly could not remember her ever speaking to him like this.

William shook his head. "You don't understand," he mumbled.

"I what?" Leah said sharply.

"You don't understand," William said louder.

"What don't I understand?" she demanded. William did not respond. "That you are afraid?" she said. "I know you are afraid. You were only a boy when Barron Braddock challenged you. Of course you retain the memory of the fear you must have felt when that seasoned, powerful warrior was shouting for your blood. But while the hand of time has weakened him, God has raised you up. I do not normally advocate such violence, you know that, but there is so much more at stake here than the pride of a foolish old man."

"No, it is not that," William protested weakly. He was disturbed by how her words reverberated in him.

"Then what, William?" Leah stepped up to him and tried to get him to meet her gaze, but he would not. "What is it, William? Is it David? Is it Salena?

"Leah—" he started in a plaintive voice but stopped.

"What is it?" she called over the wind, forcing his face back to hers.

"I killed David!" William said much louder than he had intended. Leah was stunned into silence. "I did not crush his chest, but his blood is on my hands just as surely as if I did! I reassigned him to the place that took his life, and..." He stopped, unsure if he could tell her what no one yet knew. "Even then he might have lived but for my mistake. He died saving my life. He answered my petty vindictiveness with selfless sacrifice." Tears were flowing now. "Then I repaid him by abandoning his body to be trampled into the earth and become carrion for vermin, while I fled to save my own neck... Salena was right. He is a hundred times the man I am, and he has traded his life for mine." William turned away and walked back to his horse, but his strength failed him and he slumped against the horse's flank. "I told you this would happen. There is a curse upon me, Leah. Anyone I am close to will die. My curse is to always live. I will have to watch everyone I love be taken from me, and there is nothing I can do to prevent it... I should be dead so many times I cannot count them all, but here I stand, not even a scratch upon me, and my oldest friend is dead because I returned."

Leah slowly approached William. "David knew what he was fighting for. He knew the risks. And how would a knight rather go than on the field of battle in noble service to his closest friend? There is no other way he would have wanted to go."

"Do you really believe that?"

"It is the code knights live by, is it not?"

William snorted. "The code? I was with David at the end. I looked into his eyes as he lay dying in that field so far from everything he loved. He knew the end was near, and I tell you there was terror in his eyes. There was no comfort from facing a 'glorious end in noble service'. There was only fear. So much fear. David was not comforted to settle into the rest of a noble warrior. He was maintaining his death grip on life. He did not want to die."

"Who is next if I remain? My family? You?" William demanded. "Of all blood, I cannot bear to have yours on my hands."

She grabbed William's shoulders and shook him. "Enough of that! David saved you because he saw in you something greater than himself. He saw in you what I see." Tears were still streaming from William's eyes, which renewed her own. She pulled him to her and held him tightly as they wept together, a reenactment of a night so many years ago—a lifetime ago.

It was some time before William came to himself. He stepped back from her. "It is too dangerous," he said, wiping his face with his palm. "I will not jeopardize the safety of those I love to gratify my own desires." He climbed back in the saddle without looking at her.

"William, what has all this done to your impressionable mind? You are drawing correlations between events where none exist. Your returning here did not cause David's death."

"You really are too good for this world," he smiled sadly at her. "Everything else good in my life I have corrupted or destroyed. But you have always remained supremely good."

"William, please," she pleaded softly.

"William... this was your—my last chance." Leah was visibly deflated as he shook the reins and started his horse into a trot. Then remembering something, she called after him. "Henry's wedding. You need to be here for Henry's wedding." William rode quietly into the darkness.

CHAPTER NINETY

"Break!" The trainer called. "That's enough for today," he said to Richard and his sparring partner.

Richard shook his head. "Not yet," he said while gasping for breath. "I want to keep going."

Martin seemed instantly piqued. "I said we are finished for the day! I only agreed to train you on condition that you would follow my rules," the trainer said crossly. "If you are pushed too hard in the beginning, you will ultimately slow down your recovery." Henry, who had just entered the training yard, braced himself for a row. His brother was a strong man and a skilled warrior, but above all he was proud. He did not work well with domineering trainers. But to William's surprise, Richard merely held up one hand in surrender, the other braced on his knee as he struggled for breath. "I acquiesce," he gasped. "It will be as you say."

"Come to mock the once great warrior?" Richard said lightly as he stood erect with some difficulty in order to greet Henry. He tore off his protective mask. Sweat was pouring down his face.

"Not at all," Henry assured him. "Considering a few weeks ago I was listening intently for your death rattle, I am amazed to see you in the training yard already."

Richard collapsed on a nearby bench, reaching for the water that had been set out. "I cannot believe how much I have lost," he said, wiping his mouth after a long drink.

"You have lost some bulk, but that's to be expected," Henry observed, sitting on the bench next to him.

"No, I can tell my strength is gone," he said, looking disgustedly at the fencing foil in his hand. "Even this thing feels heavy." He threw the weapon aside. "But mostly I feel it in my stamina. I am instantly winded."

"Well, you know what they say, it's easier to stay conditioned than to find it again once lost," Henry uttered sagely.

"Wonderful, thank you," Richard rejoined sarcastically as he took another long drink between breaths.

Henry felt slightly guilty for making light of his brother's difficult situation. This was surely devastating for him to be reduced to this state. For the first time in his life, he had been in need of rescuing, and now he was struggling to regain the strength that had always come naturally to him. Henry sought to reassure him. "Take heart, brother. The quality that most set you apart from your peers and, unfortunately, most of your siblings, is discipline. You achieved remarkable things once because of it, and you will again."

Richard was staring at the floor as Henry spoke. "Thank you," he said quietly.

"You know, if this trainer is not agreeing with you, I could make other arrangements for you," Henry offered.

"No, I will stick with this. Thank you, though. Martin is tough, and that's what I need right now."

A door on the opposite side of the yard opened, emitting a very striking blond woman that started toward them. Her face tapered down from high, regal cheekbones, to a finely pointed chin. She was dressed simply enough in a grey dress with a heavy cloak to guard against the chill of the late winter air. Richard and Henry both stood as she approached, and Richard's face broke out in a broad smile.

"Grace, I hope this day finds you well?" Richard said pleasantly, his exhaustion seeming to vanish.

"It does, Sir Knight. And how are you bearing up?" she said, taking his hand and moving close to him. "Training went well, I presume?"

"I am coming along, a bit slower than I had hoped, but I am getting there."

"Well, if it was anyone else, he would not even be out of bed yet. Your progress astounds me." She leaned in close, and Henry became extremely uncomfortable and began looking for an inconspicuous mode of exit.

Richard suddenly remembered himself and turned to Henry, slightly embarrassed. "Grace, I need to introduce my brother, Henry." Grace stared at him blankly for a moment, and then her eyes brightened. Without warning she stepped over to Henry, put her hands on his shoulders, pulled him close, and kissed his cheek. "My heartfelt gratitude to you," she said sincerely.

"Gratitude?" Henry said bemused, one hand going unconsciously to his cheek.

"For saving Richard. For bringing him back to me," Grace elaborated with misty eyes.

Henry was even more awkward. "Well, I had help. At least I seem to remember some other people along."

"Grace was my nurse upon our return," Richard explained. "Actually, you have met her before."

"I'm sorry, I'm sure I would have remembered," Henry shook his head.

"Well, I was a lot younger," Grace elaborated. "My father is Randall Tell. Anthony is my brother," she said excitedly. Henry searched his memory to find the cute blond girl from his youth. He could recall only limited interaction with her as a child, as she was several years younger than he was.

"Is that so? Well, it is a pleasure to re-make your acquaintance."

"Our family was visiting while my father tried to arrange a favorable match for Anthony." Her speech became very rapid as she spoke. "The ennui was driving me to distraction when I heard that Richard was in need. Well, what could a lady do other than offer her assistance? I was surprised, after all the stories I have heard, to discover this fierce warrior was really just a gentle giant."

"Yes, well, trying times will change a man, won't they?" Henry said, watching Richard for his reaction to Grace's comments. Richard did not seem at all embarrassed by her words. He merely smiled at her as she spoke.

"And with so much in common," Grace continued, as if Henry had not spoken, "we had an instant rapport."

"I can see that. How wonderful," Henry said politely, mildly amused by Grace's overly forward nature.

"You know," Richard interrupted, "I never thanked you properly for what you did. I did not deserve rescuing, but you and William..." He stepped over, put his hands on Henry's shoulders, and looked him directly in the eye. "Thank you for my life."

Henry was again uncomfortable by being put suddenly on the spot. "Do not give it a thought. You are our brother. What else could we do?"

"Well, I think you had better take it easy for the rest of the day." Grace said, taking his arm and pulling him toward the door.

Richard looked over his shoulder at Henry. "She mothers me unbearably, but she's beautiful, so what can I do?" He laughed as he let himself be led toward the door.

Henry sat down again on the bench in the training yard. This was a different side to Richard he was seeing, a kinder, gentler side. And Richard was making more of an effort at it than ever before. He wondered how deep this gentler side actually ran in him. Was it a permanent change or would he, like most people, slip back into his old character as he moved further and further away from his humbling experiences? Time alone would tell.

CHAPTER NINETY-ONE

"Lord Mayfield, it has been a long time," Martha Dawning said to Mary's father without much warmth.

"Lady Dawning, how did we ever let it get to be so long?" the large, bearded man said affectionately.

"I'm sure I don't know," Martha Dawning said perfunctorily. In point of fact, she remembered perfectly well why they had not seen each other since before Braden died, and she was positive that George Mayfield remembered as well. But there was little point in rehashing it now.

"I hope you know how deeply sorry we were to hear of Baron Dawning's passing." Sympathy was dripping from his voice. Mayfield's slip of a wife nodded her greeting to Martha but said nothing.

"Lady Mayfield, it is good to see you after all these years." Lady Mayfield was a tall, thin woman with a serious face. Lines of severity now marked what was once a very comely countenance.

She nodded again. "Lady Dawning," was all she said.

"So it seems our young ones have fallen in love," George Mayfield said expansively.

"It would seem so," Martha said evenly. She did not trust them, and she did not like this match. But there had been too much division in her family over marriage already, and she could not bear to lose Henry in that way. She had already lightly made some suggestions about waiting and no need to rush into something this momentous, but he had flown off the handle at the mere suggestion that this was anything other than what it appeared to be—a good match formed on the deepest admiration and consideration for one another.

So just this once, she decided to put her reservations aside and assume this was exactly what it purported to be, the chance meeting of two old friends that had blossomed into love, both sides blissfully ignorant of the deep rift that had opened between their parents, who had once been fast friends.

"We cannot express how overjoyed we were to hear that Henry Dawning had proposed to our very own Mary. I said, 'What a perfect way for our old friendship to be rekindled.'"

"Mmm, quite," was all Martha said.

"Now, of course there is the small matter of her dowry. Forgive my gaucheness in even mentioning it, but I always prefer to get such matters out of the way right up front. Then we can enjoy the rest of the festivities, as is fitting on such an occasion." Martha looked at him expectantly. "Now, Mary is our youngest daughter, so her dowry is necessarily not as large as her older sisters; not to say that it is small..."

"Well, it is certainly not small," Lady Mayfield supplied.

"No," George reaffirmed. "Truth be told, it is probably more than we should give for a youngest daughter; but we adore Mary so and wanted to show how overjoyed we were at the prospect of being united with the Dawnings. So we are parting with our lands in Scotland," he announced grandiosely, then waited expectantly for Martha's reaction.

Martha sat and contemplated for a moment before speaking. She knew the Mayfields very well and doubted seriously they would be willing to part with any valuable land. She wondered if they were offering her a large patch of the bog, secure in the knowledge that this close to the wedding there would be no time to have the offered land properly surveyed. But she could not outrightly accuse them of such a thing. "That is wonderful, Lord Mayfield." She forced a smile, albeit a weak one, onto her face. "Such a choice parcel of land as you have described will make the perfect wedding gift for Henry and Mary, and each time they look out over their vast tracts of land, they will know to whom they owe their gratitude."

George gave Lady Mayfield a sidelong glance. "Wedding gift, lady?" he asked hesitantly.

"Yes, is that a problem?" she asked innocently.

"Well, no, I am sure they will be quite pleased with the land, but we naturally assumed that you would want to keep Henry closer to home."

Martha raised her eyebrows in mock surprise. "And why, pray tell, would that matter?"

"Well, to help take the burden of the affairs of state off your shoulders."

"That is not Henry's responsibility. He has four elder brothers."

"Well, yes... but we understood... that they..."

"That they what?"

"Well it seems that we were misinformed." George quickly dismissed the matter. "I wonder if I might not arrogate to the honor of mentioning that to them, the wedding gift I mean, in my toast at the wedding. I will give you full credit, of course."

"Of course." Martha Dawning was all too sure that her 'old' friends were just the same as they had always been.

CHAPTER NINETY-TWO

"Do you ever imagine there could be a better life for you?" Leah asked William.

"Better?" William kicked a stone into the stream. "Look around, Leah. I have a better life than most anyone."

"You have a more comfortable life than most people, but if it does not make you happy, then it may not be a good life for you."

He thought about that for a moment. "I'm conflicted. Part of me loves the accolades that come with the life of a knight. You know, victory, glory, getting to be a hero...but part of me hates it at the same time. It disturbs me to think that the moment I ride out to defend the kingdom, my life may already be forfeit, and it is not up to me to decide. That often seems too much to bear. But at least I am fighting for my own lands and family. How much worse is it for those knights that are sworn to Dawning Court and are attached solely by oath? I cannot even imagine what it must be like to know your life may be spent on another's whim."

"That's the price they pay for a life of privilege, I suppose," Leah agreed. "But it is certainly better than the alternative."

"How so?"

"It is often argued that the serfs and peasants give up that life of privilege in exchange for the protection of the knights and barons; but the fact is, if our lands are invaded, the peasantry will be the first casualties of the invasion, and they will have less say in their fate than even the knights."

"Exactly. Therefore, when you ask if I imagine a better life for myself, what else is there? You know, when I was small I used to want to be just like my father. He seemed so powerful and so wise." William scooped up a handful of stones and began skipping them across the brook as the two of them meandered along the bank. *"I just assumed I would grow up to be him. But now the thought of having to take on the responsibilities of a barony sends shivers down my spine, and I give thanks every day that I am not the eldest son."*

"What you really want then is to be free from responsibility?"

William hesitated before answering, sensing a trap. *"I suppose that's right."* He sighed and squatted down by the side of the bank. *"I suppose I do really just want to be free. What is curious about that is that I do not know when or where I changed from wanting to become my father to being terrified of the burden of my father's responsibilities."*

Leah sat on a soft patch of earth and reclined on her hands. Her hair fell in front of her eyes as it always did, and the faded blue cotton dress outlined her shape nicely. William forced himself to look away and dismiss those thoughts that seemed to be coming unbidden with increasing frequency recently. Leah was his friend. That was all either of them wanted, and he was not willing to jeopardize that for anything, he told himself. Yet still he found himself wondering if their solid friendship would be the foundation for a transcendent romantic relationship. But then again, perhaps not. They were so young and both had so much left to experience; delving into this relationship now could only spoil it for later.

On the other hand, Leah was older than he was, and women were expected to be married younger than men. So if he did not stake his claim now, would he lose her? Did he even have a claim to stake? And what if he did pursue her and she reciprocated? Would the premature nature of such an arrangement only give the natural enemies of such a union, Leah's father for example, too much opportunity to foil his plans? William cursed himself for the thousandth time for *entertaining these wild ideas. What would make him think a girl like Leah would settle for a confused, immature, child anyway?*

Leah had cocked her head to the side and was peering at him curiously. He started to feel as if she were reading his thoughts and nervously tried to distract her. "So what about you? Do you ever wish for a different lot in life?"

"I never really saw a need to."

"You're telling me that you don't get tired of all your lessons on good grooming and etiquette; all the expectations and demands to be perfect, prim, and proper at all times and to mingle at endless functions with a bunch of people you do not know? Come, now. You have often complained of those affairs."

"I confess that I do sometimes murmur, but those stuffy affairs demand so little of me that it seems a small price to pay for everything else." She stretched and lay back on the grass. William wished she hadn't.

"Everything else?"

"Of course. A nice place to live, food to eat, a good family, a beautiful view," she said, looking dreamily at the sky. "And good friends. The other things are such a small price to pay, I just don't think of it as a sacrifice."

William lay on the ground next to her with their heads almost touching. "I wish I could see what you see."

"You can if you just let yourself; it is all right there." She waved a slender arm at the scenery.

"No, it is not. The beauty you see in everything and everyone is right there," he said, tapping her forehead with his finger.

As they lay there together, William was acutely aware of just how far outside the bounds of propriety their relationship really was, but he had known Leah too long to maintain any real formality between them. He could not even imagine only seeing her in strictly regimented meetings, as was frequently the standard in courting. "The reason everything is good to you is because you are so good." William sat up and hunched over his knees in a protective position.

"But don't you see, William? You said it yourself," Leah said sitting up after him. "The world is what you make of it. If

you want to see the beauty and good in the world, it is there. But if you look for darkness and pain, it is not hard to find."

William looked into her beautiful hazel eyes and smiled. He could not help himself. She was so wonderful, and everything she did was so picturesque. It was hard to believe there could really be a creature like this. "What?" she said self-consciously. "You are laughing at me."

"No," he said. "I am just not sure how I ended up with a friend like you. I fear that it is only a matter of time before it is discovered there is a swan in with the chickens and you are spirited away to be with your own kind." William flushed slightly at the overly sweet nature of the sentiment. It was an expression of a sincere feeling, but when he tried to articulate it, it sounded silly to his own ears.

Leah did not seem to notice his embarrassment as she looked away, blushing, at the same time. "Now stop that; you know I am not that good."

William chortled loudly. "Name one bad thing you have done in the last week."

"I can name several..." she rejoined before thinking.

"Alright," William said sitting back on his elbows and making a great show of settling in for a long wait.

"Why, just this morning..." she began, then trailed off.

"Yes?" William prodded. "This morning you... fell in with a band of highwaymen and robbed a royal courier?" he suggested. "You took over France, perhaps? You would not be the first woman to do it single-handedly, you know," William rolled on, having a great time at his friend's expense. "I know, you stole a ship—"

"I fought with my sister," Leah blurted out. William stopped mid-joke and looked at her with raised eyebrows.

"You fought with your sister?"

"It wasn't an ordinary quarrel," Leah said looking away, unable to meet his gaze. "You are aware of the fencing instructor that visits our estate a few times a week?" William nodded dumbly. He was struggling vainly to imagine where this might be leading. "Well, Eve started studying with him also a while back," she continued.

"Ok," William said slowly, still confused.

"Well, she wanted to practice with me today. She is so competitive," Leah said, anger rising in her voice as she recalled the events of the morning. "Anyway, I have been studying for much longer than she has and figured it would be a good chance to teach her some tricks I have learned along the way. But she is much more athletic than I am, and I found that I was having a hard time keeping up with her. I became so frustrated that it took everything I had just to fend off her attacks. Finally, the only trick I had left to keep from losing was a technique I knew she had not yet learned to disarm an opponent, and despite knowing it would hurt her, I did it anyway." She trailed off, ashamed. "Why is she so competitive?" she blurted suddenly. William was grinning at her. "You're laughing at me again?" she said, some of her anger flowing toward him.

"Yes, I am," William admitted. "As the pantheon of great sins go, I'm not sure this made the top three. Maybe not even the top five," he said, trying to suppress his laughter.

Leah punched him solidly in the chest. "I tell you something that is painful to me, and all you do is laugh?" He stood up, realizing that may not be the last blow that would be coming his way before this was over.

"I am sorry," William choked out through scarcely contained fits of laughter. He cleared his throat and straightened up. "I—I'm sorry," he said in a more serious voice, trying to keep the corners of his mouth from turning up with only limited success. "Please let me help you up, milady." He offered his hand to her. She looked at him suspiciously through her wayward lock of hair but offered him her hand.

William helped her up and pulled her in close. "You know, I was just thinking," he said softly. "Perhaps Eve is not the only one in her family who is too competitive," and erupted in another fit of laughter as he danced out of the way of the kick to the shins she directed at him.

Leah's lips pursed in fury as she stalked away. "Wait, wait," William pleaded. She ignored him and kept marching. "Leah, Leah," William said, catching up to her but prudently staying out of striking distance. "Do not go that way. I saw the town constable looking for you earlier. You must flee."

"You are a jerk," Leah said, though she could not completely suppress some amusement of her own. Nevertheless, her dignity had been insulted. "I'm going home. Please do not follow me." Leah cut off the main trail and headed toward her father's house. Knowing he was pushing his luck, William discontinued his pursuit but could not resist one last jab. Leaping into the crook of a tree and hanging off the trunk, he called after her: "Fear not, milady. No one will ever know of the foul deeds you have perpetrated on your own family. I will never tell. Wild mice could not drag it out of me." Leah's nose shot up further in the air as she walked primly away. "They could throw me in the dungeon and starve it out of me, and I would not talk till at least lunchtime, maybe even dinner..." He pretended to be thinking about it. "No, no, lunch. But your secret is safe with me, milady."

When Leah was out of earshot, William walked back to the castle, still chuckling to himself and feeling only slightly guilty about teasing his friend.

CHAPTER NINETY-THREE

"Now me, now me!" Hannah squealed in delight, clapping her hands as Thomas swung Harry around in the yard in front of his estate. Thomas was worn out from his day with the children. The sun was starting to set, and he was anxious to wind things up for the day, but the children showed no signs of fatigue.

"Okay," he gasped, setting grinning Harry down in the grass. He picked up his little red-headed daughter on his back and began racing around with her. It did not take long before his large belly was heaving even more than before, and he had to slow to scarcely more than a walk.

"No, daddy," Hannah ordered. "Faster, as fast as you can."

"That's easy for you to say," he muttered and forced himself to pick up the pace.

"Faster, faster!" she yelled, squealing again as he jumped a small puddle in the dirt. "Jump the fence now." She pointed to the wooden fence erected from roughhewn logs that surrounded portions of his land near the house. Thomas ran over to it and pretended to try to jump it, falling over it instead as he gently deposited Hannah on the ground while he pretended to be dead, collecting some much-needed moments of rest.

"Get up, Daddy," she said and jumped on his stomach.

"Ow." He rolled into a fetal position to protect himself from Harry, who had toddled over to them and was now preparing to jump on him also.

"Careful now, you will hurt Daddy," he said, trying to sound playful but with definite purpose.

"Again, again," Hannah said and jumped on his head, sliding off and inadvertently tearing at his ear as she did so.

"Damn it, Hannah!" he roared and shoved her away from him.

She stumbled back and fell on the ground, landing solidly on her bottom. It took a moment for the shock to wear off enough for her to start screaming. Hannah rarely merely cried. If she was unhappy, she screamed. And she was definitely unhappy.

Harry looked from his father to Hannah and back again, and not knowing what else to do began to cry himself, his cute little chubby face turning into a sad frown as he did so.

Annie hurried up to them, having entered the yard just in time to see Hannah jump on Thomas. "You cannot be so rough with them," she chastised Thomas. "They are just children."

"Well, I used to have two ears," Thomas said, holding his left hand over his painful red ear." Annie scooped up the children protectively, one in each arm.

"She was not trying to hurt you."

"Well, she did," Thomas said. "After I had asked her several times to stop."

"At least hers was an accident," Annie pointed out. "You are old enough to know better. She is not."

"It was an impulsive reaction," Thomas barked, angered at Annie's refusal to understand and dismiss this. "Just like marrying you," he added. Annie made no reply as she was accustomed to his digs, and that made Thomas angrier at having failed to elicit the reaction he was after. "And just like my marriage to you, I was sorry the moment I had done it, and you have continued to make me sorry about it ever since." Annie's large, dull eyes began to tear up, and she took the children into the house.

Thomas leaned against the fence to watch the remainder of the sunset. He regretted pushing Hannah and the effort it was going to take to mend things with Annie. Oh, Annie, what had he ever been thinking to marry such a girl? Their relationship was bad to begin with and had only declined steadily from the beginning. And each new stress was making it that much worse. He wanted to say it was all Annie's fault, but truth be told, she was the same simple-minded girl he had first married. She was not a good match for him, but he had rushed impulsively into the marriage and had only seen his folly when it was too late. They were too dissimilar, he and Annie. He was clever and scheming, she was simple and kind. He was brutally tactless in every situation, and she would never dream of hurting anyone if she had a choice.

She had definitely become more emotionally withdrawn from him since his more virulent insults had started. At first he had restrained himself, but as they continued to struggle, the insults started to come. And once they started, it was impossible for him to stem the flow. They were instantly on his tongue before he even thought about it.

He sighed his cares to the darkening sky. He felt it was an allegory of his life: once bright and hopeful and now darkening on every front. This was not what he was meant for. He was once a great warrior, a proud warrior; but when all that ended, he returned to Dawning Court for nothing. Now if he fought in the skirmishes that developed from rival barons or peasant uprisings, he did it for nothing. There was nothing in it for him except the fulfilling of his duty. It did not enrich him in any manner; in fact, all he could do was lose. If he was injured or killed, this is all that he would ever get out of this life. He would never be great, only forgotten, just as the darkening sky would be forgotten at the next sunrise.

Things definitely seemed darker since John's proposal weeks before. Thomas was finding fault with every aspect of his life. Nothing satisfied him any longer. Perhaps John was right, that was a way out. But Thomas would have to risk everything he had for such a venture, and he would still be answerable to his good-for-nothing eldest brother; and this if the Saracens did not betray him, which they almost certainly would, as John was not strong enough to keep control over them.

He understood why John was making such a choice: he had nothing to lose–no land, no wealth, no honor or status. If he were rebuffed, what could be stripped from him that he had not already stripped from himself? And if he were killed? Well, at least it would spare him the life of degradation he seemed destined to lead. But Thomas was different. He only needed the chance to be great. If he just had the opportunity, he would be baron. His wife would be dressed in the finest silks, and she would be honored to be his wife. She would boast of her husband to other women who were already envious of her. Though he still may not respect her, he would not feel trapped with her alone as he did now; he would know many beautiful women, and they would fight for his favor. He would have many concubines, but he would have one special one—one concubine who eventually would come to relish her place as his favorite, to jealously guard his affections. Leah would be his. He would control her, own her.

Thomas snapped himself out of his daydream, surprised at how far he had let his thoughts wander out of the bounds of propriety. He had often been badgered by such thoughts in his life, but since John's proposition, he found that he was dwelling on them with increasing frequency, and they were often darker than he had ever intended. What had started out as wholesome fancies about being a beloved baron with a blissful family had become something else entirely.

He stretched and stood as the last rays of daylight were sliced by the horizon. He had to accept that the answers to his problems were not simply going to glide in over the horizon. Or were they?

It was dark enough now that the silhouette coming toward him down the road was elusive. He was not sure for some moments if it was real or imagined. He waited upon the visitor as this road only led to his estate. There was nowhere else a loan traveler could be intended for. He half seated himself on the fence that was just too high to be a proper seat, folded his arms over his belly, and waited.

The robed figure walked directly up to him without hesitation. The hood was drawn over the face, but it did not take long for Thomas to realize who it was.

He was instantly nervous, and his first instinct was to step back and be on guard, but his pride would allow him to do nothing of the sort. Instead he remained motionless, trying to look as nonchalant as possible. "And what brings you to my humble abode?" he asked, again assuming his formal language but not trying to be overly polite, expecting that she hated him and had only evil designs on his person.

"I have come for you, Thomas," Anisa said, drawing back the hood from her beautiful features.

"And what could you possibly want here?"

"John tells me he has presented a proposition to assist him in regaining the barony that is rightfully his." Her hands went to the ties keeping the front of her robe closed and began working on them. Her shapely figure was not easy to make out under the robe.

"Perhaps," Thomas said, trying to be mysterious. "My brother and I speak of many things. What is that to you?"

"Why did you reject your brother's proposition? Do you not feel he is entitled to make such a claim?"

"My reasons," Thomas said, puffing up before her, "are my own."

"Perhaps you believe it to be so," she said smiling slyly. "But I believe you betray more than you realize."

"What manner of woman are you to say such things?"

"You harbor a notion that you would be a more fitting leader than Sir John." It was not a question. "He is too weak, and we are simply using him."

Thomas shrugged off his surprise. "I suppose that is true."

"Thomas, you may well be correct."

"What is this?" he demanded. "Did you come here to convince me to betray my own brother?"

"John is the rightful heir to the seat. He must be allowed to reclaim it. But should he fail, who will take his place?" Thomas did not respond. "I will grant that we Saracens need advocates in power here in Europe." She stepped closer to him. Thomas would have withdrawn, but he was backed up to the fence. "The mighty arm of the English knights," she said, sliding one finger down Thomas' large arm, "is destroying us. And we would be willing to take whatever advocate might be available to us."

Thomas was electrified by the proximity of this beautiful woman making such bold advances. He did not dare allow himself to speak for fear of betraying himself. Instead he tried to look stoically unmoved by her overtures. "We would prefer John, as he is the rightful heir and there are fewer grounds for challenging his suit. But he is not as strong as you are. And if he cannot take his place..." she left it hanging.

Thomas was floored. "Come to the point, woman!"

"Would you not make a stronger leader than John? Do I err in this?" She arched her eyebrows at him.

Thomas shrugged but could not bring himself to contradict her. "I suppose, but John's strong will is not his defining characteristic."

"Nor are his wise decisions."

"The fact that he is in league with you is proof enough of that," Thomas said loftily.

"But you are not subject to the same weaknesses," she stated matter of factly.

"My decisions are more reasoned than his, to be sure," Thomas nodded.

"Your brother," she said, stepping back a pace, "is a man of great passions. Perhaps you share in his appreciation of many of the finer things."

Thomas considered her, unsure of what she was leading up to.

"What higher compliment is there to a warrior king than a beautiful woman?" Thomas' glib reply died on his lips when Anisa released her now unfastened robe and let it fall open, revealing a form-fitting silken gown that highlighted all the virtues that nature had bestowed upon her. Thomas's voice caught in his throat. She was indeed very beautiful, and his eyes were riveted on her form. He tried to look elsewhere but could not seem to wrench his eyes from her. A slight smirk played across her face that went unnoticed by Thomas, who was not looking at her face. "I believe we understand each other," she said and let his gaze remain a moment longer as she slowly refastened the clasps of her robe. "You have the promise of greater things than you yet know," she said confidently. "And you will know when your moment for greatness has presented itself. I hope you will not let it slip away."

Thomas stood rooted in place as he watched her disappear the way she had come. The whole experience was surreal enough that Thomas may have doubted himself whether it had actually happened the next day but for the intense need to do something physical. To the now familiar training yard he went and took his well-worn weapon and his training shield, which carried more weight than usual to prepare his arm for long days of battle, in his now-calloused hands.

He stared at the well-worn pole for a few minutes, thinking of all that had been denied him in his life. A powerful, burning desire was ignited in him, a desire for all those things he had always craved but not had the opportunity to make his own. He was yearning for all the wealth, the women, and the power that had always been denied him. He unleashed on the battered post with a fury that reduced its beaten fibers to splinters. When his moment came, he would be ready.

CHAPTER NINETY-FOUR

William sat by the fire in the little hostel at which he had stopped for the night. Winter was upon them, and the travelers were few. The conditions slowed his progress as well, but that didn't matter as he had no specific destination in mind. He had felt very acutely the need to leave his erstwhile home, but he kept replaying the conversation with Leah in his mind. How after all these years did she still know him so intimately? How could she know his fears and misgivings as if he himself had confessed them to her?

He could not imagine a being that he so desired and so feared the consequences of being with than Leah. Sitting alone by the fire, he shook his head. Why was he in this place? Why couldn't he be back at Dawning Co—home? His home. There was too much risk. Risk to the family, risk to Leah, risk of Braddock. He could not accept that responsibility.

But what was going on with Leah? He had not noticed it in the emotion of the moment, but the more he thought about his mother's warning and the more he considered their last encounter, he was sure his mother was right. There was more at stake than he realized. Was he really willing to turn his back on the person that meant more to him than anything in the world? Particularly when she was literally begging for his help?

He grumbled and settled deeper into his cloak. He had never even intended to return here in the first place. If he had just stayed away, none of this would be happening. Nobody would be looking to him to solve their problems. He would not be expected to attend anybody's wedding, nor be blamed if his presence caused problems. "I hate this place," he grumbled into his chest and settled deeper into his chair.

CHAPTER NINETY-FIVE

"William, get it!" John shouted at his littlest brother, who was racing toward the ball in the grass as the sun was setting on the courtyard. It had been less than a year since Braden Dawning had died, and John would periodically call the brothers to games like this to help them feel like a family again after all the numbness that accompanied their loss.

"Get the ball!" William zipped in and scooped up the ball from where Richard had just dropped it. He ran a few steps and tossed it to John. Edward dove to block the pass but missed, just tipping it with his fingertips and sending it running wild. William darted after it again.

By now Richard had disentangled himself from Thomas, who had knocked the ball from his hand to begin with. He was racing William for the ball, and he slowed down just enough that his youngest brother could beat him to it. William dove on top of it and rolled to his feet, his natural dexterity already showing itself. Thomas, laughing, grabbed the back of Richard's tunic, knowing full well that he did not have the ball but pulling him down anyway. Edward jumped on the back of his much heavier younger brother, Thomas, and tried to wrestle him to the ground. Then John arrived at a run and tackled the whole group of them. They all went down in gales of laughter with cries of "foul" and "cheater" being fired into the air to no one in particular, as no one was listening.

William, stopping just short of the goal, realized the fun was no longer happening around the ball and ran back to his brothers and flopped on top of the pile of them. They laughed harder still and wrestled until all that remained of the day were the orange and pink clouds illuminated by the fading light of the sun.

When the moment was past, they all sat side by side, watching the remnants of the sunset. "This was fun," Thomas said first. "I'm glad we did this."

"Let's remember this," John said. "In the future, though we may bicker and quarrel, let's remember this moment when we all sat here together as brothers. Whatever differences we may have were set aside, and we were happy now. And though we lost our father, we are the brothers of a noble birthright. As we look into the sun now, so let us look ahead to our lives of prosperity and joy together, for together we can achieve more than we can separately. We are noblemen born to be protectors of our kingdom, our religion, and our people." John began to speak with confidence as his brothers caught the vision. "Through the grace of the Almighty, there is no way we can fail as six powerful warriors for God; we will protect and forge the destiny of our fair kingdom, and there is none who will be able to withstand the collective will of the Dawnings. We are and always will be the Knights Dawning. Can we all agree to that?"

They all circled around and put their hands in the center to make a pact that right at that moment they could see what was important, and they would never forget it, whatever became of them. They were part of an elite brotherhood that was destined to change the course of history.

The final rays of the sun faded behind the horizon, and they all laughed and joked as they walked back to the castle, conscious that they had just shared a special moment together—a moment that made them closer as brothers and better people in general. Each of them was equally sure things were going to be good from then on.

CHAPTER NINETY-SIX

"Are you quite sure you want to go through with this?" Thomas asked Henry.

"I don't understand. Why would I not want to go through with it?" There was a slight challenge in Henry's voice.

"I am just saying that marriage may not be the answer to all your problems. One can always get married, but once it is done, one cannot undo it."

"And why do you assume that I view it as the answer to all my problems?" This was the first time Henry had seen Thomas since returning. The conversation had started off badly with Henry demanding an accounting of Thomas' whereabouts and his reason for not accompanying them as promised. Thomas had immediately gone on the offensive and accused Henry of not looking after his responsibilities. He claimed he was with John and did not dare leave him for fear of what he might do in such a dark place as he was then. He insisted that he could have used help that day but no one came, and when he emerged again, he had been forgotten. Now the conversation was strained, each trying not to upset the other while each was looking for reasons to be offended.

"I do not assume that. But I assumed you were not so naïve as to marry for 'love,'" Thomas shot back. "If it is your natural male urges that are prompting you to follow this course, then you will regret it. I promise you."

"Is this not the next natural step in my life? I have been a student and a soldier. I have been knighted and even recognized by the king. What is left but to start a family? And wouldn't Mary make a fine match?"

"All that may be true," Thomas admitted, "but do you *want* to get married?"

Henry sighed. "I don't want to stay like this," he said. "I don't want to be trapped in this life that I am powerless to fix, living on regrets and imagined hopes that will never be realized until one day I awake to find that my whole life has passed me by and all that is left for me is the pain of the mistakes I have made and a terrible fear of those I will yet make."

Thomas placed a gentle hand on Henry's shoulder. "I understand. But marriage can be the greatest boon to man's spirits or the heaviest millstone around his neck. I am merely advising caution on the matter."

"Because your marriage is so great?"

Thomas withdrew his hand. "Because my marriage is so lousy! Who better to warn you against the pitfalls that await you than someone who has fallen into them himself?"

"Annie is no Mary."

"And Mary is no Annie!" Thomas fired back, then took a breath to calm himself. "I grant you that Annie and I are not happy. There are things about her that I find difficult to abide. But had I married someone else, there would have been other... foibles that I would have to endure. All I am saying is that marriage is the hardest thing you will ever commit to—longer than any crusade and more intense than any smith's fire. So if you are doing this for any sort of impulse of infatuation, lust, or even pride, you will regret it." Thomas saw Henry's mouth tighten into an angry line and quickly ended it. "I am not accusing you of anything. Just promise me this is a calculated decision, not an impulsive one."

Henry stood. "This is a good match, and I would be a fool to pass up such an opportunity as this."

"Maybe you are right."

"Thank you for your advice," Henry said, though he did not sound the least bit grateful. Who was Thomas to give him marriage advice?

"Anytime, little brother. Anytime," he said to Henry's departing back. "Henry, one more thing," he added quickly. "Will you remember that sometimes it takes dramatic action to break out of the rut of ordinary life? Dramatic action that everyone may not always approve of..." Thomas trailed off, sure that he was not being understood correctly.

"So it does, brother," Henry smiled, assuming this was Thomas' approval of his own marriage to Mary.

CHAPTER NINETY-SEVEN

"He's where?" Henry demanded.

"William has left Dawning Court again," Martha announced sadly to Thomas, Richard, and Henry, who were all assembled in the library. It was not uncommon for them to meet like this since Richard's return. They were all trying to re-establish a relationship as brothers, but it was proving to be a slow process.

"I am to be married in two days. He could not even wait around for that before running off?" Henry said in disgust.

"This was not his first choice either," Martha explained. "But he thought you would not want your wedding interrupted by a joust with Daniel Braddock."

"Braddock, right," he said unconvinced.

"Doesn't he know we could help him with Braddock if he would let us?" Richard suggested.

"Remember," Martha answered, "when William left the first time, it was a very different world. Thomas was still in the Holy Land, you were—" she said to Richard, "who knows where, Henry was still an untried young man, and John was not even in a position to help himself. To whom could he turn for help? Why would he expect anything different now?"

The brothers did not speak immediately. "Should we go after him?" Richard suggested.

"Go after him?" Henry asked.

"You know," Richard said, "the three of us find him and work out a plan to bring him back and deal with Braddock."

"Nice idea," Thomas said, "but remember that the challenge issued to William is between Braddock and him. Honor demands that we not interfere with that."

"William is not a knight, though," Richard pointed out hopefully. "He is not bound by our code."

"True, but all of us are," Henry pointed out. "There is nothing we can do to interfere with that."

"This is ridiculous that we are all here and we cannot bring our youngest brother back home," Richard lamented in frustration.

"He could fight Braddock," Thomas suggested. "If he survives, honor is satisfied and William could get his life back. Can he beat Baron Braddock?" He looked at his brothers.

"Braddock is a fierce warrior," Richard said dubiously. "He is much stronger than William and much more experienced."

"That's true," Thomas replied, "but Braddock is getting old, and you are remembering William the boy. What do we know about the skills of William the man?" They both looked at Henry.

Henry shrugged. "We really only had one battle together, and I had my hands pretty full. I did not have much chance to observe my brother. There were others tasked with that responsibility."

"You must have seen something," Thomas pressed. "How did he handle himself? How did he conduct himself on the field?"

"Well, he was not scared, but that could have been because he thinks more of himself than he should. Really everything happened so fast that I lost track of him, and the next time I was aware of him… he was kneeling next to David's body… William made it through okay, but he was unable to protect his friend."

"Or maybe…" Thomas said slowly, "maybe David died protecting William…" There was a moment of silence.

"Perhaps William knows that he cannot beat Braddock. What choice would he have but to run?" A long silence followed that was interrupted by a knock at the door.

532   The Knights Dawning

"Yes?" Martha said, and Sebastian let himself in.

"Forgive the interruption, Lady Dawning, but I thought you should be aware that Lord William is back and occupying one set of the guest chambers."

She stared at him for a moment before saying simply, "Thank you, Sebastian." He nodded and quietly left the room, leaving the Dawnings as he had found them, thoughtful and silent.

CHAPTER NINETY-EIGHT

"William walked into the blacksmith pavilion near the Dawning stables carrying his suit of armor. "Well met, Burt," he hailed the aging but still powerful smith.

Burt looked up from where he was pounding a strip of steel held between tongs with a heavy mallet. "William," he smiled. "I heard a rumor you were back. But I hear lots of rumors about you; never know what you can believe." He set his work on the anvil and went to greet his young patron.

"Well, do not believe everything you hear," William told him. "William Dawning would not return to Dawning Court under any circumstances. He is a wanted man, after all."

Burt smiled knowingly. "Of course. And what can I do for you, young master?"

William laid the shirt out on a table in front of him. "What would it take to repair this?"

"I remember admiring this when you first got it from Jurou. Never seen anything of the sort," he said. "Never seen anything like it. Each tiny plate is made up of a very thin diamond-shaped piece of steel wrapped in white leather. The pieces are then connected with a series of rivets that allow them to move with the wearer. Brilliant piece of craftsmanship."

"I have come to depend on that craftsmanship to keep me alive and thought I would avail myself of the opportunity of having it restored."

Burt only grunted. He was inspecting the hundreds of abrasions, dents, and bends closely with his expert eye. "Do you want it restored or simply repaired?"

"What's the difference?"

"About three months." He said without looking up.

"Three months?" William asked in surprise. "Burt, for reasons of which you are well aware, I cannot tarry long. I am here for my brother's wedding and must depart soon after."

Burt shrugged. "I am not a miracle worker," he said. "Each of these pieces is wrapped completely and the leather sealed on the back. I will have to dismantle much of the suit to re-wrap the leather and replace some of the plates."

"I do not have three months. What about just repairing it?"

"I suppose I could hammer out a few of the more damaged plates and patch the leather. Won't be able to preserve the color though."

"The color? Why?"

"Thought you noticed," he said. "Your white armor has turned grey already. The leather patches and hammer work will make it look even worse, and it will be impossible to hide the repairs if we leave it white. But if I stain the leather, I can hide it so no one will ever know."

William considered it and finally sighed. Not just any smith would be able to work on his armor, and he did not know when he might have another opportunity to repair his armor in a relatively safe place. If it started to fall apart in the field, he had a big problem. "Very well," he assented. "What color would it be?"

"Have to be something dark," Burt said, carrying the armor to his workbench. "Heavier than it looks," he commented, hefting the armor. They discussed the color options and finally agreed on one.

"And you will have that ready by the wedding day?" William asked again. "Because I cannot wait longer."

"Do my best, sir, cannot promise anything though."

William smiled indulgently. "Very well, Burt. Do your best." Burt was a brilliant smith, but one would never know it from his low-key, understated manner. Burt was another holdover from his father. When Braden was campaigning, he would not settle for the second best anything. He surrounded himself with the best craftsmen and horse trainers he could find. Many of those were gone now, but Burt remained, and William was very grateful for that. Of all the essential functions that were involved in supporting a knight, none was more important than that of blacksmith.

CHAPTER NINETY-NINE

"It has been confirmed, Father," Hans told Baron Braddock quietly. "You were correct." Hans always made his father believe all good ideas came from him. "William Dawning has returned for Henry Dawning's wedding and is present at Dawning Court now."

Braddock's face went red with rage. "Then she did not disavow him after all!"

"That would appear to be correct, Father, else he would certainly not be welcome at Dawning Court."

"After what her cowardly son did to my boy! Never was there a more blatant affront to chivalry, courage, and honor than her son, and she has the audacity to welcome that treacherous snake back to her bosom!" He was on his feet now, his eyes alive with an unwholesome light. "Very well. If Martha Dawning believes she can cross the Braddocks without repercussions—Braden Dawning himself would not dare such an affront!" he roared.

Hans was instantly standing at attention. "What orders, Father?" he asked excitedly.

"Milord," Rafiq interjected. "Are you quite sure of this information?" He could not keep the nervousness out of his voice. The two plots he and his cohorts had so long been cultivating to work in tandem, or at least as a backup if the other failed, were about to collide. "It will do little to garner sympathy for your cause among the other barons if you are to attack a wedding party."

"We ride!" Braddock said, ignoring Rafiq. "We ride with the army! Either she will surrender William Dawning and I will kill him with my own sword, or I will dismantle Dawning castle." He walked off the dais toward his armory as Rafiq stood in his way, only moving when it was clear the baron was not going to break stride. Hans ran from the room to assemble the men.

"What is the plan, to ride to the gates of Dawning Court and call William Dawning out?"

"That is exactly my plan!" he said. "I know you have always thought me a coward, Rafiq," Braddock said to his advisor. "Well, today you will see what the hand of Daniel Braddock is capable of."

"Your mind is quite made up about this then?" Rafiq was desperate. All that they had worked for could be seized by Braddock's forces in the very moment of triumph. "I certainly never considered you foolhardy before now."

He stopped and looked at Rafiq. "What is this you say?" he demanded. "You have been urging me to war with the Dawnings for years in order to satisfy some private agenda of your own. Do not think I do not know that you have your own designs. And now that I intend to do just that, you are the lone voice trying to hold me back. Why?"

"Are you quite well enough?"

"Speak your peace or leave me this instant!"

Ragiq sighed before speaking, and when he did it was in a dispassionate voice, a calm assessment of the facts rather than an emotional response. "William Dawning is going to kill you, and there is nothing you can do to prevent that unless you desist from your present course this instant."

"Wha—how dare yo—"

Rafiq cut him off. "This is not personal, milord," he told him in the same unemotional voice. "I am merely making you aware of the facts. You cannot withstand the younger, faster warrior. He is a legend."

"Well so am I!"

"No," Rafiq shook his head. "You were a legend. Now you are... nothing." Even as he said these last words, Rafiq regretted it. He knew he had just struck a terrible blow to the Baron's pride and guaranteed he would do exactly what Rafiq did not want at that moment.

"Be gone from my sight! If I see you again too soon, perhaps I will quench my bloodlust on you instead of the Dawnings!" Rafiq bowed and quickly retreated to send word to Amir. He prayed it was not too late.

CHAPTER ONE HUNDRED

"*Amir, do you know why I specifically recruited you?*" *Imam Hassan Ibn Sabbah asked casually, inspecting the blossoms in his lush garden as Amir dutifully followed him around the garden in the fortress of Mount Alamut.*
Amir suspected it was because of his great size and strength but did not presume to say as much. "No, Imam," was all the reply he made. One did not take too many liberties with the self-proclaimed mouthpiece of Allah that had thousands of assassins at his beck and call.
"Amir, what is your greatest desire in this life?" the cleric said, leaning over to deeply inhale a particularly fragrant blossom.
"To see the heathen scum crushed and driven from our lands forevermore," Amir declared vehemently without hesitation.
"Ah, and you yourself have led many men to their doom toward that end. And yet failure is all you have to show for it."
"Those men are safe in the bosom of Allah." Amir was unable to keep the resentment entirely out of his words.
"I am assured of that," Hassan said easily. "But what has come of it? Are the invaders routed? Has the tide of crusaders been stemmed, or is it greater than ever?" Amir was forced to acknowledge that there was no appreciable improvement.
"But how can that be?" Hassan asked, seeming perplexed. "Are the Muslim people inferior to the Christians?"
Amir stiffened at this. "Not one whit! The Christians are better trained and better equipped, yet our farmers still cut

them down by the scores. Should the circumstances be reversed, not a true believer would fall to the sword of a Christian," Amir declared.

"So if what you say is true, and I've no doubt that it is so," Hassan continued in that same easy style, turning now to Amir, "how then is it that we cannot stop them?"

"We will wear them down. They are waves breaking upon the shore, but the tide cannot last forever and will recede."

"Ah, but does not that same tide eventually reduce the mighty boulder to sand? Does the water not eventually carry away the pier with it?" Amir made no reply under the small intense circles of the Imam's eyes. His long grey beard over his plain grey robe made the darkness of his countenance seem even more pronounced.

The aging cleric abruptly turned and resumed his inspection of the florae around him. "Make no mistake about it," he said. "Given the chance, the Christians will rob us of our lands just as Jacob cheated our father Esau out of his inheritance. I was thus in the attitude of pondering on this when the voice of Allah came to me and showed me why we fail to fend off the invaders. We are like a child that has inadvertently stirred up a hornets' nest. We are swatting at the pests, but we shall never get them all. The only way to be rid of them is to destroy them at the nest. That is why I have recruited you, specifically, above all the able-bodied and willing men that would join our ranks given the chance. There can be no doubt of your devotion to the cause after what the crusaders did to your mother." The long scar down Amir's left cheek stood out brightly as his face colored. "Your light skin and ability to speak their language make you the perfect candidate to attack them in their nests."

A smile slowly crept across Amir's scarred visage as he considered this. "Yes," he said, catching the vision of it. "We will stir up insurrections in their own lands. Turn their people on themselves, foment rebellions. Then the wicked will punish themselves, and what thought will they give to crusades when their own people are rising up against them?"

Hassan smiled, calmly satisfied that his young ward had grasped his divine purpose. "Retire and formulate a plan. Decide how you will begin, and return to me in a few days' time."

Amir shook his head, rubbing his scar thoughtfully with his left hand. "I do not need to think about it. There can be only one choice. I will start with the Dawnings."

Hassan raised his eyebrows in surprise. "Yes, I suppose that is appropriate." He considered for a moment. "Very well, make it so." Amir bowed low. He would set out for England at once.

CHAPTER ONE HUNDRED ONE

"*If you lose your weapon,*" Jurou said, taking the practice sword from William's hand, "*what other weapons are available to you?*"

"*My hands and elbows,*" William uttered tritely, hoping Jurou would move on to some new material. Often William felt that Jurou did not appreciate the speed at which he retained information.

"*And what else?*" Jurou prodded.

"*My feet, my knees, my head,*" William finished, not trying to mask his boredom with the age-old lesson.

"*And what else?*"

William stared. "*There is nothing else,*" he said.

"*You are not thinking obliquely,*" Jurou told him. "*If you confine yourself to the traditional ideas of combat, you will necessarily suffer from the traditional limitations of combat. Everything is a weapon.*"

"*I understand that,*" William said, impatient with Jurou's indirect method of teaching. "*My hands and feet, etc. etc.*"

"*No, everything,*" Jurou repeated. "*Defend!*" he ordered and swung a roundhouse kick up at William's face. William instinctively threw both arms up to absorb the heavy blow on the thick muscles of his forearms.

He then kicked up at the side of Jurou's head, which blow Jurou easily knocked aside. But William knew he would and instantly reversed directions, swinging his heel at the other side of Jurou's head. Jurou fell back a pace to avoid it, and William *rained a flurry of strikes down on Jurou's defenses. The trick in mounting a successful attack was in a continuous barrage of attacks. Even an untrained fighter could fend off one or two strikes, but eight or ten strikes was something else entirely.*

Jurou continued to fall back faster and faster against the onslaught. He was headed rapidly for the wall, where he would be cornered. William was well aware that Jurou was not countering his attacks as he normally would have; but William also knew that he would have no recourse once his back was to the wall. He pressed him harder, jab, jab, right cross, left cross, uppercut, roundhouse, side kick. All of which Jurou deftly blocked or dodged as he fell back further still in the process.

William knew Jurou well enough to know he was planning something, but he could not figure out what. Perhaps he really was completely occupied defending against William's attack. Perhaps this was a coming of age test, and William was proving himself. Front kick, back hand, left hook. They were only a few paces from the wall when, to William's surprise, Jurou turned and ran to the wall.

William was not going to give up his advantage and sprang after him. By the time Jurou was brought up short by the wall, William expected that he would already be in the middle of an attack before his teacher had a chance to collect himself. Jurou crossed the three steps to the wall with William right behind, but Jurou did not stop at the wall. Rather he took two steps up the wall, pushed off and launched a vicious spinning roundhouse kick at William's head. William's momentum carried him directly into the path of the kick. He was too shocked to execute anything but the crudest of blocks.

Stars exploded in his vision and he felt the world tipping up to meet him. He hit the tatami floor, and everything went dark for a moment. He came to as Jurou was raising his legs off the ground. "Just relax a moment," Jurou said calmly. "Let the blood return to your head."

William was still too dazed to respond. He stared at the ceiling, waiting for his thoughts to reconvene on a central topic. "You see," Jurou said. "Everything is a weapon. My roundhouse kick you easily blocked, but when you thought you had me in a corner, that the wall was my prison, it became my weapon and my surprise attack. In battle, seeing such opportunity is the difference between life and death."

"There are not too many walls on battlefields, Jurou," William mumbled rubbing his sore jaw, vaguely remembering a similar protest to his trainer at some point in the past.

"Think obliquely," Jurou barked, recognizing that William was just being obstinate. "Never do what your opponent expects. Stepping into a blow when you would naturally shrink from it puts you out of danger and within striking distance. Punching the shoulder of an opponent drawing back for a strike will stop that strike. Breaking the finger of a much stronger man will bring him to his knees as surely as overpowering him ever will."

"What about fair play?"

"This is your life!" Jurou barked. "The time for fair play is before the battle has begun. If you should not be at odds with an opponent, you halt the situation before it deteriorates to combat. But once the battle is joined, there is only the living and the dead! Your opponents are not fellowmen, they are objects to be eliminated before they eliminate you. You are not fighting, you are killing. Never use two strokes to kill when one will do. If his groin or throat is exposed, do not spend time trying to best him at swordplay, shove your blade through the exposed spot and move on. You are not fighting with them; you are killing them. Get that straight in your mind now. There is a difference."

"So go for the weak points?" William said, trying to sum up the many lessons Jurou was throwing at him.

Jurou sighed. "Name the striking points."

Now it was William's turn to sigh. "The eyes, bridge of the nose, bottom of the nose, front of the chin," he began to recite the list of vulnerable spots on the human body with no enthusiasm. He was on his feet again but still not feeling particularly stable.

"Yes, yes, but what else?" Jurou interrupted him with a wave of his hand.

"I do not understand."

"This is what we have been talking about," Jurou said. "Think obliquely."

"I still do not understand. Pressure points are pressure points."

"Think obliquely. Everything is a weakness. Everything. What happens if you splash water in someone's face?"

William's eye narrowed. "Are you feeling alright, Jurou?" he asked.

"What happens?" Jurou snapped, his growing impatience manifesting itself.

"I don't know; he flinches, I suppose."

"That's right. He flinches. He cannot help it. It is a natural reaction. The curious thing is that even in a life and death struggle, he will still flinch even when doing so could cost him his life.

"People see what they expect to see. A man swings a weapon at you, a person sees only reacting and avoiding the weapon. You must see everything. Where he is exposed, where he is vulnerable. If you merely block his swing and strike back, you could be fighting all day with a single opponent. However, if you step inside his stroke and run your blade through his visor, it is over."

William could not help being startled by the cold efficiency of his words. "Aren't you supposed to be teaching me Eastern philosophies on peace and the sanctity of life?"

"Do you want to learn philosophy, or do you want to learn how to stay alive?" Jurou was not amused. He did not seem to be in particularly good humor today, and William told him so.

"There are certain lessons that I have to know you are learning, William. You once asked me if speed could overcome strength. Well, this is the way that speed can overcome strength. These methods narrow the gaps between the natural abilities of those facing each other. It is a pity that you do not seem to be taking this seriously. This could be the difference between your *being a legendary warrior or a head on a pike. You have the skills, William. The question is will you learn to apply them before it is too late?"*

CHAPTER ONE HUNDRED TWO

"*E*nough, John," Martha snapped at him. "*You asked for time to prepare, which I respected at the time. But that was six years ago. My hair grows greyer and my back more hunched under the burden that should have been yours, and not only have you not owned up to your responsibility, but you seem to have adopted a number of vices that are making you increasingly unfit to rule in your father's stead.*"

John's lip curled at the mention of Braden Dawning. "*My father,*" he sneered. "*He was a despicable person, and the less I am like him, the better person I consider myself to be.*"

Martha was taken aback at her son's disrespectful words. She had noted the decline in his customary humble attitude over the last year, but she had never heard him speak of his father with such open disdain. "*Your father had a great many faults, I will grant you,*" she said to her son, "*but he raised this barony to power singlehandedly. He avoided vices that he knew would put him into compromising positions. And what's this I hear of you frequenting local taverns, consorting with ladies of ill-repute? And still you persist in fraternizing with Lindsay. The baron of Dawning Court cannot marry a villein,*" she repeatedly firmly.

"*You think I don't know that?*" John demanded. "*We would have been married ages ago, but I knew my mother, the great Regent of the most powerful barony in the world, forbids it. Everyone knows that!*"

"These are dangerous times, John. Dawning Court needs a strong leader, and she needs it now. We no longer only face threats from outside. I have reason to fear that Richard's ambitions will lead him back here, where he will set his sights on this barony from which to launch his quest for power. If he succeeds here, he will march all over England in his pursuit of ever more power."

"Sounds like Richard is a son that Braden would be proud of."

"But he cannot win. He will have some success, but the other barons will unite against him, and even the crown will join them when the king recognizes that the throne is the last step in Richard's complete ascendancy. Richard will lose everything. We will lose everything!"

"Lose everything?" John's sneer was back. "What do I have to lose? You think I care about any of this?"

"You should care about this. At one time, John, I thought you would be a great leader because you did not seek for power. You did not want the responsibility, and that is what set you apart from Richard. You would have used the sword only reluctantly, and our people would have flourished under your reign. But now all I see is you bringing shame on our house with each passing day."

"That is right. Because I am shameful. Father said so; I know you must think so."

"Enough with this self-pity," Martha said coldly. "You will sever all ties with your vices and with Lindsay, and you will step up and take your place at the head of the house of Dawning!"

"Sever ties with Lindsay?" John snorted. "She is the only one that wants nothing from me. She is the only one that is not ashamed of me. Why would I ever sever ties with the one person in this world that actually loves me?"

"John, do not tell me that you did not know this was coming. I warned you more times than I can count that you needed to end that relationship. The fact that you chose to persist, well, you have no one to blame but yourself."

"*Lindsay understands me. She listens instead of just telling me what I have to do and why I am such a disappointment to everyone. I would rather be with her than here at court with all these conniving, devious manipulators.*"

Martha drew herself up. "*You walk a dangerous course that puts far more than yourself at risk. I want you to step up and be a man and accept your birthright, but I will not allow it unless you will rule with honor and strengthen our house. Unless you break off this foolish infatuation with this girl and demonstrate you are willing to get out of your own selfish desires for the greater good, then you are not fit to be baron.*"

"Not fit? And if I choose to take it, how will you stop me?"

"I will have no choice but to disavow you."

"Disavow?" John was shocked. "You cannot disavow the rightful heir."

"As regent, I carry all the powers of the office and can therefore disavow any knight I choose. And while it is true, you could make a claim anyway and try to start a civil war, who do you think the knights pledged to Dawning Court will follow: the Baroness who was at the elbow of the greatest baron they have ever known—the baron most of them pledged their fealty to—or the boozing, fraternizing son?" John glared at her defiantly. "Still believe your behavior has no effect on our reputation?"

"You would disavow me for marrying a girl I love rather than making a political match?"

"It will bring me no pleasure to do so. But I must ensure that you do not spread the consequences of this disastrous union over the rest of our family and the thousands of people that live under the auspices of the Dawnings and look to us for safety and stability in these tumultuous times."

John glared at her, and she returned his look calmly, if not sadly. At last John snorted. "Very well, you will get your wish. I cannot conceive of a worse fate than being sentenced to rot as the baron and have all the responsibility for thousands of lives heaped upon me." Martha did not speak. She only watched him sadly.

"I will not be baron. I do not even want to be baron," John said with more force this time as if the act of admitting it were strengthening his resolve. "I am going to marry Lindsay."

Martha sighed. "John, please just consider what you are doing. There is more at stake here than you and me."

"I do not care, Mother," John said. "This is not my concern any longer. I have been thinking about this for a long time, and now that you have made it a choice between Lindsay and the barony, it has become an easy choice at that."

"John, if you do not accept your responsibility, Richard is next in line. Richard will be disastrous as baron. He will wreak havoc on his people and all those around us. He is too reckless, too self-centered. You have always been a balance to Richard, and we need you in this seat."

"Sorry, Mother, my mind is made up," John said as he turned to go.

"John, if you turn your back on your responsibility, you are turning your back on everything—on everyone that is depending on you. I will have no choice but to turn my back on you as well—to disavow you for these actions. You will have no place here any longer."

John's footsteps slowed, and he stopped a few paces from the door but did not turn around.

"So be it, Mother. I will sleep better at night knowing that I did the courageous thing by not making myself baron. I hope you can console yourself with the same thought."

"John, please—" was the last thing Martha said to him, and the door clicked behind him.

CHAPTER ONE HUNDRED THREE

The congregation stood in the chapel, awaiting Mary's entrance. Henry stood at the front next to Father Garand, trying not to look as terrified as he felt. He was dressed in a regal-looking silk outfit with the Dawning crest emblazoned on it, a short cloak, and shoes that turned up at the toes.

"Stop fidgeting," Roland muttered to him out of the side of his mouth. Henry became aware that he was swaying back and forth nervously. There was ice in the pit of his stomach.

"What if I blow it?" he murmured back to Roland.

"You have to say two words. If you forget them, I will step in and marry her."

"I bet you would."

Suddenly the organ blared to life. Several moments later the door at the back of the church opened and Mary entered the hall in a beautiful flowing gown that swept dramatically out across the floor behind her. Her hair was cascading down under a corselet with white flowers woven into it. Everyone was entranced as she methodically made her way up the aisle, but none more so than Henry. She joined him on the dais, and he could not stop gawking at how beautiful she looked. She extended her hand to take his. He dumbly gave his and let himself be turned toward Father Garand.

"Welcome," Father Garand said loudly to the assembly, but Henry was not listening. He could not believe he was here. Everything had happened so fast. He had been in despair over one woman only a few months before, and now here he was marrying someone completely different. His soul sickness had not completely dissipated in the intervening weeks. He still felt a pang when he saw Leah or was reminded of that fateful day in a bloody field in Persia, but he pushed all that aside. The battle was lost and Leah had rejected him. That was the past and this was the present. And this was his moment.

Henry was still lost in his reverie when Roland nudged him. He started and noticed that Mary was looking at him with an intent expression, and Father Garand seemed to be waiting for something.

"Uh—I do," he said, embarrassed. The congregation tittered slightly.

A moment later Henry was awkwardly kissing Mary, and the ceremony was over. He had missed the whole thing, but he was satisfied with the parts he would retain in his memory forever. The way Mary looked. The awkward kiss, his friends and family assembled for the occasion. He was content.

***

William was next to the large center aisle, standing next to Richard and Thomas in the Dawning family pew near the front of the chapel. His mind was full on this occasion, and he was deliberately trying to avoid Leah's gaze. She kept throwing him long, meaningful looks from an opposite pew that made him exceedingly uncomfortable.

Then there was the matter of Henry taking Mary into the family. Though he personally had his doubts about the prospect, to say the two did not look nice together would have been disingenuous. This may be a bad situation, but it was Henry's right to choose his own companion. Not that it mattered, William thought. Henry was as pigheaded as the rest of them. The whole family could have lined up and forbidden the marriage, and he would have married her anyway. This had already happened with John, and to a lesser extent Thomas, although with Thomas it was for different reasons the family objected. Surely Henry would be no different.

William's eyes fell on Leah again for the hundredth time that morning. Wherever he looked, his eyes always seemed to come back to his friend, who looked especially striking this morning in her spring dress. He quickly averted his eyes when she glanced over, and he found his gaze resting several pews behind Leah. All at once he was breathless. William felt as though his heart had stopped. Seated there, conversing in quiet tones with those around her, was a stunningly beautiful woman the likes of which William had never seen. Her dark hair was pulled back away from her face and flowed down her back. Her bronze skin made her look exotic. She just happened to glance over as William was first noticing her, and when her dark eyes fell on William, they took his breath away. She met his eyes and deliberately looked away as if taking no notice of him. Instead, she tossed her hair, threw her long, dark locks back over her shoulder, and deliberately did not look his way again.

Throughout the ceremony William kept finding ways to sneak glances at this newcomer. He did not know her but at once determined that he must meet her. He felt guilty to think about Leah and was glad she did not know his thoughts at that moment, but he had never met a woman whose appearance alone had such a dramatic effect on him. It was like being struck by a bolt of lightning, but he enjoyed it, and he could not let that pass without further investigation.

William noted with some dismay that he had heard very little of the ceremony. John's absence was even more of a concern. There had been some quiet talk among the brothers in attendance as to whether he would make an appearance or not. John had not spoken to Martha since their falling out, and he had not returned to Dawning Court since then. His attendance, therefore, would require a great deal of humility on his part. On the other hand, this was a big event in the Dawning family, and to not be seen here would be a slight to Henry that no one would miss. John would not want that, either.

No one expected Edward would turn up, and in this they were not disappointed.

The belfry began to ring out the announcement that the wedding was complete, and Henry and Mary walked arm and arm out of the chapel, looking every inch the perfect couple. "You owe me five pounds," Thomas muttered to Richard as the congregation stood in honor of the newlyweds.

"It's not over yet," Richard muttered back. "If he even materializes for the reception, then he has 'attended'."

"I don't think so," Thomas scoffed. "The wedding is over. The couple that started out this day as individuals is now permanently joined in marital bliss."

"The reception would not be taking place if not for this blessed union, and I dare say if Henry had refused the reception, this blessed union would not be taking place either. Ipso facto, the reception is part of the wedding," Richard countered.

"You cannot change the rules of the wager in the middle," Thomas said out of the corner of his mouth. From a distance, both men appeared to be smiling happily in reverent silence. "He is most probably just waking up in a drunken stupor and trying to determine where he is. So he may very well make it to the reception. Although probably in someone else's clothes. That is the very reason I bet on the wedding."

"Tell you what. If he shows at the reception, we'll each pay each other half of the wager," Richard suggested genially.

Thomas rolled his eyes. "You know, Richard, next time I think we should pay the Moors your ransom. Then maybe they would send your brain back with you."

William tensed up at this, unsure how Richard would take joking about his terrible ordeal. But to William's relief, he only laughed.

The church emptied in an orderly fashion with the last rows exiting first out the rear doors. When it came their turn, Thomas said, "Let's eat!" a bit louder than he should have and feigned to push past his brothers to the doors.

CHAPTER ONE HUNDRED FOUR

"This is it," Anisa said, looking John in the eye. "This is the moment you are going to take back what is rightfully yours. You are going to be a man."

John smiled down at her. He still had misgivings about the morality of this course of action, but he loved that Anisa believed in him, and he could not face the wrath of her disappointment if he let her down. Anyway, he was grateful for such a strong woman who would push him into taking back his birthright. He needed her strength to complement his own weakness and crippling lethargy. And Anisa was the perfect person to fill that role, for what possible motive could she have to want him to become baron other than his own welfare and perhaps to be a baroness herself? And what a beautiful baroness she would make.

He looked around the stable at the Saracens that he and Anisa had been meeting with for months. They seemed a decent bunch, but the fact that they were all Saracens was not lost on him. "And you're sure no one is going to get hurt?" he asked dubiously.

"We already went over this," Anisa snapped, her impatience evident in her tone. She took a deep breath to regain control of herself. They were too close now to risk offending him. "Amir is gathering his men secretly outside the gates of Dawning Court. While everyone is distracted by your proclamation that you are claiming your legal and lawful birthright, we will clear the gate. And before anyone knows it, they will be overpowered and realize that resistance is useless."

"You do not understand my family very well if you expect them to just surrender," John said. Anisa did not respond. This was actually a subject of much concern among her colleagues. If they did not capture and kill every Dawning here and now, they would have a civil war on their hands. Of particular concern was Richard's rescue and safe return, but it was too late to turn back. This was their best opportunity for success. They had to act today.

John saw the irritation on Anisa's face and changed the subject. "Do we really have to do it during my brother's wedding?" He knew Henry would not soon forget such an indignity.

"We have already discussed all of this," she said. "The wedding is the perfect time. There is no other time when we could guarantee the key figures would be present in a single location. Everyone who needs to know you are taking over will have to acknowledge it here and now. Remember, this was your idea, and a brilliant one at that."

"But what if they will not submit to it?"

"They will. You have rightful claim to the seat and an overwhelming force to back you up. They will see the logic and prudence in going along with us."

"And if they won't?"

"They will!" she said in a firm tone intended to end all argument.

John did not again voice his serious misgivings about that part of the plan. Anisa seemed convinced they would all surrender against overwhelming odds, but she did not seem to realize that his family was stubborn, lionhearted, and fearless. He was very afraid of this turning ugly. He again lamented not gaining Thomas' confidence. If he had Thomas' support, then Henry likely would have followed, and the three of them together could have secured his seat. As it was, Anisa insisted his family was in no danger, but he knew it would be up to him to intervene to keep order and ensure everyone's safety.

John had suggested the idea of a peaceful declaration of his intent to take his inheritance and only escalate if it became necessary. But Anisa had insightfully perceived that such a course of action would merely provide the opportunity for the family to outfit a resistance and make civil war a certainty. This way, she pointed out, it would be over before it began. His brothers would swear an oath of fealty to him, and then they would see what a fine leader he was and have no reason to rebel.

Richard, however, was always a concern. John had known since they were children that Richard intended to take over. He had made no secret of it. But when Anisa had put these original plans in place, or rather, when Anisa had helped John realize what he wanted and he had formulated this idea, Richard had not been a factor. John had expected Richard to return from his distant crusades years from now to find Baron John firmly in control, dashing any royal aspirations Richard may have had.

Anisa handed John his sword. "Now is that really necessary?" John scoffed. "I'm not going to be fighting."

"Yes!" Anisa almost yelled at him, her eyes flashing as a mother who had lost patience with an unruly child. Her temper was getting the better of her much more frequently of late. "If you are not armed, they will not take you seriously. Do you want to be laughed all the way to France, or do you want to rule?"

Reluctantly John strapped his sword to his waist. The whole suit of armor was uncomfortably tight around his midsection. The sedentary years of drink and idleness had not been kind to his girth. With some embarrassment he loosened the leather straps on either side. It left a large gap between the plates where he was exposed, but at least he could breathe.

Anisa held his helmet for him. He took it and gazed at the large red plume sticking out of the top. He had once thought that made him appear so regal, but now it seemed so silly, not unlike a giant peacock. He slid the helmet once more over his head, the familiar scent of the cold, oiled steel filling his nostrils.

"It's almost time," Anisa said, peeking through the stable door at the church across the courtyard. John looked over her shoulder at the many servants that milled around before the church. Some were setting food on tables that had been set up on the lawn while others were simply resting, grateful to be out of their masters' view while they were in the church occupied with the wedding.

"You know, I should be in there right now," John said regretfully.

"You have to be here. Nobody is going to pay attention to a wedding guest making a claim for the barony. They will just ascribe it to inebriation and laugh at you to your face the way they have been laughing behind your back for all these years. But after your notable absence, you will arrive in glory as The Knight Dawning. They will all notice, and they will all listen." Anisa's eyes glowed as she envisioned the moment that was now so close.

"I suppose," John sighed. "But that is my brother getting married in there." Afraid she was on the verge of pouncing on him again, Anisa did not respond. John quickly changed the subject. "So where is the leader?" For months all he had heard about was this great mastermind, Amir. "The leader" was how they usually referred to him, and despite some reservations, John was bursting with curiosity. Ordinarily he would have insisted immediately on meeting the leader of a group with whom he was working so closely, but Anisa had explained that the logistics of it had made it impossible for them to meet until this occasion. He had accepted that, but now Amir was expected to walk through the door at any moment.

The leader had brought additional men with him, whom John had also not met. He was not comfortable with that either, but more men would be essential if this got out of hand. Oh, how he prayed it would remain peaceful. He took a deep breath and reassured himself that he could handle his side and Anisa could handle hers. Together they could keep control of the situation.

"I'm sure he is only doing final preparations for the soldiers outside the wall. He will be here shortly," she assured him.

"Speaking of that, all you men have somewhere to be. The time is not long, not long at all."

The Moors that John had come to know over the last months all filed out the back of the stable. They were good men; he could trust them.

John shifted his weight nervously from one foot to the other. His heart was racing now as he contemplated the task that lay ahead.

Anisa gently commanded him to be at peace. "Remember what you are doing here. For the first time you are taking control of your destiny. It is bound to intimidate you. And you are going to make some enemies, but then and only then will you be a man. You will no longer be a mouse with no enemies and no friends because no one even cares enough to pay attention to you." She pressed her body up close to him. He was disappointed he could not enjoy it for the iron between them. "You are the heir to a noble birthright. You come from generations of mighty warriors. Today you will prove that you belong among them. Today you will prove that you deserve the name Dawning." Just then the door opened on the opposite side of the stable from where John and Anisa were. A shadow moved into the dimly-lit stable.

John was instantly on his guard. He took a protective step in front of Anisa. The shadow played over the dimly lit stalls in eerie, grotesque, oversized shapes. For a brief instant the morbid thought flashed through John's mind that he was watching the approach of the angel of death. "What a way to go," he thought to himself. Standing in a stable doing something I'm not sure is right for an inheritance I'm not sure I deserve with people I'm not sure are my friends—the perfect end to a perfect life.

The shadows that leapt and played through the stable coalesced into a gigantic silhouette eight feet from where John stood with his hand on the hilt of his sword. "John," came the booming, accented voice. "I am Amir. So good to make your acquaintance at last." Amir stepped forward, and the light fell across his scarred visage.

Instantly the memory of the peasant revolt from so many years ago came crashing in on John. He remembered William fighting with the giant and the giant knocking him to the ground. He remembered tackling him and the brothers rallying around their youngest brother to protect him. "You?" John said, taking a step back and bumping into Anisa. "You are the leader? How—?" He stepped to the side in order to keep both Amir and Anisa where he could see them.

Both Nizari began a slow advance toward John. "John, we have come too far to turn back now," Anisa said calmly as she took another slow step toward him. The church bell began to peel, marking the completion of the ceremony.

"How long have you had designs on my family?" John demanded, still trying to comprehend what he was seeing. He felt like a fool. All this time he had placated his conscience with thoughts that this group was genuinely interested in his well-being. He told himself that he could control them. In that moment he seemed incomprehensibly naive.

"I see you remember me," Amir said mildly. "What a pity we got off on the wrong foot. Let us start again. I am Amir, and I am honored to be in the service of the next baron of Dawning Court." He bowed slightly to him but continued to advance menacingly.

John tore off his helmet. "Last time we met, I was united with my brothers against you. We were a family. What a fool I was to think this band of misfits was anything like a family!" he said, casting aside his helmet in a show of defiance. The sight of this giant was like the harsh light of day shining down on his misdeeds. He was filled with shame and shocked at how far he had fallen. Step by step he had let himself be led down this path until he was on the brink of an attack on the only people to whom he had ever really mattered.

"The bell has sounded," Anisa said urgently, glancing back and forth between John, Amir, and the stable door. "We have to go now!" She was afraid of what might be happening on the other side of the door if they were not there to control the situation. This was not part of the plan.

John drew his sword, both Amir and Anisa instantly ceased their advance, and Amir's hand slowly found its way to his own sword hilt. "Go if you like! But you will do so without me." John threw his weapon down at their feet. "See how much sympathy for your cause attacking a wedding party engenders among my people."

Amir raised his hands palm out to show his intentions were peaceful. "John, we have no time for this. Many people have worked for a long time to get you here. You will go out there, and you are going to take your place as the rightful heir of Dawning Court. And when you do, we will be there as your loyal subjects and advisors." Amir slowly picked up John's sword and offered it to him. "Take this weapon and seize your destiny," he whispered intensely.

"Very well," John said calmly. With a sudden movement he knocked the sword aside and slammed a furious uppercut into Amir's chin. Amir was lifted off the ground and sailed back several feet before hitting the ground in a daze.

John rounded on Anisa. "All this was to manipulate me?" He did not want to believe it but could not escape the overwhelming evidence. "Everything you said, everything you... did?" John felt as though he had been kicked in the stomach.

Anisa backed up against the door. Fear stood plain in her eyes as she regarded the considerable power of this large, angry knight that was leveled at her. "I, we—" she stammered. For the first time in John's recollection, she was speechless. John drew back one gauntleted fist, determined to send her head through the stable door. All at once the anger flowed out of him. It was his fault. He knew that it was he who wanted to believe her. He had let himself be led down this path. It was his fault as it always was. He stooped and picked up his helmet with the hand he had intended to demolish her face with. Anisa was still backed rigidly against the door, stiff with fear.

"You are nothing but an ugly mirror into my worst proclivities," he said. Just then a piercing, searing pain cut into his side. His knees threatened to buckle. He turned to see Amir sliding an antique, leaf-shaped blade between the seams of his ill-fitting armor. John felt the warm liquid flowing down his side, carrying away his strength. His knees finally did buckle, and he found himself looking up at Anisa, who stepped off the wall when she saw what was happening, his anger now replaced with the sickening certainty of death. Though he had never been here before, he had seen it all too often to delude himself into believing it was anything else.

John reached imploringly out to Anisa as the last vestige of anything good in his life. She stepped up to him, the fear vanishing from her eyes. She grabbed his hair roughly and peeled his head back.

"You cowardly, miserable worm," she said from between clenched teeth, her real feelings that had been straining to come out now flowing freely. "You are not a man! It is the ultimate in English arrogance to believe that I could ever love someone like you. You are weak, and your family is weak. We may not get to them through you, but we will get them."

"Wh–why my family?" John managed, finding himself out of breath. Amir stepped beside Anisa, and his arm snaked around her as the two of them patiently watched John's demise.

"How does that English steel feel, John?" Amir asked conversationally. "This blade was used by one of your own to deceive and murder my people." He wrenched the blade out of John's body sharply and held it up in his left hand to inspect the blood still running down its length. "I had always intended that it would gut you; I just did not expect that it would be necessary so soon. You are as big a disappointment in death as you were in life."

Anger surged anew in John. He looked for something to lash out with, but his sword was on the ground out of reach. Suddenly he became cognizant of the heavy helmet still in his right hand. Rage surged through him and he swiped the helmet up at Anisa. Surprised, she lurched to avoid the blow but was impeded by the close proximity of Amir's massive frame and was unable to duck aside. The helmet caught her in the side of the head and sent her crashing back into an empty horse stall, where she collapsed.

Amir cursed and lunged forward to intercept another blow as John stumbled to his feet, determined to strike at Amir also. Amir put his massive shoulder into John's unstable figure. The force of the blow sent him crashing through the stable door into the courtyard.

CHAPTER ONE HUNDRED FIVE

The wedding guests exited the chapel to an uncommonly beautiful spring day. The sky was clear with only the occasional white, fluffy cloud lazily drifting by with no particular place to go. It was a perfect day for an outdoor event. William stared at the sky, wondering if perhaps this union was ordained of God after all.

There were long tables set up with refreshments and food of every sort. There were many servants everywhere standing at attention, carrying trays of drinks and food. Other smaller tables had chairs surrounding them, offering a place for the guests to rest and to dine in comfort. Massive canvas pavilions stretched out to cover most of the heavily used areas.

There seemed to be an army of servants already in attendance, so William was surprised to see another group entering the main gate pushing two more loaded carts with them. What more could they possibly need that they did not already have, he wondered. Oh well, better to have too much than too little at a wedding. Still, something seemed off about this new group of servants approaching the wedding party. William could see that they were dark skinned. But it was not uncommon to find serfs or laborers who worked in the sun all day moonlighting as servers at big events requiring a larger detachment of servants than was regularly employed in the household. They were often the family members of the regular serving staff, brought on for the extra help when it was required. Still, something nagged William about these newcomers such that he could not seem to take his eyes from them.

Just then everyone's attention was gathered to the head of the table as Mary's father, a great bearded, overweight noble began to speak. "Ladies and gentleman, thank you all for coming to celebrate this blessed union..." he began.

As the baron began to expound on the mixed blessing of losing his daughter to marriage but gaining a son in Henry, William kept one eye on the servants that were slowly advancing up the hill towards them. "What is it about them that nags at me so?"

"...It is a blessing when two young people of this quality find each other..."

Their clothes were not quite right, but neither was that too uncommon, as matching servant attire was not always available for the temporary help.

"...bequeath to them fine lands in the kingdom of France..."

Their bearing! That was it. That was what was bothering him. Though their heads were bowed, they were marching almost in time. Their posture and bearing was that of a stiff military unit. And their boots were thick leather, like the boots of soldiers, not the soft boots of servants. There was some subterfuge afoot. But why? Why would they be here now?

William hesitated only a moment, knowing Henry would never forgive him if he was wrong about this, but he quickly determined the risks involved if he were correct were too high. He slammed his glass down on a nearby table hard enough that George Mayfield stopped mid-sentence as every eye turned to William. "We are under atta—" Just then, across the courtyard the stable door exploded outward as an armored body came crashing through it. They all turned toward the source of the sound in surprise.

Thomas squinted at the figure who struggled unsteadily to his knees. "That's John!" he exclaimed.

" Ha! You owe me two-and-a-half pounds," Richard said triumphantly, still not grasping the gravity of the situation.

With the last of his strength, John struggled to his knees and shouted, "It's a trap! Trap! Defend yourselves! Defe—" With that he collapsed face down on the lawn.

William was focused on the giant figure silhouetted in the gaping stable doorway. There was no mistaking that frame. "It's the giant!" William shouted. Everyone looked at him even more confused. "We are under attack!" he roared, shoving over a table both for protection and to startle the guests into action.

Upon hearing this, the men pushing the carts pulled weapons from under the tarps covering the carts. More armored soldiers jumped from under the wagon coverings and charged the last of the distance up the hill.

The giant disappeared from the doorway, and Thomas raced toward the stable. "John!"

The wedding guests began to scream and flee in panic. William looked around frantically for the guards, but there was no sign of them. Then all was pandemonium. The Moors began to cut into anyone that came within striking distance. There were about thirty of them in all. The guests outnumbered them five to one, but the Moors were heavily armed and armored. Nobody from the wedding was armed. The guests were easy prey.

William shoved through the crowds to the closest Moor as an aged aunt of Mary's was run through from behind while trying to flee. It was too late for her by the time William reached her. The implications of this moment were crashing in on him even as he struggled to gain control of the situation. John had obviously been attacked by the giant. They were being attacked on their own land while celebrating, and his loved ones were in enormous danger. His mother, brothers, friends, and Leah were all in jeopardy. Fury was boiling by the time William reached the first Moor. The habitual rage that he had fought against all his life—the rage that consumed him since discovering these personal attacks on his family—took over. William knew he was not as good a fighter when angry, but at that moment he did not care. He charged the closest Moor.

Seeing the unarmed party guest running toward him, the Moor sneered and brought his sword down in a heavy overhand blow with both hands. But rather than shrink from the blow, William charged even faster, a move that was so unnatural and counterintuitive that the Moor did not have time to react. Rather than contacting soft flesh, the Moor's swing proved useless as William spun underneath his arms, then crouched and turned his back to his assailant. William locked his hands over the Moor's wrists, which were trapped over his right shoulder, and sprang out from his crouch. The momentum from the blow was sufficient to shatter the Moor's left elbow, and a nudge from William's right hip sent the off-balance Moor up and over William's shoulder, leaving his weapon resting neatly in front of William. The Moor screamed until the hard thud on the ground knocked the wind from him. Before he could regain himself, his own curved scimitar had smote deep into his chest.

***

Richard looked around nervously amidst the crowd. He was still a shadow of his former self and felt the lack of his former strength very acutely, though he was still far larger than any ordinary man. But it was more than his diminished strength that filled him with reservations. He had not been involved in a battle since his defeat and capture; and what's more, he had not been involved in a battle since, in the clutch of a fevered mind, he had seen into Hell. He had seen where all his sins—where all the killing—was going to lead him and was loathe to walk that line again.

He hesitated, considered running, looked for the guards; but they must have been neutralized before this moment because no one was coming to their rescue. A woman was stabbed in the belly in front of him as she tried to get away, and Richard's jaw tightened. He steeled himself as he stepped forward, unarmed, to face her murderer.

The Moor was just pulling his bloody blade from the woman writhing on the ground. He turned toward Richard and drew back to strike at him. Richard stepped boldly forward and seized his sword arm with one massive hand in a vice grip that threatened to break the Moor's wrist. Richard pressed his body against his attacker, wrapped his free right hand around the helmet, grabbing the face of it, and twisted sharply. With a sickening pop, the Moor body went limp, and Richard casually took the weapon from his hand as he fell. He ignored the wrenching in his stomach as he realized how easily killing still came to him but accepted that he had no choice on this occasion.

***

Thomas had been cut off by three Saracen rogues as he ran to help John. He looked around quickly for a weapon but did not find anything. The rogues approached, and Thomas slipped behind a long table and kicked it on its side between them. He smashed one leg of the table free with one meaty forearm. The first Saracen was just jumping the table as the table leg broke free. Thomas did not hesitate to crack the heavy oak leg over the back of the unprotected head. The Saracen's eyes rolled back in his head, and he slumped to the ground. Thomas grinned at the remaining two as he caught the first blade on his makeshift club.

He felt strong again. The training was working. He had not known anything like this was coming, but he was glad now that he had been ready.

***

Henry was numb with shock and rage at this attack. Not only had these foreigners attacked his family, but they had specifically plotted to defile his day. They were killing indiscriminately any guests they could reach: relatives, friends, and well-wishers. Henry saw William charge headlong into the battle. He himself wanted to do the same but had to keep his head about him. He immediately took his bride and her parents and rushed them back into the church. He ordered them to bar the door, then spun to join the battle and came face to face with Martha, out of breath and fearful. With some amount of annoyance, he banged on the massive wooden door of the church, identified himself, and ordered them to open it. When the door was cracked, he roughly propelled Martha into the church, ordered them to bar the door again, and went charging into the fray.

He bowled over the first Moor he came to, who was busy massacring another wedding guest, with a well-placed shoulder in the small of his back. Seizing the Moor's fallen spear, Henry rammed it viciously into his throat as the Moor struggled to regain his feet.

"Henry!" William shouted at him. "Help Thomas!" Henry scanned the grounds until he spotted Thomas up toward the stables, fencing madly with two rogues. He nodded his understanding and ran toward Thomas, still clutching the clumsy spear in his hand. He did not care for this weapon. He was much more adept with a blade. As he passed by William, William threw the scimitar into the air in front of him. Henry caught it in his left hand as he slammed the fallen Moor's spear into the ground and kept running.

***

William crossed the short distance to the next assailant, yanked the spear from the ground, and brought it down in one smooth overhand motion on the unprotected Moor head. The Moor froze for a moment in surprise, then collapsed.

William spun to find Leah behind him. He seized her arm in his left hand and pulled her quickly the short distance to where Anthony was fighting with an opponent, desperately fending him off with a serving tray and meat clever. Wordlessly, William rammed the blade of his spear deep into the Moor's blind side, ignoring Leah's gasp as his stained white clothes became even more blood soaked. He propelled Leah unceremoniously toward Anthony, who caught her as she stumbled forward.

"Anthony, I am charging you with her safety," William said, stabbing his spear in the ground and retrieving the fallen Moor's sword. He threw it to Anthony, who deftly caught it in his right hand while retaining a protective grip on Leah with his left."

"But I can help you," Anthony insisted.

William, who had already turned back to the fighting, turned once again to face Anthony. "You can help me by ensuring she," he said, jabbing a finger at Leah, "and all other guests are safe! Now go!" William commanded. Anthony did not argue further. He turned Leah towards the castle and started off.

"Anthony," William called after him. "If only one person survives here today, it had better be her."

Anthony nodded his understanding and continued to guide Leah away. Leah craned her neck and watched with a horrible fascination as William yanked the spear from the ground and raced toward a small group of Moors. They were on his land, in his house, slaughtering his family and friends in the most cowardly fashion imaginable. The rage William had spent years learning to control found new channels through his body and flowed freely now. He welcomed the increased strength and renewed energy that accompanied the anger. He swung the spear in a wide arc at head level, slashing across the face of the first of three Moors and using the momentum of the spin to slam the heel of his boot into the head of the next. William brought the spear back up, spun it in an underhand swing, and ran the third Moor through the belly. The first had unconsciously dropped his weapon to tend to his deeply cut face. Leah was horrified to see William turn and run this unarmed man through the chest. And without a moment's hesitation, he spun and dropped the point of the weapon into the back of the neck of the man he had knocked off his feet with his kick, who was on all fours trying to right himself.

The whole grounds were in chaos. The Moors were quickly disappearing now and would soon be outnumbered. But there were a disturbing number of wedding guests lying in pools of blood, which was running over the green grass in grisly contrast to the beautiful beginnings of the day.

One of the effects on William of letting the anger overtake him was a kind of tunnel vision. He had a very narrow focus, and he did not see the danger from behind. Leah saw it from where she was still being removed to the castle. She shrieked a warning to William, but he could not hear her over the din of the yard. William's first visible warning came from the gleam of light off the metal of the blade that spelled his doom. The light caught the corner of William's eye. But by then the Moor was already into a side arm swing from behind. With no time to consider, William leapt straight backward. It was too late to avoid the blow completely, but the slower-moving section of the blade toward the hilt sliced into his right arm as his shoulder blades plowed into the surprised Moor's chest.

William and attacker both went to the ground, with William landing on top of the Moor. The breath exploded from the Moor's lungs, and William's head involuntarily snapped back, crashing painfully into his opponent's nose.

William was in pain but not stunned as his opponent was. He rolled to his right, seizing the Moor sword with his fresh blood on the blade, and stripped it from the Moor's hand as he rolled by. Leah let herself breathe when she saw William roll away. By then they reached the castle door, and Anthony was gently but firmly trying to guide her into the entrance. "Please go inside and barricade the door, milady, until I return." Leah was still trying to watch the battle as Anthony pushed her out of view behind the heavy door. She shoved his arm away and lunged back out the door just in time to see the now disarmed Moor climb to his knees and beg for his life. William wore a look of unbridled fury Leah could not believe as he stepped toward the Moor without a moment's pause and severed the Moor head completely from his shoulders. A crazed look was in his eye that Leah had never seen before—a mania that bordered on the verge of complete loss of control. Leah felt ill. She could not believe what she had just seen. She could not believe that William, a noble and gentle man, would murder an unarmed man begging for his life. Anthony shoved her back through the door and closed it against her back. Leah sank down to the floor, suddenly feeling weak in the knees. The tears came now at what she had seen: the violence, the terror, and the horrible reality of watching people being slaughtered. And now it was her best friend, whom she believed in above all others, doing the slaughtering.

William tore a strip of the dead man's clothes to bandage his arm that was bleeding heavily. He surveyed the battlefield as he did so. He could see Thomas, Henry, and Richard fighting in relatively close proximity to each other. They were fending off the last few assailants that stood between them and the stable where John lay. William had to get up there. He darted toward them as Richard crushed the skull of his opponent and turned on the other two.

The giant was nowhere to be seen. William knew that he must be escaping. They could not let him go again. This was at least the third time he had been involved in a direct attack on their family. This would not stand. They could not let another injury to their family pass.

William was running full tilt when off to his left he spied the breathtaking, dark-haired woman from the church. She had fallen back on the ground with a Moor standing menacingly over her.

***

Evelyn had gotten caught up in the chaos as the guests started to panic and run blindly in every direction. She had tried to find her parents and family, but there was too much bedlam and too many people screaming and crashing into everything. There seemed to be assassins everywhere slaughtering anyone that came within reach. She raced toward the church where she had seen others escape to, but it was locked when she arrived. Desperately she ran toward the castle. Where were the guards? How could this be happening?

There was an elderly woman lying on the ground in a daze but with no apparent injuries. Evelyn stopped next to her. "Are you hurt?" she said gently but urgently. Still dazed, the elderly woman shook her head. "Then we must go quickly!" Evelyn said, taking her arm and trying to help her up. A man screamed ten feet away from her, and she turned to see an unarmed guest collapse under the mace of a Moor.

Evelyn stepped in front of the woman, never taking her eyes off the Moor who now fixed his sights on her and started toward them. She took both the old woman's arms and pulled her up. "We must go this instant!"

As the old woman came to her feet, Evelyn stumbled backward and bumped into someone. She spun as a surprised Moor rounded on her. With a vicious backhand he sent her sprawling.

He stood over her with a lascivious expression and said something in Arabic that she did not understand; but his meaning was clear. He laughed to himself to see her frantic expression. She looked around for a weapon, but finding nothing she grabbed a handful of turf and hurled it into his face. He flinched, and Evelyn kicked him hard enough in his unprotected groin to lift him off the ground. He doubled over in pain and fell to his knees.

Evelyn sprang from the ground to run. Where was an empty-headed, big shouldered, would-be-suitor when she really needed one? Too busy practicing his charm in the mirror, no doubt. The Moor lashed out at her leg as she ran, and caught the side of her ankle with a gauntleted fist. The hard steel against her ankle caused her ankle to buckle painfully, and she ended up back on the ground a few feet from where she had started. She rolled onto her back and sat up.

The Moor stumbled painfully to his feet and stood over her again, this time a pace back. He could hardly stand upright as he raised his sword. "Is that painful?" she asked wickedly. "What was it you were planning on doing with that?"

The Moor realized that she was insulting him, and this enraged him further. He snarled and raised his weapon high, pausing for a moment to savor the fear in her eyes. In this, however, he was disappointed. Evelyn was too angry to be appropriately fearful, and the Moor was met only with angry defiance.

It was a pity to destroy an infidel woman of such exceptional beauty without taking the time to appreciate her fully. But like all the European women, she did not know her place. He raised himself to his full height. What a—

The spear entered the unprotected pit of his arm behind his breastplate and shoved his body violently sideways. He stumbled as his undulating limbs seemed to lose strength one by one. He lost his grip on his weapon as his arms went into a spasm from the force of the blow. Then he was unable to stand up straight. He fought his legs to keep them from giving out, but they had their way, and the ground came up to meet him.

Evelyn's defiant eyes opened wide in shock. She turned to see a figure cloaked in blood racing toward her. He leapt over the body of her assailant and tore the spear from it. He hit the ground running to assist the three Dawnings that were still fighting to get to their brother. She knew this man. There was no doubt who this could be.

* * *

Richard, Thomas, and Henry leapt over the last falling bodies of the Moors standing between them and John. The brothers raced to John's side and fell on their knees beside him. The ground around his body was drenched with his blood. His face was ominously white as Thomas knelt beside him, stripped off his armor, and pressed an ear to his chest to listen for breath or heartbeat.

"He's dead," he announced, tersely confirming what they already knew. The brothers stared in stunned silence as they absorbed the information. They had always known that the life they led was fraught with danger and that any of them could be killed at any time. But somehow it had never happened to them. The Dawnings were always spared, whatever the circumstances, and it began to look like divine providence had taken an interest in them. Richard had survived a terrible battle, incarceration, and torture. Henry had lived while every last man with him was killed. They had all survived dozens of battles in the Crusades and in local struggles. But John was dead on their own land from a fight they did not understand. Perhaps they were on their own after all. Maybe they had no divine protection at the end of the day.

Henry sprang to his feet with Richard close behind. This brief pause had allowed William to catch up to them. He did not even need to ask. The expressions and the unnaturally motionless way his brothers were kneeling told him everything. They were not in a flurry of activity, attempting to save John, because there was no activity that could help him.

Ibrahim stepped into the opening of the stable door that was now strewn all over the yard to gauge the progress of the fight. It took but a moment to register the scene before him, of the Dawnings kneeling around the body of their fallen brother. He immediately dodged out of sight, but it was too late.

"You?" William muttered, taking a moment for his mind to place the face.

Henry, Richard, and William were instantly on their feet in pursuit. Thomas, who was a bit slower, was bringing up the rear.

Ibrahim raced through the stable, calling a warning to the others who were checking each stall for Anisa. Amir had indicated that she had collapsed in here somewhere, but the stable was huge, and now it was too late. They had to escape.

The Dawnings burst pell mell into the dimly lit building, weapons drawn and thirsty for more Saracen blood to make restitution for the Dawning blood that had been spilt. But they were greeted only with the retreating backs of a small group of Moors racing for the opposite exit.

The brothers charged after them. They caught the slowest of the men just outside the opposite door of the stable. His escape had been hindered by the others vying to be the first through the doorway. Henry reached his retreating back first and ran his sword into it without even breaking stride. The Moor gasped and collapsed, and the brothers continued after the remaining five men without even slowing down.

It took Ibrahim and the others perhaps a hundred yards to realize they had the advantage unless they continued to flee. If they ran, they would be cut down one by one. But if they turned on them, everything changed. It was Ibrahim and four fully equipped soldiers against three exhausted, unprotected men wielding weapons that were not their own. Now was the time to confront them.

William and Richard were running side by side with Henry a pace ahead: William on his right flank and Richard on his left. Richard glanced over at William and was surprised at the crazed look in his eyes. It was clear that William was not in full control of his faculties at that moment, but his attention was diverted when Henry did the last thing any of them expected.

Henry charged into the center of the group of Moors, swinging wildly. Ibrahim was in the center and the target of Henry's attack. Ibrahim immediately fell back under the fierce onslaught, leaving Richard and William to try to protect Henry from the soldiers on either side of him that quickly tried to take advantage of the situation and get at him from the flanks.

This created the urgent need for them to circumvent the two men standing between them and the two Moors that were about to run Henry through. Both men met this challenge in different ways. William charged the first man with a wide swing at his head. The Moor ducked it and cut at William's waist with his blade. William leapt up and pulled both legs up and out of the way as he rotated horizontally over the deadly blade of the opponent. He landed facing the first man, with his back to the second. The first Moor's swing had spun him around, and just for an instant both Moor backs were exposed. That was all it took.

Richard took a more direct approach. He stepped within striking distance of his opponent and let the inevitable swing come. He caught the assassin's sword with his own weapon in his right hand and seized the Moor's wrist with his left. Sliding his right forearm under the Moor's leg, he picked him up and heaved him toward the back of the Moor about to cut into Henry's flank. The two collapsed in a heap.

Ibrahim's weapon flashed as he defended himself against the heated assault. He knew that Henry was not calculating his attacks, relying on passion to overcome, and that if he could just defend long enough, Henry's uncalculating passion would inevitably lead to an error in his attacks. And that is all Ibrahim would need. But the assault kept coming. He noticed his two soldiers on his left drop from what seemed an invisible hand. He then danced aside as the two on his right were hurled around like rag dolls by the oversized Dawning. They should have killed that one when they had the chance. Now they were being punished for allowing the infidel to live. As if to punctuate this thought, William descended on his two fallen comrades viciously and repeatedly, ramming his spear into unprotected body parts until they stopped twitching.

Henry's incessant attacks did not let up. After several more steps, Ibrahim stumbled over a root in the ground and fell backward. He raised his sword feebly, knowing the end was near. The tall, slender Dawning stood over him and struck his sword from his hand. Henry straddled him and pulled him by the breastplate up slightly off the ground, his sword held to his throat. "Who are you?" he demanded. Ibrahim said nothing. Henry flicked his weapon, and a nick appeared in Ibrahim's neck that immediately oozed blood. "Why are you after our family? You dare to come into my house during my wedding and kill my people?"

Fear filled Ibrahim's eyes as he stared up at Henry's enraged face. "Please, don't hurt me." He held his left hand in front of his face while his right hand stole slowly down to his boot, where he had a knife concealed.

"You murder my family in cold blood and demand mercy from me?" Henry slapped him in the side of the head with the flat of his blade. "Are you Nizari?" he yelled. "What do the Nizari want with us?"

Ibrahim's fingers closed around the hilt of his dagger. He slowly drew it out, all the time holding Henry's gaze with his own fearful expression. "No more," he pleaded. "I will tell you anything you want to know." He slowly extended the dagger to drive it into the ribs of this infidel.

"Henry!" William, who had just finished brutally dispatching the others, called. With a hop he crossed the short distance and planted a kick into Henry's side—the opposite side of the one which Ibrahim was about to pierce. Henry was not braced for the surprise hit and was picked up and hurled several feet in the opposite direction. Ibrahim swung hard at him at that moment, but instead of embedding his blade deep in the side, he slashed Henry's stomach as he was flying over the top of him. William caught Ibrahim's knife-bearing wrist in both of his hands and dropped his knee onto Ibrahim's elbow, snapping it in the wrong direction, giving vent to his own fury at seeing the face he had rescued from the highwaymen all those months before coming back to inflict so much damage on his friends and family. Ibrahim screamed, and William glared his pure rage into his face. "I saved your life!" he said between clenched teeth. "You are only here because I allowed it, and this is how you repay me." But before Ibrahim could respond, William yanked his body by means of his broken arm.

Ibrahim screamed again. The pain was excruciating, and it was impossible to resist with his broken joint. William slid behind him like a snake, wrapping his legs over Ibrahim's arms as his arms slid around the Moor's throat and tightened.

"William, no!" Richard shouted from where he was tending to the flesh wound on Henry's stomach. "We need him for information!"

William did not hear his brother's protests. His face was twisted in anger, his teeth grinding, and every muscle in his neck taut. He twisted and squeezed until Ibrahim's strangled cries had ceased and his body was still. William released his victim and kicked his limp form violently away from him.

It was all at once strikingly and uncommonly quiet. Richard's weary shoulders slumped in defeat. That was their last link to find out what happened to their brother.

Richard seemed to mutter something, but no sound reached William's ears. Tears were flowing freely down Henry's cheeks, but William could not hear what he was saying. All he could hear was the pounding of the blood in his head. Everyone was dead. The attack was over, but it was not over. There was no giant body in the pile of dead. William ground his teeth in frustration and roared, "Where is he? He is not here!" He grabbed his spear and ran back to the stable.

He kicked the large door that had swung partially closed after their rapid exit, swinging it violently open and tearing it half way off of its hinges. "Where is that miserable coward?" he shouted into the air. "Where are you?"

"William, no! No, William!" It was Henry's voice that finally broke through the pounding in his head. He and Richard dragged William back.

"It's over! It's over today!" Richard tried to soothe him as he and Henry each took an arm and pulled him away from the barn and his crazed pursuit.

"It's not over!" he yelled. "He is still here. We have to find him before he tries again." They wrestled him until they all collapsed.

"We'll get him, William. We'll get him." Richard hugged his brother's head to his chest as William slowly resigned himself to losing the giant yet again.

The three were exhausted and overwrought, trying to take it all in. They sat back to back in a circle as each thought his separate thoughts about the same moments, the bloodshed at the wedding party, the loss of their brother, the death of these remaining Moors—Nizari—the only ones who might have been able to provide answers to any of this. The chaos that had exploded their lives and changed them forever less than an hour before had just as suddenly subsided.

"You put up quite a fight," Richard forced a laugh. "We could have used Thomas' help."

"Hey," Henry suddenly perked up. "Where is Thomas?"

Just then, from the darkness in the stable, a silhouette emerged. The brothers were instantly on their feet again, ready for anything, but they were all surprised when the shape converged into the form of an exhausted, blood-covered Sebastian.

"Sebastian, are you all right?" Henry was concerned at the sight of all the blood on their aging house servant.

Sebastian looked down at the blood without emotion. "There are many that require attention, Sir Henry. But do not fret, this blood is not my own."

"Yes, of course." The immediate fight had completely pushed from Henry's mind the carnage that awaited them on the other side of the stable.

"Milord," Sebastian turned his attention to William, "Baron Braddock is at the gates with his army and says that if you do not accept his challenge to settle this blood feud here and now, he will destroy Dawning Court."

The fear, the violence, David's death, John's murder, the repeated attempts to destroy his family, all converged at once. And deep within William's mind, something snapped.

The End

COMING FALL 2012

The Knights Mourning, the gripping sequel to *The Knights Dawning.*

Visit www.pendantbooks.com for more information or to be added to our mailing list for updates and specials.